This gift provided by:

The
Seattle
Public
Library
Foundation

SUPPORTSPL.ORG

SUCH A PRETTY SMILE

SUCH A
PRETTY
SMILE

---◆---

KRISTI DeMEESTER

ST. MARTIN'S PRESS
NEW YORK

First published in the United States by St. Martin's Press, an imprint of St. Martin's Publishing Group

www.stmartins.com

Library of Congress Cataloging-in-Publication Data

Names: DeMeester, Kristi, author.
Title: Such a pretty smile / Kristi DeMeester.
Description: First edition. | New York: St. Martin's Press, 2022.
Identifiers: LCCN 2021036714 | ISBN 9781250274212 (hardcover) |
    ISBN 9781250274229 (ebook)
Subjects: LCGFT: Psychological fiction. | Thrillers (Fiction) |
    Horror fiction. | Novels.
Classification: LCC PS3604.E458 S83 2022 | DDC 813/.6—dc23
LC record available at https://lccn.loc.gov/2021036714

First Edition: 2022

10 9 8 7 6 5 4 3 2 1

For every mother who is haunted by what came before.
And the two Js. Forever.

SUCH A PRETTY SMILE

CHAPTER 1

LILA 2019

There was blood in the water—a dull pink bloom—the morning Lila Sawyer heard about the first missing girl. Macie had sent her a screenshot, and the picture showed a girl only slightly younger than they were—twelve, or a mature eleven—with lank, dark hair and deep-set eyes the color of pond water. Lila glanced at her phone as she balanced one slippery leg on the edge of the tub, her mother's forbidden razor in her hand. The cut on her ankle stung as she splashed water over it.

Holy shit. Have you seen this?

Lila set the razor down and wiped her hands on the towel hanging from the rack before grabbing her phone to pull up the picture. She recognized the girl, the plain angles of her face, how she'd hidden behind a veil of hair as she hurried through the hallways of East Pritchard Middle. Invisible as Lila had been before Macie lifted her into something that resembled popularity.

What happened to her? she typed, and then swiped the blade over her legs again, hoping that this time she'd managed to avoid cutting herself. If she came out of the bathroom looking like a horror show, her mother would know she'd been shaving—a full year before she was technically allowed, even though every other girl she knew had been shaving since ten or eleven. She'd begged when she turned thirteen, but her mother refused to budge. Shaving was something women did and never above the knee unless she wanted people to think she wasn't a good girl. Lila was tired of feeling like a yeti every time she wanted to wear shorts or a skirt. Her phone chimed again.

Dunno. Her legs were all torn up. Cops are on the news saying she probs got lost in the woods, and coyotes got to her or something. My mom says there's no way an animal could do all that, and that it's definitely a murder. It's freaky.

Lila's stomach turned over as she stared down at the girl's eyes, thinking of what she would have seen and felt in her last moments. Teeth? Pressure and pain colliding in the deeper parts of her before bursting outward like a terrible, darker growth, and then the knowledge there would be no more breath to draw. No more sun.

Lila typed out a reply, but there was nothing to say that didn't sound hollow, so she set the phone on the floor, blinking away the threat of tears. She ran the razor over her legs again without caution. The story had given her goosebumps, her prickled flesh easy to nick. Her leg opened up in three places, small entrances that allowed her blood to cascade into the water.

"Shit," she said because her mother wasn't in the room to yell at her for using unladylike language. The word felt good in her mouth. Heavy and exciting and *right*. Nothing at all like her boring mush of a life inside the tiny apartment her mother had found in Acworth. She'd wanted to get Lila out of the city and had read some article about how it was an "up-and-coming" Metro Atlanta town, only it had never really up and gone anywhere. There were a few restaurants—including Hank's Cajun Grill, which her mother said was close enough to the New Orleans cuisine she grew up on—and a Target, and a beach on Lake Allatoona that wasn't really a beach at all but a tiny stretch of dirty sand where kids in soggy diapers dribbled apple juice while tired-looking moms stared out over the unmoving water, as if just looking could change their entire lives into something that wasn't this. At the very least, Lila wished they lived closer to Atlanta, where her mother taught Art Theory and Sculpture I–IV. Her mom constantly reminded her that the city wasn't a good place to raise a kid, and she needed to be able to see the sky and stars and take a breath that didn't feel choked. It was better for her art and better for Lila, and they were staying in Acworth. End of discussion. Still, Lila daydreamed about who she would have become if they'd stayed in Midtown. Some cooler version of herself with neon hair and a nose ring and maybe an illicit tattoo she'd have had done in Little Five by some dude nicknamed something ridiculous like Bone or Animus.

She hurried and finished, then stepped out of the tub, dripping onto the tile, to replace her mother's razor in the little caddy hanging on the wall of the shower. Using a wad of toilet paper, she swiped at the blood on her legs and then tacked a few pieces onto the nicks, willing herself to heal more quickly. School started in forty-five minutes, and her mother wasn't the kind of mom who would write her an excuse if she were tardy.

"Come on," she muttered, but she was still bleeding when she tugged on a pair of dark leggings and then pulled her favorite dress over them. It was the color of an emerald with fabric delicate as a moth's wing that fluttered around her when she moved. Once she got to school, she'd take the leggings off. If her mother saw her chewed-up legs, she'd be able to tell Lila had shaved them, so she put the leggings on even if it meant she was stifling in the late-spring heat. Sweat pooled against her lower back, and she fanned the dress away from her, already imagining what Macie would say when she saw her bare legs. If her eyes would go wide, a smile curling at the edges of her lips in the way that made her look dangerous and beautiful at the same time.

Lila scanned her face in the mirror and wondered if there was anything hiding there that would betray her feelings about Macie. What had started as awe over this girl who'd offered Lila her friendship had become a kind of agony; a need that had evolved into something larger than calling Macie her best friend. But she knew how Macie saw her. A passion project or a play-thing she could hold up and examine like an insect pinned in place before nodding in approval. Yes, hadn't she done a good job with what she'd created? Hadn't she taken something drab and made it beautiful? Made it better? But Lila was still the same person her mother had given birth to: the squirming, awkward girl who was treated as if she were five instead of thirteen. No matter how she tried to find the right clothes or the right makeup or the right hairstyle, Lila couldn't change that.

Lila's bedroom was painted baby pink with a ballerina border—a leftover from whoever had lived in the apartment before that the leasing company hadn't bothered to change before they moved in. She hated it. Wished her mom would let her paint it bright teal with a canopied bed and tulle curtains she could close at night and feel like she was sleeping in the middle of the clouds. Maybe some twinkle lights. Or at least some posters. Anything that would belong only to her. But her mom said she didn't have the money, even though it wouldn't be *that* much, so Lila had never asked Macie to sleep over. She'd rather die than have Macie see her room before their friendship had gone any further.

Everyone already talked constantly about Lila's mom. Caroline Sawyer didn't bring orange slices to soccer games, or go to PTSA meetings, or talk to any of the other moms if there was a recital or a concert or a potluck, or gossip about whatever someone named Susan said on Facebook that week. Instead, her mother hovered at the back of everything like something you could see through. Like some painfully lovely ghost wearing the skin of something alive. But they all talked about Caroline. All the other moms chattered on and on about the artist who was semi-famous and *known* in the city, who made those disturbing sculptures that looked like something you'd see in a scary movie or in a haunted house. How strange to think that Caroline with her impeccable makeup, her shining hair, her toned body, which made the other mothers narrow their eyes whenever their husbands made no secret of staring at her, was capable of making such awful things. Tucked inside their voices was the discordant combination of awe and disgust, and whenever they started up their babbling, Lila would shrink further and further into herself, willing herself invisible, but of course, they always saw her, were forever asking in their syrupy-sweet voices what Caroline was working on now? Or marveling aloud how they would have never guessed that Lila was Caroline's daughter since they looked nothing alike. "Your mother is so pretty! Funny how genes work out sometimes." And there was Lila shrugging her shoulders before excusing herself, the inside of her mouth aching from biting down on her cheeks.

Every morning, Lila hoped she would wake up magically transformed into the kind of girl who looked or behaved like her mother's daughter. Effortlessly beautiful. Talented or athletic or intelligent. Or even just one of those things. Anything to set her apart. Instead, every day was a reminder of exactly how average she was. Her plain face, devoid of her mother's high cheekbones and full lips and large eyes. The constant parade of

Bs and Cs on her report cards. The complete lack of any artistic talent—her childish attempts relegated to the trash can before anyone could see them. If she hadn't seen her own birth certificate, she would have wondered if she'd been adopted.

Lila grabbed her strawberry lip gloss and swiped it over her mouth and then dragged a brush through her hair and hoped it would dry straight instead of the frizzy mess it normally was. She'd inherited her dad's curly, dark strands, and it was yet another thing to resent him for. Knowing her luck, her hair would go crazy the second she stepped outside, and Macie would sigh and tell her she should try harder or at least get up earlier and straighten it before school; Lila was *so* lucky because her skin was fucking *flawless,* but she *had* to do something with her hair.

She left her bedroom without glancing at the mirror again. It was pointless to imagine she was going to look like anyone other than herself, and anyway, she was already cutting it too close with the time. Soon enough, her mother would come barging in, hurrying her along. In fact, Lila was surprised she hadn't done exactly that already, but her mother's bedroom door was closed, and the voice leaking from beneath was the kind of hush that didn't want to be heard. Lila crept closer, pausing after each footstep, and then pressed her ear to the door.

"It's just like before," her mother said. "There were bite marks on her thighs. And there was a woman on the news who said she saw the girl with a man. Tall and wearing a dark coat. That doesn't strike you as too similar to be a coincidence?"

Lila's heart leapt into her throat. Her mother was talking about the girl whose body had been found. That much was normal. Probably that's all anyone was going to be talking about for a while. But it was the *before* and *similar* that made Lila hold her breath so she could hear more clearly.

"I know there are terrible people everywhere, Daniel, but it's just . . . eerie. Something about it doesn't feel right . . ." Her mother paused and let out a loud sigh. "Well, you don't have to be an asshole about it." Lila pictured her father on the other end, a frown dominating his face, his forehead creased in frustration. "I'm perfectly aware of what you're going through, and I understand how difficult it is, but you have another daughter, too. Or have you forgotten again?"

Lila withdrew quickly, tiptoeing down the hallway and into the kitchen to search for a granola bar or another distraction. She didn't want to hear the rest, didn't want to hear that same argument rehashed for the hundredth time.

Before. Her mind snagged on the word like something thorned. Her mother never spoke of her past, of her life in New Orleans, where she'd met Lila's father. All Lila knew was it hadn't worked out, and Caroline had moved to Atlanta shortly before Hurricane Katrina to finish art school. Now, she taught at the same university, and life had fallen into a comfortable rhythm. Whenever Lila brought up her mother's past or asked about it, her mother only shrugged and said it had been a long time ago, and it hurt too much to think about. Leaving her father had been messy and left more emotional baggage than she cared to unpack.

There were the rows of orange pill bottles in the medicine cabinet, and the days when her mother could not get out of bed and ignored her artwork, and the hours Lila had spent in a waiting room, flipping through the same *Highlights* magazines while her mother offered up her secrets to her psychiatrist. Eventually, Lila had learned to stop asking. But now, that word, that *before,* had brought forward an unrecognizable piece of her mother, and Lila unwrapped a granola bar and bit down. It was stale.

"Morning," her mother said, and Lila turned, waited for her mother to spill out everything Lila had ever wanted to know, to explain how this missing girl was similar to something her mother had once known, but her mother didn't say anything more, the dark circles under her eyes she'd tried to cover with concealer evidence of her lack of sleep. But that was how it had always been. Always busy. Always working. A never-ending line of classes to teach or students to advise or projects to finish or galleries to visit.

"You ready? We're going to be late if we don't get a move on," her mother said, and Lila waited another beat—to give her mother the chance to explain, to say anything that might be real—and then she nodded.

Once they were in the car and buckled, her mother brought her fingers to her eyes and patted at the dark circles as if she could get the blood there moving to lessen the appearance of fatigue.

"I talked to your dad this morning."

Lila tucked her hands underneath her thighs to keep them from fidgeting. Her mother would tell her now, about *before*, and there would be no more mystery. "Yeah?"

"He said you weren't returning any of his calls. He wants to see you, Lila. It's been months since you were out there. He misses you."

Lila let her breath hiss out of her. So that's what this conversation was going to be. A continued silence about her mother's secret past and a reminder of something Lila would prefer to forget.

"Misses me so much he said maybe five words to me the last time I was there."

Her mother sighed. "Rebecca had just had Brina. Having a preemie with a heart condition is a lot to deal with."

Lila stared straight ahead, her lips pursed tight. It wasn't just that her dad and stepmother had been distracted or concerned about the health of their new baby. It was like Lila had actually been invisible. He was so completely absorbed by his new daughter that he was four hours late picking Lila up from the airport. The attendant, with her pinched face and sad, drooping eyes, had led her away from the crowds streaming to their cars and into a tiny room that smelled of reheated food and coffee, so she could call and remind Daniel of his forgotten daughter. After that trip, her mother had finally caved and bought Lila a cell phone.

Even after her father finally picked her up, he didn't apologize but spent the car ride in silence, drumming his fingers against the wheel as he sped back to the house, where he dropped Lila off with instructions for how to find the spare key.

"I'll be home later. There's a pizza in the freezer. Call my cell if you need me. Reception isn't great in the hospital, but you can call the NICU if you have to. You can look the number up online," he said as he popped the trunk so she could grab her suitcase. He didn't even get out of the car but lifted his hand in a wave as he backed down the driveway.

For the rest of the trip, she'd stayed inside the extra bedroom they kept for her, with the plain white walls, and the plain navy sheets, and the boring dresser that held extra pillowcases for when guests came to visit. It had never been her room. Even with her clothes hanging in the closet and her books scattered next to the bed, her dad and Rebecca had never kept it for her. Not really.

She'd stayed in the room and read her books and came out at night like some nocturnal creature to watch television and eat the takeout her father brought home, and Rebecca would stare around her with bleary eyes as if seeing Lila for the first time. Her father would sometimes ask Lila how her day had been, and then Rebecca would ask for something or mention something about Brina, and her father would stop listening to anything Lila had to say.

The week passed, and when her father dropped her off at the

airport, he didn't walk her to security like he normally did. "Love you, kiddo," he said, and then left her standing there at the automatic doors.

She did not cry until she got onto the flight and then covered her face with a blanket so no one would see.

"You should call him, Lila," her mother said. Lila felt her face growing hot, and she bit down on her tongue. She would not cry. Not now.

"Why are you taking his side? You were mad at him, too," she said.

"I'm not taking his side. I'm just saying he wants to talk to you." Caroline dropped her voice to a whisper. "Even if he is being a jerk."

Lila smirked, and Caroline nudged her with an elbow. "I'm not going to force you to call him if you don't want to. Just passing along the message. I don't blame you for being angry with him. Just try to give him a little bit of a break. He's under a lot of stress."

Her mother went quiet then—no further mention of the *other* thing she and Lila's father had talked about—and Lila stared out the window. Everything growing green and lush and humid and thick. She wanted to tug off her leggings and let the air run over her skin. Instead, she fidgeted against the seat and pretended that the silence hanging between her and her mother wasn't at all like a blade pushed deep inside her gut. There was something else to know, and she wished her mother would just tell her what it was.

"You heard about the girl they found? The one who'd been missing?" Lila asked, turning to Caroline so she could watch her mother's face, watch for the twitching of a muscle, a slight frown, anything that would indicate there was an actual person behind this bland mask of calm.

"I heard."

"You heard how they found her?" Her mother winced then, and Lila pressed on. "All torn up?"

"Stop it, Lila. I don't want to talk about that."

"You think they know how he did it? Like with a knife or something? Or maybe it was worse than that. His teeth or his fingernails." She felt sick with her own words, unable to keep her need to talk about what happened from bubbling out of her, but she couldn't stop. She needed her mother to tell her about *before,* something to fill out the hurt she felt over her father, but her mother set her jaw.

"I said stop it."

They both went quiet then, Lila's fist pushed against her stomach to keep everything she wanted to say contained.

Only when they pulled up to the front entrance of the school did her mother speak again. "Look at me," she said, but Lila was already pulling her backpack over her shoulder, her weight pushing against the door.

"Lila, look at me."

Lila paused and turned to stare at her mother. *Tell me. Tell me about before.*

"What happened to that girl is terrible. It's disgusting, and the thought of it makes me sick and angry, and I don't know what I would do if something like that happened to you." Her mother's breath caught and hitched, her eyes going glassy, and Lila wished she could pull everything she said back inside of her, swallow it back down and bury it so her mother would not hurt like this.

"I worry so much. How I can't be there to protect you, and you're older now, and I can't . . . I can't . . ." Her mother dissolved into tears then, and Lila leaned over the console, the gearshift jabbing against her ribs, and hugged her mother. Her hair smelled of mint and rosemary. The way a mother's hair should smell. A smell that reminded Lila of how her mother used to carry her, to sing her to sleep, to sit beside her when she had a nightmare until they both drifted off.

"I'm sorry," she mumbled, and her mother nodded into her shoulder.

"I love you, my girl." Her mother's hands fluttered against her back and then her shoulders, pushing her away as she dashed the tears from her eyes. "Now go or you'll be late. I'll be right here to pick you up after school. Only early classes today and no advisement sessions," she said, and Lila climbed out of the car.

Only when she knew her mother was gone did she realize she had not responded. "Love you, too," she mumbled, already guilty over not saying it when her mother was still there.

"Where the hell have you been? We were supposed to meet early so I could do your makeup." Macie appeared at Lila's elbow, her golden hair shining in perfect spirals.

"Nowhere. Running late," Lila said, trying, without success, to hide the thickness in her voice. Macie rolled her eyes and reached out to fluff Lila's hair.

"I guess it's fine. You need some eyeliner though. Andrew would die if he saw you with eyeliner. Super sexy. And ditch the leggings. It looks weird. We can tell Ms. Shakib you're on your period and do it in the restroom real quick."

Lila cringed at the mention of her period. Here was another thing Macie had that she didn't. Another reason Lila felt like a kid instead of a teenager. "She'll never buy that. I haven't even gotten my period yet. And I don't like Andrew that way."

"Um, she can't tell us we can't go to the bathroom if we're bleeding all over ourselves. And how's she going to know you haven't gotten it yet? Plus, Andrew's got the mega hots for you. Trust me."

Lila let Macie tug her forward. Somehow Macie never got in trouble for being in the hallway after the bell. She'd bat her eyes and say she'd forgotten an essay on her desk at home or she was running an errand for a teacher, and the administrator on hall

duty would smile back at her and do nothing. Macie lived in a
world where everything was uncomplicated, and Lila envied her
for it. Macie never questioned herself, never doubted whether
or not she would get exactly what she wanted, and Lila understood it was because Macie was conventionally pretty. No one
ever imagined the pretty girl doing anything wrong.

When they got into the bathroom, Macie took Lila by the
shoulders and turned her this way and that. "Okay," she said.
"Close your eyes. I can do this quick."

Lila held her breath as Macie leaned into her. She smelled
of cinnamon gum and cotton candy body lotion, her mouth so
close Lila wanted to press her own to it and let whatever would
happen unfold, but she could not bring herself to do it.

"Don't make it too thick, okay?" she said, and Macie huffed.

"Just hold still," Macie said, and then pulled Lila's eyelid taut.
"Listen, my mom said you could stay over tomorrow night. So
we can finish the poetry project."

"On a school night? At your house?" Lila's heart pounded.
She and Macie hung out at school and texted and followed each
other on every form of social media, but there'd never been a
sleepover or one-on-one hangout. Never the chance of isolated
hours together spinning outward.

Lila could practically hear Macie roll her eyes. "We're working on school stuff. It's completely fine."

"No way will my mom let me go. Not with everything that's
happened with that girl."

Macie sighed and pulled Lila's eyelid tighter. "Your mom's kind
of lame, you know?"

Something sharp twisted inside of Lila, and there was a terrible feeling building in her mouth, pushing her tongue against
her teeth, but she didn't say anything at all. She understood her
silence was a kind of betrayal of her mother. She should have
defended her, but she would not argue against Macie.

Macie continued. "The cops will find whoever did it. It's, like, *their job*. Besides, we'll be in my house, behind a locked door, with an alarm system. Plus my mom has a gun in her bedside table. Keeps it loaded."

"I'll ask," she finally said, and Macie tapped her on the forehead.

"Okay. All done. Andrew's going to love it," Macie said, and Lila turned to face this new girl in the mirror. This girl with kohl-smudged eyes who looked sleepy and mysterious at the same time. This girl who was not Lila. It wasn't a bad thing. Not at all.

Lila grinned, her mouth filled with slightly crooked teeth, and the sight of this normal part of her ruined everything. Ran a crack through the beautiful thing she was trying to be.

"Get rid of the leggings and let's go," Macie said. Before Lila could respond, Macie rushed out of the bathroom. She would never be anything other than Lila Sawyer. Forever the embodiment of almost but not quite.

Lila let Macie do the talking when they walked into the classroom, kept her head down and headed to her seat while Macie whispered to Ms. Shakib. Andrew was already in his desk. He stared at her as she passed, but it wasn't his gaze Lila was concerned with.

Stupid, stupid, stupid.

For an hour Lila practiced breathing in small sips and curled her fingers against her wrists. Anything to keep from screaming because Macie couldn't even see what was right in front of her. Lila didn't want Andrew. Not at all. She wanted *Macie*. Sweat clung between her thighs. She'd forgotten to take off her leggings.

When the bell rang, she gathered her things slowly.

"Andrew definitely looked at you," Macie said as they left.

"No, he didn't."

"Shut up. He totally did. Ask your mom about tomorrow.

Don't forget!" Macie said, and then the crowd swallowed her as they separated for second period.

Lila spent her classes swiping at her eyes, leaving her fingers stained and her skin raw. She probably looked like a freak, but it didn't really matter. She could never tell Macie how she felt. How when she closed her eyes at night, she thought of Macie beside her, their breath rising in ragged peaks as they stared at each other, their fingers skimming over each other's shoulders and collarbones, everything lit up and electric in the need for more. But she knew Macie. How she would never talk to Lila ever again; how she would call her a dyke behind her back and then in front of her. She'd done that exact thing three months ago when Cassidy Truman cut her hair into a pixie cut that was less pixie and more troll. If Macie knew how Lila really felt, she'd let Lila drop away. Used and disposed of. And if that happened, Lila's heart would shatter.

She passed the rest of the day listening to everyone talk about the girl, their fear dropping out of them like hard stones. Hours of hoping her mother would say she could stay at Macie's, hoping that for once, her mother would allow Lila this one thing. Just this once.

After the final bell, Lila wiped off what remained of the eyeliner in the restroom and drifted outside, but Macie was already gone. Some days her mom would pick her up, but most days Macie rode the bus or walked home so she could pass the high school with its horde of older boys who had their own cars. Lila checked her phone, but it was empty. No messages. No notifications. Her mother was already at the curb, the ancient, forest green Saturn idling blue smoke.

"Good day?" her mother asked.

"Yeah. Nothing new," she said, but there were two questions burning inside of her, two things she wanted so deeply they deleted everything else: there was the dead girl, and the secret her mother was so obviously keeping about the murder, but more important was Macie's invitation. She would wait until they got home, her mother focused on the new sculpture she was working on, to ask her about staying over at Macie's. After dinner. While her mother was working. That would be the best time. Her mother's mind would be elsewhere, and maybe she would forget about the dead girl and just say yes.

Through a dinner of flavorless chicken and frozen vegetables, Lila stayed quiet, nodding or saying "yes" or "no" to her mother's questions as she poked at her phone, desperate for something from Macie. A text message. An Instagram comment. Anything.

"Something major happening inside that thing?" Caroline said as she took a delicate bite of her chicken.

"Sorry." Lila slid the phone across the table and focused on pushing her food around her plate until enough time had passed for her to dump what remained in the garbage. Almost every night was like this. The silence stretching between them as they pecked at her mother's best approximation of a healthy, balanced dinner. Caroline's reasonable portions a reminder of the calories Lila shouldn't consume.

"I'm going to work for a bit, if that's okay. Want to finish this piece before the month is out. Brenda will have my ass if it takes much longer," Caroline said.

Lila nodded. "I have homework anyway," she said, but it was a lie. She'd finished everything in that afternoon's study hall, so she paced the length of her bedroom, listening to the distant sound of her mother pulling out the old tackle box where she kept her materials. The twigs and leaves and pebbles and other shredded portions of nature that made up her artwork. Once, Lila had gone through the tackle box and found the fully preserved body of a stag beetle. At the time, she hadn't known to think it was strange. At the time, it was only an odd, beautiful thing her mother would use to make another odd, beautiful thing.

For forty-five minutes, Lila sat in her bedroom counting the seconds until she knew her mother would be distracted enough to say yes. Her phone pinged once ten minutes in. Macie asking if she could come. She forced herself to wait the full forty-five minutes even though she wanted to leap up right then and tell her mother she was going whether Caroline said yes or not.

Finally, she wandered out of her bedroom and stood behind Caroline, watching as her mother bent a thin, transparent wire into a hook. Going slowly, she pierced a magnolia leaf with the wire and then threaded it through. The sculpture was a woman, but her legs were transparent, vanishing into nothing, and her mouth . . . Lila didn't like to look at the mouth. It gaped and seemed to be forever locked in a scream. The lips looked like the legs of large insects dyed scarlet. Probably they were.

"Mom?" she began, and then stopped, waiting for her mother to look up. It was better if she didn't, but she did.

"Hmm?" Caroline's hands continued to work automatically, and her eyes were distant, glazed.

"So Macie and I have this project in English. Poetry. It's due next week, and she asked if I could go over there tomorrow to work on it, and then, you know, stay the night? Since we'd be working on the project," Lila said. Her mother flicked her eyes back down to her hands.

"Absolutely not. It's a school night, Lila," her mother said.

"We're working on a project, *for* school. You want me to get a good grade, don't you?"

"You can get a good grade without staying at your friend's house on a school night."

"We're going to be working the whole night. I promise. We'll just be in Macie's house, and her mom will be there, and they have a security system. It's super safe," Lila said, leaving out the part about Macie's mother's gun.

Caroline sighed, and set down the wire, the leaf. Not good.

"I'm in the middle of something, Lila. You know about not interrupting me. And I said no."

"Please? It's for school."

"Jesus Christ, I guess I won't be finishing this tonight." Her mother's hand brushed against the leaf, and it went skittering across the table. "There's too much happening now. The police don't even know what really happened to that girl, or what it is they're dealing with. This just isn't a good idea."

"We'll stay inside, I promise. It's just Macie's house. Please, Mom? Please?" Lila hated the girlish whining in her voice and how like a child it made her feel. Like she was incapable of finding the correct, adult words. Yes, there was a girl who'd been killed, but that wasn't going to be Lila, not tucked away in Macie's bedroom with music and popcorn and pajamas.

Her mother's face tightened, and again Lila thought of the *before* her mother had talked about, but there was Macie and an entire night together, and in the face of that possibility, so little else mattered.

Her mother sighed.

"Fine," she said. Lila squealed, and her mother held up her hand. "Conditions first. I drop you off at the door. No riding home with Macie or walking to her house from the school. You'll call me twice. Once at six, and again before you go to bed. And then I'll be the one to pick you up for school in the morning. Seven o'clock sharp."

"Yes! Sure, I can do that. No problem," Lila said, unable to control the stupid grin on her face.

Sighing again, her mother stared down at the sculpture. "Help me clean this mess up at least. Since you distracted me. No way I'll be able to get back into the zone tonight."

"Sorry," Lila said, and she truly meant it. Her mother smiled so infrequently except for when she was working. Then her mother became a different person altogether, lit up and glowing.

They cleaned up, Lila still avoiding looking at the sculpture's mouth, and then they watched television together, their bodies uncomfortable on the lumpy green couch her mother had bought thirdhand at a yard sale. Some old sitcom with jokes that were less than funny. Lila had already started to doze when the late news came on, the bleach-blond newscaster grimly staring into the camera as she recounted the top story. The screen flashed to a police officer surrounded by microphones as reporters shouted questions.

"We have no reason to think this is anything other than an isolated incident at this time," he said before pointing into the audience at a reporter the camera didn't pan to.

"And what about similarities to other killings? The ones attributed to The Cur?"

"Again, we have no reason to suspect this case has any connections to anything else at this time, but we are closely examining all leads," the officer said. Her mother shifted beside her, her hands scrambling for the remote.

"It's late, Lila. Time for bed," she said as she clicked off the television, and Lila pretended not to notice the tremor in her mother's voice. She slid across the couch and hugged her mother. She did not pull away when the hug lasted longer than normal.

"Love you. Good night," she said.

"You too, my girl. Sleep tight."

When Lila finally pulled away, there was no denying the fear in her mother's eyes.

CHAPTER 2

LILA 2019

"I still can't believe your mom let you come." Macie was draped across her bed, her hair fanned out behind her so it looked like a halo. Lila's fingers itched with the need to touch those curls, to slip her fingers through the heavy strands, but she kept her hands still, her fingernails pressing half-moons into her palms.

They'd spent the afternoon and evening talking about the project without actually doing anything. They'd made their own dinner—some pasta and a half-empty jar of marinara Macie found in the door of the refrigerator. Five times they'd sneaked into the kitchen to take long pulls from one of the many bottles of wine Macie's mother had in the refrigerator and then tiptoed giggling back to Macie's bedroom. Macie's mother was late getting home from work, and when she did, she'd poured her own glass of wine and gone straight into her bedroom, Macie directing a middle finger at the woman's retreating back.

Forever the dutiful daughter, Lila had called her mother as instructed, Macie making a point to roll her eyes as she chatted with her mom, reassuring her that yes, they were working, and no, they weren't doing anything else. At ten, she'd called to tell her they were going to bed, but of course, they didn't. Instead, Macie had poured more wine into a plastic cup before hustling Lila off the phone and back up to her bedroom.

At midnight, they were tipsy, giggling and falling over each other as Macie tried to teach Lila some dance move that involved complicated, quick steps, and Lila never wanted the night to end, wished she could will the sun to stay dark and cocoon herself in this moment until her breath stopped coming. At some point, Macie had reached under her T-shirt and stripped off her bra because the underwire was cutting into her. As Macie pressed her body to Lila's to show her the dance, Lila's heart was a raw, aching thing, and she wondered if this was what approaching the shimmering edge of love felt like.

Macie had finally collapsed on the bed, her chest rising and falling with their efforts, and Lila had followed her down, their bodies touching but featherlight so it almost wasn't physical connection at all.

"I'm bored. We should do something." Macie sat up and scooted off the edge of the bed, and Lila willed her to come back, to never leave that spot again.

"Like what?"

"I don't know. Sneak out or something. My mom always takes a sleeping pill at night. Trust me, she's out cold. She wouldn't even hear us leave."

"And go where?"

Macie groaned. "I don't know, Lila. Does it matter? It sucks just sitting around. Maybe I'll text Cameron. See if he wants to meet us."

"As in Andrew's older brother, Cameron?"

Macie bounced forward to grab her cell phone. "I'll see if Andrew wants to come, too. Like a double date!"

Lila shook her head. Her tongue suddenly felt heavy, her limbs dead things she couldn't lift. Outside, the world was painted in dark. She didn't want to go out there into all of that terrible, moonless black, out there where something or someone had taken a girl apart and left her in pieces.

"My mom," Lila said, but her brain was fuzzy, her skin hot. "She wouldn't let me."

"It's done!" Macie tugged on her hand. "And your mom isn't here, is she? She won't know. Put your shoes on and let's go. I told him to meet us at the end of the street if he wants. No response yet, but I bet he'll come."

Slowly, Lila pulled on her black ballet flats and stood. Her mother would be furious if she found out, but Macie's mom was asleep and would stay asleep. She'd seen before how sleeping pills worked on her own mother. Lila could have screamed in her ear for hours, and her mother would have kept snoring.

"I can't believe you have Cameron's number. It's kind of weird, don't you think? Why would he want to talk to somebody in eighth grade if he's a junior?" Lila flexed her legs, her neck, but still she felt disconnected from everything that was happening. Like the world had slipped behind a darker veil. It was exciting and scary at the same time, and she pushed against the butterflies forming in her stomach. Never before had she dared to step outside the prescribed life her mother had placed over her. A bell jar meant to stifle and display. She was going to do this because it was Macie, and she wanted Macie to think she was daring: the kind of girl who did crazy things and then laughed about them later. But there was her fear rising, and her skin was clammy and cold. Outside, there were teeth and pain and ghosts who were once girls. In the dark, they would whisper of what happened to them.

"I've been texting him for like two weeks now. We talked at a basketball game for a little while. He said I was mature for my age. And how cute is it if you date Andrew, and I date Cameron? Best friends and brothers. We can have a double wedding." Macie pursed her lips. "Plus he has a car. Let's go already. Jesus, you're slow!"

Somewhere in the distance, a dog barked. Lila jumped, her heart hammering in her ears.

"It's just a dog," Macie said. Lila swiped her damp palms against her shirt. Her mother was terrified of dogs, and that anxiety had seeded in Lila as well. From her earliest memory, she understood that running underneath those growls and barks was a thread of violence. The dog barked again, lower this time and more guttural, and Lila squeezed her eyes shut.

"Come on," Macie said, and Lila shivered. There was no reason for her to feel so afraid. It was just a dog. And they were just going outside. There was nothing to worry about, but her armpits had gone damp, and panic fought in her belly. If they went outside, something terrible would happen.

Since she was little, she'd had small moments like this. Dread squeezing at her heart as she lay panting on the floor and imagining there was a monster at the door or lurking under her bed. But she'd learned to force herself through these episodes and breathe until her alarm subsided. She'd never told her mom or dad. Already, there were the psychiatrist appointments and the medication, and Lila didn't want to add to her mother's burden. And her dad would blow it out of proportion the way he always did.

She hadn't realized until she was older why her father seemed to watch her so carefully at times or to question her on particular points that didn't seem to be important. As if he was always waiting for some damaged thing inside Lila to finally reveal itself. For him to finally see that she was, in fact, her mother's daughter not only in blood but also in brokenness. So she kept herself as quiet as she could and hid in the bathroom with a towel stuffed in her mouth if the panic overwhelmed her while she was at her dad's house. Because she understood her father's belief that the darkness coiled deep in her mother's brain could infect Lila as well. But more important was the need for her silence. To be his "best girl." Even if he hadn't called her that in years.

Lila let her eyes open and glanced over at Macie, her hair golden and hanging down her back. She took a deep breath and let it out, imagining it would stain the air with her weakness. A sulfurous yellow mist.

"Cameron still hasn't said anything back." Macie frowned and slid her phone into her back pocket.

"Maybe he's sleeping."

"I guess." Macie turned toward the window. There were no blinds, only two sheer panels. Framed by that murky square, she looked not real. A girl drawn in miniature.

"He's probably sleeping," Lila said again, desperate to keep Macie focused on her instead of on the outside, slumbering world. On her, instead of Cameron.

Macie let her head tip back, her neck pale and smooth, and closed her eyes. It hurt Lila to see how beautiful she was.

"Are you ready yet?" Macie said. Lila bit down on her tongue, but she wasn't brave enough to do it hard enough to draw blood. To make it hurt enough to force the words she didn't want to say up and out.

"My mom would be so pissed." Better to blame her mom than to have Macie know the truth. That she was afraid of whatever unknowable monster lurked outside.

"Oh my God. Don't be such a fucking baby."

"I'm not," Lila said, stung by the severity in Macie's voice. Lila looked down at her hands. It didn't matter if it had only been a dog barking. The night had grown strange, as if somehow she'd momentarily shed her skin, and she wished she'd never come to Macie's house, wished she was home and safe in her own bed.

Tears pricked at the corners of her eyes, and she didn't bother to wipe them away.

"I can't," she said, louder this time, and Macie's face went hard.

"No fucking way. I already texted Cameron. If he comes, and we're not there, he'll probably never talk to me again." Macie paused and took a step forward. "Jesus. Are you actually crying?"

"No. Don't be mad," Lila said, but her voice was thick.

"I swear to God, Lila, if you mess this up, I'll never talk to you again. You can go back to being the weirdo sitting alone in the corner."

Lila curled into herself. She sank onto Macie's bed and hugged her arms over her abdomen as if she could somehow hold in the hurt of what Macie had said.

"Sorry," she said, but there were other things raging inside of her. Harder, sharper things that could wound, but she couldn't say them even if the desire to do so burned in the deeper parts of her. She couldn't go back to being completely alone. Macie wasn't the most popular girl in school, but most people liked her, and when she'd sat next to Lila at lunch at the start of the year, Lila's entire world had changed. And now there was that deeper feeling that turned her heart liquid. If she lost Macie now, Lila imagined the blood moving through her would solidify, her heart useless in its breaking.

"You are the literal worst. If he texts, I'm going without you. And if Andrew's there, I'm telling him what a bitch you are." She flopped onto her bed. "Just go to sleep then. I'm waiting to see if he texts back."

Lila paused, considering if she would be allowed to sleep next to Macie. She purposely hadn't brought a sleeping bag, hoping . . . for what, she couldn't be sure. Had she actually thought Macie would let Lila sleep in her bed? It had been stupid to hope. Stupid to imagine she could bring herself to confess her feelings to Macie.

Stupid to think there would be something more than the disappointment the night had become.

"There's an extra blanket and pillow in the closet since you didn't bring anything," Macie said, and Lila ducked her head even though there was no way for Macie to see the flush of shame creeping over her neck.

"Thanks," she said, going to the closet.

"Whatever," Macie said, and then the girls were quiet.

From her spot on the floor, Lila watched as Macie stared at her phone. Lila's own phone remained quiet beside her, and finally, at one thirty, Macie rose and switched off the light.

So Cameron had never responded. A bitter victory for Lila.

Eventually, Macie's breathing evened, but Lila could not sleep. Her skin felt too tight, the air around her too thick, the sensation of inherent wrongness pressing into her as if it could invade her lungs. She turned onto her side and forced her eyes closed.

At first the sound was small. An animal come awake in the night and scurrying through fallen leaves. Something without teeth and claws. Something safe. But it grew louder as if whatever it was had come close to the house.

Lila sat up, her breath catching in her throat as she peered at the window. Again, the sound rippled through the dark, but it had changed. It had grown quieter, more elusive. Like the moment before something draws breath.

Looking through the window, Lila could see the dim outline of the tree line across the street, how the shadows bent toward each other, tangling into a nightmarish landscape. The sound crested, and outside, among the trees, something shook itself loose. Yellow eyes winked back and then vanished.

Lila clutched at the blanket, but she could not speak. From the darkness, those yellow eyes flashed again. They were too high off the ground to be a dog. Maybe an owl? Lila crept forward, her palms slick against the carpet. She pressed her face to the window as fear grew hot in her throat.

Outside, something howled, and Lila pushed away from the window and back toward her makeshift bed. She wrapped herself in the blanket as if she could hide herself, as if something so flimsy could keep her safe. *Just a dog. It's just a dog.* She repeated the words to herself again and again as if they could calm her.

Eventually, she dropped into a fitful sleep, and she dreamed of yellow eyes, of Macie leering over her with a mouth full of sharp teeth.

When morning came, the room lit in a soft glow, Lila rose and showered, embarrassed to face Macie, and angry, too. So frequently now, she was angry at herself, angry for her own silence, for her own limited ability to say exactly how she felt. She was brushing her teeth, Macie still asleep in her room, when the doorbell rang, and Lila jerked, the toothbrush jabbing her gums.

She waited for someone to stir, Macie or her mother, someone who belonged here, unlike Lila, who imagined she belonged nowhere. The doorbell rang again, and the house remained silent. Lila padded down the stairs, the doorbell sounding a third time. There was no way both Macie and her mother had slept through the bell, but still no one appeared, so Lila made her way to the door, standing on tiptoe to peer through the peephole. Her mother stood on the porch, bleary-eyed, her fist raised to hammer against the wood.

Lila went to open the door, then paused, remembering she didn't know the alarm code. She pressed her mouth to the door, hoping her mother would be able to hear her through the thick wood.

"Mom? I don't know the code, and everyone else is asleep. What are you doing here? You're super early."

"Get your things, Lila. Right now. We're going."

Lila's skin went cold. It wasn't possible for her mother to know Macie had texted Cameron. No way.

"What's wrong?" she said, and behind her, a bedroom door opened.

"Everything okay?" Macie's mother stood at the top of the stairs, her hair slicked against one side of her head.

"It's my mom," Lila said.

"Could have at least called first," she mumbled as she shuffled down the stairs, her fingers punching in the code before pulling the door open and blinking into the sunlight.

Lila's mother stepped forward and grabbed Lila into a bear hug. "Jesus," she said as she folded Lila against her. Her mother smelled of sour sweat, and Lila wondered if she'd even bothered with showering that morning. This was not the flawless version of her mother she knew.

"Is something wrong?" Macie's mother stood off to the side, wrapping her arms around herself.

"Go and get your things, Lila," her mother said, and when Lila didn't move, she snapped. "Now."

Lila took the stairs quickly, listening as the two women talked in low, hurried voices. Something was wrong, and Lila thought of her father and immediately felt sick. If anything had happened to him or to Brina, she would never be able to forgive herself for the resentment she felt toward them. It wasn't exactly Brina's fault, but it was her birth that had led to her father's absolute disregard of Lila.

Macie had woken up but made no movements as Lila gathered her few things and then crept back to the top of the stairs, pausing to listen to her mother's lowered voice.

"She was just like the first one," her mother said, and Macie's mother murmured something that sounded like alarm. "Found her three streets over. I was terrified and came straight here. I'm so sorry to have woken you."

"Don't even think of it. I completely understand."

Lila descended the stairs, making enough noise so the women would know she was coming. Another girl. She thought of those yellow eyes staring back at her from the woods and wondered if the howling she had heard was the sound of that girl being torn apart. She stared at her feet to keep herself from falling. Around her, the house felt too small, as if she were tucked inside the contracting stomach of some beast.

"Ready?" her mother asked when she saw her. All Lila could do was nod. "Thank you again, Kelly. I didn't mean to scare you."

"Y'all be careful," Macie's mother said, and then Lila's mother was hurrying them to the car, her grip on Lila's elbow tight enough to hurt.

CHAPTER 3

LILA 2019

At first, Lila couldn't bring herself to speak, to ask her mother about this second girl. Locked inside her memory was the vision of those yellow eyes staring back at her, and the overwhelming, unexplainable terror she'd felt. Her insides constricted around her fear and curiosity. She shouldn't want to know what had happened to the girl, but she did.

"They found another girl?"

Her mother twitched her hands against the steering wheel before she opened her mouth and then closed it so hard Lila heard her teeth clack together.

"Yes."

"The same as before?"

"Yes," her mother said again.

Lila hesitated, tested the weight of her question in her mouth, the possibility of the connection to what she'd seen the night before. "Do they think it's dogs that are doing it?"

"I don't know, Lila. I don't want to talk about it. You're safe. That's all that matters."

"Probably not dogs though. Not now that there have been two of them. Maybe it's more than one person. Or a group of people. Or maybe they do it and then have dogs mess them up so it's harder to figure out what they did to the girls?" The questions streamed out of her, filling up her mother's silence, but for all of their heft, they did no good. Her mother did not respond but looked like she would be sick.

Caroline drove on, the trees exploding around them with greenery and dribbling dying blossoms toward the earth as whatever hid inside the wooded areas huddled safe in the newborn screen of leaves. Her mother turned on the radio, and voices filled the car, harsh, discordant eruptions arguing back and forth.

"At this point, police should be looking for a serial killer. There were those cases in New Orleans. The Cur—"

"But that was over a decade ago. Serial killers don't just stop for, what, fifteen years and then turn back up in a completely different city."

"Maybe he was in prison for something other than the murders. Or he could've been hiding out somewhere else, but it's clear he's active again, and the cops aren't—"

The voices vanished, her mother's hand trembling as she punched at the radio's power button.

Her mother's face was stricken, her eyes focusing on the distance as she made the next turn automatically. "I'll be here to pick you up right after school. Stay where there are other people. Other kids and teachers. If you see . . ." She trailed off, her fingers fluttering over her mouth, before shaking her head as if to clear away whatever it was she'd almost said.

"If I see *what*?" Lila asked.

"Right after school. Come straight out." They turned into the drop-off lane, and her mother took the curve too quickly, her tire scraping against the curb.

"Tell me what you were going to say."

"I'll pick you up right after school. Love you," her mother said, staring ahead, the conversation clearly over. Lila climbed out of the car but then leaned back inside.

"Love you, Mom," she said, closed the door, and watched as her mother drove away, taking her unspoken words with her.

Macie didn't sit next to Lila in first period or at lunch. Lila picked at the crust of the sandwich her mother had packed her and then stuffed the uneaten food into the garbage. Across the cafeteria, the girls Macie sat with instead giggled behind their palms, their heads pressed together as they whispered. Only once did Macie look up at Lila before immediately glancing away.

Lila wanted to shout across the cafeteria that Macie was being stupid. She hadn't done anything. She'd only been nervous, the dark night and the dog she'd heard scaring her because of what was going on. Cameron probably wouldn't have come anyway. She kept quiet, her fingers twitching over her split ends and despair heavy in her chest.

Everywhere, there were whispered conversations about the dead girls and the possibility of a killer. They rose like a vapor that the students swallowed greedily down, gobbling the tragedy because it was not their own and because they had not been the ones violated and left to rot in the dirt. Some of the students folded into themselves, wearing their fear and paranoia like a blanket, as they darted nervous glances over their shoulders and bent inward to hide away the softness of their bodies.

A woman walking her dog had found the second girl. This one was thirteen. Horses and a family stable. Private school uniforms and knee socks. The kind of girl you noticed, as opposed to the first girl, who was so starkly invisible. The kind of girl who

came from the money and wealth and privilege that was supposed to prevent things like this.

There were bite marks on her newly formed breasts; one nip-
ple missing. Her vagina split open as if whatever had wormed
its way inside her was not made of flesh and blood. Lila caught
snatches of the same phrases again and again until she wanted
to scream at all of them to shut up, to stop talking forever, but
the whispers rose and fell, the horrors spilling outward so it was
hard to breathe.

Without Macie to talk to, Lila distracted herself by reading
the news stories about the girls on her phone, but there wasn't
anything new to learn, and the more lurid details turned her
stomach. Police were investigating connections to similar killings that happened fifteen years before, in addition to a handful in the '80s, but those murders had occurred in a number of
different cities, none of them in Georgia. The only connections
between the older murders and the current ones were the ages of
the girls and the torn wounds on their bodies. No one had ever
been caught, and the killer they called The Cur had vanished
into obscurity. Lila closed her phone and put it away. She didn't
want to read about death anymore. Not with the memory of the
barking and howling she'd heard the night before still impressed
into her brain.

When the final bell rang, Lila felt once again as if she'd come
untethered from her own skin, and she floated toward the entrance. At home, she could go to bed, fall into a dim, blank sleep
where she wouldn't have to think about Macie's silence, or the
girls, or her mother's secret, or terrible, yellow eyes staring back
at her.

"Lila!" It was Macie's voice. Macie, calling to her and asking
her to wait. Macie, no longer silent, hurrying down the hallway
toward Lila, who had frozen, not sure if she should be apprehen-
sive or ecstatic or angry. Macie had ignored her all day over some

stupid *boy*. And look what had happened. Lila had every right to be freaked out, and Macie was making her feel terrible about it. It was bullshit. She opted for a blank expression and hoped her face held none of the warring emotions she carried inside.

"Cameron finally texted me," Macie said, catching Lila's arm and squeezing. "His mom caught him trying to sneak out, and she took his keys and his phone. He had to text me from a friend's phone because she told him he couldn't have it or his car for two days. That's why he couldn't come."

Lila nodded, waited for Macie to say she was sorry or she had been wrong, but of course, that wouldn't happen. It was stupid to hope.

"So anyway, that's what happened. Crazy, right? I thought he didn't like me or something, but it was just his mom." Macie took a small step forward, and Lila caught at the smell of her perfume, so sweet it was almost cloying. She breathed it in, wishing she could lick the scent off of Macie's skin. "Anyway, I didn't get a chance to tell you this morning that I like your shirt."

Macie's voice wavered, her meager olive branch extended, and she reached between them to tug at the hem of Lila's shirt, and of course everything was forgiven because Macie was there, and she was smiling and *touching* Lila, and of course Lila would let all of this go.

At the front of the school, her mother was probably already waiting, staring at the clock and starting to panic that she had not seen Lila spill out of the front doors with the rest of the students, but Lila didn't want to leave, didn't want to walk away from Macie now that she finally had her back, but Macie gripped her elbow and guided her out the main entrance.

"We didn't really get much of the project done, huh?"

Macie giggled and rolled her eyes. "It'll be fine. I'll FaceTime you when I get home, and we can work on it. There's your mom." She waved at the car and then turned away. "I'll call you later, 'kay?"

Giddy, Lila drifted toward the car, her mouth twitching into a smile. Macie wasn't angry with her, and the dark weight of the rumors about the girl fell away.

"Was that Macie?" her mother asked as Lila sank into the passenger seat. The interior of the car smelled of coffee and her mother's orange blossom perfume. Some stupidly expensive brand available only at Phipps that required an every-three-month pilgrimage to Peachtree for a new bottle.

"Yeah. She's going to call me later." Lila couldn't keep the smile from her face, and she tucked her chin into her chest and let her hair fall down around her. She knew if her mother saw, she would understand exactly how Lila felt about Macie, and Lila wasn't ready for that conversation. Not when her relationship with Macie still felt so fragile.

"I have class until eight tonight. There's leftovers in the fridge. Or you can make a sandwich. I'll drop you off, and you go straight inside and keep the door locked." She paused and glanced in the rearview mirror, her fingers smoothing her eye shadow and lipstick. "And don't open the door for anyone. No one. You hear me?"

"No one. Got it," Lila said, and her mother sighed out a long breath.

Fifteen minutes later, she was standing outside of the apartment door fumbling through her backpack for her key when her phone rang. Lila abandoned her backpack and grabbed her phone instead. Macie's face stared back at her. Lila smoothed her hair and tried to calm her fluttering heartbeat and then accepted the call.

"Hey! I'm just walking in. Give me a second," she said.

"Are you by yourself? You should invite Andrew over." Macie laughed, and Lila fought to keep herself from grimacing.

"My mom has to teach tonight. It's only a few hours." She ducked down to retrieve her backpack. An awful heat rose up her neck, and she hoped Macie wouldn't see the red splotches on her skin. The physical manifestation of her frustration stamped there for anyone to see. Why did Macie always have to make it about a boy? Why couldn't she see just Lila? Why couldn't that be enough?

"That's plenty of time."

Finally her fingers closed around her key, the metal cool against her heated palm, as she tried to keep the phone angled in a way that didn't make her look like a bloated monster with eight chins.

She changed the subject. They would not spend this time talking about stupid Andrew. "We only have the poetry analysis left, so I thought I could—"

"Holy shit. Oh my God. Cameron is calling me. I have to go." The call disconnected. Lila blinked down at the blank screen as the key slid into the lock. Her chest went tight, and the heat worked its way from her neck to her belly. Her skin felt like a thing separate from the meat of her. Something she could tear away and drop to the earth. Something she could shed.

Macie had hung up on her. Abandoned her again for some asshole that couldn't find a girl his own age, so he had to go sniffing around for someone easier to dazzle with his mediocrity.

Lila blinked, her eyes suddenly dry and aching. Closed the door behind her and locked it. Told herself to breathe. Told herself not to cry. She let her book bag fall, not caring if everything spilled out of it. Fuck Cameron and fuck Andrew, but mostly fuck Macie.

She took a few stumbling steps forward, but then stopped. Again, she blinked, unable to fully comprehend exactly what it was she was looking at. The kitchen was a disaster. Her mother's tackle box was spilled open over the table. Sticks, leaves, small rocks, and tufts of grass were spread over the surface and on the floor. Paintbrushes and tubes of acrylic paint also littered the space while pieces of hornets' nests and some gossamer material that looked like a bridal veil draped over the kitchen counter.

Lila lifted the thin, veil-like material in front of her face before letting it flutter back to the countertop.

Her mother never left her materials out. She always cleaned up immediately. Everything in its proper place. Not even when she'd seen her mother completely lost in her work, the world she was constructing in miniature the only thing that existed. She would have never left her precious materials scattered all over like this.

Lila let her fingers drift over the countertop and took a delicate step forward. There was something behind the kitchen table. A dark mass that set her blood thudding in her ears.

She knelt and peered at the shape on the floor. She'd grown up seeing her mother's sculptures, but she had never seen this one, had never seen anything quite like it. The sculpture reared upward on hind legs, standing as tall as Lila's knees, small sticks fashioned into legs that looked somehow powerful, the bent angles of the wood leaving the impression of musculature. Here and there, small tufts of what looked like animal hair drifted away from the sticks, and the feet were arched with brittle, translucent claws extending outward. The body was equally bulky, the small bits of wood twining together to create a torso, two cruel-looking arms.

It was the face that made Lila uneasy. The sculpture's face was of a man, his mouth opened impossibly wide to reveal fangs. Animal teeth. She lurched backward, her hands scrabbling against the linoleum. How would her mother have found claws and teeth? Animals lost teeth sometimes, but what it would require to find them . . . Lila didn't like thinking about it.

"What is this?" she whispered, and her tongue ached with the effort of speaking even those few words. The teeth and claws . . . they couldn't be real. Her mother had to have made them out of plaster or something. She brought the tip of her finger to the point of one of the teeth and then snatched back her hand as she hissed in a breath. *Real.*

Her mother had always worked with natural materials—things she found on her many walks. The combination of those items to create something new always struck the eye as odd, as if looking at something normal through a prism. All the elements the gaze would naturally seek out somehow distorted. Her sculptures and installations always created a feeling of disquiet, but Lila had never seen her mother create anything like this. Something so blatantly vile and threatening and macabre.

She didn't want to look at the sculpture anymore. Didn't want to see those teeth and claws. She set the tackle box upright before slowly gathering together the twigs and leaves to return them to their proper places.

Don't look. Don't look. Her mouth was dry, her head gone suddenly light. Her thoughts melting one into the other. Nonsensical, inchoate things. Yellow eyes. A man's mouth as it chewed. The outline of Macie's neck. Her mother's reddened hands as they twisted among leaves and thorns. Teeth.

She shook her head. She needed water. To cool her throat, her face, her belly. *Don't look,* she told herself, but there was something inside her that wouldn't listen. Something that turned her head back to the sculpture, her eyes gobbling up the claws, the ropy, muscled legs, the *mouth.* Always, the mouth. Her stomach clenched, a deep heaviness settling in her lower abdomen and creeping into her thighs, and her fear dropped away from her like a shed mantle. She thought of Macie. How it would feel to bury her face between Macie's legs. How it would feel to run her teeth along Macie's throat, to trace her fingers over Macie's collarbone. She stared at the sculpture, her mouth watering, and she did not know when it was she'd begun to pant, but she heard the sound, and a part of her that was only dimly aware wondered if it was she making the noise or if it was something else entirely. There was only the sensation of separating from herself, of floating upward to stare as her hands danced over the button of her jeans, as they dipped further down, and a disconnected sense of fullness that bordered on pain. *Yes. You want this. You want her.* That mouth opened wide, the teeth ivory and sharp, and yes, Lila wanted to touch that private part of herself while Macie's name died on her lips, but there was the sound of a key in the lock. Lila scrambled backward, her fingers fighting with the button on her jeans so her mother wouldn't see what she had been about to do, and how long had she been standing there if her mother was already home? She glanced up at the clock. Nine. Four hours gone.

"Lila, why aren't you answering—" Her mother stood at the threshold of the kitchen, her hands gripping a grocery bag. A deep flush rose up Caroline's cheeks, and her gaze locked on the mess behind Lila, the spilled contents of her life's work.

"What the hell did you do? Why were you in my things?"

"They were like this when I came in. I thought you were working on something and had lost track of time. I didn't take anything out. I swear."

Her mother took another step into the kitchen, letting the bag drop to the floor. "Where did you find that?" Caroline's hand trembled as she pointed to the sculpture.

Confused, Lila shook her head. "I didn't. It was out when I came in. Just like I told you." Could her mother tell what had happened? Scent the darker portions of her thoughts on the air? See the guilt in Lila's shaking hands?

Her mother bent, tracing the curves of the legs, the arms, staring at the sculpture as if she feared its fangs were something that could sink into the warm meat of her skin and transmute her into something bestial. Carefully, she touched the chest, her fingers stroking over the tufted fur.

"What is it?" Lila asked. Her mother didn't respond, but her shoulders rose and fell, the sound of her breath quickening. "The claws and teeth—are they real? You found them, didn't you? You didn't . . ."

"Yes, they're real." Her mother's voice was even, measured. Every word parceled out carefully. "But I made it a long time ago. In New Orleans. It wasn't anything I ever intended to show anyone."

Lila's head swam. Four hours. She'd somehow been staring at that sculpture for four hours, and she'd felt so strange. Like something else had been working through her, her blood pumping into a vast heart that was not her own. She shoved the feeling away and focused on her mother.

"I'm not working on it now."

"Then how the fuck did it just show up in our kitchen?"

"Watch your mouth, Lila Sawyer." Her mother's eyelids fluttered, her gaze flicking from the sculpture, to the table, to Lila.

"Why won't you just tell me? Why won't you tell me anything about when you lived in New Orleans? Why is it such a big fucking secret?"

Her mother's voice dropped low. "I don't know why you pulled all of this out, but go to your room."

"I didn't do it!"

"Goddammit, Lila, I said go. Now!"

Already there were tears forming, and they threatened to spill. Lila held them back as she rushed past her mother, leaving her standing amid the bits of wood and fur, and down to her bedroom, where she slammed the door and threw herself onto her bed.

For a long time, the apartment was quiet except for Lila's own muffled sniffling, but then there was the sound of her mother crying, and somewhere in the distance, in some hidden apartment, the sound of a dog barking. The sounds seeped into Lila's mind, shading her dreams in a darker tint.

When her alarm finally rang the next morning, everything seemed disconnected as it had the night before, her body independent from her mind as she floated through showering and brushing her teeth. She told herself not to think of those lost hours. Not to think of that strange feeling of disconnect she'd felt. It had been nothing. She had to believe it had been nothing. The precipice of any other possibility was far too frightening to approach.

Neither Lila nor her mother spoke on the ride to school, and Lila stared out the window, imagining she could still hear her mother's sobbing somehow threaded through the dog's barking. Sadness and anger married together and coiling tight in her chest.

In first period, Macie sank into the desk beside her. "You look like shit."

"I barely slept. Some idiot's dog was barking all night."

"I could never live in an apartment. All those people around you all the time."

Fuck you. These were the words she wanted to say to Macie. To call her a snob and tell her she wasn't such hot shit, but she stretched her mouth into more of a baring of teeth than a smile. A dim idea crawled through her mind—an image of her twisting Macie's hair away from her scalp until the girl cried out in pain.

"You really do look sick. Go to the nurse or something. At least it would get you out of class," Macie said, and the image faded as quickly as it had come.

Lila brought a hand to her cheeks and then her forehead. They didn't feel warm, but she'd never known exactly what it was she was supposed to be feeling for. Maybe she really was getting sick? Maybe that was why she hadn't felt like herself lately, like her body was responding without her.

But there was the thought again, of Macie's hair in her fist, and another, of Macie's face with blood dripping from her mouth and nose as her mother's sculpture rose above them, man-sized now with that terrible mouth stretching open, the jaws creaking as it stared down. Again, Lila's mouth watered, and she swiped her hand across it, darting a glance at Macie, terrified she might have seen, but Macie was staring down at her phone, completely absorbed.

She was fine. Macie had been a total bitch to her yesterday. She'd had a major fight with her mom and not slept well. That was all. There were no parts of her mind that were starting to atrophy. She had not inherited her mother's illness. She was nothing like her mother. She was not.

Lila floated through her classes, paying the minimum amount of attention. At lunch, Macie chattered on and on about some new sneaker line, and Lila said yes and no in all the right places.

"Anyway, you want to go to the movies with me tomorrow night?" Macie nibbled at a pretzel, her eyes large and wet.

"Huh?" Lila's head felt as if it had been stuffed with cotton.

"The movies. Do you want to go? Tomorrow night?" Macie purposely slowed down each word. There was a part of Lila that envied Macie's ability to live in the superficial world—to not live too long in her own worry, her own insecurity—but it grated on her, too. That nothing bothered Macie very deeply and that she was so focused on the exterior of things. Like making Lila prettier. Like Cameron. Like those were the only things that mattered. It seemed to point to the fact Macie would never truly care about anything beyond what it could immediately get her. A movie was unimportant in the face of so many things, but since Macie had deemed it so, it was *so*.

"I'll have to ask my mom, but with the other girl they found, there's no way she'll say yes." She was thinking, too, of their argument, of how she'd spoken to her mother. If she were grounded for the next month, she wouldn't be surprised.

Macie rolled her eyes. "Whatever." She spun away and flicked her hair over her shoulder. "Maybe one day, your mom won't suck so fucking much, and you'll learn how to have some fun, and maybe then we can go. I mean, you would think someone who was an artist would be more chill."

Lila's mouth flooded with the taste of something bitter. "She'll probably let me go," she said, but she knew the lie for what it was.

"Sure. Text me when she tells you that you can't." Macie walked away without looking back. Lila blinked back tears and crumpled her shirt inside her fist. She wondered if all of these small crimes she'd committed were tallied somewhere. All of these small, pointless indiscretions that left her confused and Macie angry, with Lila still holding on to the shreds of their friendship she was trying to craft into something more.

The rest of the day passed in a blur, with Lila catching at snatches of conversations about The Cur. How he must like little girls. How he must have raped them before he killed them. How he tore them up from the inside out. How no one had been arrested yet. The final bell rang without Lila noticing, and her teacher had to tell her the day was over. Lila threw her books into her backpack, apologizing awkwardly. Outside, her mother was waiting. The sun cast a wet heat over everything. Lila was too tired, and her thoughts circled and slipped, dissolving before changing again, and she wanted sleep and to find a way to make her mother understand, to make her say yes to the movies. To Macie. To everything she didn't yet dare tell her.

On the drive home, Lila dozed in the passenger seat, the air conditioner doing little more than moving the heat around, glad, for once, for her mother's silence about the dead girls. They made dinner, drifting together and apart without speaking, and Lila waited. There would be no right moment to ask her mother about the movie, but she could not make herself open her mouth and ask. The dull star of a headache began to form in the center of her forehead, and she gnawed at the cuticles on her thumbs as she watched her mother load the dishwasher.

"Macie asked if I can go to the movies with her, and I really, really, really want to go," she finally said. Her mother did not look up.

"You were just at Macie's house."

"Yes, but that was for school. I never get to do anything fun."

"You just had fun. At Macie's house."

"That's not the same!" Lila's voice pitched louder, and her mother looked up with eyebrows lifted.

"We're not doing this again. You honestly think I'm going to let you go running around town when there've been two girls murdered?"

"I'm not running around town. It's the *movies*. She's my only friend, and you never let me do anything. Like I'm some freak." The words built in her—heavy and awful—but she couldn't stop herself. "It's like you want me to end up like you. Never going out. Never doing anything. Just sitting in this shitty apartment with your pills and your sticks and your paint."

Lila clapped her hands over her mouth, but it didn't help. Her mother squeezed her eyes shut—her face gone pale—and the room felt too small, as if it were going to fall down around them and crush the breath from their lips.

"Oh my God. I'm sorry. I'm so sorry, Mom. I didn't mean it. I didn't—"

"Stop talking."

"I didn't mean it, Mom. I swear. I barely slept last night—"

"I said shut up, Lila!" Her mother's voice was sharp. The kind of yelling you did when there were other people living above and beside you. "There are things that I've seen . . . Things I can't ever forget. I close my eyes every night, and I still see Jazzland, and sometimes, there are dreams where it's you, and I have lived every fucking *moment* since you were a baby terrified that those dreams are going to come true." She drew a breath, a tiny moment before everything else spilled out of her. "And I hope, and I pray, Lila, you never have to feel like this. Like at any moment every part of your life is going to be pulled apart by a thing you don't even fucking *understand*. I hope you don't. So I'm sorry things aren't what you want them to be, and I'm sorry I'm not the kind of mother you can be proud of, but this is all that I am, and I'm doing my best, okay? That's all I can do."

Lila told herself to go to her mother, to hug her and tell her again how sorry she was, but she couldn't move. Her mother had finally acknowledged the *before*. That she'd experienced something that had marked her. And still, her mother would not tell her about this thing she had seen. Lila wondered if it was possible whatever had happened was the reason for her mother's irrational fears. The dogs. Her overprotective need to keep Lila trapped in little-girl-dom for as long as possible.

Her mother stared back at her. She sighed, and the sound echoed hollowly over Lila. "I will drop you off ten minutes before the movie starts, and I will pick you up exactly when it's over. No hanging out in the lobby. Absolutely under no circumstances are you to do anything other than go into the movie and come back out again. I should come with you, but you're right." Her mother offered a weak smile. "You're growing up and should be able to do stuff like this."

"Yes. Absolutely," Lila said. She knew she should be excited. She'd wanted this, after all, but a sense of uneasiness and guilt settled over her, and she squirmed.

"One other thing. You need to talk to your dad. He called again today."

"Sure. Okay. Thank you so much, Mom. You have no idea."

They sat together for a long while in a quiet that wasn't comfort but an anxious kind of confusion. Lila thought several times she should say something else, but in her head, everything sounded dumb, every apology and explanation insincere.

Eventually, they fell asleep curled around each other. Lila dreamed of dogs with bloodied teeth, and she woke in the middle of the night, her heart fluttering and her mouth dry. Her mother slept on, but Lila could not find sleep again. Only when the room began to turn light did she ease out from beside her mother to run the shower as hot as she could stand it and then force herself under the stream. She brushed her hair. She put on lip gloss and dug her purple shirt out of the hamper. It still smelled fine, so she pulled it on. Her skin felt itchy.

Still quiet, her mother drove her to school. "Love you," she said, and Lila felt her skin grow hot.

"Love you, too," she said, and turned away before she started to cry.

Stupid. There was no reason to feel sad, but she bit the inside of her cheek and hurried inside. Macie wasn't in the cafeteria, but groups of kids huddled together, staring down at their phones as they passed whispers back and forth about what they thought they knew about The Cur. He was a softball coach. He was a daycare janitor. He ate the parts of the girls he tore off and carried their flesh around in his belly.

Macie was already in Ms. Shakib's room, her phone on her desk as she stared at it, her eyebrows furrowed.

"My mom said I could go. She's going to drop me off," Lila said, and Macie glanced up.

"Excellent!" She clapped her hands together. Relief turned Lila's arms and legs to water. Everything would be okay. Macie was still her friend, and everything would be okay.

Macie leapt up and wrapped her arms around Lila. "This is

going to be so perfect. You have no idea. And your mom doesn't have to worry either. The news said this morning the cops have the guy they think hurt those girls."

He did more than hurt them, Lila thought.

"Good," she said, wishing Macie would hug her again.

The day passed slowly, but finally, the last bell rang, and Lila was back in the car with her mother, who drummed her fingers along the steering wheel.

"Macie said she saw on the news they caught the guy who did it," she said, but the tension didn't drain from her mother's face.

"I want you to call your father before we get home. Before the movies."

"Fine," she said, and turned to stare out the window. She'd call, but she wouldn't do anything except answer questions. Keep the conversation one-sided. If her dad gave a shit about her, he would apologize right away and only then would she say anything more.

She pulled her phone from her bag and brought up the number, her hands damp so her touch smeared across the screen. She dialed the number and waited. Three, then four rings, and Lila hoped he wouldn't answer. She could toss her phone back into her bag and tell her mom that she'd tried, but the phone clicked, and she listened as something on the other line shuffled.

"Yeah?" Her father's voice was clipped. Had he not looked at who was calling before he answered, or was he irritated that Lila was interrupting his time with his new family?

"Dad? It's me."

"Lila? Jesus, kiddo. It's good to hear from you. You doing okay?"

"Fine. Mom said I was supposed to call you," she said, and listened as her father cursed under his breath.

"Good. That's good to hear." A car honked in the background. "That's good," he said again. There was a quick burst of muffled sound, as if her father had covered the receiver to say something out loud, and Lila waited for him to take just a fucking *second* to talk to her, to his first daughter, whom he hadn't spoken to in months. She thought about asking him if he'd heard about the abductions, something that would shock him or force him to care that there was the possibility of a serial killer in the same vicinity as his daughter. She could easily be the same as all those other girls who'd been left in pieces. She listened again to the sound of him shuffling and decided against it. If he ignored her, still distracted by anything and everything, she would crumble under his carelessness.

"School's fine. Mostly Bs," she said, filling in the places where his questions were supposed to be, but still there was only his silence.

"Math is getting better. Still some Cs though," she said, and it was like the space in her head was filling up with water, heavy and light at the same time, and muddling everything that was supposed to be.

"Okay," her father said, and then muttered something that sounded like *Jesus fucking Christ,* but Lila's skin was hot and buzzing, her mouth thick with anger, so she couldn't be certain of what she'd heard.

"Lila, I'll have to call you back. I'm driving to the hospital. We got a call about Brina. She had a bad night, and they're worried there's something else that's wrong. But I'll call you back. I prom- ise," her father said.

"Sure. Okay. Bye," she said, and hung up before he could spew any more of the lies he told himself so he would feel better.

"Everything okay?" her mother asked.

Lila shoved her phone back into her bag. "Yeah. Baby stuff. They think something else happened."

"I'm sorry, Lila. It's hard—scary—having a baby. When there are complications, it's even harder." Caroline squeezed her shoulder. "But it doesn't mean you're not important, too. It'll get better."

"Will it?" Lila asked, and her mother didn't respond but pulled her lips into a thin line.

Lila turned away and stared out the window. She could feel her mother's eyes, her ever-present anxiety, thick in the air. Her thoughts turned away from her father and refocused on Macie. On the dark of a movie theater, their arms touching. The fragrance of Macie's hair, her skin all around.

But then her mind shifted again, and she thought of the secrets her mother held. Of what she'd hidden from Lila. That single word her mother had offered up.

Jazzland.

CHAPTER 4

LILA 2019

There were two hours until the movie, and her mother was absorbed in a new project, so Lila closed herself in her bedroom and opened her phone. There was still that single word floating in her brain. *Jazzland.* Some link to *before,* to whatever it was that had made her mother afraid.

From her phone, she did a search for *Jazzland, New Orleans* and scanned through the first couple of links. A Wikipedia page told her Jazzland was a theme park in New Orleans that had been abandoned after Hurricane Katrina. The park still stood but had been overrun by nature and vandals, and Lila clicked over to images and looked through a handful. Gaudily colored buildings made out to resemble the French Quarter stood amid overgrown grass, their edifices covered over with graffiti. Everything shaded in the color of death. She flipped to the next picture—a giant, grotesque clown's head with a gaping mouth rested along what appeared to have once been a fairway—and she shuddered as a chill worked up her spine. It was only an abandoned park, but the photos were ominous, somehow threatening, and she exited out of the page and pushed her phone as far away from her as she could.

There was a dim fear building in her gut, but she couldn't identify what connection Jazzland had to her mother or to her. Her mother used to live in New Orleans, and she must have gone to Jazzland at some point and witnessed something disturbing. She curled a foot beneath her, wondering what her mother had seen at Jazzland that had stuck with her for so long. Her phone chimed, the text message a happy reminder of what was coming. Wear something cute! followed by two grinning emojis and a purple heart.

Lila pulled shirts Macie claimed to like over her head only to take them off again. She was exhausted and nothing looked right on her body; every item of clothing made her appear like an elementary school kid who'd just come off the playground. Finally, she settled on a blue dress with leggings and told herself it wouldn't matter what she wore because she and Macie would be in the dark.

If she'd wanted, she could have sneaked into her mother's bathroom and into her makeup bag. Dabbed some concealer under her eyes and swept some mascara onto her lashes, but her mom would have wondered why she was doing something so out of the ordinary just for Macie, and then she would have guessed, and Lila wasn't ready for that. Not yet.

Instead she pulled at the skin on her face, pushing it this way and that as if the mere act of doing it could somehow change the bones beneath. She leaned forward and pressed her forehead to the coolness of the glass and breathed out, and for a moment, the face before her wasn't hers at all but something else altogether. Lila reeled backward. It was only her face after all, but she couldn't quite catch her breath, and she blinked rapidly, trying to clear her vision and telling herself she'd seen nothing unusual. She was *fine*. She was more than fine. She was going to the movies with Macie.

On the drive to the theater, her mother repeated the rules again and again as if they were some mantra to ward off evil. A charm to hold up when the darkness descended. When they pulled up to the theater, her mother's eyes darted over Lila's face as if this was the last time she would see it. "Don't talk to anyone you don't know. Don't go with anyone you don't know. I don't care if Macie says she knows them. Lila," her mother snapped, taking Lila's chin in her hand. "No one. You understand? I don't care if Macie says it's okay. No one."

Lila nodded her head. "Yes, ma'am." Her mother sat back in the seat and sighed. She slumped over as if all of the air had been let out of her lungs. For a second Lila wanted to hug her mother and tell her she wouldn't go after all. She'd stay home, and they could watch old black-and-white movies and make popcorn and fall asleep on the couch, but Macie stood out front, smiling and waving, her hair falling around her shoulders in a way that made Lila's heart slam against the cage of her chest. She got out of the car.

"Eight o'clock. Sharp. I'll be right here," her mother said as she shut the door, and Lila turned to wave and then her mother pulled away, and she watched the taillights until she couldn't see them anymore, and again some strange feeling tugged at her. She felt the need to call her mother back, but Macie yelled her name, and she turned and pushed her uneasiness away.

"Did you already get your ticket?" she asked. Macie laughed.

"Ticket for what?"

"The movie."

"Oh my God. That's cute. You thought we were actually going to a movie?"

Lila's stomach turned over. "We're not?"

"You're going to die. Absolutely die. Cameron's coming to pick us up. And he's bringing Andrew. Double date!"

Lila fell silent, and Macie grabbed at her arms, her hands, and Lila could have screamed this betrayal into the sky. The movie had never been about wanting to be with Lila. Macie didn't want her. Not *that* way. Probably not even as a real friend. Above, the stars blinked in and out—their white fire raging against the dying light—and Lila let her gaze go slack, the light blurring until everything was painted in a dim halo.

Lila's leggings clung to her damp places. She should have worn shorts, but then her mom would have seen she'd shaved her legs earlier in the week. "I can't. My mom would kill me."

"So your mom won't ever know. It's not like we'll be gone forever."

Lila forced a smile. "Seriously. She'd commit actual murder."

"It's not that big of a deal, Lila. It's not like we're taking off with some creep show. You owe me this after the other night."

"But Cameron didn't even come."

"Come on, Lila. This is Andrew we're talking about! The guy you've only had a crush on for a thousand years," Macie said, but it wasn't true. It wasn't true, and Macie knew it, but she locked her arms around Lila's neck and pressed their foreheads together, her face close enough to dazzle, and all Lila could do was nod. Of course she would do what Macie wanted. Of course.

"This is going to be *amazing*. Wait and see."

"Okay," Lila said. Behind them, a group of little kids squealed and chased each other through the lobby. Their mothers stood off to the side, absorbed in their own conversations.

The sky had gone gray, and the sunset was not beautiful, a bruised rose trampled in the dirt. A thin slice of moon already shimmered, but it looked insubstantial; something Lila could crush between her fingers and then grind to dust.

"Aren't you excited?" Macie asked.

"Yeah," Lila said. She was still too hot, but she'd leave her leggings on. The thought of taking them off and having her legs exposed made her kind of woozy, so she ignored the sweat sticking to her thighs.

Macie drew out a tube of lip gloss the color of a plum and applied a coat, puckered and simpered into the camera on her phone, and Lila wondered if Cameron would be able to smell Macie when she got into the car. A hot, feral thing trapped in steel and rubber and unable to run away. Like an animal in a cage.

"There he is," Macie said, pointing, and Lila turned to look.

Cameron's car was a dented sedan with a strip of primer running down the side, and he pulled it to the curb of the movie theater and grinned as he lay on the horn. "Ladies! Hop in," he said, and Macie smoothed her skirt and climbed into the front seat. Lila followed and climbed into the back next to Andrew.

Cameron's hair was buzzed close, and it looked speckled, as if he'd dyed it but not been successful. His jaw was strong, and his nose crooked, but he had a mouthful of white teeth and a nice smile. And he could *drive*. Lila could understand why a girl like Macie would throw herself at him. He was what mothers wanted for their daughters. The kind of boy worshiped on the altar of "nice." Handsome in a way that was safe. Reasonably charming. Destined for some mid-level corporate job that paid for a three-and-a-half bedroom home in the suburbs. Boys like Cameron and Andrew were a sure thing. They guaranteed a safety that was palatable. As Macie giggled over absolutely nothing, Lila understood, too, exactly what girls laid at their feet in return.

"Hey," Andrew said, and combed a handful of dark hair away from his forehead. Andrew looked nothing like his brother. He was small, the delicate planes of his face what the girls at school called "pretty."

Lila's voice died in her throat. Andrew blinked back at her, clearly waiting for a response she could not give him. Cameron turned his massive body and thrust it between the seats so he hung partially in the backseat.

"Aww. Is your friend shy?" Macie swatted at Cameron's arm and giggled again. "Don't worry, darlin'. We'll have a great time. Andrew, tell your girl how pretty she'd look if she smiled."

Andrew studied his hands. Cameron let out a barking laugh, and then the car was moving too fast out of the parking lot, and her heart lurched. In the front seat, Macie was squealing and putting on her cutesy, baby doll act. Lila wished she could slap her. She shouldn't have done this. Shouldn't have gotten into this car with this older boy for him to drive them to some desolate place where prying eyes couldn't see. Shouldn't have followed Macie the way she always did like a dumb, besotted puppy.

There was no air conditioning in the car, and it didn't matter that the windows were down. Lila sweated, her palms slick, and she wiped at her upper lip, at the dip between her breasts. She tried to do it quickly, but Andrew watched her, and he smiled. She looked away, angry that he probably believed the lie Macie had concocted. Idiot. Her body was not for him.

Cameron turned onto a side street and then turned again, and Lila knew where it was he was taking them.

Three years ago, an area just south of Highway 381 had been cleared to make room for an office park, but the buildings never found tenants, so they sat empty. Concrete monsters with quiet hiding spots tucked into discreet corners. This was where Cameron was taking them. Lila thought of the dead girls, their mouths permanently silenced, and the world came together and apart.

Cameron turned into the first lot. Lila faced the window and stared out at the endless walls of gray. It was like being swallowed, and she shivered despite the heat.

"Who would want to work in a place like this? It's depressing," Andrew said, and Lila felt dizzy. Closed her eyes and tipped her head back and tried to gulp down any of the air that moved through the windows, but it didn't make her feel better. The smell of something decayed clung to the air. Lila imagined she could feel the scent bead against her lips, and she coughed to rid her throat of the taste.

Macie leaned across the seat, pressed her chest against Cameron's shoulder, and whispered something in his ear. Cameron smiled, but he didn't laugh, and his jawline was hard. Andrew shifted in his seat.

"Here we go," Cameron said, and guided the car into a parking space. He reached across Macie's seat, grazing against her thighs as he did, and into the glove box. He drew out a plastic bottle with clear liquid.

"Vodka. No smell," he said, and opened it up and offered it to Macie. "Ladies first."

Macie took a tentative sip and winced but then took another. She kept her eyes on Cameron the entire time. When he handed the bottle into the backseat, Andrew took it and held it between his hands, but he didn't open it. Lila mouthed a *thanks* at him, and he nodded and passed the bottle back into the front seat.

"We're going to take a little walk. Y'all want to come with, that's cool. Or stay here. Have the car to yourselves." Cameron winked and opened his door.

"Are you forgetting two girls were just killed?" Lila's voice finally broke through, her teeth sharp around the words. She glanced at Macie, who already stood outside the car, her arms crossed in irritation.

"Do I look like a hairless, prepubescent girl to you?" Cameron chuckled at his disgusting joke. Lila imagined herself cheerfully tearing out his throat. His blood slick on her chin. Of course, he had no reason to worry. He was large. Muscled. Walked with a swagger that said he'd never been afraid of walking down a street alone. "Besides, you two have plenty to keep you distracted." He closed the door with another laugh and crossed to Macie.

Macie pawed at his arm, looping herself around him as she tugged him away. The creeping dark of the tree line in front of them opened a hole wide enough to pass through, and then they were gone. For a second, Lila imagined she saw something like teeth opening, but then she blinked, and it was just the parking lot. Andrew sat beside her, and her heart beat a sluggish pattern in her chest.

"Did you do that homework for Mrs. Kemp?" Andrew asked, and all of her air whooshed out of her.

"Not yet. Figured I'd wait for Sunday."

"Yeah. Me, too."

She watched the gray haze surrounding the buildings, the air shimmering in the heat. Out of the corner of her eye, she thought she saw something move. Something with fur and a tail streaking across the parking lot. She blinked, and her entire body felt too heavy, and she wished she could go to sleep and wake up in her own bed, but she was here, and Macie was somewhere else, and there was nothing she could do.

Andrew didn't talk, and she watched the buildings. They seemed to shift and change in the heat, growing larger and larger until they blotted out what was left of the sun. Night grew long and deep, and Macie still wasn't back, and the dark swirled outside of the car, tried to reach inside for her, but the windows were up, and the doors were locked, and the shadows couldn't get inside.

"Too hot," she said, and glanced over, but Andrew wasn't there. When had he left the car? The door was closed and locked from the inside, but she didn't remember him getting out, didn't remember him leaving her there. Sweat pooled beneath her, and she reached underneath her skirt, grasped at the waistband of her leggings, and peeled them off. She gasped for air, but it did nothing to cool her.

When Andrew came back, she could get him to find Cameron and Macie, and they could go home. She would tell her mother they'd gone to the movie, but she'd gotten sick; spent the rest of the time in the restroom, and her mother would press a cool washcloth to her forehead, her neck, and let her sleep in the next morning. She would forget she'd come here.

She opened her door, but the air outside wasn't much cooler than the air inside, and she pushed herself upward and stumbled forward so that her foot caught against the curb. The concrete scraped her skin, her blood beading but not falling, and she pressed her fingers to the spot and brought them away. She didn't want to look at the smeared red on her hand. If she did, her chest would constrict, and she wouldn't be able to breathe ever again.

"Macie?" An owl answered her, and she stepped away from the car and farther into the never-ending concrete and asphalt. Somewhere deep inside, machinery started up. The sound of metal grating against metal flooded through her, and Lila brought her hands to her ears. She didn't want to hear this. It hurt her to hear it. Like something was turning her inside out; as if her entire body were on fire as something alien moved through her blood and settled behind her skin. She knew in the logical parts of her brain she should be frightened, but there was the sleek, wonderful sensation of something inside her waking up for the first time. Whatever strangeness had occupied her body wouldn't let the fear totally surface, and she grinned. It felt so *good* to let go, to give in to whatever tugged her forward like an automaton made of flesh.

"Where did you go?" Lila said, but she knew there was nothing there to answer her, and that it hadn't really been *her* who'd spoken, but this thing that had come to live inside of her.

A dog barked and then howled—long and low—and she thought of curved teeth and wet tongues and missing girls, and she was still too hot. Her fear of dogs felt dim and far away. Like an inconsequential memory floating to the surface after years filled with more important things. She pulled her dress over her head so she stood in only her bra and underwear. The air didn't feel right as it slid over her. It wormed instead of drifting and felt like so many damp mouths. She scraped her hands over her belly and thighs. Her skin seemed to hang from her bones, thick and loose, and she took another step forward.

"Could close my eyes and still find you," she said, but her voice still wasn't her own. She went down on all fours, and it felt good to move this way. Easy and right as she slipped farther into the dark.

She could smell Macie and Cameron before she saw them. Smelled their sweat and need and naked want. It stank and made her mouth water at the same time. She filled herself up with their scent. They tasted of thousands of little deaths buried and hidden in a wrapping of skin. They disgusted her, and she spat. The girl—Macie—turned at the sound, but the older boy forced his mouth on hers, and he was hungry, and it didn't matter if the girl was afraid. He was hungry and would have what he'd come here for. She owed him that.

Lila watched him rake his teeth over her neck, her small, developing breasts, and behind him, Lila watched yellow eyes open and close in the dark. A blurred place where something had stood only a moment before vanishing. It moved quickly, its claws churning up the dirt. Lila grunted and pushed her fingers under fallen leaves and dropped pine needles until she touched cool earth and then she, too, buried her fingers inside of it. Had she ever been frightened of those yellow eyes? She couldn't remember, and it wasn't fear coursing through her now, but recognition.

Again, Macie's head snapped up, and Lila heard the worry in her voice and the boy's irritation as he pushed away from her and zipped his pants. He didn't look back at the girl he left on the ground as he walked away.

Branches tore at Lila's skin as she ran back toward the car, and she dropped blood into the dirt, but it didn't matter. She couldn't be caught, and she ran without thinking, a dim part of her coming back into some awareness, but still there was this new thing alive beneath her skin. When she came into the parking lot, she pulled her dress back on. She didn't like the way it rubbed against her skin, but it couldn't be helped.

Andrew stood outside of the car, and he turned to her, his eyes taking in the dirt smeared across her mouth and cheeks, the blood on her arms. "What the hell happened to you?"

"Nothing. Where the hell were you?" She threw the curse word back at him, and he winced.

"I had to pee. I told you."

The memory of what she'd seen in the trees had already begun to fade, and she touched her face, her hair, but she wasn't quite sure if the thing behind her skin was actually her. Something had taken her over, and she told herself it was just the heat, but she knew it had been more than that. It had been animal and hungry and desperate for violence. It would be normal to panic, to collapse into confusion in the face of what she'd done, but that foreign thing was still coursing through her blood, and whatever normal reaction she should have had drowned in a strange kind of numb euphoria.

"You're bleeding." He reached out a hand to touch her, and she recoiled, her lips pulling back to show her teeth, and he stopped, his hand frozen in the air. They stayed locked in those positions, a tableau of defense and supplication, until Cameron came crashing through the woods.

"Get in the car," he mumbled.

"She's bleeding," Andrew said, and Cameron glared back at him.

"I said get in the damn car. Now. Or I'll tell Mom about the little stash in the back of your closet."

Flushing bright pink, Andrew moved toward the car. Macie came out of the woods, mascara streaked and her shirt on inside out. Andrew looked at Lila again, and she climbed into the car without glancing at him. He didn't understand. Wouldn't understand what she'd seen. What she'd felt. Those teeth opening inside of her and what it meant to move through the woods without being noticed.

"Something happened," she said, but no one heard her. She rolled her window down and leaned into the night air and breathed until her head went light.

In the front seat, Macie said something, her voice whining and needling, but Lila couldn't hear, and Cameron turned up the radio. Macie tried to reach for him, but he shrugged away from her.

Lila's head swam. She remembered yellowed eyes and fur. Her tongue felt heavy. When they got back to the theater, she'd go to the bathroom and wash herself off, wet her face and hair, pull her leggings back on, and hope her mother wouldn't notice the small tear on her dress. Her mind told her again that she'd gotten too hot and wandered off into the forest, confused and looking for Macie, but there was another part of her that felt as if this wasn't the person she'd always been. A girl capable of violence. And what did it say about her if she liked it?

When Cameron pulled the car into the theater's parking lot, Lila glanced at the digital clock glowing on the dash. Forty-five minutes. They'd only been gone for forty-five minutes. She put her hands over her mouth to keep herself from burbling with idiotic laughter.

Lila pulled herself out of the car, but Macie stayed behind, her hands still grasping at Cameron's shirt, his face, and he turned away from her again. Lila let the door close behind her. She didn't bother to say good-bye. Andrew didn't either. She'd probably freaked him out, but she didn't care. Not anymore. There was something alive inside of her, and it felt nice to let this new cruelty free.

The air inside of the theater's lobby was cold and teeming

with the greased smells of popcorn and butter. Her skin prickled, and she felt the thing shift inside of her. She brought her hand to her stomach and pressed it flat. "Shh," she whispered.

The bathroom was empty. All the kids and their moms, the couples on dates, were still locked inside dark theaters. She ran the water and shoved her head under the tap, opened her mouth and drank until her insides went all sloshy and she thought she would burst. She twisted her hair tight to wring the water out and pulled it back again. With a wet paper towel, she wiped the dirt from her skin and dabbed at the scratches on her arms and then tugged her leggings over her legs.

Her eyes looked different. The pupil larger than the surrounding brown, and she blinked at her reflection. It didn't blink back, and she smiled. There were too many teeth for her mouth. She looked exciting. Dangerous. All the things she'd never been but had always wanted to be.

When Macie came in, she went straight into one of the stalls and didn't look at Lila when she passed. The sound of her retching bounced off the tiles, and Lila's ears pricked up. Her mouth watered.

"Let me in," she called. Macie opened the stall door, and Lila crammed her body into the space. "Jesus. That's disgusting," Lila said, not caring if her comment hurt Macie's feelings or made her angry. A darker part of her had roused and didn't care about Macie slutting it up with some guy three years older than her; didn't care about Macie and her dumb, swollen face as she heaved and then threw her arms around Lila, who was supposed to be her best friend. Lila who was in love with her and hated her at the same time, wishing she could kiss her and then bite her lips until they bled.

"I thought he liked me," Macie said, and Lila drew her hands over Macie's hair.

"He sucks. He only goes after younger girls because everyone his own age probably thinks he's a perv," Lila said. She wound her fingers in the girl's hair and wiped the salt from her cheeks and surreptitiously licked her fingers, the sadness slick on her tongue. A pretty thing she could carry home with her to taste again and again.

"He's not a perv, Lila. He *likes* me." Macie drew a deep, shuddering breath. "Everything was fine, but then I heard a sound and got all freaked out, and Cameron was so pissed because I 'killed the mood.' I kept trying to talk to him the entire way back, but he wouldn't say anything at all. And you weren't exactly the most fun either. Andrew looked weirded out."

Whatever had come awake inside shifted in Lila's belly, and there was only red and anger and red. A need to hurt Macie for leaving her behind for some boy who didn't care about her; who would have left Macie in the dirt if it meant saving himself.

"You're a really shitty friend. You know that?" Lila pushed Macie away, and her stomach flipped. It would be easy to slap Macie—her palm left stinging—but instead, she opened the stall and walked out of the bathroom. Macie was probably still in the stall, her mouth hanging open in disbelief, but Lila didn't care anymore. She wondered why she ever had. It felt *good* to say what she felt, to finally let the truth out of her instead of pushing it all down. To let her anger bubble up and fling it out into the world.

Lila bought an extra-large popcorn and a bottle of water with the money her mother had given her for the movie and sat at one of the benches. She shoveled handful after handful of the hot, greased kernels in her mouth. Butter dribbled down her hands, and she licked at it. A guy sweeping up the lobby stopped and stared at her, and she grinned up at him, butter smeared across her chin. "Fuck off," she said, the power of the phrase making her giddy. He ducked his head and went back to sweeping.

There was still an hour until her mother would come to pick her up. If Macie ever emerged from the bathroom, Lila was going to have to listen to her pick apart the nuances of everything that happened in the woods. Every part of her humiliation torn to shreds and examined until it was paper-thin. How small Cameron had made her. The pain over his rejection of her body. A body that likely still carried small bits of shameful baby fat. Lila stood and dumped what was left of the popcorn in her mouth.

"What the hell, Lila." Macie's voice was hot in her ear. Lila turned to face Macie and shrugged her shoulders. "What's wrong with you?" Macie's face was blotchy. Red and white and bloated.

"You look like shit," Lila said, and her heart pumped inside of her, happy to say this terrible thing. Happy to watch as Macie's eyes grew large and her face more red. "No wonder Cameron didn't want to fuck you," she said. She crunched down on the words, and they burst in her mouth like something sweet.

"Know what I would have done if it was me? What I would have done if you were wriggling around in the dirt underneath me like some whore?" She leaned close and whispered in Macie's ear. "I would have split you open. Like a worm. Peeled back your skin and left you there to rot," she said, and the thing inside her skin roiled in ecstasy with the awful violence of her words.

"There's something wrong with you," Macie said, and backed away. "Really fucking wrong."

"Run home to Mommy, Macie. Tell her all about how Cameron couldn't get his dick hard, and you put it in your mouth all soft, and it didn't matter what you did, he didn't want you."

"Is that what you were doing? Watching us like some pervert?"

"Poor little *girl*. Did he laugh when he saw those nubs you call tits?"

"Fuck you, Lila. I'm telling everyone how fucking weird you are. Everyone."

"That's fine. I'm tired of you acting like a bitch all the time,

Macie. I'm tired of not saying how I feel, and you not even stopping to *ask*. All this time together, and you have no idea, no fucking clue, how I feel. And what's worse is you don't care. I can tell everyone that Cameron would rather use his own hand than put himself inside of you." Lila grinned, and her mouth and chin were still slick from the popcorn, and she wiped her hand over it. Macie's face crumpled, and then she pushed past Lila and through the exit.

The thing inside of her squirmed, and she licked her lips. She wished Cameron had hurt Macie; wished she could have crept up on them and watched while he was doing it. Black blood flowing out of Macie and into the dirt, and she could have lapped it up, put Macie's flesh between her teeth and bitten down. A beautiful thing to push down and feel Macie open up just for her. Like a good girl. Lila would have parted Macie's legs and felt the heat pulsating there. She could have tasted all the sweetness Macie had hidden, and it was Lila's, and no one could take it from her. They would have been wed in flesh. Finally together the way Lila wanted.

Maybe later, after Macie had forgotten and forgiven her, she could take her back into the woods and teach her about beauty and pain and blood, and sweet Macie would bloom under her like a flower. The thing inside her roared its approval. Her fury and desire like dark sisters.

Lila looked again at the clock. Her mother would be there soon, so she went back into the bathroom and cleaned her face again and stared at herself in the mirror. Her stomach heaved, the butter making her queasy, and then, as quickly as it came, whatever had come loose inside her drained away.

Guilt flooded through her, and she pressed her forehead against the mirror. She didn't understand why she'd said all those horrible things. Why she'd been so awful to her very best friend even if she had been so angry with her. Macie would never forgive her for the horrific things she'd said. For not pretending to be the cute, fun friend who would make out with the younger brother while Macie sneaked into the woods with the older. Lila had just felt so disconnected from herself—from the person Macie, her mom, the entire fucking world expected her to be. It had been wonderful to finally say what she wanted, and now she had fucked everything up because she'd gotten overheated and drifted into some kind of semiconscious state. Tears pricked at the corners of her eyes, and she swiped at them with a paper towel in her trembling hands.

None of what she'd seen in the woods had been real. None of it. Fear turned her skin cold, and she huddled into herself, thinking of her mother, of her father's careful observations. Would the rest of her life become nothing more than an endless series of appointments and pills and worry that at any moment the potential illness locked in her head would seep outward? And if people knew, if people could see inside to the dark, pulsating heart of her, how simple would it be to lose herself? To give in to their definitions. Their qualifications of what she should do. Who she should be.

She pushed her fingers against her temples and then up into her hair. No. Her life wouldn't be like that. She could fix things. She could make it better. She wasn't going to be like her mother. She wasn't confused about what was real and what wasn't.

She hurried back to the lobby to find Macie, to apologize, but she was already gone, and Lila sank down onto one of the benches to wait for her mother, her face buried in her hands. She'd call Macie when she got home and explain. She'd been too hot in the car. She hadn't meant any of the things she'd said. She was so sorry. So sorry.

When her mother pulled up, she climbed into the car and buckled her seat belt. Routine. Nothing out of the ordinary. Careful and precise. She did not want her mother to know there was anything wrong. She would not tell her about the thing that had come awake inside of her. If she did, her mother and father would force her to see a doctor, and life would be forever changed into something beyond her control.

"How was the movie?"

"It was okay, I guess."

"What was it about?"

"Some guy likes some girl who doesn't like him back. He does a bunch of stupid stuff to get her attention. He falls in love with her best friend instead. You know. Okay."

Her mother nodded, and Lila sank back into the seat and watched the streetlights bleed into each other, and beyond that, a black sky that stretched on and on.

"Macie's mom pick her up?"

"Yeah. She came right before you did."

Lila pushed the fleshy pad of her fingertip against her collarbone, marveled at how thin the skin there was. Almost as if she could dip her fingers beneath and pluck out the bone without much effort. So easy to turn herself inside out. Become someone else. Someone who wasn't losing her mind and terrified of what that could mean.

"Homework tomorrow. No exceptions."

"Yeah. I have math."

Her mother paused. She sighed, and silence filled the space between them.

"Only math? What about that project? The one you were working on with Macie," her mother said.

"I said I had math."

"I thought—"

"I already *said* what I had. Jesus. The project is over. I did it. Basically the entire thing. Because Macie . . ." Lila trailed off, and it was like something inside of her skin turned over. Her frenzy dying off as quickly as it had come on.

"Everything okay?" her mother said, and Lila turned her

body farther toward the door. Of course her mother was able to tell something was wrong. She should have known better than to have thought she could cover it up.

"Yup."

Something bad happened, she thought, but she couldn't bring herself to tell her mother about what had happened with Macie.

They didn't speak the rest of the drive. Twice, her mother's hands fluttered away from the steering wheel as if she were thinking about reaching across and touching Lila, but then she'd wrap her fingers around the wheel again, her eyes trained forward and unblinking.

When they got to the apartment, Lila moved past her mother—left her standing in the living room squeezing her keys tight in her fist—and locked her bedroom door behind her. In the morning, she would call Macie. In the morning, she would make everything right. But for now she was too tired, and she didn't think Macie would talk to her anyway. Not after all of the horrible things she'd said.

She climbed into her bed, pulled her sheets against her chin, but she didn't sleep. Instead, she watched dark shapes gather against her ceiling. Eyes and mouths and tongues and teeth coming together and apart, and she wondered if she had actually fallen asleep, if all of these lovely and terrible things around her were nothing more than a dream. From somewhere deep down, a voice began to speak.

CHAPTER 5

CAROLINE 2004

One year before the storm they called Katrina, before those dark floodwaters pulled up New Orleans's dead and set loose a leviathan of hunger and rage, Caroline Sawyer asked her doctor for something to help her sleep.

"Ambien," Caroline told him, and he looked down at her, his bare skull shining in the morning light coming through the window behind him.

"You poor thing." He squeezed her shoulder, and Caroline held herself still under the unnecessary physical contact and smiled up at him.

Forty minutes later, the slip of paper pressed tight in her palm, Caroline waited for the prescription at the Rite Aid desk, bought a six-pack of Abita Purple Haze and a bag of Skittles, and drove herself home, the pill bottle tucked in her purse. She drove with little awareness, focused only on the thought of rest, so she almost passed the exit off I-10 and had to quickly cut over two lanes, horns blaring around her as she raised a hand in apology.

Around her, the streets grew smaller, the colorful shotgun houses of Mid-City crowding together as she turned onto Baudin. When she and Daniel had moved in together, Caroline had looked specifically for one of those vibrant houses—painted Pepto-Bismol pink or the color of deep ocean water—but they'd had to settle for something more typical. The place they'd rented had been a shotgun subdivided into two apartments—tiny enough for them to afford—and the white paint had needed a fresh coat since the '80s. Inside was similarly shabby, but it was close to Finn McCool's, where she downed black and tans and pretended she gave a shit about cheering on the Saints. Even though the roads were terrible, the sidewalks were plentiful, and there was easy access to the streetcar, and a general, pervasive sense of fun and excitement. People lingered outside, laughing and talking, and when they'd moved in, Caroline had envisioned herself working by the front window, her sculpture materials scattered about her as she listened to the neighborhood come to life. She parked out front, palming her keys as she hurried up the walk, and then let herself into the musty dark of the living room that led to the tiny kitchen.

Pulling the bottle from her purse, she turned it over, tracing the lid with her fingernail. Probably the doctor wrote her the prescription because she'd done herself up pretty; because she had curled her hair and taken the time to line her eyes and put on a lipstick that was brighter than her normal shade. Probably hadn't hurt that she'd worn a push-up bra. She'd imagined getting the prescription would be difficult. There was no way she could waltz in and simply say she hadn't been sleeping and expect the doctor to do anything but tell her it was all in her head and she would be fine. So she'd gone the extra mile, remembering how his gaze had slid over her body at her last checkup. And now she had the bottle in her hand.

Daniel wasn't due home for at least another two hours.

Caroline hoped she would be asleep before then, and he would tuck himself in next to her, his lanky body outlining hers, his hands still splattered with oil paint. In the morning, maybe she wouldn't feel like the world was turning inside out, and he would let her sleep a little longer, and she could put off his questions for at least another day.

At least Vivian Kellum hadn't questioned Caroline when she asked for the day off. Normally she would be putting another boring session of landscape and still life painting instruction for Vivian's daughter Beth behind her before driving to Helping Hands Hospice Care to sit with her father until the nurses kicked her out. She glanced at the clock on the microwave. If she left now, she could still make it to her father's room before his evening medication made him too drowsy to visit, and the immense guilt crawling through her gut would perhaps ease. But she needed the sleep, and there was deliverance in her hands.

Indecision gnawed at Caroline. Given how advanced her father's cancer had become, how much of it had eaten into his colon, one night was enough to lose him. But if she didn't get some sleep, she'd be no good to anyone, and the questions and the paperwork and the bills were enough to drown her. The lack of sleep and the pressure of paying her dad's medical bills were why she'd felt so out of it lately. She'd spent most of her life fighting unexplainable anxieties, but this was something more than her terror whenever she heard a dog bark. More than the unease she carried with her at all times that left her skin crawling and her heart feeling as if it were going to push its way out of her body, her sternum making a sickening crack. At night, she'd stare at the ceiling, not sleeping but feeling as if she'd come untethered. Hours passing as she drifted, panic running through her body, so there was never any rest. And now it was happening during the day, too. With her father or at the Kellums', she'd feel herself start to separate, her jaw clenched and aching as she lost small gaps of time. Thirty minutes. An hour. Her body and mind like so much dead weight under her alarm. She couldn't let it go on. So there was the prescription and her flaring hope it would help.

She'd barely swallowed the single pill and a mouthful of still-warm beer when she heard the lock click.

"You're home," Daniel said, and she turned to face him, swiped her hand across her mouth, and swallowed. The humidity had made his hair curlier throughout the day, and he needed a shave, but it still surprised her how handsome he was behind all the scruff.

There'd been a few of her snottier friends who'd expressed surprise or disdain when they'd started dating. "A painter? Really? Who's supposed to make the money if you're both artists?" Caroline hadn't stayed friends with them, and two years later, even after everything with her dad's illness, he'd offered her a ring, and she'd said yes.

"I am. You're early," she said.

"I was going to surprise you with dinner." He lifted the paper grocery sack he carried. Whole Foods. Caroline inwardly groaned. That meant something sugar-, fat-, dairy-, carbohydrate-, and joy-free.

"That's sweet," she said, but the words were hollow things on her tongue. She reminded herself to be thankful even though she'd anticipated an afternoon of quiet. She spun the small diamond on her finger and told herself to smile even though doing it required more effort than she wanted to use. She'd been doing this more and more lately. Putting on a mask. Perfect makeup. Perfect hair. Smiling when she wanted to scream. Anything to keep the outside world from seeing how broken she felt.

"Vivian gave you the day off?"

"Yeah. I . . . um . . . I went to the doctor."

He frowned. "What did he say?"

"Not much. That I was stressed out. Makes sense given the

circumstances . . . with Dad. He gave me something to help me sleep."

"I wish you hadn't done that." Daniel swung the grocery bag onto the countertop, unpacking a box of red quinoa, a small red onion, a bottle of organic extra-virgin olive oil.

"I really don't need your anti-medication manifesto right now."

"You have no idea what that shit can do to your body. Melatonin does basically the same thing. Trent told me—"

Caroline held up her palm. "Stop. I haven't slept for more than three hours in weeks now. *Weeks.* I told you how disconnected I've been feeling. I can't afford to be like that around a kid. Or around Dad. I don't really care what one of your art snob colleagues has to say about how putting impure things in our bodies somehow limits creativity. It's a load of bullshit, and you know it."

"I just wish you had talked to me about it first. We could have found a better way. Something more natural than pumping chemicals into your system."

Caroline clenched the hand not holding a beer into a fist. "There was an opening this afternoon, so I took it. And I don't need your *permission.*"

"I didn't say you did. I just wish you'd talked to me." He shrugged and turned back to the groceries.

"I'm a grown-up, Daniel. I think I can handle it."

"I know you are. Don't be mad. I'm worried about you is all." He pointed at the beer in her hand. "Any more of those?"

She stared at him. "Mr. Holistic-Living-and-Hot-Yoga is going to lecture me about sleeping pills and then drink a beer?" He grinned back at her and wiggled his eyebrows. She sighed. "In the refrigerator." She took another long sip, remembering she probably shouldn't be mixing the pills with beer, but she told herself she would stop at one. And Daniel didn't need to know she'd already taken a pill.

"Anything new with Vivian and Beth?" His voice echoed back to her from the confines of the refrigerator, and she shrugged.

"Same old, same old. That woman really loves paintings of boring-ass bowls of fruit." There was barely ever any sculpture or anything remotely close to anything Caroline was interested in. Painting had never been her favorite, and poor Beth—she got the technical stuff, but it was clear she didn't love it. The kid painted like a Stepford Wife. Still, her mother, Vivian, insisted on a "classical education in art."

"I don't understand how you put up with it. I wouldn't be able to handle doing that Mickey Mouse, paint-by-numbers bullshit."

"Dad's bills don't pay for themselves."

"You could take out a loan. Go back to school and use what's left over after tuition to help."

Caroline rubbed at her temples. "You know I can't do that. Not with Dad the way he is. I have to take care of him. After Mom died . . ." She trailed off, and Daniel crossed the room and crushed her to his chest.

"I know. But you have to take care of you, too, and you're too good of a sculptor to just let it all go. People are constantly asking me if you're working on anything new. It's like I'm invisible." He paused, chuckling, his palms warm against her back.

Lila kept her face buried against him so he wouldn't see her frown. She knew he didn't mean to hurt her with his last comment, but it was like he couldn't help himself. This constant comparison between them. They were different artists. She told him that all the time—that it was like comparing apples to oranges—but she knew he didn't believe it. The passive-aggressive comments that he laughed off as teasing spoke a truth he would never reveal to Caroline.

"What if you looked into something cheaper? Helping Hands isn't the only hospice care in the city. And then you could maybe go back only part-time. You only need like twelve credits to finish, don't you?"

Caroline pushed away from him. "I'm not putting my father in some shithole just so I can go back to school. You know I can't do that. Jesus. My father—the person who *raised* me—is dying. His insides are being eaten up, and I can't do anything about it but sit there and *watch,* and you want me to go to class and studio like none of it's happening?" She pressed her lips together, furious that he was bringing this up again, that for some reason, he couldn't understand that those things were no longer important to her in the face of her father's illness, that his need to be the *it* couple on the art scene didn't occupy her thoughts nearly as much as it did his.

She drained her beer, her throat still dry. She wanted to get another but held herself back. "I'm going to bed. Back to work tomorrow, and I'll be headed over to see Dad after that."

"It's so early. You don't want to eat?"

"Not hungry." She spun on her heel and stalked down the hall to their bedroom. She changed into an oversized T-shirt and a ratty pair of gym shorts, listening as Daniel banged angrily around the kitchen. Let him be angry. He had so little to be angry about whereas she had so much. If he was frustrated, she felt no guilt in not apologizing. Daniel was the one who *had* finished art school; the one who had taken a fairly lucrative consultant job at Antoine's Gallery. The job that had originally been offered to Caroline. She'd had to turn it down—she'd still been the sole caregiver for her dad at that point—and she knew it was still a raw spot for Daniel. That he had been the second choice. But he was the one who was still painting and selling work semi-regularly. Working round the clock to try to prove himself worthy to the local art community—a closed loop of narcissists who looked for every reason to exclude anyone they deemed unworthy of their attention. And Daniel was desperate for their attention. To prove that he was worth the weight of his own ambition. It grated on her, but she understood. Before her father's diagnosis, she'd been the same way.

Even before her father got sick though, she'd been frustrated with her work. She recognized her sculptures' merit. Saw that they were fundamentally good. Interesting and compelling. But there was always something missing. Some integral part that would reveal a deeper emotion. Subtext and hints at a larger truth she could feel bubbling somewhere inside but never translated to her sculptures. She would work—her fingers pricked and bleeding—and she would feel so near to expressing something larger, more impactful, but she could never quite get there. Her brain would get foggy and confused, losing the thread of exactly what it was she'd hoped to say, and she'd grow increasingly frustrated until she gave it up.

In the beginning, she'd been content to go on her nature walks. Happy to gather whatever struck her eye and tuck it away, a treasure only she could see. Satisfied to craft her small sculptures that were strange, fairy-tale mimics. A princess made of feathers. A dragon from straw and paint and plaster of paris. But as she'd gotten older, even as her sculptures gathered attention and then accolades, a deeper need tugged at her. Couldn't she do more? Say more? *Be* more?

At night, while Daniel lay breathing next to her, asleep while she was awake, she told herself she didn't begrudge him any of it. If her father hadn't gotten sick, she and Daniel would have been moving tangentially. But at least both of them *moving* instead of this daily stagnation.

Eventually, Daniel went quiet in the kitchen, and she watched the shadows crawl across the ceiling and wondered how long it would be before she finally dropped off, and then she was gone. Sleep rose up, quiet and insistent, and pulled her down into a place she would not remember. Outside, something howled, and in her sleep, Caroline trembled.

When Caroline woke, it was still dark. Beside her, Daniel shifted, the sound of his breath carrying her up out of sleep. She swiped at her face and hair. Her hands felt numb, her touch something that passed through without feeling. She panicked for a moment—her fingers fumbling with the sheets, her mouth opening to gulp air—and she tried to call back the dream she'd been having. Something with teeth. Something that left her with the taste of blood still wet on her tongue.

Daniel reached for her, their argument forgotten in the dimness of his own slumber—and pulled her tight against his chest. The sleep-sweet smell of him brought her back to the moment. The clock on her nightstand glowed faintly, and she had to squint to see the hands, but it had been ten hours since she'd gone to bed. Even if she hadn't immediately dropped off, it was more than she'd slept in ages. Relief sheared through her, turning her muscles liquid. Loose and slippery under her skin. She wondered if she'd collapse onto the floor if she stood.

She slid out from under the sheets, and Daniel's hands groped at her T-shirt, catching the edges of the fabric and pulling. "Stay here. I'm sorry I was an asshole," he said, and she leaned over him and dropped a kiss against his cheek.

"I know you are," she said, and he grinned without opening his eyes. "I'll make some coffee."

She touched her arms, her legs, her face. Every part of her was solid. Sturdy. No trace of headache. No desire to bury herself back under the covers. She stretched her fingers and flexed her calves, waiting for something to hit her, to remind her that she shouldn't feel this normal. With her hands splayed before her, she waited for the same haziness she'd been feeling, but there was only a sense of lethargy, as if she'd stumbled into a dream she'd eventually wake from and forget.

She smiled. It was good to feel *better*. A simple, clear thing to carry her through a morning of art instruction with Beth and then the afternoon with her father. Where she would be able to do more than move through the hours as if she were in a trance.

She brewed the coffee strong, the dark liquid swirling against the chipped mug she pulled from the cabinet. She left hers black. It burned her tongue as she drank, but she ignored the pain and took another sip. She pulled down another mug for Daniel and filled it, dumping three spoonfuls of unsweetened vanilla almond milk in before topping off her own.

"Hey, pretty lady."

At the sound of Daniel's voice, she jumped, the coffee sloshing over the edges of the mug and stinging her hand.

"Sorry. Thought you heard me coming."

"No."

"You burned yourself." He reached for her hand, drew it to his mouth, and kissed it.

"Not really. It's cooled off a bit. And I'm feeling much better." She smiled, and it felt good to smile and mean it.

"Did you sleep?"

Caroline threaded her fingers through his and squeezed. "I did."

"I'm glad. I may disagree with how you did it, but I really am glad." Daniel drew her into his chest, and she wrapped her arms around him. "Let's just stay here like this. I don't want to go to work today. Gemma is coming in, and her ass will be on fire when she does. Guaranteed," he said, and laughed, the rumble in his chest vibrating through her.

"No can do," she said. He dropped a kiss on the top of her head and pulled away. "Come back," she said, grasping at his shirt. Daniel let her tug him back to her. "Now don't move."

"But there's coffee," he whispered into her ear. Caroline released him, swatting his backside as she did, glad to have this playfulness between them returned. It had been too long since they'd joked or teased each other.

"How did you know *coffee* was the magic word?" she asked.

Daniel tapped the side of his head. "Brain implants. It's how I got you to agree to marry me."

"So maniacal."

They drank their coffee leaning against the counter, their arms touching, and Caroline wished it could always be like this. Simple and easy and without the pressure of the outside world drawing them apart.

Reaching out, Daniel tucked a strand of hair behind her ear. "I'm glad you feel better. And things will only go up from here. A couple more nights with some decent sleep will set things right."

"Yeah. Definitely," she said, and set her coffee down before leaning into him, her lips on his shoulder. Even this—this physical need—had been ignored lately, and phantom threads of desire wound their way through her abdomen.

"Keep that up and you'll be late," he said, and she brought her mouth to the delicate skin at his neck.

"Maybe tonight then. Don't forget about me."

"Never." He buried his fingers in her hair, and she pressed into him and reminded herself that she was supposed to be getting ready for work. That she hadn't gone to see her dad the night before, the way she had every single night for months.

"You be good today," she said, and unwound herself. He grabbed at her, and she giggled and slapped his hands away. Tonight, they could cook dinner together. She would come home, and they could spend the evening eating pasta—gluten-free for Daniel—and then, in the quiet before sleep, relearn the angles of each other's bodies.

"Always," he said, and she forced herself to go back down the hallway and into the shower, where she washed herself quickly and climbed out. She toweled off and did her makeup. Blew her hair dry and straightened it. Her jeans were too loose—she'd lost more weight since her father had gone into hospice—and she covered the gaping waistband with an oversized tunic. Good enough.

She drove in silence, the trees sliding past in a rain-washed blur. The humidity had just begun to slip, cooler weather still hiding even in late September, and Caroline let her car windows down and breathed in—the deeper swamp smell of rot and decay mingling with the night smell of Confederate jasmine and, floating above all of it, the faint reminder of a thousand people's morning cigarettes. The scent comforted in a way only someone native to New Orleans could understand.

The city dropped away behind her, the ugly gray-brown of the buildings fading as she exited off I-10 and steered her car toward Metairie. Small bungalows gave way to gabled, bricked monsters that offered green lawns, palm trees, and gated gardens. Inside those massive homes lived ladies who lunched at the country club and gossiped about whose children had to be given a scholarship to the Metairie Park Country Day School.

The Kellum house stood back from the street. It was one of the only homes without brick; more traditional with its second-level porch, pale yellow paint, dark shutters, and dormer windows. The yard was meticulously landscaped with trimmed boxwoods next to the front door and a colorful bed of annuals lining the walk. Once a week, a team would descend on the yard with their mowers and edgers and pruners, and Vivian would write a check, which she slipped through the mail slot when they came knocking for payment so she wouldn't have to actually talk to the men cleaning up her garden beds. Vivian was the kind of woman who only spoke to "the help" when absolutely necessary.

Beth stood at the front door already. She was dressed simply in a long-sleeved white shirt and dark jeans. With her pale hair and skin and dark blue eyes, she was the kind of fragile beauty described in books by dead white men as elfin and delicate, but today that loveliness was hidden behind a deep scowl.

Caroline smiled to herself. She remembered using exactly that kind of scowl when she was twelve. Her dad told stories about how he had to bribe her to talk; how he'd used canvases and nature walks and oil paint to extort conversation and the occasional smile from his daughter.

But where Caroline's adolescent anger at the world had been withdrawn and quiet, Beth was anything but. The kind of girl the local, snobbish mothers whispered about, refusing the play dates and outings Vivian had tried to arrange when Beth was younger. The kind of girl who was "not nice." The kind of girl who was a "bad influence." Their daughters were bound for the Junior League. For debutante balls and homecoming tiaras and five-carat, colorless engagement rings.

Meanwhile, Beth had been kicked out of the Day School after an incident with a popular boy. Well-known last name. Captain of the middle school boys' tennis team. Vice president of Student Council. Always on the honor roll. A good boy according to the mothers and teachers and administration. A bright boy with a promising future.

Beth claimed he'd been taunting her for weeks, calling her "Mosquito Bites" because her chest was flat. Then, on a Tuesday afternoon, he'd pretended to stumble into her while she stood in the lunch line. His hands landed directly on her breasts, which he squeezed. Behind him, his buddies cackled and high-fived each other.

"Oh, gosh! I'm so sorry." Every word coated with sarcasm as he backed away. "I'm just so clumsy."

For the next two minutes and thirty-eight seconds, Beth Kellum punched and kicked the ever-loving shit out of him. What neither the boy nor his buddies understood was that Beth was working toward her blue belt in Tae Kwon Do—perhaps the only progressive thing Vivian would ever do for her daughter—and it took three teachers to pull Beth off him. She'd split his lip and almost broken his nose. His ribs were bruised.

And he'd fucking deserved it. Even when the school's administration threatened expulsion unless she apologized, Beth refused. He was the one who had been harassing her. The one who had put his hands on her first. She had nothing to be sorry for, and she hoped he remembered the lesson she taught him for the rest of his miserable life.

Vivian was mortified. She canceled her lunches. The cocktail hours and charity benefits. She threatened Beth with months of grounding, with boarding schools for troubled teens, but nothing worked. Beth wouldn't budge. Let them expel her. It wasn't fair that he'd started it but wasn't in trouble at all.

So when the school's administration called Beth and her mother in for the tribunal, Beth was ready. The small tape recorder her mother had bought to help Beth with taking notes was tucked in her bag, the microphone strategically uncovered so it caught every single word.

Yes, the Day School would be expelling Beth while the boy would remain enrolled. He would serve two days of lunch detention as punishment for teasing her. He was a good boy, after all. He was involved in sports and clubs and had big things ahead of him. Beth was a known troublemaker. Her discipline file was two inches thick. She was a problem—a blight—on the school's immaculate reputation. This kind of behavior was not acceptable for a young lady. Besides, he'd probably been teasing her because he liked her. He'd brushed up against her, and she had overreacted. She'd had no right to physically assault him, and no, he had most decidedly not sexually harassed her. That was absolutely not the case. They were very sorry, but effective immediately, Beth Kellum was no longer welcome on campus.

Beth had it all on tape. She mailed a copy of the tape and a

letter blasting the school for their hypocrisy and clearly sexist pol-
icies to WDSU. But it was Vivian who unwittingly answered the
reporter's phone call when it came, and within three days, Beth's
plan crumbled. Vivian's attorneys threatened to sue if WDSU
aired the tape, which incidentally featured a minor *and* a group
of individuals who'd never consented to be recorded. WDSU sent
the tape back at Vivian's demand, and Vivian forced Beth to de-
stroy it, her mouth set in a grim line as Beth cried so hard she
gagged.

Since then, Beth had been homeschooled. Locked away in
that lovely house so Vivian could keep a close eye on her. The
quintessential princess in her ivory tower.

Plus there were the weekly visits to a highly recommended
child psychiatrist where Beth was repeatedly advised on how to
better control her anger. "That old fart doesn't actually care about
anything I say," Beth told Caroline after almost every mandated
appointment. "He just wants me to shut up. And I know he tells
Mom everything even though he told me he wouldn't." Caroline
would listen as Beth railed against him and remind her that
Dr. Bryson was incredibly intelligent and only wanted to help
her. Beth would glare at her until Caroline dropped her eyes and
suggest they get started on the day's project.

"Good morning, Beth," Caroline called as she climbed out of
the car. "Everything okay?"

"Same as it ever is." She jerked her chin toward the house.
Caroline hadn't had a day at the Kellums' yet that wasn't thick
with tension between mother and daughter. She brightened
momentarily. "I have something I want to show you later. Something secret."

"That right?" Caroline said, and the front door opened.
Vivian Kellum stepped onto the porch. She was dressed in a
peach-colored twinset and cream slacks. Pearls twisted along her
collarbone.

"I'll be back in a few hours. Senator Williams called a meeting and asked me to take notes. I left a print of what I'd like to see today on the kitchen island. Very classic," Vivian said, smoothing her hands over her slacks.

Inwardly, Caroline groaned. Classic meant Monet. Classic meant more boring as hell. But Vivian had explicitly laid out her goals for Beth when she'd hired Caroline. Traditional art instruction. Some art history. Practical work in paint and sculpture. Mostly paint, even though she knew Caroline specialized in weird kinds of sculpture she didn't quite understand. Nothing avant-garde. None of that Surrealist, experimental stuff Caroline was known for. Yes, she knew Caroline was the youngest artist to ever have a piece accepted at the Ogden Museum of Southern Art, but Beth was a difficult child and needed structure. It was so exciting to know that Beth was going to receive lessons from a local artist who was practically a celebrity! How jealous all the girls at the club were going to be when they heard that Caroline Sawyer, the artist *everyone* seemed to be talking about, was working for her!

It made Caroline uncomfortable to know she was part of Vivian Kellum's redemption tour. If it wasn't for the sizable paycheck that covered her dad's bills and for actually *liking* Beth, Caroline imagined she wouldn't have lasted very long at the job.

Vivian breezed past them in a storm of powdery perfume. "Be good!" she called, and then was gone. Caroline and Beth stood in the foyer, watching as Vivian pulled away, and then together, they turned back into the darkness of the house.

CHAPTER 6

CAROLINE 2004

Caroline turned to Beth. "What is it you wanted to show me?"

Beth looked up at her, and for the first time, Caroline noticed the dark hollows under the girl's eyes. "Maybe later. I need to go and get my paint," she said, and without looking back, disappeared down the hallway.

"Okay then," Caroline mumbled after Beth, and then closed the door behind Vivian, making sure it was locked.

Inside, it was still dark. Regardless of the numerous windows, the sun never seemed to find its way into the house. The trees outside blocked most of the light, but Vivian loved them and would not even allow them to be trimmed.

The hallway led to a living room and dining room done up in colonial grays and whites; heavy, expensive furniture was swept artfully through the room, and china and polished silver was tucked carefully inside an antique hutch. At the back of the house, the kitchen opened onto two opposing sets of stairs. Up to go to the four bedrooms, and down to go to the basement.

Hooks hung from the wall going up the stairs. Empty places where pictures once hung.

Caroline had asked about them when she'd first started working for the Kellums. "It was too hard for Beth after we lost her father. She cried every time she saw a picture of him. Said his ghost was trapped inside. So I took them down, but I couldn't bring myself to take down the hooks. Something about it felt so final." Vivian twirled the band she still wore on her finger as she explained. Upstairs, Beth had grown quiet, but if she'd heard any part of their conversation about the father she'd lost, she'd never let on.

"I lost my mom around Beth's age. It can be hard on a kid. I don't remember much about it, but my dad says I stopped talking for a while," Caroline said, and Vivian nodded. Caroline never asked Beth to talk about her father, and the girl had never offered anything up. The hooks remained, their stories untold, and eventually, Caroline forgot to see them.

There was a pot of coffee on, and Caroline poured herself a cup even though she knew it would make her jittery. The two mugs she'd already had were still circulating through her system, but it felt good to hold on to something warm, and she cupped it between her hands.

The door to the basement stood open, a draft feathering over Caroline's arms, and she pushed against the door with her toe until it clicked. The basement was a large, damp room that Vivian called Beth's playroom, but Caroline had only ever seen Beth reading down there in that shadowy, cool place before clattering upstairs for her art lesson. Probably, the girl had outgrown the need for a playroom within the past year or two.

She drank her coffee and waited for Beth to come back downstairs with her paints. She glanced over at the island and did groan aloud then. She'd been right. A print of a Monet landscape

sat on the granite countertop. Irritated, she took another sip
of coffee and flipped on the small television Vivian kept in the
kitchen.

A perfectly coiffed reporter filled the screen, gesturing to a
small wooded lot behind her, and then a picture replaced it. The
photo showed a girl with hair cropped at her chin and bangs that
needed a trim. There was a smattering of freckles across her nose,
and she had her arms flung around the neck of a fluffy golden
retriever as she grinned into the camera.

THIRTEEN-YEAR-OLD GIRL MISSING FROM LOWER NINTH WARD,
the headline read, and Caroline turned up the volume.

". . . taken from her backyard. Her parents were inside as
the girl played in their fenced yard. Anyone with any information is encouraged to call the hotline on your screen or nine-
one-one immediately. It is possible McFurrow is in extreme
danger."

Caroline clicked the television off and poured the remainder
of the coffee down the drain. She couldn't be sure if it was the
excessive caffeine or the news story that had nauseated her. How
frequently had she allowed Beth to go into the gated backyard
while she cleaned up their materials? It could have easily been
Beth. The thought made her skin crawl.

Behind her, Beth pounded down the stairs, her paints and
brushes spilling out of her hands and clattering to the floor.
Caroline winced at the sound, her head suddenly light, and she
gripped the countertop and forced herself to breathe deeply as
she pressed a hand over her mouth. It was just a news story. She
had no reason to feel this unnerved.

"Are you sick, Ms. Caroline? I can call my mom if you need
me to," Beth said. Caroline shook her head, afraid that if she
opened her mouth, she would be sick. It had to be the combination of the Ambien and the caffeine, coupled with the awful

news story. She hadn't exactly eaten a proper dinner the night before. Her blood sugar had dropped, and that's why she felt so terrible.

"Are you tired? Do you want to lie down for a little bit? I can paint down here by myself. I'll be really quiet, and I'll paint what Mom left. Promise," Beth said.

Caroline spoke from behind her teeth. "No. It's okay. I just need a snack. Didn't really have breakfast this morning." She did not want to tell Beth about the abduction. Not because she was afraid of scaring her, but because Caroline was afraid even mentioning it would make the panic cresting through her even worse.

"I can make you something. Toast, maybe? My mom always makes that for me when I'm sick." Already, Beth was striding across the kitchen, purposeful in her movements, and Caroline sagged against the counter. Her shirt clung to her back—wetslick with her own sweat—and she pulled it away from her.

"Here." Beth stood before her, a glass of ice water in her extended hand, and Caroline took it, let the water flow over her tongue and down her throat until she thought she would choke.

"Thank you."

"The toast should be ready in a few minutes. Are you sure you're okay?"

"Hey, I'm supposed to be the adult here, right?" The joke was feeble, and Beth didn't respond, only looked up at Caroline as she took back the glass.

"I'll be okay, Beth. Really. I just need to eat something. I'll be right as rain after that."

"Promise?" She held out her pinkie, and Caroline closed her own around it.

"Sure."

"Good. There's something I want to show you. A secret."

"You mentioned that earlier. What is it?"

Beth shook her head. "Not today. I'm not ready yet."

"Okay. I just figured since you brought it up, you wanted to show me now." Again, Beth shook her head. Caroline felt she would never understand children. The secret world they occupied; their nonsensical rules.

Caroline dutifully swallowed the heavily buttered and honeyed toast under Beth's watchful eye, and only when the plate was clean did Beth nod in satisfaction. For the remainder of their time together, Beth sat in the kitchen and followed Caroline's instruction—her glorified paint-by-number like Daniel had said—but Caroline could feel the girl's eyes on her. It was sweet that Beth was so concerned, but Caroline wished she'd stop staring at her like she was something that could shatter.

By the time Vivian pulled into the driveway, Caroline had washed her water glass three times too many and wiped down every counter even though there wasn't a speck of paint anywhere.

"Have a good time?" Vivian asked as she came into the kitchen, her hands tucked around a paper bag, the top of a bottle peeking over the edge.

"Yup," Beth said before Caroline could respond. "I finished my painting." She pointed toward her easel and peeked at Caroline.

"A wonderful time," Caroline said, and Beth nodded her head.

Vivian drew down a wineglass and set it on the counter. "Beth, tell Ms. Caroline good-bye and then go get washed up," Vivian said, but already her back was turned, the wine opener in her hands doing its work. A bit early for a liquid lunch, but Caroline supposed everyone had a poison. Even hypocritical good Christian ladies.

Beth scrambled down from the table, grasped Caroline's hand, and led her down the hallway as if Caroline was the child. "You'll feel better tomorrow. You'll sleep in since it's the weekend. No nightmares. And on Monday, I'll show you something that will make you forget how bad you felt today."

A chill shuddered through Caroline's belly. "How did you know I have nightmares?"

"Don't you?" Beth cocked her head to one side. "Sleep tight tonight, Ms. Caroline," Beth said, and opened the door. "Sweet dreams."

Before the door closed, Caroline thought she heard Beth laugh.

CHAPTER 7

CAROLINE 2004

She drove, wondering what could have possibly made Beth laugh after she'd closed the door. Why in the moment Beth had looked up, her head tilted and eyes sunken, Caroline had wanted to run. As if what stood before her wasn't Beth at all but a monster wearing little-girl skin. Caroline sighed and pushed the thought away from her. Illogical. She wasn't living in a horror movie. Beth's head wasn't going to start spinning, her mouth spewing pea-green liquid as a priest screamed his pointless incantations.

She made the turn that would take her past a CC's Coffee House. If her father was awake, she wanted to sneak him the chicory blend. Something to make up for not coming to see him the day before. After retiring from the Navy, he claimed he would never drink anything other than real NOLA coffee ever again if he could help it, and her childhood memories were infused with the acrid reminder of his coffee brewing in the kitchen.

The parking lot at Helping Hands was full, as it always was. Caroline's visits most always coincided with a shift change, and she usually ended up following a nurse or front office staff person to their car and then taking their space. Today was no different, and it took a couple of loops around the lot before she located a nurse on her way out. She parked and hurried inside, passing the coffee back and forth between both hands so she would not burn her fingers. The automatic doors slid open, chilled air rushing out as she went inside.

"Hey, Ms. Caroline," a nurse at reception called, and she raised her hand in greeting. Normally, she'd stop to chat, but today she wanted no delays.

Her father's room was on the first hallway. She was grateful, as always, that he was not on one of the farther hallways. They all connected like a maze, the walls painted the same bland shade of oatmeal with prints of cheap watercolors hung here and there. Even though Helping Hands was the best hospice care in the city, the faded pastels did little to cheer the place up. At least on the outer edges of the building there were windows and daylight. The interior rooms spilled bright, fluorescent light into the hallways. An artificial sun that added another depressive layer.

Her father's door stood open, the television a low susurrus, and she went slowly inside. Even now, the sight of his wasted body—the bulk and muscle of his years in the Navy withered away—frightened her. This was not the man who had hugged her with the kind of ferocity and strength that made her ribs ache. The man who had been able to lift her into his arms when she got her acceptance letter to art school, cheering as he shouted that his daughter was a goddamned genius. The man who rose before the sun every morning to go for a run. The man who spent the first year and a half of his retirement learning how to speak Italian, so he could finally take the vacation he'd always wanted and come home fifteen pounds heavier. The man who'd used art to coax her out of her silence after her mother's death, his old tackle box suddenly appearing one day on the kitchen table filled with rocks, grass, and a few acrylic paints. A canvas set beside it. This man who drifted in and out of consciousness, the pain confusing him and taking him away from her, was not her father. She didn't want to remember him like this but feared it had been so long that her memory would be permanently stamped with this version of him.

"My girl," he said, lifting a hand toward her that she took between her own as she tried to ignore the tissue-paper thinness of his skin, how the veins jutted out in stark relief. Caroline leaned down to plant a light kiss on his cheek. She didn't like the fevered heat she felt there. There was no aspect of his dying she would ever get used to.

"You'll have to drink it quick before Cee comes in, but I brought you a little something," she said, holding out the coffee.

"You are a godsend. Just a few sips, yeah? Our secret. Even if they let me have it, I wouldn't drink the mud they brew here."

Caroline brought the cup to his lips and tipped it, watching to be certain she didn't spill, and her father swallowed two small sips.

"That's good. All I need to tide me over and to keep from messing with my innards. Not that they can be much more messed up than they already are." He laughed, but it was a hollow wheeze.

"Next time, I'll see if I can get some crawfish back here."

"What I wouldn't give for some of your mama's boudin. I'd do shameful things to get another taste of that woman's cooking. Lord knows," he said. Caroline stared down at her hands. More and more frequently now, he was talking about her mother. As if she hadn't been gone since Caroline was a teenager. As if Mom had been a shining example of a wife and parent—as if she hadn't spent all of Caroline's childhood acting as if Caroline was something to be ashamed of.

In Caroline's memory, there was still the image of her mother standing over her, shaking as she held out the chicken bones Caroline had dug out of the garbage. With hammer, glue, and wire, Caroline had fashioned them into a crude throne small enough to seat a miniature evil queen.

"What the hell is this, Caroline?" Her mother had closed her fist around the throne, and Caroline had kept her eyes trained on the floor.

"Nothing."

"It's not nothing. Did you make this?"

"Yes." Caroline's voice fell dead on her lips, and her mother reached down and grasped her chin, her fingernails digging into the flesh there.

"No more of this. You understand? It's disturbing. Can you imagine what people would say if they saw this? They'd think there was something wrong with you. Look at me. Say yes ma'am."

"Yes, ma'am," Caroline said, and her mother dropped her hand.

"Good. Now go wash your hands. And brush your hair. It looks like a damn rat's nest. Dinner's almost ready." Her mother had turned on her heel, the sculpture still clutched tight as if she could exert enough pressure to not only break it, but to turn it to dust.

And Caroline had listened. She was a good girl. She didn't want to upset her mother. Didn't want her mother's gaze to fall on her that way once more, so heavy in its judgment. Instead, she went quiet, the images and sculptures she carried inside of her wasting away as she forced her hands, her fingers to be still. She would walk, her guilty hands shoving interesting, illicit things into her pockets. A leaf pocked with mold. A thorned seed pod. But she always emptied her pockets before she got home. Eventually, she learned if she bit down on her cheek hard enough, she wouldn't cry.

Caroline savored the warmth of the coffee cup between her

palms, wishing as she always did that the memories of her mother weren't tainted with shame. "I know, Dad."

"You finish that for me, love. No point letting it all go to waste just because I can't have more than a few swallows."

She did as he asked, the earthy flavor of the chicory a lovely bitterness blooming over her tongue. "I miss this. Daniel won't drink anything except light roast."

"I'll try not to hold it against him," her father said. He passed a hand over his face. "Sorry, chérie. Mind if we don't talk? Feeling a bit more tired than normal."

"Of course not." She set the coffee on the small table beside him and reached across to squeeze his hand. He smiled back at her and let his eyes flutter closed. After a few minutes, her father's chest rose and fell, the skin of his face stretched tightly over the bones—a reminder of what he would become when the cancer ate enough of him to delete his existence. Caroline turned her attention to the television so she would not have to imagine her father as a corpse.

The set was tuned to the local public station—a nature documentary with a calming British voiceover detailing the migratory pattern of butterflies—and Caroline let herself drift, the warmth from the afternoon sun spilling through the window and over her legs. For the first time in quite a while, she was on the verge of sleep without having to take a pill. Relief carried her down, and she let her eyes slip closed. She could doze for thirty minutes. Her father was beside her. If anything happened, she would hear the machines beeping.

Her sleep was light; she could still hear the murmur of the documentary, the sound of her father's breath, so when she heard the voice, she assumed it was the television. A commercial or the program changing. Normal. But it grew louder, more insistent, a thin whine that grew into a hoarse scream.

Caroline jerked awake, searching for the noise, her heart dully thumping out a pattern of panic as she looked at her father. His eyes were open, and he stared at the ceiling, but there was no comprehension in them. His teeth were bared, and the cords in his neck stood out against his graying skin.

He was screaming Caroline's name.

"Dad?" she said, and shook him, tears already streaming down her cheeks. "It's just a dream. I'm right here." Still, his eyes were distant, and she knew he couldn't see her.

"Don't go with him. Please don't." He moaned and pulled his lips farther back from his teeth, blood beading against the cracked skin. "Stay away from him, Caroline." His voice rose back into a scream, and then one of the nurses, Cee, rushed in and pushed Caroline back.

"Give me some space, sweetie." Cee swept her gaze over the machines, checking vital signs. "Mr. Sawyer? Can you hear me? Come on back to me now. You had a dream." The nurse attempted to hold down his arms, but her father thrashed.

"Please don't," her father said again, and Caroline clamped a hand over her mouth. There had been days where the pain was enough for her father to take a bit longer to recognize her, but he'd never had hallucinations or whatever the hell this was.

Two other nurses ran into the room, one pushing a metal cart, and Caroline backed away. She didn't want to see this; didn't want to watch a nurse punch a needle filled with even more sedatives into her father, to see the dim confusion that would settle over his features as it took hold.

"I'm sorry," she said, but there was no one listening, and the nurses went about their work, every movement methodical and precise. Her father continued mumbling, but the words were nonsensical, and the nurses spoke in soothing tones and settled him back into his bed.

"Just a bad dream." Cee turned to face Caroline and straightened her scrubs. "It happens all the time. Nothing to worry about.

Sometimes patients get confused when they wake up and bring whatever they found down in their sleep back with them. It looks scarier than what it is."

"I was just sitting with him, and I drifted off, too. I'm so sorry. I didn't mean to do anything," Caroline said.

"Sweetheart, you didn't *do* anything. Don't go blaming yourself," Cee said. The other nurses were busy resettling her father, checking to be sure nothing was amiss. "You need some good rest. I know you want to be here as much as possible, but you're going to hurt yourself trying to watch over him when he's got people taking care of him round the clock. That's why we're here. He's resting comfortably now. Why don't you go on home? Get some sleep and a hot meal that doesn't come out of a can or a vending machine, and he'll be here in the morning." The nurse's voice was still comforting, but there was an edge in it, too. She didn't expect an argument or a refusal.

"You're right. You'll call though? If anything else happens?" Caroline said.

"Of course. But he's stable, so I doubt you'll be hearing from us today. And I know we'll see you tomorrow, Ms. Caroline." Cee chuckled, and reached across to squeeze her arm. "And please don't give it another thought. It was just a dream," Cee said.

"Thank you, Cee. I'll see you tomorrow."

Caroline scrubbed a hand over her eyes as she walked, but it did nothing to remove the image of her father's bloodied mouth from her mind. She stepped through the automatic doors and into the cooling evening. Around her, the parking lot lights were kicking on, washing everything in an unnatural amber glow, and she slid behind the wheel, determined to put her father's dream out of her mind, but there was a lingering strangeness she could not shake. She pressed a hand to her chest, but it did nothing to calm her racing heart.

Daniel's car was already out front as she pulled up to the

house, and she parked behind him and leaned her forehead against the steering wheel. She would have to go inside and recount everything that had happened when all she wanted was to take an Ambien and fall into bed.

She walked slowly, the muscles in her legs tense, but it did no good to delay. Daniel was in the kitchen when she entered, browning something that smelled bitter in a frying pan, and he turned, setting down the wooden spatula he was using on the counter. She'd wanted to make dinner with him. She imagined her mother's pursed lips. The small, dismissive shake of her head if she'd seen Daniel cooking instead of Caroline. The mess of dishes in the sink. Another series of failures.

"You okay?"

"No," she said.

He turned and switched off the burner. "What happened?"

"He's getting worse. He had a dream, I guess? But it seemed like more than that. He was so scared. For me. Because of me. He kept saying my name, and I've never heard him like that." Her voice caught and then she was sobbing into Daniel's shoulder.

"It's okay. I got you. It was just a dream, yeah? Just a bad dream. Nothing to get upset over."

"But . . . ," she began, and he pulled her even tighter and shushed her.

"You don't have to worry." Inside his arms, Caroline tensed. He was right. Of course he was. She let herself fall into silence in the name of comfort. Willed her anxieties to drop away because Daniel was doing what he could. Still, his solace felt empty in the face of everything she'd wanted to say.

He shifted backward so he could look down into her face. "Plus, I have a surprise for you." He grinned, and she forced herself to return it.

"What is it?"

"No way, sister. Not telling until tomorrow morning. It

would ruin the whole thing if I made the big reveal now," he said, and dropped a kiss on her forehead.

Again, she made herself smile, made herself pretend she was excited. Even if Daniel hadn't listened to her, he was trying to do something nice. The least she could do was be grateful for that. He prattled on as he drained what she saw now was spinach, and she nodded where she was supposed to, her smile still frozen on her face.

By ten, they were both in bed, Daniel already snoring beside her, and she watched him, marveling at how they had somehow found each other in a city that profited on depravity and disconnect. She was thankful. She was. She nuzzled into him, and then, finally, she slept.

CHAPTER 8

CAROLINE 2004

In the morning, she woke while the light was nothing more than a dim gray smear against the walls, and she lay still, willing sleep to return. After thirty minutes, she rose and started the coffee, her body feeling disconnected and loose in its skin. The vigor she'd felt the morning before was gone and replaced with a dim, untraceable ache in muscles she couldn't identify.

"Caroline?" Daniel's voice sounded from the bedroom, and she turned and forced a brightness she didn't feel into her voice. She didn't want to spoil whatever Daniel had planned for her with her bad mood.

"In here," she called, stepping back into the kitchen. Daniel was already dressed in a T-shirt, shorts, and running shoes.

He pointed to his feet. "Get your dancing shoes on, girl. We've got plans." He was hopping from one foot to the other like a kid who'd had too much sugar.

"Hiking?" she said, pushing past him.

"Just get ready. Comfortable shoes," he called after her.

She hurried through a shower, tugging a brush through her hair and then pulling it into a bun. She went lighter than usual on her makeup. Some concealer and mascara. A swipe of lip gloss. If Daniel had told her to wear comfortable shoes, that meant something active, and she'd sweat it all off anyway. It seemed as if the coffee she'd had was starting to kick in, or maybe it was the shower that had perked her up, but she felt better.

"Okay. Ready," she said as she walked down the hallway. Daniel was by the door, keys already in hand, still bouncing back and forth on his toes.

"You are going to love this. Promise," he said, and opened the door. Outside, the air was a touch cooler but still humid, and she followed Daniel to the car, feeling a slight fluttering of exhilaration herself. It was unlike Daniel to show this sort of childlike excitement, and it soothed her further. She smiled—a real one this time.

"Do you plan on letting me know where you're taking me, or are you going to make me wear a blindfold, too?" she said as she opened the door and climbed into Daniel's car.

"There'll be two stops this morning, Ms. Sawyer. Hope you brought your appetite."

He turned up the radio—some song she didn't recognize with a driving bass line—and let down the windows, screeching along. Soon enough she was laughing and attempting to sing with him, the malaise she'd been feeling temporarily lost in the sudden freedom of this day Daniel had planned for her.

"We have to go a little out of our way first," he said, guiding the car onto 61 North.

"Tell me we're not headed toward the Kellums'. No work today. You promised," she teased, and he shook his head.

"Metairie, yes. Kellums'? Absolutely not. Before we get to the main event, I wanted to take a little walk down memory lane. And get some food in our bellies. Two birds, you know."

Ahead of them, the highway opened, signs for shops and restaurants littering the view, and she clapped a hand to her mouth as the memory came flaring up. "No way. Our first date," she said, and Daniel wiggled his eyebrows and grinned.

"Chocolate, right?" he said, and she smiled back at him as he pulled into the parking lot of the Krispy Kreme where he'd taken her all those years ago. "Be back in a second. Don't go anywhere." She watched as he jogged inside, remembering the butterflies in her stomach the first time he'd brought her here. They'd been in their second year of art school, both drowning under the same pressure from Dr. Rimbard's art studio when she'd stumbled across him late one night, bleary-eyed with bleeding fingers as he tried again and again to slice a bilateral cut along a thin piece of clear plastic.

She'd offered her help. He'd accepted, and they'd spent the rest of the night ignoring his project in favor of talking. When the sky outside turned lighter, he'd asked her to breakfast, and driven her here, where they'd lingered over coffees—his without sugar and just a splash of skim milk. Watching him order, how purposeful he was in refusing a donut, she understood that even in his creativity, there was rigidity to him. An asceticism that served as something holy. She'd been self-conscious about her single double-chocolate donut and picked at the edges while they talked, but he seemed not to notice. He wanted to paint, to live more deeply than the people he said were sleeping through their lives, and she understood. When she sculpted, she felt the same way. Like she'd tapped into an undercurrent that could only be glimpsed in fleeting moments, the flesh of the world peeled back to reveal glittering shadows. Everything beautiful and dangerous as she pushed further in and further down. After that, they'd been inseparable.

Daniel emerged, a bag crumpled in his left hand and two

coffees balanced in his right. Reaching across the center console, she opened the door for him. She took the coffee he handed her, and then grabbed the back of his neck and drew him in, her mouth seeking his. It was as if she could finally take a breath.

"There's more where that came from," she said.

"Save it for later. There's one other thing," he said, and she kissed him again.

"You sure about that?"

"Positive. Trust me," he said, and then opened the bag, pulling out two donuts—a glazed and a double chocolate—and sank his teeth into the glazed as he handed her the chocolate.

"Sweet baby Jesus, did you just actually eat sugar? Refined carbohydrates?" She dramatically placed her hand over her heart and pretended to swoon. "Ladies and gentlemen, he's putting junk in his body. I never thought I'd see the day that Daniel McHough would backslide into eating processed foods." He flashed her a glaze-smeared grin.

"If you tell anyone at the gallery, I'll deny it."

"Tell me there's real cream and sugar in that coffee, too."

He winked at her and lifted the cup to his lips. "Maybe. Guess you'll never know."

"I'm going to tell everyone. Whatever the next party or gala or charity fundraiser is, I'm going to wait until every single art snob is present and then scream it to the whole room, you wheatgrass-loving *faker*."

He leaned over and planted a wet, sloppy kiss against her cheek. She squealed and swatted at him as he put the car in reverse, craning his neck to look behind them as he turned the radio back up. He drove, and they ate their donuts and drank their coffee. She relaxed into the seat, the music washing over her. She wished it could always be like this. That her father was well. That she was finishing her degree, her work on exhibition and garnering attention that went beyond the local scene. Today, she could pretend. Today, she could shed that weightier layer of herself and fall into something lighter.

The music faded, the DJ coming on to announce the morning news, and a more serious voice flooded through the speakers.

Early this morning, dispatchers were alerted to the possibility of human remains in Couturie Forest. Police can now confirm that the remains are those of thirteen-year-old Anna McFurrow, who was reported missing last week. Police Chief Dan Bellinger will conduct a press briefing later this afternoon. Anyone with any information is encouraged to contact the City Park Police Department.

Daniel changed the station, flipping through the channels until there was music again. "Nothing sad today," he said, and drummed his fingers along the steering wheel.

Caroline's stomach churned as she remembered the news story from the day before. She willed the feeling away. Daniel had planned something just for her, and she would enjoy it no matter what. Beneath her, the highway droned, and she let her eyes drift closed, but the sharp edge of foreboding lingered, and she breathed deeply, counted to fifteen, and then opened her eyes. They'd gotten back on I-10 and then I-610, the city behind them and Lake Pontchartrain ahead.

"Beach day?" she asked, and Daniel shook his head.

"Guess again," he said.

Ahead of them, the twisted steel of roller coasters emerged from the trees, and Daniel signaled to exit onto Michoud.

"Jazzland? No freaking way." She laughed and stared out the window as the park grew closer. "I haven't been here since I was a kid. My dad used to bring me."

"I figured you could use a day to completely let loose. Act like a kid. Drink Coke and eat junk food. The works."

Leaning across the car, she kissed him again. "This is perfect. Thank you."

Already the parking lot was filling up. Minivans stuffed with tired parents and hyperactive kids. Groups of teenagers milling by their beat-up hand-me-down cars, as they jostled one another or shouted back and forth. Everyone flooded toward the entry gates, and Caroline climbed from the car, reaching to clasp Daniel's hand as they joined the stream of people.

Brick columns with turnstiles in between stretched upward toward a wrought-iron gate fashioned after the fleur-de-lis iron scrollwork found in the French Quarter. Atop the gate, the neon sign for the park was lit, the brightly colored letters spelling out *Jazzland* topped with stars that shone dull in the morning light. Already, the scents of popcorn, cotton candy, and funnel cake filtered through the air, and even though she'd eaten, her mouth watered.

"Mega Zeph first. And I fully plan to make out with you while we're waiting in line," she said, and Daniel laughed and handed her a ticket.

"It's your day, lady. You're the boss."

Ahead of them, the park opened into an old-fashioned main street, shops on the left and right pumping ice-cold air conditioning against their legs as they moved toward the center of the park, which opened on a large water feature. Together, they wound their way to the back of the park with the rest of the older kids who were determined to be among the first in line. Caroline had the sudden compulsion to run, to fully sink into an abandonment of her adulthood, and she sped up, tugging Daniel along. When the green-and-purple buildings of the Mardi Gras area appeared, she did begin to run. It had been years since she'd done anything like this, since she had not felt immobile under her duty to her father—the year of caring for him on her own before she couldn't do it anymore, leaving school, and taking the job at the Kellums'. So many small portions of herself buried under the person she had to be instead.

But here, under the bright sky, with the energy of the crowd buzzing around her, she was able to let all of it collapse. She rode the Mega Zeph, clinging to Daniel's hand the entire time, and then she rode it again, her hands in the air as she screamed and laughed, her breath coming hard and fast, and she never wanted to do anything other than this. To fade into the simplicity of her sudden, brilliant happiness.

As she came tumbling off the ride for the third time, she pulled Daniel to her and buried her face in his chest. "You're the best. I love you," she said, and he tucked his chin on the top of her head.

"You, too."

The day faded into late morning, the light shifting into something more golden than gray. They made their way through the park, stopping to pop in and out of the shops, laughing at the kitschy items for sale, sharing a funnel cake and two slices of pizza as the day wore on, and then going back to the rides.

They'd paused for some shade, staring beyond the rides and out toward Pontchartrain Beach, the water still and flat as glass, and Caroline leaned against Daniel and sighed. "Dad would love this. I think he liked coming here more than I did," she said. Thoughts of her father formed into a painful knot of guilt. Tomorrow, she would stay with him all day. Tomorrow, she would tell him how much fun she'd had, how she'd thought of how they used to come here together. Tomorrow, she would be the good daughter again.

A group of teenagers ran past, their screams a mockery of one of the girls who lingered at the back, her hair pushed forward to hide her face, her head tucked down in shame or embarrassment or any of the hundreds of other reasons a girl will feel that her skin does not fit her. Caroline watched the girl, watched how she lingered on the fringes, how it was so obvious these people she'd selected as friends didn't see or hear her. Caroline should have felt recognition and sympathy, should have felt some kind of compassion for this girl who seemed so much like herself at that age, but instead what crept upon her with slow, insistent steps was a growing sense of disquiet. Watching the girl, she shivered. There was nothing here to fear, nothing to explain this sinister feeling, as if she stood over an abyss staring downward. The feeling grew despite there being nothing to feed it, and it rose up, quiet and insistent, to swallow her down.

"Doing okay? You went a little quiet there," Daniel said, and she nodded.

"Yeah. Of course," she said, forcing the lie out of her. Her skin prickled, and she glanced over her shoulder, but the girl and her group had vanished into the depths of the park.

"Anything else you wanted to ride?"

"I'm a little worn out," she said, and swallowed against the bitter taste on her tongue. "Let's maybe just hang out here for a bit longer."

Even when Daniel reached for her and wrapped an arm around her shoulder, she couldn't shake the chill that had worked its way under her skin.

Nothing's wrong. Everything's fine. She closed her eyes and repeated the phrase to herself as a mantra, as something she could hold on to to keep her heart from leaping into her throat, the pain of its rapid beating enough to make her choke. Around her, the air seemed to expand and contract; the humidity invasive. The screams from the kids on rides grew into an awful shrieking, and a deeper fear unspooled in her belly.

When the sound of dogs—what seemed like hundreds of them—snarling and snapping emerged, she told herself it wasn't possible to hear what she was hearing. That there was no feasible instance that would allow those distinct noises. As if the dogs had happened upon an animal and opened it up, the blood spilling over their lips as they tore into its flesh.

Her entire body tensed, her fingers clawing at Daniel's arm, and he looked down at her in confusion. "What is it?"

"You don't hear that?"

"Hear what?"

Her legs trembled, and she tried to straighten them, tried to keep the panic out of her voice, but all that came out was a whisper. "The dogs."

"Dogs? I mean, I hear kids yelling and stuff, but they don't sound like dogs."

She could envision them, hundreds of bodies moving as one, saliva dripping from their muzzles, their bared teeth, and together, they howled, the sound worming into her so that it seemed the world would break apart with the violence of it. There was her terror unfolding like shards of glass, and her lungs ached, the interior parts of her body feeling scraped raw. She forced her mouth to form words, but she could barely hear herself.

"Jesus. How can you not hear that?"

"It's kids on the rides, Caroline. I promise. You're probably just overheated or something. We'll get you some water, okay?"

She let Daniel guide her away, his hand firm against her back as she trembled, the noise growing louder with every step as if the dogs were just behind her and snapping at her heels. She clenched her fists so she wouldn't clamp her hands over her ears.

Daniel hustled her inside the pizza shop and guided her to a booth. "I'll grab you a water. Just take some deep breaths," he said, and she listened. Forced air in and out of her lungs and then drank the water he brought her as she tried not to see the look of concern on his face. Eventually, the noises faded, but the vague, ominous feeling remained.

"Feeling better?" Daniel said as she drained the water.

"Much. Sorry about that. Got too hot, I guess."

"You scared me there, Linny." He reached across the table and squeezed her hand. "You were talking some crazy shit for a minute. We can stay in here for a while if you want. Or if there's anything else you wanted to do, we could head back out."

"It's fine. I'm okay now."

He furrowed his brow, and she knew he didn't believe her. "Are you hungry? For something other than junk? I could get you a sandwich."

"No. I'll be okay."

He stood and slid in next to her, and she tucked herself into the crook of his arm. How many times had her father brought her to Jazzland when she was a kid? Six? Seven? She'd been young, but she felt like she would remember if she'd ever heard or felt anything like that. All those visits, and she'd never experienced anything close to what had just happened. But she'd gotten too hot. Confused. Conflated the sounds of the rides with her own childhood phobia. The explanation was simple, but she found it difficult to accept. The sounds had felt so *real*.

Her legs ached, and she needed to move, to stretch, to get out of this artificial air even if it meant going back out into the park. Even if it meant she would hear the dogs again. If she did, she'd ask Daniel to take her home.

"Mind if we just walk around?" she asked.

"We can if that's what you want. You sure you're okay?"

"Positive," she said, and he helped her out of the booth, his hand steadying her as they made their way to the door. She held her breath as she stepped out into the sun. There were no sounds, no dogs, and she exhaled, the air rushing out of her so it felt like she might collapse. Daniel kept her upright, and she walked beside him, pretending she was not afraid.

For another hour, they wandered the park, the air thick now

with the spoiled odors of fried food and garbage. Daniel kept asking again and again if she needed a break. There was a part of her that wanted to scream at him that she didn't need him to treat her like a child. He only wanted the best for her, had wanted this day to be something special, and she'd ruined it. It was a lesson her mother had made sure Caroline understood from a young age—this burial of emotion in the face of bruising a man's ego. She bit down on her tongue, the sharp edge of the pain keeping her quiet. When Daniel's cell phone rang, she was thankful for his momentary distraction.

"Everything okay?" he spoke into the phone, and Caroline turned away, watching a group of obviously exhausted moms argue with their children. Behind her, Daniel mumbled something that sounded like sympathy and then snapped his phone closed.

"That was Gemma. There's some issue with the caterer for the Aversion Gala. She has to run out and deal with it, so I'll need to cover the gallery for the rest of the day. I'm so sorry, Linny."

"Of course. Don't be sorry," Caroline said. The gala was a career boost—an opportunity to impress the upper echelon of the art world. And Gemma was the person who decided if Daniel was formally invited or not. If Gemma told Daniel to stop sleeping and live in the gallery, he would have done it. Besides, Caroline wanted to be away from the park. To be in the dust-coated quiet of her own home.

She wanted to forget the sounds she'd heard, and the fear loosened in her blood. She wanted to sleep and forget.

CHAPTER 9

LILA 2019

Lila's phone had stayed quiet all night. There were none of the usual texts or notifications that drifted in until early morning when Macie finally went to bed. Lila had not been able to sleep, had tossed and turned, determined not to look at her phone, not to check Macie's Snapchat or Instagram Stories to see if she'd posted anything about their trip to the movies, but around four, she couldn't help herself and snatched her phone from the nightstand.

But Macie was missing from her Instagram feed. Lila clicked on her followers list, but Macie wasn't there. Searching her name yielded no results either, and Lila closed out the app and opened Snapchat instead. No Macie.

She already knew what would happen, but she dialed Macie's number anyway and waited. Two rings before the message. "The number you have dialed is unable to receive calls at this time. Please try your call again later."

Numb, she let the phone drop away, tears pooling in the corners of her eyes. She deserved this. To be cut out so completely that she was erased on every front. She'd said horrible, *horrible* things. Of course Macie would block her, but it didn't make the reality of it hurt any less. Everything inside of her felt raw and exposed, and she stood, desperate to run, to move, to do *something* other than curl into herself and sob. She went and sank down at her vanity, flipping on the small lamp that sat there, and stared at her bloated, splotched face.

She leaned forward and pressed her mouth to the mirror, the condensation of her breath fogging the glass, distorting her eyes and the planes of her face until this thing looking back at her wasn't her at all but some other girl. For a moment, the color of her hair seemed to shift, to grow lighter until what reflected back at her were long, blond curls instead of her own halo of frizzy brown strands, then the face of the first dead girl, then the second. She blinked and her reflection went back to normal. Maybe if she *were* someone else, all this awfulness with Macie would have never happened, but she was frightened, too. Was this how it began? Her hold on reality slipping away in small moments?

She figured her mother wasn't sleeping either, but she couldn't bring herself to go to her, to tell her what was happening, and she sat wearily back down on her bed. Whatever secret her mother was hiding was likely going to stay safely locked away in her mother's memory. If she told her mother what had happened, she would tell her father, and her father would insist she go to the doctor to be pumped full of pills, just like her mom. Numbed up and distant and unable to feel even small happiness.

Again, she unlocked her phone and stared down at it. She could refresh the apps as much as she wanted, but Macie wasn't going to reappear. Instead, she opened the browser and again typed in *Jazzland, New Orleans.* That small clue that could lead her to the *before* her mother had hinted at. The first few links didn't tell her anything she didn't already know. There were a few videos on YouTube of people in the park, the screams of kids on coasters rising and falling over jazz music playing from unseen speakers. Buildings painted in vibrant pinks and greens, a hallucinogenic version of Mardi Gras. Every link covered the same information: that it had been abandoned after Katrina, that there were rumors every few years about it being rebuilt, that they filmed scary movies there, that the surrounding swampland had reclaimed the park and gators swam in the waterways.

Lila went back to the main search page and scrolled down. There was nothing new here. Nothing to give her any kind of clue to what her mother was hiding about Jazzland. She scrolled further, the headlines bleeding one into the next, and then stopped. At the bottom of the page, buried under all of the generic information, was a link to what looked like a PDF file. "Bleached Burial Grounds: An Investigative History" was the title, and there, highlighted by the search engine, was the word *Jazzland*. Excited, Lila opened the file.

The article was someone's graduate thesis essay; her name and the professor's name were still emblazoned on the title page. Lila scanned through the opening paragraphs, looking again for Jazzland, but it did not reappear until the fifth page. She traced upward to the start of the paragraph and began to read.

The earliest history of New Orleans includes hundreds of instances of white landholders lashing out in prejudicial terror against black practitioners of Louisiana Voodoo ceremonies and religious traditions. One cannot step foot in the city without stumbling over land where blood was once shed in the name of blotting out the perceived threat of the Voodoo religion, but the land where Jazzland now stands was perhaps the bloodiest spot of all.

In the early 1800s, fifteen black women, accused of being

Voodoo Queens, were lynched by a group of white men on the plot where Jazzland now sits. The women ranged in age from teenagers to grandmothers, but all were known for being sharp-tongued and fiercely independent in an era when such behavior was unacceptable for women, much less a woman of color. This despicable act was ignored by the all-white police force, and for approximately a hundred years afterward, the spot—then known as the Queen's Grave—was the preferred place to purge accused women. There is no formal or reliable record of the names of the women who died at the Queen's Grave over the years, but a conservative estimate, based on diaries, letters, and other contemporary source material from the eighteenth and nineteenth centuries, puts the number at approximately 250 to 300 women.

The murders that took place at the Queen's Grave were an open secret well into the twentieth century. For years the 140-acre parcel that sits slightly northeast of the city could not be sold. In addition to the sordid history of the location as a site of torture and murder, there had long been rumors of bizarre goings-on. Multiple sources reported strange noises emanating from the property, likened by more than one witness to the sound of hundreds of snarling, panting wolves gathered in one place. Wildlife safety investigators were called repeatedly to the property in the first decades of the twentieth century, but they never discovered a wolf pack or any other like predators in the area. Eventually, the land sold cheaply to the development group that turned it into Jazzland. As much as the developers tried to erase the history of the property, they could not completely escape it. The mysteries and rumors surrounding the Queen's Grave continue to be shared among those who still remember the murders that transpired there.

The paper went on for another thirty pages. Other locations were explored and analyzed, including a surprising number of theme parks and tourist attractions. Lila skimmed through them, taking note of a few paragraphs that discussed a pleasure garden in Atlanta where two women were beaten to death in the 1960s. The women had been lovers, and there was ample evidence that the alleged murderer had made sexual advances toward both of them, had been twice rejected, and had threatened violence as a result. But the predominantly male jury in the case was sympathetic to the defendant, and the state had not been able to secure a conviction for the murders.

Lila set her phone down and rubbed a hand over her face. Even with this new knowledge, she didn't feel any closer to understanding what it was her mother was hiding. She closed her eyes but did not sleep, her thoughts circling back again and again to the moments in the woods. Flashes of Macie's bare skin; the dim sensation of movement in her belly; sweat pooling under her breasts, in the center of her back as she became something monstrous.

"I'm not like my mother," she whispered, and her voice drifted up and up as she repeated herself. "I'm not like her."

CHAPTER 10

CAROLINE 2004

By the time Daniel dropped her off, the heat had become more invasive—the car's air conditioning straining as he made the drive from Jazzland back to the house.

"I'll be back as soon as I can," he said.

"I'm going to lie down. No rush," she said, and then he kissed her and was gone. She let herself inside and then fell onto the couch. She stretched out, hoping for sleep, for any kind of rest for her body, but her mind raced. She closed her eyes and breathed slowly, but still, in the back of her mind, she heard the dogs, the screaming of children, and there was no rest. There was never any rest. And tomorrow, she would get up and do it all over again, and the next day, and the next, until her father died, and what would happen then? She drifted, following her memories down and down into the snarling, discordant noise from the park. Her body felt feverish and clammy, and her hands ached and her head ached, and there would never be anything other than this confusion and deep pain in her heart. She floated, there in the dark, and wondered if this was what slipping into death was like. Confusion and shadow.

She sat up, and her fingers twitched over her face. Her mouth. Her hands suddenly tender, burdened with a need she hadn't felt since her father had gotten sick. The tackle box was in their closet, stuffed behind a stack of clothes she'd meant to donate. Hidden away so she would not have to suffer the daily reminder of the artist she was supposed to be. Of the work still boiling in her and how she could not discover how to bring it fully out of herself like a beautiful act of bloodletting.

Her body burned as she pushed herself up. She went to the closet, not bothering to turn on the light, and pulled out the tackle box, her fingers passing over the lid in reverence. She did not feel the pressure she normally did when she approached her work. There was nothing but the musty scent of her materials, the way every piece molded to her palm as she held them up.

She began to work. Threading together leaf and wire. Scarlet paint and torn fabric. Letting her hands dip in and out, her brain given over to euphoria she'd not felt since she was a kid. What she was creating would be only for her, and she felt the world open beneath her. An infinite, golden place where her anxieties drowned under honey-coated air. This was what she'd been searching for. This secret key to her own interior.

Around her, the room grew darker, but she didn't need to see clearly. Her hands knew what to craft. There was only the drive to move faster, to ignore the sting and ache of her fingers. What she was making would not wait.

Above her, blinding light invaded the darkness, and she flinched and blinked her eyes in confusion.

"Caroline?" Daniel spoke from behind her, but her neck felt stiff, and the light was so bright that she couldn't turn to look at him. "What the hell are you doing in the dark?"

She shook her head trying to clear it, but it still swam, and the light hurt her eyes. Behind her there was the sound of rustling and then a sharp intake of breath. Daniel was beside her, his hand resting lightly on her shoulder.

"Holy shit," he whispered, and she looked up at him, trying desperately to make sense of how much time had passed—it couldn't have been that long since she'd begun working, but if Daniel was back, it had to have been a few hours at least. "It's amazing, but why were you working with all the lights off?"

Caroline glanced down. Spread before her was a chaos of leaves and thin wire and bits of torn rags covered in crimson smears that looked sickeningly like blood. A lone figure stood before her, the wire bent to form the body of a woman wearing a delicate dress fashioned from leaves and cloth that drooped toward the floor. The fabric and leaves appeared torn and bloodied. Incorporated within the dress were the transparent, thin blades of insect wings. In her hands, the woman held the dismembered head of a dog. Its teeth were bared, and they, too, were painted crimson.

She lifted the sculpture, feeling the lightness of it, how breakable. But it was everything she'd wanted it to be. Dark and lovely and moving. Her fears made manifest and visible to the world. Her hands fluttered to her throat, pride surging through her. This was the kind of work she'd always wanted to do. Art that spoke of something deeper. Art that bled out the portions of herself she'd kept hidden for so long.

"Can I see?" Daniel extended his hand, and he took the sculpture carefully from her and held it up to the light. "It's beautiful. Really insanely good. Why didn't you tell me you were working again?"

Her tongue felt thick in her mouth. "I didn't plan it," she said, and at least it was an honest response.

He gave a low whistle. "I mean, Jesus. How long did it take

you to make this? The wings?" He traced a finger lightly over the dress.

"I wasn't sure what it was going to be when I started it. Didn't want to block myself if it didn't end up being anything special," she said, unsure of why she was withholding from him, but she felt the need to protect herself. If she told him it had only been a few hours, his comparison between their talents would surface, and she didn't want to deal with it.

He set down the sculpture, and an expression she couldn't quite identify flickered over his face. "You're going to blow past me if you keep this up. They'll start calling me Mr. Caroline Sawyer." He said this lightly, jokingly, but Caroline could hear the edge of jealousy in his voice. She'd hoped to avoid his teasing, but this felt different. More aggressive. He turned away. "You hungry? I've got stuff for salads."

"Sure," she said, and he went into the kitchen, opening and closing cabinets, the refrigerator. He babbled about something that had happened at the gallery, about Gemma and the forthcoming gala, but Caroline wasn't listening. Instead, she stared at the woman and at the head of the dog in her hands. Something about it tugged at her memory. Slowly, she began putting away the materials, her cramped fingers struggling to grasp the leaves and fine wire.

Again, a dim memory flitted through her mind, and she lifted the sculpture and carried it to their bedroom, where she set it gently on her nightstand. When she did, the memory came back to her full force—sour breath on her neck; the close, animal smell of unwashed bodies; her own body limp and useless as her brain screamed that something was terribly wrong. She shuddered, her hands gripping the nightstand, but as quickly as the memory came, it vanished.

She sank onto the bed, going over those disconnected pieces, trying to thread them together, but nothing made sense. There was nothing she could remember that seemed revelatory, but she was certain these were portions of something she had seen, something that had happened, but there were too many things missing, too many components left in the dark. Her father had told her once that she'd had nightmares when she was younger. Maybe she was remembering pieces of them? Some combination of stress, lack of sleep, and the strange experiences in Jazzland dredging up these past fears?

That night, she slept locked around Daniel, but the comfort his body offered did not keep her mind still. She rose around three in the morning and watched television until it was time to go back to see her father. Daniel went with her, and they spent the hours playing cards and reading magazines they had already read. By the time they got home, Caroline felt as if her eyelids were sandpaper, every movement an irritant and increasing her longing for real sleep.

That night was no better, and when she woke again around three, she was standing in the kitchen, the phantom sensation of teeth on her throat. The remainder of a deep rotted smell that made her gag and press her hand to her mouth. Frightened, she booted up her laptop and searched for side effects of Ambien, already certain she would see sleepwalking listed, and with her suspicions confirmed, she snapped the computer shut and drummed her fingers across the top.

Somehow, whatever nightmares her sleeping mind conjured had wormed their way into her subconscious, and the fear lingered like some awful hidden thorn. Since Jazzland, she'd listened for the dogs, listened for confirmation she had not imagined all of it, but wherever the sounds had come from, she could not find them again, and the silence around her had never felt so heavy.

CHAPTER 11

CAROLINE 2004

She and Daniel both floated through their morning routines on Monday, brushing their lips together before saying good-bye. She didn't have the energy to do much more than that and felt guilty for expecting him to do any more either. He'd been with her the entire day at Helping Hands, and she knew how even though sitting with her father involved no real physical activity, something about the place siphoned the energy from the body and left you feeling hollowed out.

Not too much longer, and you won't have to do it anymore, she thought, and immediately hated herself. Hated the reality and the weariness of her thoughts, how she felt buried under them. Her exhaustion had grown into a tangible burden that the Ambien seemed to be doing little to help.

"Fuck off," she said, mostly to herself. "It's going to take longer than a few days." There was obvious logic in what she'd said, but still, it was hard to trust that the Ambien would eventually help her more than it was. She listened to the hum of her wheels against the road as she drove.

When Caroline pulled up to the Kellum house, Beth wasn't outside like usual, and the house looked completely still. Normally, Caroline could see lamplight spilling through the front windows, but everything was dark, and her skin tingled. She didn't have a key, but the front door was unlocked, and she let herself in, the door swinging shut as if sucked from behind.

"Hello?" she called into the emptiness of the house, terrified to take another step. Closing her eyes, she could not stop herself from picturing blood pooled over the kitchen floor, streaking away and forming some grotesque kind of beauty. Her mind could not bear the unwanted intrusion of such a thought. There was only so much weight a person could carry before dropping, and Caroline was close to complete collapse.

"Caroline? That you?" Vivian's voice sounded far away, and Caroline moved toward the kitchen.

"It's me. Everyone okay?" A dull throb started up in the center of her forehead. She brought her fingers there and pressed down, but it did nothing to alleviate the pressure or fear that had become a permanent part of her awareness.

"Sorry. Running a bit late. Someone has been more than a little grumpy all day." Vivian tried to make her voice light, but there was the edge of frustration in it. She emerged from the kitchen, her hands tugging at the sleeves of a cashmere sweater.

"It happens."

"Not on days you're supposed to have huge meetings, it doesn't. She"—she gestured over her shoulder at the stairs—"has spent the morning dawdling instead of doing her schoolwork." Vivian turned to face the base of the stairs that led up to the bedrooms. "Beth Kellum, if you do not get down here this minute, it'll be a full month of being grounded instead of two weeks." She turned back to face Caroline and clapped her hands together. "Well. I have to run. If she's not down in the next ten minutes, make sure to tell me."

Caroline nodded, because there was nothing else to do. "Of course. Sure."

"I'll call if I'm going to be late tonight. The senator may ask me to stay a bit late after the meeting," Vivian said, and patted her hair. She breezed past Caroline in a blur of perfume and hairspray. The front door opened and closed, and the house went quiet.

She waited for Beth, but upstairs, there was no movement. "Beth?" Caroline called up the stairs, and the girl responded by letting out a grunt. Caroline's headache dug in a little deeper.

"You have to come down now, okay? Your mom said you're grounded if you don't. Come on. We have things to do."

"No, *we* don't have anything to do. *I* have stuff to do. You just get paid to sit and watch me do it."

"Someone's in a mood." Caroline put her foot on the bottom step, but there were no more sounds coming from upstairs, and she sighed. She'd needed an easy day. "Right now, Beth. I mean it!"

A loud groan floated down to her along with the slamming of a door. "Fine!"

"Good. Bring your stuff. Looks like your mom wants you to focus on portrait work today." The print on the island was classical—a knockoff Rembrandt.

"Whatever."

Caroline pinched the bridge of her nose, remembering herself at Beth's age, reminding herself of the mood swings and the sudden outbursts of anger, but it didn't help the irritation blooming in the pit of her stomach that rose to mix with her unease.

"I don't feel good." Beth stood behind her, her hair disheveled and her eyes puffy. This was not the carefully groomed, impeccably dressed girl Caroline had come to know.

"Don't feel good how?"

"My stomach hurts."

"Should I call your mom? You think you need to go to the doctor?"

"No. It'll be better in a minute. This happens sometimes. You just don't know about it."

"Is it cramps? If it's cramps, some ibuprofen would help."

Beth shook her head. "I haven't gotten my period yet. I'm like the only one who hasn't. It just happens sometimes. Like I said." Beth glanced out the window and licked her lips, and Caroline had the sudden feeling there was someone standing there. She whipped around, but there were nothing but trees at the window.

"Did you hear about that girl they found? Anna McFurrow?" Beth stared down at her hands, her fingers twisted together. Caroline swallowed, not wanting to answer, but Beth stared up at her, her brow furrowed as she waited on a response.

"Yes, I heard, and I don't really want to talk about it. It's awful . . . what happened."

"The news said she was cut up. All on the inside of her legs. Like somebody had clawed her open."

"Stop it, Beth."

"I met her at riding camp. None of the other girls would talk to me. Because of what happened at school. But she did. Said she would have kicked his ass, too. She was cool." Her voice dropped to a whisper.

"Oh, honey. I'm so sorry."

Beth turned away and quickly swiped at her eyes. "S'okay. What did you do this weekend?"

Caroline didn't question the subject change. She wanted to let Beth talk about how she felt, but she didn't want to push it if Beth wasn't ready.

"I went to Jazzland with my fiancé, and yesterday we went to see my dad," she said.

"You went to Jazzland? I've wanted to go there for *forever*. Like, for my whole life. Mom says it's trashy." Beth jerked her chin toward the portrait on the island. "I'm so tired of painting all of this boring stuff. You don't even like it. I know you don't."

The sudden shift in Beth's mood—melancholy to irritation—was disconcerting. *Teenage hormones,* Caroline told herself. Or maybe something happened with Vivian. Or she'd had a frustrating appointment with her psychiatrist. Beth put on a good show, but after what had happened with the boy at school, she'd frequently slip into irrational and drastic attitude changes. Caroline sighed. She was too tired to deal with this.

"Beth—"

"But you don't! I looked you up online. I saw your sculptures, and they are so badass. Why can't we do stuff like that instead?"

"Because your mother would fire me. And then maybe kill me. Not sure which would come first."

"It's such bullshit how you just give in to her like that," Beth said, and Caroline raised an eyebrow and let the second curse word slide. She wasn't Beth's mother.

"She told me nothing outside of the classics. She pays me, so what she says goes."

"You're just like her. I thought you weren't, but you *are*."

Caroline stared down at Beth, remembering her own mother's face when she'd found Caroline's first attempts at sculpture. The anger, fury, and deep humiliation that there was something *wrong* with her. Beth already had so much stacked against her: a father who'd died years ago. A mother who enforced rules and restrictions designed to keep Beth in line and ensure her development into a sweet, Southern young lady.

Caroline bit down on her cheek. She did not want to become her own mother; someone who would stifle instead of encourage. It went against everything she loved about art.

"Fine. We can go for a walk, and I'll show you how I find

materials, and we can put something small together. *Very* small. But then we still have to do the portrait, and not a single word of this to your mother. Deal?"

"Totally!" Beth bounced onto her toes. "This is so awesome. I want to see if I can find some dog hair. We can go now, right?"

Already, Beth was running for the door. Caroline's memory caught on Beth's mention of dog hair, but there was no time to give it any further thought because Beth was already out the door, and Caroline had to scramble to keep up.

Together, they moved under the dim sunlight, the cloud cover chilling Caroline so she shivered. The grass was damp, and the air tasted of water.

"The best thing to do is to pick a small spot. Something you know you could walk around in a few steps. And then look close. Deep and then deeper. Sometimes, the most interesting things like to hide. It looks funny, but I get on my hands and knees a lot, too," Caroline said. Beth nodded, her face already set in the most serious of expressions, as she bent toward the earth.

Together, they knelt, their fingers tracing over the grass, Beth a miniature imitation of Caroline as they lowered their faces close and then closer. Letting out all of her breath, Caroline let her vision blur, the green and brown running together into a single mass. The old process of this thing she loved so much felt like sinking into warm water. She inhaled and let her gaze sharpen, taking in the small area she'd focused in on. Each blade of grass. Each twig and rock and leaf seemingly growing larger so that the rest of the world vanished as Caroline inched forward, touching and exploring. She'd forgotten how much she loved this part. The discovery. The single-minded focus that let everything else drop away. When she was gathering material, there was nothing else. No worry or fear or pressure. Only the finding and the joy that came with that simple action. Again, she moved forward, her knees damp from the ground.

A breeze lifted her hair, and she smiled to herself. She should have done this sooner. Should have brought Beth outside and given her a true lesson. Let her understand that art wasn't only painting piss-poor imitations of old, dead, white men. Again, she shifted forward, and there, caught against the grass, was a small gray feather. Her grin widening, Caroline reached for the feather, drawing it up delicately to prevent damage, and held it up to the light. Black striations ran across the barbs, the subtlety of its pattern only visible upon close inspection.

Caroline sat back on her heels. "Beth, look," she said, and turned, but Beth was not there. There was no adolescent girl crouching anywhere near Caroline or standing under one of the trees, her fingers tracing over the bark.

"Beth?" Caroline's voice cracked, but she called out again, her knees buckling as she tried to stand. "Beth?" She spun, scanning the tree line, desperate for a flash of blond hair, any movement that would lead Caroline to where Beth had gone. Her heart stuttered in her chest, heat flooding up her neck and into her face as she thought of the girl who'd been found. Anna McFurrow. Beth had known her, and now Beth was gone. Louder, she called Beth's name, telling herself not to panic, but she couldn't keep the fear out of her voice.

When Beth popped out from behind a tree not more than fifteen feet away, Caroline felt the energy drain out of her, her heart pumping uselessly under the sudden lack of strain.

"Yeah?" She stared back at Caroline, her hands tucked behind her back. Her expression was clearly guilty. Caroline had the sudden need to grasp Beth by the shoulders, to shake her until her head lolled and snapped like a doll's.

"You scared the hell out of me. Don't ever go where I can't see you. Ever."

"You were busy. I was just right there." Beth pointed behind her, and Caroline saw her hands then, saw the deep red smeared over Beth's skin, and she lurched forward into a panicked run. Immediately, Beth shoved her hands behind her back again, but Caroline was on her, grasping at Beth's arms to draw her hands forward.

"What happened? Did you cut yourself on something?" Beth shook her head—her jaw set in a fierce clench—and tried to pull back against Caroline's grip, but Caroline held her tight. "You're bleeding everywhere, Beth. You have to tell me what happened." Caroline did shake her then, lightly, and the girl's eyes widened.

"Nothing happened. I found a dog and was petting it."

"A dog? Did it bite you? You might need stitches or a shot."

"It didn't bite me. Jesus. Let me go," Beth said, and jerked her body away. Caroline dropped her arms to her sides.

"Was the dog hurt? Is that where the blood came from?" Beth glowered back at her. "Absolutely not. You are not going to ignore me," Caroline said, and grasped Beth's shoulder. "Where was it? Show me."

"Fine," Beth said, and vanished once more behind the tree. Caroline followed, her fury building. Beth walked a bit farther and then stopped. "There." She pointed at the ground. "Just a dog. See?"

The small form lay on the grass, curled in on itself, the tawny fur matted and stained with blood and buzzing with flies. Caroline clamped a hand over her mouth.

"Jesus Christ. What the fuck?" she said, not caring that Beth was standing beside her. The dog looked as if it had been struck by a car and then dragged itself to that spot to die. And Beth had been petting it. She'd been petting a dead dog.

"Have you gone crazy? Why in the world would you touch it? Your mother is going to lose it when she finds out."

Beth screwed up her face. "It's not like you have to tell her. It was your idea to come outside. To come looking for stuff for a sculpture."

"Don't you dare, Beth Kellum. Don't you dare even *imply* that this was my fault. And to think I felt sorry for you," Caroline said.

Immediately, Beth's face crumpled, tears pricking the corners of her eyes. "I just . . . I felt so bad for it," she said, and remorse flooded through Caroline. What Beth had done was odd and disgusting, but Caroline could understand Beth's reasoning. Sometimes confronting death made people think or do weird things. If anyone understood that, it was Caroline.

"Listen, let's just head back, okay? Get you cleaned up before your mom gets home."

Beth nodded, and they trudged back toward the house. By the time they rounded on the driveway, Caroline could make out Vivian's sleek black Mercedes sedan. "Shit," Caroline muttered.

Vivian stood at the front door, her arms crossed in front of her as Caroline approached, searching for the best way to tell Vivian her daughter was covered in blood because she'd been petting a dead dog. "I'm so sorry, Vivian. We went on a little walk. I thought it would put Beth in a better mood, and I know I should have called to ask, but I didn't think we'd be gone very long, and then Beth—"

Vivian held up a hand to stop her. "Not now, Caroline. Beth Kellum, get up here right now."

Beth approached, no longer bothering to hide her bloodied hands, and Caroline steeled herself for the onslaught of Vivian's anger.

"I thought she'd hurt herself, but it's not her blood," Caroline began, and Vivian's eyes narrowed as she looked at Beth. "It was a dog. She touched it, and it was . . ." She hunted for a word that would lighten what Beth had done, but there wasn't one. "Well, it was dead."

Vivian stared at her daughter, her eyes blinking rapidly as if she couldn't process Beth's bloodied hands or what Caroline had said. "What in the hell is wrong with you?" she asked, her voice a horrified whisper. "You think that's normal? Petting a dead animal? It's sick, Beth. It's the kind of thing that gets you locked in a goddamn loony bin."

Beth took a single step forward, her face red-streaked and blotchy. "I *hate* you. I wish you were exactly the same as that fucking dog."

Vivian flinched and jerked backward as if Beth had struck her. Her face drained of color. Caroline looked away and wished the earth would swallow her up.

"Get inside. Now," Vivian said, but her voice shook.

Beth glanced at Caroline and then stalked into the house. Guilt rose up to overtake Caroline. She had not meant for this to happen. She'd assumed Vivian would be upset, but Caroline *had* been the one to take Beth outside. She opened her mouth to take some of the blame, but Vivian whipped around and motioned for Caroline to follow her.

"Come inside, please," she said, and Caroline followed, readying herself for the dismissal that was likely coming.

Vivian led Caroline to the front sitting room and motioned to one of the chairs. "Sit down," she said, and Caroline hurried to obey. She could explain. She could get Vivian to understand. She couldn't afford to lose this job. If she did, she wouldn't be able to afford her dad's hospice bill. Not on minimum wage. She had to fix this.

"I'm sorry you had to witness that little performance, but you should have left a note. Do you know what it's like to come home to find the front door unlocked and your child gone?" Vivian asked.

"I'm so sorry, Vivian. I got distracted—just for a minute—and then she was with that dog, and—"

Vivian turned and faced the window. "There was another little girl taken. Last night. She lived two streets up. Her mother let her go check the mail, and she never came back. They think it's connected to the other girl they found in Couturie the other day. Police are looking, but they haven't found her yet. I heard the news and drove straight home. Didn't even make it to the senator's office. I couldn't keep myself from thinking . . ." Vivian's hands twitched together and apart as if the movement could contain the horror hiding somewhere among them. "And in a neighborhood like this. A *nice* neighborhood. I mean, certainly things like this happen in other parts of the city but not here. Can you imagine?"

Caroline shook her head. Vivian deeply believed that pain and violence were things that happened only to those without money or privilege. The unsavory portions of her life were so small compared to the larger horrors of the world. But Caroline understood terrible things did not discriminate. Their tastes were wide. Greedy. Never-ending.

"Well, obviously I'm not going to the meeting. The police are talking about a serial killer, how what's happening is a lot like some cases back in the late eighties. He had some disgusting name . . . The Cur. It's awful. Just awful. You'll take the rest of the day, of course. Since I'm home," Vivian said.

"I'm so sorry. I would have never imagined Beth would do something like that."

Vivian turned back to face Caroline and lifted her lip into a perfectly lipsticked sneer. "I would. It's not your fault. You shouldn't blame yourself. Sometimes I worry. That she might be . . . disturbed. Mentally." Vivian spat out the words as if they pained her. "Dr. Bryson has been suggesting medication. I'm starting to think it would be for the best."

Caroline stared down at her hands, hating this woman for the way she was talking about Beth. But she couldn't say anything. It wasn't her place. She cleared her throat. "We didn't quite get to the painting."

"Tomorrow then."

"Okay. Yeah. I'll just get my stuff," she said. From upstairs there were no sounds, and guilt wrenched through her once more. Beth would blame her. She understood that. Beth would likely be irritable with her in the upcoming days, but at least she was safe. If another girl had been taken, and so close to the Kellum house, Beth's disappearance could have been so much worse than some blood on her hands. Caroline sighed and gathered her purse and keys from the kitchen counter where she'd left them.

Vivian saw her out. "Be careful. See you tomorrow," she said, and closed the door.

Caroline made her way down the porch steps and then turned to look up at the windows, but there was no sign of Beth watching her leave. "Take it easy on her, Vivian," she said, and turned back to her car, but then froze.

On the driver's side door was a bloody handprint.

Beth must have brushed up against the car before they came inside, but still, seeing it there jarred Caroline. The mark looked too clean, too perfect to be an accident. Caroline opened the door and examined the front and back seats, but they were neat and empty as they always were.

Or maybe it wasn't an accident at all, and Beth had left the print there as a threat. A reminder of how easy it would be to get Caroline fired. She knew how capable Beth was of manipulating a situation. The handprint felt like an ugly reminder of how far Beth was willing to go to punish those who slighted her.

Caroline would clean the mark off when she got home, but still, she felt deeply unsettled and upset by the morning's events. The second missing girl. The worry she'd felt for Beth when she couldn't find her. The blood. The dead dog.

By the time Caroline was inside her car, the dome light switching off, she could not stop the tremor working through her muscles. Everything felt too close, too much like a swirl of memories she couldn't quite identify.

Turning on the heat did nothing to soothe the chill that had crept under her skin. It was still early. She could go home and take three or four Ambien. Fuck being responsible. She wanted to melt down into the nothingness it promised.

When she let herself into the house, she went immediately to the medicine cabinet and shook three pills into her palm before placing them in her mouth. She turned on the sink and stuck her face into the stream and drank and drank and drank until she was gagging, but there was nothing inside her that would come up, and she turned off the sink and stumbled into the bedroom.

She left the lights off and sank onto the mattress. Outside, a car horn sounded. She couldn't keep her body from jerking, and she shrieked into a pillow, her breath heating her face as the darkness fell over her. She drifted but did not dream.

It was the pain that brought her back to herself. The fleshy pad of her thumb in sudden agony, and she opened her eyes. Blood flowered over her fingers and wrist, and she brought her thumb to her mouth. She'd cut herself. But that was impossible. She'd been sleeping. There was nothing on the bed that could have cut her, and there was too much blood, the crimson stain of it materializing before her. It smeared across the floor, appearing here and there and leading toward the kitchen.

She blinked into the muted light, saw the coffee table, the television. She wasn't in the bedroom, wasn't tucked safe and sound into bed. Open before her was her tackle box, the dim outline of her utility knife set beside it.

"Jesus," she whispered. Another sculpture stood before her, but she had no recollection of working on it. She reached over and turned on the closest lamp.

The sculpture stood on hind legs, sticks and twigs twisted together to resemble the cording of muscle. Tufts of hair covered the exterior, and the body was certainly of an animal, but the face was of a man, its mouth opening, and there were fangs and claws. Her stomach lurched as she saw how *real* they seemed to be. She'd never kept anything like that in her tackle box. Sometimes she would find animal hair or feathers but never claws. Never teeth.

She shifted forward to reach for the sculpture, the blood on her arms swimming into focus, and she recoiled. *Jesus. The blood.* Her thumb still stung, but she looked again at the claws, the fangs filling the mouth, and there was blood smeared against the hardwoods, too. She scrambled backward, desperate to put as much space between her and the blood as possible, the need to turn away, to hide overriding the nausea threatening to overcome her, and as she turned, she saw the front door. It was standing wide open, evening shadows leaking into the house, the humidity pooling near the entrance as it wormed its way inside.

She stood, pitching forward, her hands outstretched and fumbling for the door. She closed it and leaned her forehead against the surface. Behind her, bound up in wire and fur and teeth and claws, there was an abomination wrought by her hands. There was nothing inside her that could unstitch what she had done, and she did not want to turn to look upon it. But she did turn, her body moving as if underwater, and there was the blood turning dark on the floor—the countertop was stained with it as well—and she looked. And she screamed.

In the sink, there was the dog Beth had found in the woods. The one she'd been petting. Resting beside the sink were Caroline's pliers, a screwdriver, and two broken teeth. Cast-offs. Not good enough for her sculpture.

"Oh Jesus. Oh fuck," she said, but there was no one to hear her, no one to see this horrific thing, and she moaned, low and guttural. How had the dog gotten into the house? How had it come to be *here* when she and Beth had left it lying in the grass? But there was the sculpture, and she knew she had taken the dog's teeth, its claws, and built her sculpture from those small pieces, and she'd not known she was doing it. She moaned again, and then bit down on her hand to keep herself from shrieking or losing consciousness.

It was her own fault. She'd taken too many Ambien even though she knew she'd been sleepwalking. In her medicated, twilight fog, she'd somehow gone back to retrieve the animal, then brought it back here and built this . . . *thing*.

But that would mean she had driven back to Metairie— walking was out of the question—and the thought turned her skin cold. It was one thing to sleepwalk in her own home, but the thought of what she could have done, what could have happened, terrified her. Already there was the dog's stiff body, and the pliers, and the claws, and the teeth, and she couldn't imagine herself going through the motions of such a horror, but she *had*. It was possible there had been other things she'd done while unconscious.

Standing, she pushed away from the sculpture, grabbed her keys, and then went outside to her car, hoping she would not find any other evidence pointing toward whatever darkness had come pouring out of her. On the driveway, she stood, hesitating, not wanting to see what lay hidden in the shadows of her car, but she forced herself forward, to move and open the doors. The front and back seats were empty as they had been when she left the Kellums'. No trace of blood.

She circled back to the trunk and stopped. On the lid, there was another partial handprint, now darkened to the color of rust. Her heart hammering, she opened the trunk, avoiding touching the print, and looked inside. Small traces of blood were streaked here and there, and clumps of hair clung to the carpet.

Her throat grew thick, and she slammed the trunk closed and looked again at the handprint.

Beth. Beth had put the dog in her car. While Vivian was talking to her, Beth had sneaked out of the house, gone back for the dog, and put it in her trunk. Caroline had not locked the doors, and Beth could have gotten into the trunk by pressing the release button in the glove box. And Beth had been angry. Had wanted to punish Caroline for the perceived betrayal. Maybe Vivian was right in thinking Beth was starting to lose it. The trauma of what had happened to her leaching from her like a slow poison.

But had there been enough time for Beth to do that? Her head spun. Logically, it made no sense, but there was the handprint on her trunk. Either she or Beth had done this, but it was Caroline who was the monster. The one who had torn out its teeth and claws and left its defiled body in her kitchen sink.

Somewhere in the distance, a car honked, and she came back to herself. Around her, people were coming home, having dinner, going about lives Caroline would never see. Like she and Daniel should be doing. Daniel, who could be home any time. Daniel, who couldn't see this. She could not let him see this.

Back inside the house, she reached under the sink and took out three garbage bags, placing one inside the next, the plastic falling over her hands—this unlovely shroud she was crafting seeming to glow loud and bright as an accusation.

She didn't breathe when she touched the dog, her gorge rising as she remembered that she had been the one to defile its small body; didn't breathe as she lifted it inside of the bag; didn't breathe as she carried it out to the garbage can to bury as far down as she could; didn't breathe as she scrubbed at the blood, as she filled another bag with paper towels dyed scarlet and then carried it out as well; didn't breathe as she cleaned the handprints from her car and wiped the trunk as clean of the blood and hair as she could. Through all of it, her mind settled somewhere just beyond awareness, fading into another kind of sleepwalking. It was the only way she could do what she needed to without screaming. Three times, she wiped down the countertops and floors, and when there was nothing remaining, the pliers and screwdriver also cleaned and put away, she turned to the sculpture. She knew she should wrap it in its own bag and throw it away as she had everything else, but she couldn't bring herself to do it.

How she had made it was horrifying, but it was beautiful, too. Fascinating and unlike anything she'd ever done. Somehow it was even more refined and visceral than the sculpture of the woman, and there were parts of her that wanted to save it, to not see it swallowed up by death and waste. Shaking, she gathered the sculpture and carried it to her and Daniel's closet. She imagined herself sitting in front of it in the way supplicants prostrate themselves before an altar, and her body longed to do it. Her mind recognized her disgust, but it felt far away. Less important than seeing the sculpture for the gruesome work of genius it was. She sank to her knees, but the front door was opening, Daniel whistling as he let himself inside, and she shoved it under a mountain of dirty T-shirts.

"Linny?" he called.

"Back here," she said. She lingered, watching the fabric, waiting to see if it would twitch or swell with breath, but there was nothing, and she reluctantly backed out of the closet, closing the door softly as she went before hurrying down the hallway and back into the living room.

"Sorry I'm late. Doing okay?" he said, and dropped a kiss on her cheek.

"Mmm," she mumbled, and there was only her fear and obsession with the closet, and what she had hidden inside it.

Daniel stared down at her, his mouth moving, but she could not hear the words. The room tilted, colors separating and then coming back together, and her skin went hot. She shook her head, trying to banish the confusion, but the light spiraled out, fracturing into a thousand pieces.

Slowly, the room righted itself, and Daniel was in front of her, her fingers resting against his chest. Heat dropped between her legs, and she traced his lips, the angles of his jaw. Even after all this, after all the strange moments of the day, she still wanted him. She wasn't sure if she should hate herself for this unbending, bodily need, but right now, it could make her feel better. Make her feel human again.

She bit down on her tongue to keep it from spilling any of her secrets, and he gathered her close, his hands hot and slick as he pulled her into his chest. She breathed in the scent of him. Like ocean water and pine and the faint chemical smell of oil paint. She felt the full length of him, the hardened muscles under the button-down he wore, and how he shifted to allow for the space she occupied.

It was easier to let their bodies come together than to tell him what she'd done. She lifted her mouth to his and kissed him hard enough for him to gasp, his hands pressing at her chest in surprise before he kissed back.

Together, they tumbled down and down, pulled at each other's buttons and zippers, and she let the natural responses of her body weight her to the earth, her legs hitching around his hips, her hands tangled in his hair. She let her eyes drift closed and pretended the darkness she saw was an empty night sky.

Daniel wrapped himself tighter around her. The room was too hot, evening shadows sneaking through the blinds and dyeing the room the color of ash, and her body seemed to detach from itself, her mind trapped in something that felt like a fever dream.

Daniel moved inside her, and she opened her eyes and stared over his shoulder at something that should not be.

A man stood in the corner, huddled into himself, his shoulders curving toward the floor, his arms slack at his sides. Caroline's breath caught in her throat, a shriek wanting to form but dying as shock muted it. The man's mouth was the mouth of a dog, and his eyes reflected at her, the lips pulled back in a kind of obscene grin. She clawed at Daniel's chest and neck, trying to get him to stop, to see what it was she was seeing, but the words would not come. Around her, the air in the room buzzed, the dust drifting through the dim light leaking outward, glittering pieces of her life caught in the process of their dying, and she blinked, forcing her vision back to what it was supposed to be. The image of the man shimmered and then vanished into shadow.

Caroline closed her eyes, but the vision still felt real. Her skin was burning, and she felt ill like the time when she was little and had gotten pneumonia, her fever spiking at a hundred and four, before her father rushed her to the emergency room.

Daniel slowed, his fingers grasping at her hips. When he came, everything tasted of death and strangeness. Her head pounded, her blood buzzing in her ears with an electric heat, and she sank her teeth into his lower lip.

"Fucking Christ, Caroline," he said, and tore himself away, her body aching with the sudden emptiness. She did not move but traced her finger along her jaw, a thin line of blood streaking from her mouth and down her neck.

He swiped at his mouth, and she felt herself drift out of her body and then back as if caught in a hallucination.

"Sorry," she whispered, and he stared back at her, his eyes dark in the dim light.

"The hell was that?"

"Got carried away," she said, her tongue rolling over the hot, iron tang of his blood. The taste of him made her want more, and she curled into herself. "I didn't mean to," she said.

Something's wrong, something's wrong, something's wrong.

"I mean, *Jesus*. You got me good." He pressed his hand to his mouth, but already, the blood had slowed. He went to the kitchen and tore off a paper towel, and she watched as the blood soaked into it in the same way it had when she'd cleaned up the dog's blood.

"That hurt like a bitch," he said.

"Sorry." Her voice was too low for him to hear, and around them the room seemed to bloat, the edges of twilight leaking through the curtains the color of old bruises, and she ran her tongue over her teeth, the taste of him still burning in her throat.

"I'm going to lie down," she said, and Daniel pulled the paper towel away from his lip and stared down at it like he didn't understand what he held in his hands.

"Aren't you going to eat anything?" he said. She stood—her hands pressed tight against her sides so he would not see her trembling—and she didn't look back at him. "It's not a big deal, okay? It's fine. I'm not even bleeding anymore. See?"

"I'm tired," she said, and then she went past him, was inside their bedroom, and he was reaching past her to grab the door.

"You have to tell me what's wrong, Linny. Fuck, this is me we're talking about. We tell each other everything. You've been acting so out of it the past few days—and you've been taking those fucking *pills*. I told you they're not good for you."

If her body hadn't felt frozen, she would have laughed. He wanted her to share herself with him but couldn't keep himself from ranting about the Ambien.

His hands found her neck, her face, and he wiped his thumbs under her eyes, but there were no tears there. "You're freaking me the fuck out, Caroline."

She pulled herself onto her tiptoes and reached for him, palms outstretched. To bless him. The holy Eucharist of his blood still coated her teeth, and her mouth opened and her tongue lolled. He jumped to catch her as she fell, his arms around her as she shook and shook and shook.

CHAPTER 12

CAROLINE 2019

Caroline poured herself four fingers of whiskey and sipped, letting the smoky flavor roll over her tongue. It had been a long time since she drank hard liquor, but tonight she wanted the flame of it in her belly. Still, there was something inside her that wouldn't quiet even with her senses dulled, and she roamed through the tiny apartment, her fingers leaving dust trails over the furniture.

In the room at the end of the hallway, her daughter slept. For thirty minutes, Caroline had stood outside her door and listened for Lila's breath. Of course, she couldn't hear anything other than the dull thud of her own heart and the dim sound of the Beatles album Lila played while she slept, and she remembered how she used to stand over Lila's crib, her hand underneath the baby's nose as she tried to reassure herself that Lila was still breathing. Still alive.

Something had happened with Macie; Caroline had felt the deep hurt of it rolling off Lila in waves all weekend, but she couldn't bring herself to ask. It was Lila's secret to tell, and she didn't want to push her into revealing her true feelings before she was ready. She'd known Lila was infatuated with Macie probably before Lila would even admit it to herself, and now the look on Lila's face when she talked about Macie—a dazzled kind of defiance—was something stronger than a girlhood crush. She would wait for Lila to come to her in her own time, and when she did, Caroline would wrap her up, tell how proud she was to have Lila as a daughter, how much she loved her.

Carrying the whiskey bottle in one hand and her glass in the other, she tiptoed down the hallway and into her own bedroom, easing the door closed behind her. She set the bottle on her nightstand and sank onto the mattress, taking another pull from her glass. Her phone was on the charger, and she stared at it. Gnawing at a loose cuticle, she grabbed her phone and selected Daniel's number, wincing as she listened to the ring.

"Caroline?" His voice was hoarse. She listened as sheets rustled. A door opened and closed, and when he spoke again, it was still in that throaty whisper.

"Everything okay? What's going on?"

"There was another abduction. Another little girl," she said.

"I heard about that, but Caroline—" he began, but she cut him off, the words rushing out of her.

"It's too much like before. They're even calling him The Cur, and I keep thinking that it's not possible. He'd have to be an old man. Too old." She finished off what remained in her glass, the ice clinking.

"Are you drinking?" Daniel asked, and she reached for the bottle to refill.

"So what if I am?"

"Listen to me. This is all a coincidence. It's awful what's happened to those girls, but you can't connect it with what happened in the past. The police are on the case. You and Lila are fine. Some of us are dealing with actual problems and not just ones we've built up in our heads."

"Fuck you, Daniel. I'm not—"

"You have to stop this. You're sounding hysterical."

Caroline gritted her teeth. "I'm on my meds. I'm not imagining things. There've been two now. Two girls abducted and killed . . . and I'm worried about our daughter." She gulped more whiskey.

"Great. On medication *and* drinking—" The phone went muffled then, Daniel's voice blending with another, and she pictured Rebecca standing bleary-eyed in the doorway, wondering if something was wrong.

"I have to go," he said, and hung up without saying good-bye.

Caroline dropped the phone onto the bed, but she wanted to throw it against the wall, to tear it apart with her hands until every part was broken. Fuck Daniel. Fuck him and his mansplaining and his inability to see beyond his immediate situation. She knew he was having a hard time with Brina, with the scary complications following her birth. But there was Lila, too, and shouldn't he be concerned for her?

Rising, she went to the small window and stared outside. Her vision blurred, and she remembered another street far from here and a man with the teeth of a dog huddled in a corner, but there were no such things here, and she knew now that the awful things she'd experienced had only been delusions brought on by depression and stress. She'd spent years watching Lila, worrying that her daughter would one day inherit what had plagued her all those years ago. Fearful that one day Lila would vanish into a secret world where she saw things that did not exist. Every morning Lila emerged from her room with her eyes clear and her voice steady was another quick breath of relief.

The parking lot was quiet. Caroline sighed and turned away, grabbing the whiskey bottle as she went to pour herself a bit more into the glass she'd left beside her bed. She sank back onto the mattress and checked her phone even though she knew there would be nothing to see. No texts from Daniel with reassurance or even dismissal, no missed calls from anyone who cared about her. Her only friends were other art professors and the gallery directors who bought her sculptures, and those relationships were largely professional. She sipped the whiskey and leaned back into her pillows, drowsy and dreaming of what her life could have been had it not crumbled before it even began. The pristine vision she'd had before she and Daniel broke. Before her hallucinations began. Her fingers slipped against the glass, and she caught it, set it on the nightstand, and let her eyes drift closed.

She woke in a cold sweat. The room was still dark—no early-morning sun peeked through her blinds—and she sat up. She'd heard a noise. Something not part of the dream landscape her sleeping brain had constructed for itself and was already quickly fading. Something else.

Groggy and still a little buzzed, she tried to reconstruct the sound, piece it together so it made sense, and she held her breath and listened. Again, she heard it. The wet sound of a mouth opening. And then a dog panting.

Leaning forward, she crept onto hands and knees and peered into the darkness. The room spun, and she thought she'd be sick, but she stilled herself and closed her eyes, and the feeling passed.

Her dresser sat before her like a fat toad; her perfume bottles lined the surface like bulbous growths. The top drawer was still slightly open from dressing herself the previous morning, and the edge of her navy bra poked out. Again, the sound filled the room and faded, and she pushed herself backward, her hands fumbling for the lamp on the nightstand as she knocked the whiskey bottle to the floor.

The light was dim and didn't make her feel better, but she searched the room from her spot on the bed. There was nothing.

No shadowed dogs lurking in a corner. She sank back onto her pillow and rubbed her eyes. Her mascara flaked off under her fingers, and when she drew her hands away, her fingers were streaked black. She drew air into her lungs, but it didn't make her feel better, and she swallowed against the gorge rising in the back of her throat.

She'd dreamed it. That was all. Her mind unsettled and drifting through nightmares, she'd dreamed the sound, had woken and imagined it still in the room with her, but there was nothing there. She closed her eyes and let her hand drift back to the lamp, and then remembered the whiskey.

"Shit," she said, and sat up again. The bottle. She hadn't put the cap back on. Whiskey would be soaking into the carpet. "Shit, shit, shit," she said, and swung her legs over the side of the bed. The room threatened to tip again, and she steadied herself and then pushed herself off the edge so she knelt on the floor.

She reached underneath the mattress, but her fingers brushed against nothing, so she leaned forward, drew up the white, ruffled bed skirt, and peered into the gloom.

The smell hit her first. Underneath the sharp bite of the whiskey was the foul stink of urine and shit, and she brought her hand to her mouth. A pair of eyes reflected back at her.

"Lila?" she said, and the girl looked at her and opened her mouth wide and wide and wide. Lila looked at her and panted. Like a dog. Her tongue lolled and spittle flecked the corners of her mouth, and her hands lay rigid at her sides, the fingers splayed outward, and the knuckles arched unnaturally as her body jerked.

"Mommy," Lila said. Caroline reached for her daughter, tugged at her dead weight, until finally, Lila's body emerged, her T-shirt and flannel pants soaked with urine, and she gathered her daughter's body to her and held her tight, and her daughter shook and shook.

"It's okay. It's okay," she said, and hugged the girl to her. She needed her cell phone. Needed to call 911. Get an ambulance. Lila retched against her, and Caroline bit down on her tongue, smoothed her daughter's hair, and brought her lips to her forehead. The skin there was hot. Feverish. Her phone was still on her bed, lost somewhere in the tangle of sheets. Her daughter's eyes rolled, the whites shot through with red, and Caroline laid Lila's head against the carpet. Her feet slipped as she rose, and she pitched forward, her hands raking across the sheets as she searched for her phone. A thin moan rose and fell behind her, and her hands skittered over her phone, and then she grasped it, her breath ragged in her chest as she unlocked it and stared down at the blurred screen.

She bent to reach for her daughter, bent to reassure Lila that she hadn't left, but she wasn't there. The space where Lila had been only moments before was empty. She reached out, her fingers clawing at nothing. There was only a hollow space that still carried the ghost of Lila's fever.

"Lila?" she said, and dropped the phone to the carpet, her hands raking against the bed skirt as she yanked it up to look beneath at more emptiness. The darkness yawned before her, and she feared she would tip into it and drown. It had taken her less than a minute to find her phone. It was impossible for Lila to have moved so quickly, impossible for Caroline to have not seen or heard her creeping from the room.

"Lila?" she said again, but her daughter did not answer, and Caroline rose, went to the door, and leaned against the frame. The hallway was empty, and she shrieked Lila's name into the emptiness once more. When the door across from her creaked open, she sagged, her muscles turning to water.

"What's wrong?" Lila stood in the doorway, her dark hair floating around her. Caroline reached for her daughter's hands, her face, and thought for a moment that her fingers would pass through her. Lila's body like something incorporeal, the impression of a shade, but Caroline's fingers wrapped around warm flesh, and she pulled Lila against her.

"What happened?" Lila said, and Caroline brought her lips to her daughter's hair and let her tears fall without wiping them away.

"I had a dream. I thought," Caroline began, but then her words failed her, and she sobbed against her daughter.

"It's okay. It's okay," Lila said, and Caroline thought again of her trembling daughter on the floor in her bedroom when she thought . . . she wasn't sure now what it was she thought had happened. Lila having a seizure? A fit of some kind? It had been so long since she'd had a delusion, so many years since her mind had constructed something that wasn't there. There had been doctors and pills to guarantee the hallucinations would stop, to push and mold her brain into what it was supposed to be. But she'd been so consumed with the abductions, so worried for Lila, it was possible her anxiety had triggered it.

Locked together, they sat, and Caroline traced her daughter's face again and again, unable to forget how real it had seemed. The limp weight of Lila's body, the damp stain spreading over her legs, and the smell, that awful smell that lingered in her throat. "You were under my bed, and it was so real. So much like . . ." She stopped herself before she could say anything else. Lila didn't need to know about the man she once saw in the corner of another bedroom. That was one burden the girl shouldn't have to carry.

"Like what?" Lila said, but Caroline stayed silent. Even with her daughter there with her, she still felt like she was sitting on her bedroom floor with the girl's head cradled against her lap. The memory a transfixed, immutable thing.

"It's nothing. It was just a dream," she said again, but the words were empty, were husks of false memories, and they burned inside her like something real.

Lila frowned. Around them, the air went thick with all the things they could not bring themselves to say. Secrets Caroline had hoped she'd never have to reveal. She opened her mouth and closed it, unsure of what to say. Lila stared back at her, the hollows under her eyes too deep. Her daughter's shoulders sagged. Caroline hated herself, but she couldn't tell Lila what had happened.

"I'm tired," Lila said.

"Of course. Sure," she said, and her daughter turned and padded back to her room. When she reached her door, she looked back.

"You going to be okay? You want me to stay with you?" Any other time, Caroline would have laughed at the role reversal— her daughter stepping into Caroline's place as a mother—but the sound stayed locked in her chest.

"No. Go to sleep." The lie burned, but she said it anyway. It would be stupid and selfish to ask her thirteen-year-old daughter to stay awake with her. "I'll see you in the morning."

"Okay. Love you," Lila said, and then she was gone, the door clicking behind her, and Caroline bit down on the cry building in her belly. There was no reason for her hands to shake.

When the sun rose, it would be better. She could lose herself in sunlight, bury the vision of Lila under her bed behind daytime sounds and smells, and eventually it would fade. But for now, it was close as skin, and she could still feel her daughter's body shaking against her, the sharp odor of urine still thick in the air. She wrapped her arms around herself, but there was no warmth in it.

She stood and crossed to the closet, where she flipped on the light. The man-and-dog sculpture sat where she'd left it. She grasped it, her hands squeezing as the sticks popped and cracked. She squeezed tighter, and then she was slamming it again and again on the floor until it came apart, but still there were the teeth and the claws, and she scattered them with her hands.

She'd hoped destroying the sculpture would make her feel better.

It didn't.

CHAPTER 13

LILA 2019

When her phone finally showed the time as 6:00 A.M., Lila dressed and went out into the living room to wait for her mother to drive her to school. She could have probably gotten away with staying home, with telling her mom she didn't feel well or even letting the full story of what happened at the movies spill out of her. But as sick as it was, she wanted to see Macie's face, to let the full degradation of what had transpired between them descend on her. She wanted to wallow in it. Telling her mother would mean having to admit to blatantly disregarding her rules, to admit to the things she'd been hearing and feeling and seeing, and that would only lead to pills and doctors and being locked in a room for the rest of her life. Even though the thought of Macie never speaking to her again hurt unlike anything she'd ever felt, there was a part of her that didn't fully regret what she'd said.

On the ride to school, her mother didn't mention the dream she'd had the night before. When they pulled up to the drop-off area, Lila scanned the front of the school for Macie, but she wasn't there.

"Macie not here yet?" her mother asked, and Lila squeezed her hands into fists.

"No. Not yet."

"Lila." Her mother pressed a hand to her shoulder. "You can tell me anything, and I'll listen and handle it with care. You know that, right?"

Lila nodded, her tongue sticking to the dry roof of her mouth, and she almost laid it all down then—Macie, sneaking around, the dog she thought she saw, the strangeness that had descended on her, all of it—but she wasn't sure how to begin, what it would mean if she told the truth, and the moment came and vanished in an instant. Maybe later, after some time had passed, and it didn't feel like everything was going to implode, she would tell her mother all of it.

"I know. Love you," she said, and climbed out. Signs plastered in the main hallway directed students to go to homeroom for progress report distribution instead of first period, and Lila's stomach sank. That meant two periods where she would have to be in the same room as Macie. Plus lunch. Her heart lurched painfully, and she wished she'd faked sick after all. Lila thought she'd wanted to see her, but now she would do anything to avoid the possibility of feeling Macie's eyes on her as she whispered about what a fucking *weirdo* Lila was. She found her way to her seat and pushed herself down. Small. Unnoticeable. Someone you could pass by and forget you'd seen.

Ms. Sellman started talking, and Lila forced her eyes straight ahead. Her head ached, and her stomach felt shredded. Like she'd swallowed a mouthful of razor blades. She put her head down and wished she'd dressed differently today. Something more comfortable. But her navy hoodie had been dirty, and all of her clean T-shirts were rumpled from sitting on the spot on the floor where she'd tossed them after pulling them out of the dryer. The black button-up she'd chosen was a little too tight. It pulled across her back and breasts, and she tugged the hem down so it covered the line of skin above her jeans. Her eyes felt burned into her skull. She rubbed at them, but the movement did nothing to lessen the sensation, and she pressed her face against her arm.

When the bell rang, Lila grabbed her backpack and left the room without looking behind her. The hallway stank of sweat and cheap body spray and the fried grease of today's cafeteria selections of chicken nuggets or square pizza. A group of guys yelled back and forth to each other, and the sounds echoed off the cinderblock walls, loud and invasive, and she wanted to grab them by the hair and kick their teeth in. The thought made her smile.

In first period Ms. Shakib handed out a worksheet about symbols in *The Giver* and told them to hop to it. After, she disappeared behind her computer, so everyone fell into a quiet chatter about the latest missing girl, the worksheets mostly ignored as they listed out all the things they'd heard. One girl with a mousy face and glasses said only a pervert could do something like that, while another who could have been her twin said two murders meant that it was definitely a serial killer, and it was probably The Cur. Her mom watched a lot of cop shows and had said she'd heard about him on one of the episodes. How he'd killed a bunch of girls back in the late '80s and then disappeared only to pop up again about fifteen years later. He'd never been caught. It could be him again, or someone who'd been obsessed with him. A group of boys with artful swoops of long hair laughed, saying they'd heard the second girl had her tongue torn out and her *clit* had been bitten off. They lingered on the word, drawing it out as if it felt good for them to say it even if they had no idea what it was.

Three times, Lila glanced behind her at Macie, but she kept her head down, her worksheet untouched, and around her the awful chatter rose. Lila clapped her hands over her ears, but it did nothing to drown out the endless discussions of those atrocities. The same wooziness she'd felt at the movies flooded through her, and she brought a hand to her mouth, breathed deeply through her nose, but it didn't make her feel better.

When the PA bell sounded, everyone jumped. Embarrassed laughter rippled through the room as the voice crackled over the loudspeaker.

"Can you send Macie Kemper to Dr. Wilson's office, please?"

Macie rose, her shoulders thrust back, her gaze fixed straight ahead. Lila watched her go, every muscle in her body clenched. There could only be one reason for Dr. Wilson to call Macie to the counseling office, and Lila suspected it had to do with her. Lila shrank further into herself, but there was no part of her that would vanish.

Andrew was sitting at her table when she walked into science. He'd pulled the chair to the very edge, his backpack thrust into the aisle, his body arching away from her. His fingers white-knuckled and straining as he gripped the table so there was no chance he'd touch her. Even by accident. Like she'd stain him just by breathing the same air.

"Hey," she said even though she really didn't want to, and he grunted and lifted his chin. She could smell the fear rolling off of him. Great, stinking waves of it, and *she* had been the one to make him afraid. The invisible girl. She wanted to open her mouth and breathe in his apprehension. Let it roll over her tongue like some forbidden luxury. Men were not frightened by women. Women were not meant to be fearsome. These were the rules Lila had grown up understanding, and there was delight in breaking them.

Lila knew she shouldn't think things like this; knew these

were not things *nice* girls thought about. She should apologize; the rules she'd upended put back in place. Girls who disturbed the natural order were supposed to say sorry. But she liked feeling this way. All squirmy and excited and as if she couldn't catch her breath. It was the same way she'd felt when she'd finally unloaded all her anger on Macie, and it felt strong and powerful. She wasn't sure she wanted it to go away again even if it did mess everything up.

He flicked a glance at her and then away. Up front. The ceiling. Anywhere but directly at her.

Her stomach hurt, and she wished she had some water. Something to distract her from the feeling of teeth ripping her insides out.

When the PA bell came on, Lila went cold.

"Could you send Lila Sawyer to Dr. Wilson's office, please? Have her bring her belongings."

Andrew pulled his chair farther away as she rose, every pair of eyes trained on her. The only thing missing was an audible "ooooh" as she made her way to the door with her backpack slung over her shoulder.

Her footsteps echoed as she made her way through the emptied hallways. Behind the closed classroom doors, indistinct voices rose and fell, and she felt as if she'd tumbled into some foreign world. She could run. Walk straight out of the school and keep going until she was back in her own bedroom, the covers pulled tight over her head. She could convince her mom to let her change schools, and she would never have to see Macie again. She could become someone else. Work harder. Be a better student, or try out for a sport. Be more charming. Smile even when she didn't want to. Be prettier.

But her feet carried her to the counseling office, and the receptionist pointed her toward Dr. Wilson's closed door. "He's expecting you," she said, and turned back to her computer. Lila's mouth tasted like something acidic, and her face and neck went hot as she knocked.

"Come in," Dr. Wilson called, and Lila turned the knob.

Dr. Wilson sat behind his desk, reclining in a large, dark leather chair. Behind him, gilded frames covered the wall—an ostentatious reminder of his prestigious education. He stood, tugging at the bottom of his blazer, and gave her a careful smile as if she was something that could bite. He pulled a pair of wire-framed glasses from his breast pocket and settled them on the end of his nose. The glasses made his face even more angular and severe, and his thinning, pale hair was combed over a pink scalp.

Lila had only caught glimpses of her mother's psychiatrist a handful of times, but he looked much the same as Dr. Wilson. Like every other older man to ever sit behind a desk and pass judgment. Their commandments masked with caring, paternalistic tones. Their age and degrees and inherent *maleness* offered up as some kind of key to unlocking feminine ills.

"Ms. Sawyer. Close the door and have a seat." He waved to a chair on the left. Lila turned to do as he asked and then went utterly still. All sound dropped away; the only thing audible was the rush of blood in her ears as she stared at her mother, who was seated in the other chair.

"What are you doing here?" Lila asked.

"I asked your mother to be here, and thankfully, she was able to accommodate," Dr. Wilson said.

"But you have classes today," Lila said.

"I canceled them."

"Why don't you have a seat, Lila?" Dr. Wilson settled himself back into his chair and shuffled through a stack of papers sitting in front of him.

"But you—"

"Sit down, Lila," her mother snapped. Lila sank into the chair, fighting her urge to inch away from the both of them.

"Now then. Let's talk about Macie Kemper."

Lila gazed down at her hands. "Macie?"

"She came to see me this morning. She was very upset. Would you like to say anything about that?"

"We had a fight," she whispered. She could feel the weight of their eyes on her. Their judgments. But they didn't understand. And neither her mother nor Dr. Wilson, with all his degrees, could fix it.

Dr. Wilson leaned forward, his face a placid mask of feigned sympathy. "Anything you say here will be kept in strictest confidence, Lila. It's okay."

Lila darted a glance at her mother, but she stared straight ahead, her hands clenched in her lap.

"I was mad at her and said some . . . mean things."

"People can say cruel things when they're angry. But sometimes, even if we don't mean it, it's possible that the things we say can scare people. And maybe those things we say are really about something bigger than only being mad."

Lila made herself nod, and he turned to face her mother. "Ms. Sawyer, I do appreciate your being able to come in. I hope you understand that East Pritchard takes situations like this seriously. We have to treat any threat as if it's a real one. And what Macie relayed to me this morning is particularly concerning."

Lila's breath caught in her throat. She didn't want to sit through this, to hear what she'd said sharpened even further. To have it cast back as a reminder of how she'd wanted to hurt Macie. To cause what little damage she could.

Dr. Wilson lifted one of the papers from his desk. "I asked Macie for a written statement. Common procedure in situations like this. She says Lila called her a whore. That she told Macie she wanted to 'split her open like a worm and peel back her skin.' I'm sure you can understand the cause for apprehension, Ms. Sawyer. Why Ms. Kemper fears for her daughter's safety."

"Of course," her mother whispered.

"I would never hurt Macie!" Lila shouted. Dr. Wilson held out his hands, palms up.

"There's no reason to get overly emotional. Overreacting isn't the answer."

Again, Lila glanced at her mother and wondered if her mother was going to defend her at all. She knew Lila would never do anything like that. Even if she had thought about it. But her mother's gaze was vacant: the look of an appropriately submissive woman.

"Lila." Dr. Wilson's voice had gone soft. "I'm going to ask you a hard question, and I want you to know it's okay to tell the truth. I only want to help you. Do you ever think about hurting other people? Or yourself?"

She wasn't sure how to respond. Didn't everyone have thoughts like that? But that didn't mean she would actually do it. If she told him yes, he would label her suicidal. Or violent. If she told him no, he probably wouldn't believe her.

"Sometimes. But I wouldn't—"

Frowning, he scribbled something on the paper before him and resumed speaking without looking at her. "What you said to Macie about hurting her. How frequently do you have thoughts like that?"

"But I don't—"

He looked up at her then, the light winking off his glasses so she could not see his eyes. "You have to understand the severity of your comments, Lila. Ms. Kemper wants you expelled, but I can make that go away. It's imperative you tell me the truth now. Otherwise, I can't help you."

Shame burned through her. She wished her skin would catch fire, her bones crumbling to ash, and spread to the wind. An immolation to purge her of the sins Dr. Wilson saw inside her.

The thing that had come awake in her had shriveled back into itself, and whatever ecstasy she'd found in its presence dwindled to nothing.

"Lila?" he prompted.

"Not all the time. Just when I'm angry."

"This seems to go beyond angry, doesn't it?" he asked. A desire to leap across the desk and slam his head over and over onto the desktop surged through her. She didn't know why he was asking her questions, since he'd clearly already arrived at a conclusion about her.

He turned to her mother. "Have you noticed any marked changes in Lila's behavior at home?"

"We've had a few fights. But it's been stressful lately. With everything in the news."

"Have you been arguing more than usual? Or maybe more intensely?"

"Yes," her mother whispered, and in that moment, Lila hated her mother. Hated her for being so spineless. For not seeing that Lila was sitting right next to her as Dr. Wilson told them both what to think. How to feel.

"Sleeping normally?" he asked.

"I'm not sure . . . I think so," her mother said.

"Any history of mental illness within the family?"

The color drained from her mother's face. "I was diagnosed with paranoid schizophrenia in 2004."

"Mmm." He scrawled another note on the paper. "Auditory or visual hallucinations?"

"Both." Her mother's whisper was paper-thin.

He glanced up, his hand still moving across the paper. "Medication?"

"Haldol."

Lila thought about the yellow eyes she'd seen outside Macie's

window. The dogs she'd heard in the woods. The sense of disasso-
ciation she'd felt. Already, she knew what Dr. Wilson was going
to ask next. And already she knew she was going to lie to him.

But he didn't give her the opportunity. "I'd like to make a
recommendation, Ms. Sawyer. I think we'll all see it's the best
solution."

"Of course."

"I can convince administration to lighten Lila's punishment
to a temporary suspension rather than expulsion. And I can talk
to Ms. Kemper. Reassure her that something like this will never
happen again. I'll alter Lila's schedule so she and Macie no longer
share teachers or a lunch period for the remainder of the school
year. But it would be under the condition that she begins weekly
sessions with me. We can arrange it for before or after school.
Whatever is most convenient." He turned back to Lila then and
smiled. His canine teeth were too long. Too pointed. It made her
sick to look at him.

"In the meantime, and this would be strictly for your convenience until you can schedule Lila an appointment with a
psychiatrist." He opened a desk drawer and withdrew a large
pad. "I might only be a school counselor, but these still come
in handy for emergency situations. Of course, you understand,
this would remain between us. As a favor. A thirty-day supply of
Zoloft. The lowest dosage and no refills. It should help stabilize
her mood until we can begin working to see if the problem goes
deeper than that."

"But I didn't do anything!" Lila said. Her mother held up her
hand, and Lila went quiet. This whole thing was bullshit. How
convenient that Macie had left everything about Cameron out
of her tattletale session. And now, her only choices were getting
expelled or letting Dr. Wilson dope her up.

"I shouldn't—" her mother began.

"Ms. Sawyer, I can't imagine how difficult it must be to be a single parent. Raising a child alone and having to work a full-time job. The guilt you must feel. Especially considering your . . . condition." He paused, and her mother recoiled as if struck. "It's important to do what's best for Lila, isn't it?"

Her mother nodded, but her hand shook as she took the prescription.

"Thank you," she said. Again, Dr. Wilson flashed his teeth.

"My pleasure." He stood and straightened his blazer. "I'm afraid you'll need to take Lila home for the rest of the day. Administration will be in touch after they've reached a decision regarding consequences." He stepped to the door and opened it. They were dismissed.

Her mother rose, and Lila gathered her backpack. She couldn't hear anything except the sound of her own heart sliding wet and liquid through its beats. Anger and guilt and dread churned inside her. There was something wrong with her. Dr. Wilson thought so. Her mother thought so. Macie thought so. And Lila couldn't even hold on to her emotions long enough to identify which was the damaged one.

She followed her mother with her hands tucked against her stomach. The raw, aching parts inside of her pushed back, and they stretched against her skin, and it hurt. She thought about screaming, but it wouldn't do any good. Whatever was inside of her would eat the sound up, would leave her screaming forever without ever being heard.

Together they made their way up the empty hallway and out under a sky the color of mercury. Rain fell against her cheeks like tears, and she tried to memorize the feeling of water on her face. She didn't think she would ever feel it again. Not like this.

Her mother kept glancing over at her as she drove, but she didn't speak. Lila wished her mother would yell at her, or question her, or do anything other than hold her body so rigid it seemed as if she was terrified of her own daughter. Within fifteen minutes, her mother was pulling into their assigned space and heading up the stairs to their door that looked like all the other doors. All the other entryways that led to empty lives and rehearsed moments that were supposed to count toward happiness.

The apartment was quiet, and Lila lay down on the couch. She would not be the first one to speak. Her mother had not defended her. Her mother had dismissed her. She curled into herself and closed her eyes. Everything inside her churned, her blood and bones shifting into new arrangements. There was pain and pleasure in becoming something different than what she used to be. She pressed her lips together so she wouldn't scream or laugh aloud. Because she was certain that was what she was doing. Becoming something else. Something *not* Lila. Underneath that awareness was the thought that her mother had something to do with it. The *before*. The things that haunted her. Whatever her mother wasn't telling her was part of it somehow. As if her mother had planted some poisoned seed in Lila, and it had finally bloomed.

Lila closed her eyes and pretended to sleep, and still her mother was silent. Her body needed the rest, but her mind raced through a sequence of disconnected thoughts. The outline of teeth and glowing eyes she'd seen in the forest; Macie's face at the movie theater; her mother's half-filled secrets.

When sleep finally crept upon Lila, her body fell into it. She did not dream, but woke with the metallic tang of blood in her mouth and the sensation that there had been something moving inside her belly. Something independent of her. It woke her, but she did not open her eyes. She brought her hand to her abdomen, wondering if she'd truly felt it or if she only needed to eat something.

"I'm hungry." Lila sat up, and her hair fell around her face and over her right eye. She didn't bother to brush it away.

Her mother jumped, her hand jerking to her throat. "Jesus. You scared me." Her hand fluttered and then dropped. "I think we have some soup."

"Okay." So they weren't going to talk about it at all. Her mother was going to make her an appointment, was going to drive her to school early once a week so she could spill her guts to Dr. Wilson, was going to force her to swallow a pill, but she wasn't going to bother with asking Lila how she fucking felt about it all.

Standing, her mother made her way to the kitchen as if soup was the bandage that could fix everything. Lila listened to her open and shut cabinets, the sound of the can opener and the wet plop as the soup fell out of the can and into the bowl. Of course the soup was canned. Everything in their life was prepackaged and cheap. Lila passed her tongue over her teeth as the microwave beeped. She was *hungry*.

Her mother stepped out of the kitchen and looked at Lila. Her eyes were tinged with red, the skin beneath puffy and raw. Lila's stomach growled. She drew her legs up underneath her so she almost crouched and then licked her lips like some feral creature. She needed to eat something, and her mother was taking so long. The muscles in her thighs quivered, readied themselves as if to spring, but she didn't move, waited instead for her mother to carry the bowl into the living room, but she moved slowly, slowly, and Lila ground her teeth so she would not scream.

"Careful. It's hot," she said. Lila took the bowl from her, ignoring the heat searing her fingers, and tipped the dish to her lips. She drank greedily, the dark tomato red dribbling from the edges of the bowl and staining her mouth as she slurped at the liquid. It burned her mouth, her tongue, her throat, but she didn't care. There was only this act of eating, of filling herself. Her mother watched, her eyes widened in shock, and still Lila drank the scorching liquid, her tongue lapping at what remained in the bowl.

When Lila was finished, she leaned backward and let out a

belch, wiped at her mouth so that the red liquid smeared over the back of her hand. She was still hungry, and the thing inside her squirmed and stretched itself outward like some great beast. It whispered, and Lila heard.

"Still hungry. Is there more?" Lila stood, pushing past her mother and into the kitchen. Her mother drew away from her as Lila went. She was still afraid. Good. Let her be confused and anxious in all the ways Lila had been. Let her not understand. Let her know that Lila had a secret, too, that it was flowering inside of her.

"I think there's another can. Chicken noodle though," her mother said.

"Yuck." Lila opened the refrigerator and closed it. Looked for something that wasn't there. It was never there. Always just enough to get by. Never extra. Never enough to make Lila all the things she would never be. To make her the girl who wore the right clothes or had the right hair and makeup. To make her noticeable. To make her a girl someone could fall in love with. A girl Macie could fall in love with.

"Sorry," her mother whispered, and to Lila, the word tasted like something dead. For years, her mother had been apologizing. For not being able to do the hundreds of things other parents could do for their children.

Still hungry. Lila hunted down the can of chicken noodle and dumped it into the bowl. The thing inside of her wanted her to eat it like that. To bite into the congealed mess of noodles and gristly bits of chicken, but she put it into the microwave. She still wanted it hot enough to burn. Swallowing the boiling liquid would mean she could still feel something other than this *thing* creeping through her.

Her mother was silent while she waited, and when the microwave finished, she withdrew the bowl, ignoring the blistering of her own skin as she made her way back to the living room, where her mother sat with her eyes closed. Lila knew then, understood implicitly, that it was likely that the madness she'd been running from for so long had finally thorned itself in her mind. But she didn't care. A part of it felt like honesty. Like tearing away the veil of secrecy that had darkened her entire life.

"Why don't you ever talk about it?"

Her mother snapped her eyes open. "About what?"

"New Orleans. Anything about your life before you came here. About Jazzland."

"I can't do this right now, Lila. Not after today."

Lila brought the bowl to her lips. Steam clouded around her face, and her mother lifted her hand, opened her mouth to tell her daughter to be careful, that the soup was hot, but Lila drank and drank, and again the liquid dribbled around her mouth and down her neck.

"You burned yourself," her mother said. Stupid. A stupid thing to say. The thing inside whispered again, and Lila curled her mouth into a snarl. Lila let the bowl slip, and it clattered to the floor, the ceramic shattering. The thing inside of her gobbled up the discordant sound and smoothed the edges of it so there was no feeling, and it was so wonderful not to feel.

"Don't move. I'll get the broom," her mother said, but Lila took a step toward her mother and then another, her feet pressing down on the broken bowl. She waited for the sharp bite of pain—knew she would welcome it—and when her skin opened, the blood pattering against the floor, she smiled.

"No. There's something else. I know there is," Lila said, her voice suddenly too loud for the space. "I know there is. I know there is. I know there is. I know. You should just fucking *tell me*. I know there is. I know there is. I know there is; *I know there is; I know there is*." She was shrieking, and her mother brought her hands to her face, her eyes, covering them so she could not see Lila's mouth opening and opening and opening.

"You don't understand. When I was a kid . . . Oh my God. Oh God." Her mother moaned, and the sound was pain and terror, and everything inside Lila went cold, the world snapping back into itself as her skin closed over the open wound the thing inside her had left. She scrambled backward as her mother crumpled.

What had she done?

"I'm sorry," Lila whispered. "I'm sorry," she said again and again, but the words could not take back anything Lila had said.

"That's enough, Lila," her mother snapped, her eyes flashing for the first time in anger rather than fear. "I don't know what the hell is going on with you or what in God's name that performance was, but that is *enough*."

Lila stared down at her hands and nodded, shame washing through her. She was sick, probably feverish after the stress of the day. That was why she'd felt so strange, like there was something inside her that didn't belong, forcing her to do and say all those terrible things. She was sick. That was all. But even as she told herself that, she saw how easy it was to be dishonest with herself. How she could convince herself to believe the lie because doing so meant she was normal.

"Lila, I need to ask you . . ." Her mother took a deep breath, her jaw settling into a hard line. "If you ever don't feel like yourself? Like you're not exactly awake and maybe seeing things that aren't really there? Or like you come to and don't remember what it is you were doing? Anything like that?" As she spoke, her mother's words grew more and more clipped, as if there were a mania building beneath them.

Lila shook her head and whispered the necessary lie. "No."

Silence took up space between them as her mother studied her face. As if her mother could peel her open and see all the rot hiding inside. "You would tell me though. If something like that happened?"

"Of course." Her guilt settled hard, but she couldn't tell her mom about what had happened with Macie. About that *thing* creeping through her. She couldn't.

"Good. That's good," her mother said.

Together they sat in the gathering quiet, neither speaking to the other, both keeping their secrets tucked away where they would not be discovered. Both choosing to believe the other's lies because it was simpler to not have to face them.

Again, Lila felt herself seem to disconnect; that strange feeling dropping once more over her like a heavy blanket, and then a part of herself snapped. It was like going to sleep, and it was so much easier this way. To just let go.

But her mother was grasping her hands, her breath shuddering as she began to speak in a low whisper. And then she told Lila about Jazzland.

CHAPTER 14

CAROLINE 2004

The hospital wristband was too tight, and Caroline worked her fingers beneath the plastic and stretched it away from her skin, but it didn't break. She'd already gone through discharge, the paperwork signed, her head nodding as she listened to her after-care instructions. No alcohol. No driving for at least a week. After the fourth commandment, Caroline lost the thread, but Daniel had asked all the questions she should have asked. She knew he would have already committed to memory every small instruction from the doctor who'd examined her, as well as her test results.

Daniel walked behind the nurse who was pushing Caroline's wheelchair. Outside, his car was already pulled to the curb. She dreaded being locked inside it with him and the questions he'd been holding back since the ambulance had brought her to the hospital the night before.

There had been blood draws that left her arms burning, and then an EEG, which had come back with a negative diagnosis for epilepsy, and then a placidly smiling doctor who squeezed her knee over and over while he talked to Daniel about what was wrong with her.

"Non-epileptic seizures are fairly common in women. Especially if there's any depression or anxiety, which I gather from what you've told me, Mr. McHough, there has been. We're waiting on blood results to check for diabetes, but I have a feeling that's not what we're dealing with here. We'll want her to follow up with her primary care physician for a psychotherapist recommendation. That should help her better deal with any anxiety or depression, and get all this"—he waved his hand at Caroline prone in the hospital bed—"under control. No one wants a repeat performance of that, do they, sweetheart?" He looked at her then and winked, and she stared back, unable to do anything other than open and then close her mouth like some dumb cow—a perfect imitation of what he probably thought of her.

"Mind your head now," the nurse said as she and Daniel guided her into the passenger seat, and then the door was closed, a vacuum of silence dropping over Caroline like a bell jar.

She'd not told Daniel about the dog. The sculpture. The man she'd seen huddled in the corner with his long, curved teeth. Even after the seizure and the trip to the hospital, she didn't think she could explain all of it to him. The doctor who'd examined her had mentioned something about dissociative periods and how even those were a form of seizure, and that it was possible she'd been having them without even knowing.

"I thought I was sleepwalking," she'd said, and Daniel had glanced at her sharply as the doctor made another note on his chart.

"Mm-hm. Plenty of people assume that," he'd said, and then left the room.

The interior light blinked on, and then Daniel was beside her, and they were leaving, the car picking up speed, and she could feel the energy gathering between them, all of Daniel's unspoken words thickening the air in the car.

"Caroline—"

"I want to see my dad," she said, and kept her gaze trained in front of her.

"I should take you home. So you can rest. And then you need to call your doctor. Get in to be seen as soon as possible. Then an appointment with a psychiatrist."

"A psychotherapist."

"A psychotherapist, a psychiatrist, a psychologist, I don't really give a shit. You need to see somebody about all of this. It's too much. It's too fucking much. The insomnia. Thinking you heard things at Jazzland that weren't there. And now a seizure? Oh, *and* the sleepwalking, which you very conveniently didn't tell me about. I mean, what the *fuck*, Caroline?"

"Why are you the one freaking out right now? All of this is happening to *me*," she spat, and Daniel tightened his fingers against the steering wheel. "I thought it was the Ambien. Sleepwalking was one of the side effects. I didn't know—"

He swiped a hand across his face. "Stop. Just stop. You don't get to explain this away. Something is *wrong*, Caroline. You need to talk to someone. Get this straightened out. You have to."

Caroline let her head rest against the window. She didn't want to deal with this right now. To have to think about making more appointments and then dealing with the insurance company and stretching herself thinner and thinner when there was already so little left to give.

"Take me to see Dad. I need to see him. I'll be okay. At least for the rest of the afternoon. Please?" Caroline asked, her voice barely audible over the scrape of the tires along the asphalt.

"You'll call. Later," Daniel said, but he made the turn, and fifteen minutes later, they were in the parking lot of Helping Hands.

He helped her out of the car but did not follow behind her, and she paused and turned back to him. "Are you not coming in?"

"I need some time. By myself. There are nurses inside. I mean, you'll be okay, right? Just like you said." He folded himself back into the driver's seat and slammed the door—whatever response she'd wanted to give him cut off.

As she walked toward the entrance, she wasn't sure if she wanted to scream or cry. More than anything though, she needed to see her dad. To sit beside him and hold his hand even if he couldn't hold it back.

"Miss Caroline!" Cee stepped out from behind the front desk and folded her into a hug. "You are a sight for sore eyes." She glanced down, her forehead creasing as she took in the hospital band. "You doing all right?"

"Nothing seeing my dad won't fix," Caroline said, forcing a weak smile, and Cee reached across to rest her hand on Caroline's shoulder.

"Of course," she said. "Your daddy has been up since this morning. He's been asking for you. And listen, if *you* need anything, just hit the button, okay?"

"Thank you, Cee," she said, and stepped away, her footsteps clicking against the vinyl flooring as she hurried toward her father's room.

The door stood open. Her father's head jerked toward her, and he held out his hands, his mouth shuddering open as a deep whine worked its way out of him and into the space between them.

"Dad?" Caroline rushed forward, the room blinking in and out as her breath shuddered in her lungs. This could not be it. She could not have returned from her own kind of death, her body and mind weakened beyond compare, only to bear witness to her father's.

"Oh God. Caroline. My girl," he said, and his voice was like glass. Something to break. He opened his arms, and she fell into him, remembering the smell of him—sweat and the scent of his aftershave—and he clawed at her back, her shoulders, his chest heaving as he cried.

Without thinking, she reached for the emergency button, but he grasped her wrist and held it still.

"I was afraid you weren't going to come back. Afraid that you were gone again. That whoever had taken you when you were little had found his way back—" He tightened his grip on her wrist, but she couldn't bring herself to tell him he was hurting her.

"Everything's fine. It was a bad dream. I'm right here."

He shook his head. "It sometimes feels like it's still happening, and I can't do anything to stop it."

"Dad, please—"

"Goddammit, I am not confused, Caroline!" His voice was a harsh bark, and she flinched away. "The nightmares you had when you came back. Jesus. Even now, I can hear how you would scream. It was the most terrible sound in the world because I knew you were remembering whatever had happened to you, and I couldn't do anything to keep it from happening again every time you closed your eyes."

Caroline breathed in the antiseptic air and told herself it was not like swallowing needles, but it burned, and she pressed her teeth down against her tongue to keep from speaking. The terror in his voice was like ice, thin and heavy all at the same time.

What happened? What happened to me?

"When your nightmares started, I'd sit beside you and try to wake you up, but it never worked. I had to listen to you scream about the Kingdom, begging me to not let them take you, and I couldn't do a goddamn thing. You'd finally wake up and not be able to remember anything at all. I asked you about the Kingdom—what it was or what it meant—but you'd only stare back at me like you didn't understand what I'd asked, and I had to pretend like there was nothing wrong. Not even when you got scared of dogs. You remember Mr. Perron's dog, Missy? Anytime she would get to barking, you'd start crying and shaking, just *terrified,* but you could never tell us why. And you'd never been afraid of dogs before."

Caroline thought back to her date with Daniel at Jazzland. The sensation of a deep, inherent wrong she had not been able to shake. The snarling dogs only she had been able to hear.

"And there'd been all those other little girls. All those rumors about The Cur. We just felt so lucky to have you back," he whispered, and a memory flashed through Caroline. She remembered something about girls going missing when she was younger. At school, there had been a mild panic among the students, and parents kept their girls at home, locked in their proverbial towers as if wood and locks couldn't be opened. Or broken. Those pure, innocent girls kept from anything that defined them in the name of protection, while their brothers carried on as if there was nothing to fear. But for them, there wasn't. They would never understand the inherent trepidation that came as a result of being wrapped in girl flesh.

But for Caroline the year between eleven and twelve was a blur. She'd never remembered much about that time in her life, but she'd always attributed her faulty memory to the death of her mother when she was thirteen. Then her father had brought her back to life with that tackle box filled with art material, and she forgot she wasn't supposed to have a blank space in her memory.

And now, there was the dog Beth had found, and the sculpture, and the man she'd seen, his teeth long and curved. The mouth of an animal. A mouth of pain.

She kept her voice low. "What happened to me?"

Her father covered his face with his hands, the words spilling out of him little more than incoherent noises. She waited for him to answer, for him to explain, and his breathing grew ragged. He dropped his hands, his face a mask of pain. He opened and closed his mouth as if trying to articulate a response to something he didn't fully understand. "We thought it was better that you'd blocked it out. Better to forget whatever had happened instead of carrying that suffering with you everywhere you went. The police couldn't find any substantial evidence, and they turned Jazzland upside down. We took you to a therapist a couple of times, but you weren't that interested in talking to him, so we told you that you didn't have to go. He agreed that if you were choosing to forget, we should let your mind do what it needed to do. We figured with all those degrees, he knew what he was talking about. And then the nightmares stopped, and things went pretty much back to normal. Except you never did like dogs. And then there was the accident with your mom, and you stopped talking again, and I had no idea what to do. It took so long to bring you back to me, and even then it wasn't through talking. Not at first. You would paint or build something, and then eventually you started talking again, and I tried not to ever think about that dark time or to remind you of it," her father said. There was logic in his words, but they did nothing to alleviate the panic flooding through Caroline's belly.

"What the fuck happened to me, Dad?" Her father reached over to place his hand over hers. If anyone had wandered by the room, they would have imagined they were seeing the two of them locked in the sweetness of a typical family tableau instead of drowning inside an awful secret.

Her father spoke, and his voice was agitated. He was lucid but also lost and flailing in the confusion of what he was telling her. "I keep dreaming about it. About something clawing its way up out of the ground and dragging you away from me, and I try to hold on, but it takes you anyway. I'm so sorry." He turned his face away as he cried. "We didn't want it to be like this, Caroline.

You have to believe that. We thought we were protecting you," he said, and Caroline let her head drop into her hands.

She wanted to scream that he wasn't telling her anything solid, to smash anything she could put her hands on, but she had no energy left. "I've been seeing and hearing things that aren't there. I had a seizure, Dad. A fucking *seizure*. And now whatever this is? Just tell me what happened. Please."

Her father's hysteria rose, his crying dissolving into shaking sobs, and the guilt that she was the cause for his distress burrowed deeper into her, and she willed herself to be calm and still. To swallow down the heat of her tears, so her father would not see them.

She sank to her knees and leaned toward him. "It's okay, Dad. It's okay," she said. Her father was exhausted. His talking had robbed him of what little energy was propping him up, and Caroline watched the lucidity drift from his eyes. He would sleep soon. Cee or another of the nurses would probably give him a sedative, and tomorrow he would be worse, and the day after that would be different yet again, and she would chase his death on and on like some inconstant lover.

She hugged her father, and he whispered something in her ear, but it meant nothing anymore. What came out of him was just a sound. His secret or apology locked away behind his exhaustion and pain.

"I have to go now, Dad. You should rest," she said, and he nodded and swiped at his eyes with a shaking hand.

"Of course. I love you, my girl."

She walked out of her father's room, blind to the hallways, the doors, aware only of the sound of her own breath, the dampness on her cheeks. Another memory floated to the surface of her awareness. Waking in a dark place, her thighs burning; her body shuddering with fever. She'd had scars on the fleshy interior of her thighs since she was a girl but had always assumed she'd gotten them playing—climbing over a fence and falling or any of the other hundreds of ways kids hurt themselves when they are too rough for their own small, breakable bodies. She thought of the sculptures, of the last one, of the man who had the body of a dog, of those teeth and claws she had wrenched from a once-living creature, and she stifled a moan.

Daniel had left the car running and watched as she approached, as she stumbled, unable to keep herself from sobbing, and he threw open his door and rushed to her side to usher her back to the car.

"Hey, it's okay. Just breathe. I got you," he said as he knelt beside her. He smoothed her hair away from her face, and she struggled to breathe, to put into words what he'd already told her earlier. To admit to him that he'd been right.

"I saw something last night. A man. In the corner of the room. I swear to you, Daniel, I saw him. Just like what I heard at Jazzland—"

"It's not real, Caroline. You have to know that," Daniel said.

"Just let me fucking finish!" She heaved in a breath, reminded herself he was just trying to help, but it did nothing to quell the fury building deep inside her. She forced a calm she didn't feel into her voice. "I do. I do know that, but it doesn't matter. I still saw him, and I still heard those dogs. And Dad. I don't know. He was talking like something had happened to me when I was younger, but he got so upset, and I didn't want to push it. But something happened and it's still there, it's still there, and I heard the dogs, and saw that man, and it felt so real—"

"Shhh," Daniel said, and he moved closer to her, putting his arms around her shoulders. Her breath hitched in her chest, and she swallowed against her rising panic. "Listen to me. He's not real, okay? He's not real."

He rocked her until her breath quieted, until her hands dropped still in her lap, and then he pulled away, his fingers pushing her hair back, wiping at the dampness on her cheeks. "You need to talk to a doctor about all of this," he said.

"I know."

"Listen, the hospital gave me the name of a psychiatrist. Dr. Walters. He's supposed to be good. I want you to call him." He dug into his pocket, pulled out his cell phone, and flipped it open. "Here. I have his number saved."

She took the phone, the screen glowing up at her. Daniel reached over and hit the Call button, then put the phone on speaker.

"Leave a message if no one answers," he said, and he watched her as the phone rang and rang and then the voice mail picked up. She pulled away from him slightly. There was no reason for him to watch over her like she was a child.

As she left the message, pronouncing the digits of her own phone number, she told herself this was for the best. She needed help, and Daniel had offered a solution. She should not be angry with him for hovering over her, for hitting dial on the phone, for ensuring she'd done what he told her. He was only looking out for her. Only wanted what was the best for her and for her to get better. She should be grateful. There was no reason for this sudden surge of frustration. No reason it should fester in her belly as he put his cell phone back into his pocket. She smiled at him, making sure there was gratitude on her face, so he would never suspect her true feelings.

But she would make the appointment, and she would keep it.

Daniel drove her home and helped her inside and into her pajamas, having her lift her arms so he could drop her shirt over her head. She hated how helpless it made her feel, but she didn't have the energy to do much herself.

When she was eleven, something had happened to her. The edge of that reality bit into her and refused to let go.

In their bedroom, she closed her eyes but did not sleep, thinking again and again of the man with the mouth of the dog, of the sculptures she'd made, the blood a transparent stain on her hands. Daniel came and went somewhere in the house, and when she finally slept, she forgot to listen for him, and there was only the sound of dogs howling.

CHAPTER 15

CAROLINE 2004

In the morning, Dr. Walters's office returned her call, and three days later, she was sitting on a lumpish tan couch, staring at a cheap framed reprint of Monet's *Water Lilies,* and waiting for her name to be called. Light, acoustic music leaked from a hidden speaker, and a delicate-voiced singer whispered about how he didn't feel it anymore. Underneath these things designed to soothe the addled minds in the waiting room was the chatter from the reception desk and the distinct odor of someone's lunch that made it difficult to take anything other than small sips of air.

Caroline tapped her fingers against the clipboard that held a pile of documents she was supposed to present to Dr. Walters when he came to gather her. Her medical history, a questionnaire with comments that detailed her reasons for seeking treatment, her family history. Every secret of her life scrawled on paper and reduced to the barest of details. It made her feel insignificant, and she focused on the painting, willing her heartbeat to slow.

Daniel had driven her here and would return in a little over an hour to pick her up. She had drawn the line though when he'd mentioned coming inside with her to wait in the waiting room, and he had agreed. She flicked a glance toward the large window and wondered if he was, in fact, still in the parking lot, waiting to see if she would emerge too early, but then the door that led back to the offices opened.

"Ms. Sawyer?"

She stood, gathering her things, and the man stepped toward her and extended his hand. "I'm Dr. Walters." His grip was firm, but his skin was thin and wrinkled, the veins standing out in stark relief. He was dressed carefully but simply in a navy suit that had likely once fit him but had grown large as he lost portions of himself to age, his shoulders stooped so the jacket fell slack over his chest. A cluster of moles on his left cheek gave him the appearance of perpetual imbalance, the gray eyes watery as he took her in and smiled.

"Thank you for seeing me," she said, and he turned, gesturing for her to follow his shuffling footsteps, and she went carefully, head down, not wanting to inadvertently overtake him, to step beyond him into a place she didn't belong. He paused, opening the door for her, that smile still pasted on, and she wondered if at the end of the day his face ached from the effort of false contentment.

A teakwood desk dominated the small office, the surface dusted and polished. There were no framed photos, no stacks of paper or file folders spilling over the surface, only the slim silver gleam of a laptop, which he opened before settling into an oversized chair.

"Now then," he said, and cleared his throat, offering his hand, the palm upturned. He kept his gaze on the laptop. Caroline wasn't sure what he expected of her. He'd already shaken her hand, but it was possible he'd forgotten. She placed her palm on his, waiting for a grip that didn't come, and he glanced up.

"No, dear. Your paperwork," he said.

She immediately withdrew her hand. "Of course. I'm so sorry. This is the first time I've ever done anything like this." Her cheeks burned as she thrust the paperwork toward him.

"Seen a psychiatrist, you mean?"

"Yes . . . I mean no. At least as far as I can remember. My dad says I went to a therapist when I was younger. That's part of why I'm here, but I don't remember that, so I didn't think to mention—"

"Have a seat, Ms. Sawyer," he said, and began flipping through her paperwork, glancing up now and again to type something on his laptop. Caroline fidgeted. She hadn't expected it to be like this. Wasn't she supposed to be talking? Guiding his finger down the page in front of him, he finally looked up. "Now. Tell me about what's been happening with you. The things you've been seeing and hearing."

She told him everything. About her father's illness; the sleeplessness; the vision she'd had of the man in the dark coat, how he wore the face of a dog; the sounds she'd heard at Jazzland; her fugue states and the sculpture she'd created without awareness; the bare hints of what her father had told her. All of it, she laid at his feet in a breathless rush, and at the end, she feared her heart would fall out of her with a wet slop. Throughout, he typed away on his laptop, his eyes never leaving hers. It unnerved her, and she could not keep herself from looking away.

"The man you've seen. Do you recognize him?" He leaned backward and folded his hands over his stomach.

"No."

"Often, when people undergo trauma, those memories will manifest in delusions. More specifically, persecutory delusions, where the person emphatically believes that someone or *something,* as in your case, is pursuing them. This can, of course, take on myriad forms. People report seeing dark shadows following them, or they believe their loved ones have turned on them, are trying to poison them or kill them in their sleep. That whatever is hunting them, it intends them harm, and they are frightened. And rightfully so. Delusions, no matter that they aren't real—and they are, in fact, not real, dear—have the power to intensely sway perception and emotion."

She shook her head. How easy it was for him to dismiss her. He hadn't heard, hadn't seen what she had. He didn't even bother to try to disguise the patronizing tone in his voice. She hadn't seen any dark shadows. The man's shape, his mouth . . . they seemed real. And she didn't believe Daniel was trying to kill her. This was something else. She opened her mouth to tell him, but he cut in.

"Delusions are manifestations of forms of paranoid schizophrenia. Trauma, particularly childhood trauma that has been repressed, as it seems to have been in your case, develops this way later in life. It's quite common to see instances of paranoid schizophrenia in cases of significant repressed trauma. Seeing and hearing things that aren't there. Like the dogs you say you heard."

"So you're saying I'm psychotic?" Her voice rose in pitch and volume, but she didn't care.

"No need to become hysterical, dear." He cleared his throat and looked at her sternly. "It's quite common among women, following an upsetting event, to become highly emotional. It allows the woman to delve inward into the mind as a method of protection against the thing that happened to her. And this heightened emotional state leads to . . . well, a prevalence of visual or auditory hallucinations."

"So this is all my fault? Because I'm too emotional. That's what you're saying." She'd been through this song and dance before. Her mother's regular reminders that any kind of angry outburst wasn't ladylike.

He chuckled. "If you want to look at it so starkly, then yes. But it's more complicated than that, of course. There's quite a bit of literature that has been published regarding hallucination as it pertains to women, but I digress. You don't need to understand the particulars of psychiatric research, nor could you given your background in . . . art, was it? But trust me when I tell you, dear, that everything you've seen, everything you've heard have only been products of your overly emotional, distraught mind."

Caroline bristled. Buried within his explanation, he'd insulted her. His dismissal of her stretched between them, palpable and sharp. "You don't understand. I heard those dogs, and there's no logical explanation for that. I heard them, and it felt absolutely real—"

"Of course it did, you poor lamb. That's the nature of it. You don't have to prove your illness to me."

She ground her teeth at this patronizing bullshit. He may as well have told her to shut her mouth. The mass of her fear was something he could put into a box and then forget. In his esteemed opinion, she was an easy fix. A series of checked boxes he could then ignore. She could have started screaming, and he would have batted his eyes and offered up some professional variation of "calm down, sweetheart." He would pat her on the head like a nice kitty and send her away without attempting to understand the nuances of what was happening to her.

She shoved the thoughts away and filled her voice with a calm she didn't feel. "What if I went back? To Jazzland. My dad mentioned something about the police looking for evidence there. Just to see if . . . anything in the park sparks a memory?"

"I would not advise that. It could lead to severe distress and disorientation. In your state, which is highly sensitive—if not overly so—the reaction could be devastating. No. I cannot recommend that you return to Jazzland. I'll start you with a low dose of an antipsychotic. Ten milligrams once a day, and then we'll reassess in a month. I'll want to see you back then. My girls up front can take care of that appointment for you." He reached into his desk and withdrew a pad, scrawling his signature across the bottom. He stood and opened the door, and Caroline rose as well, her body responding automatically to his control. Was that all he was going to offer her?

He placed his hand in the hollow of her back and gently guided her out. Before she could turn to ask anything else, he had closed the door, and she was alone in the hallway, the prescription in her left hand.

"Fuck," she muttered, and turned away. Up front at the reception desk, a frosted-blond receptionist made Caroline her follow-up appointment. "That's all?" Caroline asked as the receptionist handed her a reminder card.

"That's all. We'll give you a reminder call about a week before your appointment, and if you need to cancel, call the number on the card."

"Thanks," Caroline said, tucked the card into her purse, and turned to go. She'd had her appointment, had spilled her guts like she was supposed to, so why did she feel like nothing had been done for her at all? Sure, Dr. Walters had asked her questions, had jotted notes about her on his computer, and had given her the prescription, but she felt unsatisfied. As she left, she checked the large clock hanging in the waiting area. Forty-three minutes from the time she arrived. All those years of damage, the hallucinations she now understood she was having, boiled down into less than an hour and a prescription for an antipsychotic. And the way he'd spoken to her. Like she was a child or a small animal. Something he could pet.

Daniel was already in the parking lot, the windows down and some song she didn't recognize leaking a soft bass line.

"That was quick. How'd it go?" he said as she climbed in.

"It was fine."

"That's all?"

Caroline leaned back, the reality of everything Dr. Walters

had said crushing her against the seat. This man had told her she was crazy. Schizophrenic. Delusional. Psychotic. She bit down on the inside of her cheeks. She didn't want to talk about it yet, but she knew Daniel wouldn't let her alone until he knew she was going to get better. She was starting to understand that their relationship had always been a subtle maneuvering of her own feelings in favor of his. "He said it's common in victims of trauma to experience delusions. To hear and see things. I think I want to get a second opinion. He was so . . . dismissive."

"He listened to what you said, right?"

"Well, yeah. But—"

"He knows what he's talking about, Caroline. He's a very smart man. He wouldn't have been in practice for so long or be so highly recommended if he wasn't."

Guilt settled over her. How often had she said almost the exact same thing to Beth whenever she complained about Dr. Bryson? "I'm not saying he isn't intelligent. He just brushed right over everything I said. I've been confused and stressed, but psychotic? I mean, Jesus Christ, Daniel. What the hell am I supposed to do with that?"

"You were hearing things at Jazzland, and then you tell me that you've seen a man who isn't there in our *home*? You aren't exactly experiencing reality right now. It's hard. I know it is. But you have to trust him and trust that he can make you better."

She opened her mouth to tell him about wanting to go back to Jazzland but then snapped it closed. He would side with Dr. Walters. Would *forbid* it. If she was going to have any control, she needed to take it for herself. Otherwise, she'd stay in the dark.

She steered the conversation back toward Dr. Walters. "He talked to me like I was a little girl. And he kept calling me *dear*. That doesn't strike you as just a little bit . . . I don't know . . . gross? Or sexist?"

"Give me a break. He comes from a different era. He didn't mean anything by it. Please, please, Caroline. Just do what he says. He's there to help you. That's what we all want. So you can be *you* again. For us. For your dad. I would have thought you wanted that, too?"

"Of course I want that." She stared out at the horizon, the buildings and sky a hemorrhage of gray. "Of course I do." She pulled the prescription from her bag and held it up. "He gave me a prescription. For an antipsychotic."

Daniel set his mouth in a grim line and backed out of the space. "We'll go fill it. Right now."

She stared back at him, but he kept his eyes trained on the road, his fingers clenched around the steering wheel. "Seriously? You had a problem with me taking a *sleeping pill,* but you're suddenly okay with an antipsychotic?"

"This is different."

"How is this different?"

"You told me you were fucking *seeing things,* Caroline. How am I supposed to feel about that? Knowing my fiancée could turn up anywhere, babbling about dogs or men in dark coats? Do you have any idea what that looks like? I'd have to be the one to clean everything up, to explain it all away."

"You're worried about what this is like for *you?*"

"That's not what I mean."

She drew in a tight breath, her lungs, the muscles in her stomach aching. "That's what it is. You're ashamed. Because you can't take me to your fucking art galas and fundraisers and parties to rub elbows with every poseur in the goddamn city."

"Jesus, Caroline—"

"How many weeks until the Aversion Gala? Two? Just enough time for the pills to work their magic, huh? Just enough time for me to get numb enough so you can parade me around and let everyone marvel at how perfect we look."

"It's not about that. Not at all. You could hurt yourself. Could hurt somebody else," he said, but his jaw was set in the hard line that betrayed his dishonesty. She knew she'd spoken the truth, but he would never acknowledge it. Disgusted, she turned away and stared at the blank, ugly expanse of the highway.

They rode together in silence, and Caroline curled her fingers into her palm, the nails biting into the flesh, but her anger floated just beneath the surface. She dug her phone out of her bag and flipped it open. A missed call and voice mail. From Helping Hands. Her heart lurched, her breath catching in the back of her throat.

Not yet. No. Not yet. The phone slipped from her grip, and she caught at it, her vision swimming, the trees dividing and re-dividing into an amorphous leviathan of verdant growth. But if there were something wrong, wouldn't they have tried to call more than once? Or when they couldn't get in touch with her, have called Daniel? She pulled up the voice mail, telling herself everything was fine, but the animal heat of her body lingered.

"Ms. Sawyer, this is Tricia at Helping Hands. I was calling to check up on your bill, which was due last week. Please give us a call back so we can get it taken care of for you."

Shit. She snapped the phone closed and ran a hand through her hair, tugging hard at the roots. She wasn't going to be back at the Kellums' for the rest of the week. Daniel had made sure of that, standing over her yet again as she phoned Vivian to ask for some time off. So there was one paycheck she could no longer depend upon, and there was only so long Helping Hands would offer her their charity. The director had taken particular pains to emphasize that point with her during the interview process. Going back to the Kellums' was an impossibility. She'd never be able to convince Daniel she was well enough to go back to work so soon. Not after having told him she'd been prescribed an antipsychotic and with him slavering after whatever prestige he could find at the gallery. He would push for her to move her father to a different facility. Somewhere cheaper. Somewhere that would only draw her dad's end closer. After everything, after trying so *hard,* in the end, she would be the one responsible for her father's erasure.

Leaning her head against the window, she let Daniel drive her toward this new, second fate she would find in the bottom of a pill bottle. Her father displaced, the vermillion and gold of her disillusions reduced to a drugged numbness, a vacuity that would swallow her whole. Her hands would go still under the dullness of the medication in her blood, and her father would be dead, and her skin would forget the shallow prick of wire, the papered dampness of leaves as she built her art, and the delicate machine of her heart would churn on, bloodless and cold. Never again would her muscles know the vivid ache of sculpture, the lovely pain of her work.

Her work. Her cheeks flushed as the idea fluttered in the back of her mind. The sculpture of the woman with the dog's head— Daniel had seemed genuinely impressed by it. Other people may feel the same way. People who would *pay.*

For a moment, another, darker vision crossed her mind, but she pushed away the memory of the second sculpture. If she could get Daniel to show the first sculpture to Gemma, it was possible she might buy it. And the check would likely be enough to float her until she started back at the Kellums'. As Daniel drove, the idea fractured and re-formed, the question she would ask Daniel broken into fragments and discarded and then replaced with a more subtle variation. Yes. This was her only answer. It had to work. But she could not ask him now. Not with the anger between them still thick and heated, the knowledge she carried now of how Daniel felt about her burning through her.

With Daniel beside her, she filled the prescription. He drove her home, and once they were inside, she opened the orange bottle, her hands chilled as she took the glass of water he brought her. She let the pill rest for a moment on her tongue before swallowing. For a moment, she thought Daniel would force her to open her mouth, to show him she wasn't hiding the pill under her tongue, but he only watched her carefully without speaking as she took another sip of water.

"This will be good," Daniel said, and he pulled her to him, his cheek against hers, his skin smelling of cedar, but she could not bring her body to soften. His body as an apology was not enough, but she forced herself to shift so she fit against him. She would swallow the medication, would listen to what Dr. Walters had told her. She needed to do it if she wanted to ensure her father's place at Helping Hands. She would do these things because she couldn't let her father down.

"It will be. And I'm sorry." She forced the words out of her and felt him relax. She breathed deeply. "I'm going to ask you a favor. I hope you'll say yes."

"What's that?"

"The sculpture of the woman—"

"The one with the dress made out of leaves?"

"Yeah. You . . . liked it, didn't you?"

"I . . . did."

She ignored the hesitation in his voice. "I was wondering if you would show it to Gemma? Get her take on it. See if she'd be willing to buy it for the gallery?"

"I don't know—"

"I *need* to sell it. Dad's bill is due, and I'm not working. I need the money. And there's not enough in what the gallery pays you to cover it plus everything else."

Daniel paused, an emotion Caroline couldn't identify flaring and then fading across his features. "Of course, Linny. Of course.

We can snap some pictures, and I'll show her the next time I see her. It'll probably be later this afternoon. You'll be okay if I head in for a little bit?"

"I'll probably lie down. Watch a movie. I'll be fine." Now that he'd taken her to the doctor, had watched her swallow her pill, he was safe to leave her alone. She didn't want to think it was true, but she knew it was. He'd been hovering over her, every part of his body attuned to hers, his movements orbiting the twitching of her muscles. The knowledge she would be rid of the pressure of his gaze was enough to unwind the tension in her shoulders.

"I'll show Gemma if she's there," he said.

An hour later, she was alone, the dust of their lives settling over her skin as she sat beside the front window. The sculpture was still there, arranged just so for the photographs she'd taken and then sent to Daniel. She could not bring herself to move it. Even with the medication flooding her bloodstream, she was afraid if she touched the wire, the dress, it would twitch to life beneath her fingers, would breathe outward all of the fear and paranoia Caroline had been carrying.

But it did not move, and she did not move, and she thought of Dr. Walters, and she thought of Jazzland, and she thought of Daniel, and she thought of all the things her male doctor and her future husband didn't want her to do, all the things she had been told to ignore, all the things expected of her and this ideal artist, this ideal *woman* she was supposed to be, and she stood up before those things had the chance to settle their teeth into the deeper meat of her.

Fuck Dr. Walters. Fuck him and his opinions that she shouldn't understand what had happened to her, and his calling her "dear," and his insistence that she shouldn't go looking into her own past. It had happened to *her*. She was entitled to know what it was that had happened to her own body.

Opening the search engine, Caroline typed in her name and then *New Orleans*. For years she'd avoided searching for any mention of herself on the Internet. Too many people imagined themselves critics, and she had no desire to see what they thought of her artwork. A list of news articles popped up. The first titled "Girl, Eleven, Missing." Her heart in her mouth, she clicked on the first link and read. Her disappearance and then presumed abduction were laid out in a series of no-nonsense paragraphs. A childhood photo of her captured in newsprint, her own eyes staring out and through the years like a ghost that had forgotten what it is it's supposed to haunt. Beneath the photos were pleas for anyone with any information to contact their local police department.

Other articles linked Caroline's disappearance to the disappearance of five other girls. Rebecca. Nicole. Amanda. Ashleigh. Heather. All of them had been found in various states of decomposition. All of their bodies torn at the thighs and lower bellies as if attacked by an animal. Their faces stared up at her, the pupils of their eyes dark smears of ink that seemed to bleed into the sclera, and she looked away, not wanting to see those girls, not wanting to acknowledge that they had been the ones who had not escaped, their lives reduced to a handful of words, a history of cruelty.

Caroline had been the only girl to return.

The speculation that there was a serial killer targeting young girls had rippled through the NOLA communities. The killer they called The Cur was the monster that lurked in the places no one wanted to look. The name materialized here and there in the articles, linking him to Caroline and the other girls. Without a confirmed tragedy, the media had lost interest in her story, so there were no other mentions beyond two articles that briefly reported on her return. How she'd been found disoriented and wandering around Jazzland, unable to remember how she'd gotten there. How thankful her parents were. How grateful. The final photograph was of her mom and dad with their backs to the camera, hurrying toward a set of double doors that could have been a hospital or the police department.

Again, Caroline combed through the articles, searching for anything that would make her *remember,* but she was hunting something that didn't exist.

The recent disappearances—those other girls who had been discovered—had likely triggered her, loosening whatever nightmares Caroline had buried in her mind. The delusions serving as the dark marriage between her memory and those stolen girls.

The names blurred before her. The girls'. Her father's. Her mother's. Her own. There had only been one article to mention any other specific name in connection with her case, and there was a grainy photograph beneath the headline: a petite, dark-skinned woman with hair slicked into a bun stood beside Caroline's father and mother, her head slightly inclined toward a microphone, an audience of reporters in front of her, their hands thrust in the air. The caption indicated the woman pictured— Lydia Doucette—was the lead detective on the abduction cases.

If anyone knew anything more about what had happened to Caroline, it would be this woman. She could have asked her father, but she didn't want him suffering any more than he already had. Opening another tab, Caroline went to the White Pages's home page and typed in the detective's name. Within seconds the listing appeared on her screen. There was one Doucette, L. listed in New Orleans, and Caroline opened her phone and punched in the number before her nerves could take over.

Even though Daniel wasn't due home for another couple of hours, she couldn't keep herself from darting a glance over her shoulder as the phone began to ring. She had no idea what she would say if the detective did pick up. *Hi, I was abducted when I was a kid, and you were on the case. But I came back, so there wasn't*

*ever really anything to investigate, but I was hoping you could tell
me anything you know about it since I can't remember?* It sounded
stupid even as she ran it through her mind, but she had nothing
else to go on at this point.

On the fifth ring, the voice mail picked up, the automated
voice telling her to please leave a message, and she gripped the
phone to her ear, breathing steadily so her voice would not shake.

"This message is for Detective Doucette. My name is Caroline
Sawyer. I'm hoping you remember me? You were the lead detective on my case when I was a kid. I was . . . well . . . I was hoping
you'd be willing to talk with me about it. I don't remember much,
and I'm just trying to piece it all together. To remember what happened to me." Caroline left her number and then disconnected
the call.

Probably she had the wrong number, and even if she didn't,
her disappearance was more than a decade ago. Unresolved despite the happy ending and shelved away to molder in some back
storage room. The likelihood of the detective bothering to call
her back was small.

Sighing, Caroline turned back to her computer and typed
Jazzland into the search bar. As she waited for the page to load,
her phone rang, and she didn't look at the number as she answered, not wanting to hope too much for the improbable.

"Hello?" she said.

The voice on the other line didn't speak in the terse, clipped
tones Caroline had expected, but in the long drawl of the Bayou.

"Ms. Sawyer? This is Lydia Doucette. I'd like to talk with you.
In person."

CHAPTER 16

LILA 2019

Lila woke with the deep taste of earth on her tongue. In her dreams, there had been her mother as a girl, her hair loose around her shoulders as she wandered away from Lila. No matter how Lila had called, this child version of her mother wouldn't listen, wouldn't turn back. Lila wondered if it had been like that when her mother had disappeared and then returned, wandering around Jazzland, confused and frightened and unable to talk about what had been done to her. And then there had been a voice that whispered, and she'd recognized the rise and fall of it, no longer concerned what it meant that she could hear something so distinct, so *real*. Maybe it was only a part of herself coming alive. A part she'd denied herself for too long. The voice slid over her vulnerable, limp body, and she woke with its words gathered in the pit of her heart. She wasn't allowed to go to school today. Or the next day. Or the next. When she did finally return, there would be the forced sessions with Dr. Wilson. And the pills.

The voice unfurled inside her, slow-moving as honey, and *she*

didn't want to see those assholes. They all thought she was crazy—
Macie had told them that. Even though Lila had only been angry
with her, and she'd had every right to be angry. Lila wasn't crazy. Of
course not. Better to linger here, to stay hidden.

Lila gnawed at her cuticles and listened as the voice hummed
inside of her. It was right. She didn't want to see Macie or anyone
else. She burrowed under the blankets.

"Lila?" Her mother was at the door. Lila wanted to scream at
her to go away, but she called back to her.

"I'm awake," she said. Her mother opened the door and
crossed the room to lift the blanket and stare down at Lila. She
pressed a cool hand against her forehead.

"You look flushed. I can cancel my classes again if I need to."

"I'm not sick. I'll be fine," Lila said. *Go away. Go. Go.*

"I don't want to leave you here by yourself. Not after . . ." Her
mother trailed off, but Lila knew what it was she wanted to say.
Not after last night. Not after what she'd told Lila; her fear finally
voiced. And still, there was something Lila felt was missing. Some
other part her mother had not told her the full truth about. A
larger secret waiting to be discovered. Lila could see it in the way
her mother's eyes had shifted away from her as she unwound her
story. How her gaze drifted, the lashes flicking open and closed
too rapidly, her fingernails pinching the skin of her wrist.

"I'll be fine. It's not like I haven't been here by myself before.
And I'm just going to sleep." Lila curled into herself, and her
mother tucked the blanket down around her and sighed. She
knew her mother was struggling, knew she was hesitant. Lila had
been suspended. She was supposed to be in trouble, not huddled
under her blankets while her mother fretted over her. There was
so much that had happened, so much that seemed *wrong,* but
Lila knew her mother already felt guilty for canceling her classes
the day before. Too many cancellations wouldn't look good on
her evaluations.

"I want you to call me at lunchtime to check in," Caroline said, and Lila nodded. "I'll be home later in the afternoon. It's my late day. But I can come home anytime if you need me to."

"Okay," Lila said. Her mother bent, dropped a kiss on her forehead, and Lila forced down her need to push her mother away.

"Love you. Call if you need anything," her mother said. Lila listened as her mother gathered her purse, her keys, and then the door latched closed. She counted to three hundred and swung her legs over the side of the bed. Her body felt weighted. She shuffled forward, her arms limp at her sides as she drifted through the apartment.

There was nothing to look for, nothing she felt would point toward the truth of her mother's story, but she went into her mother's bedroom where she flung open the dresser drawers and rifled through their contents. Socks and underwear and the old T-shirts her mother wore to bed. She tossed them at her feet as she dug deeper into the drawers, but there was nothing to find. Her mother's closet door stood ajar, and Lila opened it fully, scanning the hanging clothes, her fingers passing over the fabric, as she looked for . . . what? She swept her gaze over the racks and then toward the floor.

There, tucked against the doorjamb, was a single claw. She searched through the rest of the closet, but the claw was the only remnant of the sculpture she had found. Her mother had either hidden it or trashed it because she didn't want it in the apartment. Or she didn't want Lila to see it. Because it had something to do with whatever her mother was still hiding. Lila smiled to herself. Yes. This was the key. The thing that could connect what had happened to her mother in New Orleans to what was happening with Lila. The reason her mother seemed to be so frightened not only for Lila but *of* her.

Palming the claw, Lila went back to her bedroom, opened her

phone, and typed *Caroline Sawyer New Orleans* into the search engine.

A handful of news stories popped up, and Lila quickly read through the first couple. They were brief and offered very little information other than that her mother had vanished from her backyard and turned up days later at Jazzland. She'd been happily reunited with her family, and the articles indicated that her disappearance was associated with a string of other abductions and murders. Twice, Lila noticed a mention of The Cur. She clicked another article, and a picture of Jazzland loaded, and she stared at it, the voice inside her seeming to come awake once more. Whispering that this place would finally reveal everything her mother was still hiding.

"Jazzland," she said, and heat dropped into her abdomen. Of course. That was where the answer to all this was. She needed to go there, to see for herself if there was something in the abandoned park that would stitch everything together. Something that would explain why Lila had begun seeing and hearing things that weren't there. Why the voice inside her hinted at some larger transfiguration.

At Jazzland, the dark chain between mother and daughter would reveal its final link.

CHAPTER 17

CAROLINE 2004

The next morning, Caroline sat in her car, the slip of paper with an address scrawled across the surface slick between her fingers. She'd been sitting out front for the better part of fifteen minutes but hadn't yet been able to force herself out of the car and up the front walk.

She'd told Daniel she planned to see her father, and she would—later that afternoon. After he'd left, she'd taken a hurried shower, tugging her shirt and jeans over still-damp skin, and then driven into Touro, the houses growing larger, white columns stretching upward and balconies overlooking manicured lawn space as she followed the instructions Lydia Doucette had given her.

Her mouth was dry, but she had not thought to bring any water. She swallowed, staring again at the house where the detective lived. The gray-and-white Victorian was nestled between two oak trees, their shade dappling the white pea-gravel path that led to the front door. A wrought-iron gate with brick columns enclosed the front yard where hostas and immaculately trimmed holly grew. Beneath a turret, a stained-glass window caught the light, winking back ocean water and crimson. This was a home of someone who took care, of someone who noticed small beauties, and still Caroline could not get out of the car.

When twenty minutes had passed, the front door opened, and a small woman stepped out and squinted into the sunlight. Her hair was cropped short but still dark, and she lifted a hand that was wrapped around a white mug.

"If you're not planning on coming inside, you may as well drink the coffee I made you out there in your car before you go. But if you're coming in, I'd appreciate it if you'd get your ass in here. Sit out there much longer and some nosy busybody is likely to call the cops on you."

Caroline flushed and climbed out of the car, fidgeting with her shirt and hair as she hurried up the walk.

"I'm sorry to have kept you waiting, Detective," Caroline said. Lydia nodded, reaching for Caroline's hand, which she shook once, her grip firm and cool, and then handed her the coffee.

"I thought you might have decided against it. Plenty of people who go poking into their pasts realize at the last moment that maybe they don't want to know after all. Wouldn't have hurt my feelings if you'd took off, but since you were still sitting out there, I figured I'd throw you a line. Call me Lydia, please. I haven't been Detective for about three years now."

"Thank you for seeing me. And for the coffee." Caroline shifted her weight from one foot to the other.

"Well, come inside. Shoes off at the door." Lydia led the way, and Caroline followed, wishing she had worn socks that weren't stained.

Inside, the house was heavy with dark wood, but morning light flooded through the entryway so the space still felt bright. Caroline stepped forward, imagining a kind of ancient dust nesting into the deep marrow of her body; the spirits of those who once lived in these rooms watching from their hidden places as she took small steps toward her own past.

"You have a beautiful home," Caroline said, attempting to fill the silence.

"Inherited it when my father passed. Not exactly the kind of place I could afford on a retired detective's salary. And thank you. We'll have a seat in the kitchen. Not as many steps to the coffeepot, and I'm going to need mine warmed up in a minute," Lydia said.

The kitchen was old-fashioned but charming. Another large picture window opened onto overgrown flora—a violent, wild explosion of color disparate from the quiet, soothing white and pale blues of the kitchen.

Lydia jutted her chin toward the small table sitting in front of the window. A coffeepot sat on a trivet, the ceramic stained from frequent use. "Have a seat. You take cream or sugar?"

"No, thank you."

Lydia snorted as she opened the refrigerator. "You enjoy that hot bean water then. Sugar's on the table if you change your mind." She withdrew a small pitcher the color of pale sunshine and poured, her lips moving as she counted to five. She replaced the pitcher and crossed to the table, refilled her mug, and dropped in two spoonfuls of sugar from the bowl. "Now," she said, taking a sip of her coffee, the steam curling around her face, obscuring her eyes, an oracle breathing in her visions and spilling them from behind clenched lips. "You had something to discuss with me."

"Yes, and thank you again for seeing me—"

"Mmm." Lydia waved a hand. "You've already said that."

Again, Caroline's face went hot, and she forced herself to continue. "Right. I think I mentioned on the phone . . . about that time. What happened. I can't remember anything. Not disappearing. Not where I went. Not coming back. I've tried and tried, and there's nothing there. I was hoping—since you were the lead detective—that you could tell me about the investigation. That maybe it would help me remember something other than what I've read or the little my father told me."

Lydia paused, studying Caroline. "What 'little' he told you?"

"Up until a few days ago, I had no idea that anything like this had even happened to me. He and my mom thought it would be better if I forgot."

"Repressed the memory is more like." Lydia shook her head. "Why not ask him to fill in the blanks? Seems to me he owes you that much."

"He's . . ." Caroline searched for the right word. She did not want to say *dying* even if it was accurate. "Ill. I don't want to make things any harder for him."

"I'm sorry." The detective placed her hand over Caroline's. "When my father passed, I spent a long time hating him for having the audacity to get sick. For leaving me. Grief is a strange thing. Has a way of pulling old bones up out of the ground and then not caring how they shock you." She sighed and withdrew her hand. "If you tell me what you do know, I'll fill in the gaps."

Caroline drew in a deep breath. "I know that I disappeared from my own yard. That I was gone for five days and then just showed back up at Jazzland. That there were other girls who were . . . killed around the same time, but that I came back. And they never caught the guy they thought was doing it. The Cur."

"Jesus. That fucking name," Lydia said, setting down her mug so that some of it sloshed out. "The media had a field day with that one. We called him lots of things internally—those of us on the case. The Bayou Butcher. The Swamp Slasher. Stupid stuff like that. But The Cur was the one that stuck—and then some moron accidentally said it in front of a reporter, and well, once you step in shit, it gets all over, you know?"

Caroline nodded. The coffee was too hot and burned going down, but she sipped it anyway and waited.

"You say you read the articles?" asked Lydia. "So you know how the bodies were discovered."

"Yes. As much as I could stomach, anyway. All of those other girls . . . I have the same marks on my inner thighs. Like scratch marks."

"It was after we saw those wounds on the second victim that we started calling him The Cur. What he did to those girls . . . Christ. It was hard to believe a human being could do something like that. The lacerations had more in common with predator bite marks than knife wounds. They looked like something a wolf would leave—or a wild dog that had lost its mind. I stayed in Homicide for another twelve years, but I never saw anything that shook me the way that case did."

Lydia cleared her throat and glanced out the window. There was only the sound of their breath between them for a few moments, and then Lydia blinked rapidly and shook her head.

"And then there was you. We didn't have a lot to go on as far as physical evidence—we combed your yard and the surrounding streets for days, but the crime scene was clean. And you were practically catatonic when they brought you in. Eventually, you knew your name, how old you were, your address, but that was about it. We tried to get what we could out of you, but you wouldn't talk, and whenever we tried, you'd start crying so hard you'd choke. We ended up turning to other sources, and then your part of the case went cold, and there were other bodies to deal with. Other cases. And we all moved on. It happens more often than I'd like to see, but that's the nature of detective work."

"So if I could have remembered anything . . . anything at all, it would have helped you find him? Everything went cold because of me."

"Well, that's overstating things a bit. You *might* have been able to give us a good lead, if you'd remembered where you'd been or who had taken you. But, then again, maybe not. Lots of witnesses are useless, especially kid witnesses, not to mention kids we suspect have experienced trauma. That makes everything trickier. And I didn't quite give the case up, even after you weren't involved in it anymore. I probably would have kept at it even longer if my lieutenant hadn't told me to give it a rest. He said the higher-ups were starting to complain that I was letting my emotions run my work. I was the only woman in Homicide back then, and only one of five Black people on the force at the time. I didn't want anybody thinking I was too soft, so I let it drop. But I couldn't ever really let it go."

Lydia's expression was mild, but her outrage was palpable. Caroline wondered how many times this serious, thoughtful woman had been forced to swallow her instincts because the men she worked with felt threatened.

"Thank you for wanting to do more," said Caroline. "It means a lot." Lydia raised an eyebrow, and curved her mouth into a wry smile.

"I'm not sure it does. But I do have something that might help—and that's why I wanted to see you in person. You'll need to keep this completely quiet, and I mean it. Not a single person. But if you think you can do that, I'll show you some things in the original case file that bothered me. Mind you, I'm not supposed to have any of it, and we won't talk about why I do. This is only between us."

Caroline nodded. "Of course. Thank you."

Lydia pushed back from the table and then returned moments later with a dusty document box. She slid it across the table toward Caroline and sank back into her seat. Caroline's fingers trembled as she flipped open the lid and withdrew the manila folder on top of the stack. Lydia moved closer and pointed to the first document.

"One of the first things we do in any public case is set up a tip line and broadcast the number on all the local news channels. Anyone with any information is encouraged to call. Most are crank calls or dead ends, but we have to cover all our bases to be sure. Sometimes a random detail that someone thinks doesn't matter is the thing that breaks a case wide open.

"When we were looking for The Cur, there were two calls that were of interest to us, or at least, to me. On the very first day, we received a call from a woman who lived in the Garden District. She only gave us her first name, but we traced the call and knew who she was pretty quickly. Old money, serious family. She claimed to know what had happened to the girls, and her story was so outlandish, we dismissed it at first. But the next night, we got a call from another woman from Pines Village. She'd driven a bus for a while and then had some kids and was a homemaker by the time the murders started happening. She had zero connection to the other woman—and believe me, I checked. But their stories lined up almost word for word. It was uncanny.

"Given the similarities, we asked both of them to come in to recount their stories, and there was something about the way they spoke, the look in their eyes . . . they were telling the truth. Even though I never had any hard evidence they didn't know each other, I believed them.

"Both women said there are beasts—they used that specific word, *beasts*—that take girls. Angry girls. The ones who act up. The ones who can't be controlled. And these beasts take the girls away to teach them how to act right. How to behave. And if the girls don't learn, the beasts kill them. The women wanted us to understand that the murdered girls we'd been finding were the defiant ones; the ones who didn't learn how to behave."

Caroline paused, the seconds unwinding, and the words she wanted to say stuck in her throat. If she spoke this thing that shouldn't be into existence, there would be no taking it back. The silent tension stretched on and on, and a chill worked its way up her spine. When she finally opened her mouth, her voice was light. Quiet. But the words felt torn out of her, and an ache formed deep in her chest. "Beasts?" Caroline asked.

Lydia stared back at her. A quiet acknowledgment that they had crossed into the inexplicable. "We couldn't get them to be any more definitive than that. They just kept coming back to that word. And of course, it was easy for most of my fellow detectives to dismiss the women as crazy. Because that's how it sounded. Crazy. But you could tell. They were upset, but not altered. Completely lucid. Still, after some cursory internal review by the team, I was the only one who thought they were worth listening to. Everyone else said it was a hoax."

Under the table, Caroline clenched her hands together until her fingers ached. Sweat clung to her lower back. She cleared her throat and forced herself to speak. "What if . . . what if those women were like me?" Caroline asked, and Lydia sat back in her chair.

"How do you mean?"

"If they were connected to The Cur somehow. Like I was. If maybe they'd repressed whatever happened to them, but some things—like their stories about the beasts—came through."

"I wondered that myself. If they'd both been victimized by the killer. Maybe it happened when they were really little, and they both came up with this 'beasts' story to handle the trauma. But when I asked if they'd ever experienced anything traumatic in their childhoods, they just insisted that there were beasts, and that they took girls. Then everyone else was moving on, and if I wanted to keep up, I had to, as well. But it never sat well with me. Those women and their stories about the beasts. I think about them from time to time. Wonder what they're doing now. If the beasts still haunt them."

Lydia glanced out the window, and Caroline pushed her now-empty mug back and forth in front of her. "I've been hearing and seeing things. A man with the mouth of a dog. Barking and snarling in places where there are no animals. The psychiatrist I went to see told me it was likely something I'd repressed. Something to do with the disappearance."

Lydia narrowed her eyes. "That's interesting." She leaned forward and flipped through the documents in the folder as Caroline watched. Some of them were pictures, and she held her breath as they flickered past in darkened shades of gore.

"There was something else in here, too," Lydia said, and pointed. The document under her finger was brief—two pages of tightly printed text—with a letterhead from Animal Control. Several women had called in reporting that they'd heard packs of what sounded like wild dogs in and around Jazzland. They were concerned for the children. If there was violent wildlife in an area frequented by families and kids, something should be done about it. But Animal Control had gone out to Jazzland and scoured the area. They'd found nothing to substantiate anything the women said about the sounds of wild dogs. Further calls were not responded to. Dismissed as crazy theories from overly sensitive mothers who don't have anything better to do than pack their kids' lunches, worry over every little bump and bruise, and stare out their windows, fretting over any strange car that drives past.

"Jazzland," Caroline whispered.

"What's that?"

"That's where I heard the barking, too. At Jazzland."

Lydia tapped her fingertips along the surface of the table. "There's something to that. Other than that being the location you were found."

"But there hasn't been anything else that's happened there,

right? No other disappearances or abductions have been at Jazzland?"

"No. And the recent abductions have been scattered all over the city. No defined pattern. Just like last time."

"So you think it's him again? The Cur?"

"I can't say for certain, but the similarities are too glaring to ignore. But I'm retired now. I get itchy every now and then, especially with cases like this, but I have to remind myself that I'm older. Slower. Better to leave it to the young and sharp." Lydia closed the folder, pulling it back and resting her elbow on it. She pushed the box toward Caroline. "The documents in there are basically more of the same, but look through whatever you like. Take your time. The beauty of retirement is that I don't have anywhere to rush off to."

Caroline drew the box toward her and pulled out another handful of files. She flipped through the pages, her eyes barely taking in the series of recorded statements, the photos and descriptions of the missing girls. There was too much here. Her brain felt sodden.

Again, she dipped into the box, her hand brushing against a hard plastic edge. She dug her fingers under it, and pulled out a cassette tape that had been hidden under the manila folders.

"I'd forgotten that was in there," Lydia said. "I think I have an old player around here somewhere if you give me a minute."

Caroline turned the tape over in her hands. The label was faded, but she could make out a series of dates. Written beneath them was her father's name. Immediately, her hands began to tremble, her neck and face going hot as she stared at the tape. As much as she wanted to hear what was on it, she also wanted to break it in half. Her father's words forever lost to her fear of what he would reveal.

"Here we are." Lydia reentered the kitchen, a small player in her hand. She set it on the table and then paused as she looked at Caroline. "You sure you want to hear it?"

Caroline squeezed her hands into fists and nodded. She needed to hear it. Even if it tore open every unseen, raw part of her. Lydia took the tape from her and loaded it. There was an aged crackling as the tape began, followed by a shuffling, and then Lydia's voice.

"We're recording now, Mr. Sawyer. I know we've been through everything several times. But if you would please, walk me through it again."

Her father drew in a deep, shuddering breath, and Caroline's heart broke. "We were in the front yard. Caroline was reading under the big tree, and I only remember because the police found the book later. *Anne of Green Gables*. Caroline told me she was hungry, and I'd gone inside to grab the both of us an apple. Some water." Her father paused, and there was the sound of him inhaling and then clearing his throat. Caroline pictured a younger version of her father sitting in a nondescript room, his hands trembling beneath the table as he tried to describe the worst moment of his life. She swallowed, but it did nothing to keep the tears from forming.

"I was inside maybe five, seven minutes. When I came back out, she was gone. I called her name like crazy. Damn near turned the house upside down, but she was nowhere. Jesus. Eleven years old and just swallowed into nothing." A sob choked out of him. "I'm sorry," he said. There was a shuffling on the tape and then a mumbled phrase Caroline couldn't make out.

"Thank you. I'm sorry. This just . . ." He cleared his throat again. "We'd hoped she'd just wandered off, but three hours passed, and I was losing my mind worrying about her. The police came and said they'd be on the lookout. There were those other girls who'd disappeared. The reports about their bodies. I couldn't even listen to the news anymore. And all anyone was talking about was how it was a serial killer who'd taken them, the one they were calling The Cur. All I could think about was how he'd found Caroline. That he'd taken her away from us, and I hadn't been there. I hadn't been there to protect her." The despair and anguish in his voice was so clear. Caroline curled forward, her nails clawing at her jeans as she continued to listen.

"Every day we looked for her. Drove around and around, handing out photocopies of her school picture and asking people if they'd seen her. Five days came and went, and she was still gone. I don't think I slept the entire time. We were eating dinner when you called us. I was the one who answered it, and I could hear Caroline screaming. I don't think we could have moved any faster. There's something about the day you become a parent that burns the sound of your child's voice into you.

"She couldn't stop screaming. Not even when she saw us. She just settled down into a kind of moaning. She had bite marks on her legs." Her father paused again.

"Take your time, Mr. Sawyer," Lydia said. Several moments passed, and Caroline listened as her father wept, her heart hammering in her chest.

"She still won't talk about it. We figured she was in shock while we were in the hospital. We asked her what had happened, where she'd been, but she only stared past us like she was looking at another world. And the nurses were so good to her, you know? Got her cleaned up and medicated so she would sleep and let us stay beside her the entire time. And they had to . . . they had to be sure. That nothing else had happened to her. She's just a little girl, but they told us they had to be sure nothing had . . . Jesus. The tests came back negative, and I thanked God then. Because the thought of anyone doing that to her . . . hurting my girl like *that*. I would have killed the son of a bitch with my bare hands."

Caroline reached forward and hit the Stop button. She did not want to hear any more of her father's agony. She'd come here to learn what she could about her disappearance, and she had. She could listen to the rest of the tape, but she did not think it would be the key that would unlock her own memory.

"Thank you for talking with me. For letting me see all this. I just can't . . ."

"I know. You don't have to explain anything." The two women stood, and Lydia stepped around the table as they left the kitchen. "I admit I wanted to see if there was anything you'd remembered since then. Anything that might shed more light on what happened. There's a strong detective on the case for the girls who have recently gone missing. If it's okay with you, I'll pass on what you said about the dogs to her. You never know. It might be of some help."

"Sure," Caroline said, and then Lydia walked her to the door and bid her farewell. Stepping back into the sunshine, Caroline paused. Jazzland. There were other women who'd heard the same sounds she had; other women who'd been dismissed and told what they heard wasn't real. She needed to go back, to see if the sounds would return, if the snarls and howls were only in her mind, if the medication pumping through her would mask the hallucination.

Yes. She would go back.

CHAPTER 18

CAROLINE 2004

On the morning Caroline was due to return to the Kellums', she woke in an empty bed. Daniel had risen early and left without disturbing her. She stared at the wall, trying to push aside the thought that he had never done this before, never left without kissing her good-bye, without telling her he loved her. He was frustrated, had told her more than a few times in the days leading up to this morning that he thought she should take more time off. But she needed the money, and he had not mentioned anything about Gemma or the sculpture. She did not want to remind him, was fearful Gemma had not liked it, and he was trying to decide how to tell her in the gentlest way possible. Maybe it wasn't as good as she thought. It had been so long since she'd finished a sculpture. Her anxieties smothered any confidence she'd ever had.

She'd gotten another call from Helping Hands; another reminder of her overdue bill, and they agreed to wait a week, but they had warned her they were making a singular exception. This could not happen again.

Without Daniel, she rose and showered and dressed and swallowed the pills Dr. Walters had prescribed. If she didn't think about what she was doing, she could almost vanish inside the practiced movements of driving to the Kellums', but when she cut her engine, a small flutter of panic danced along her spine, and she had to force herself out of the car.

She'd expected Beth to be waiting for her outside as she had in the past, but the door was closed and Beth was nowhere to be seen. Vivian answered the door and led Caroline back to the kitchen.

"She's upstairs. Been refusing to come out of her room, but she'll come out now that you're here. She's not the only one who's missed you. I'm glad you're back," she said as she poured coffee into a travel mug. "I'm sorry for her behavior. She's been refusing to take her medication. Dr. Bryson says she'll understand why she needs it eventually, but I just don't know. It's like nothing makes her happy anymore." Vivian sighed as she snapped the lid onto her mug and set it next to her purse.

A flood of heat passed over Caroline. Jazzland. Beth had wanted to go. Had complained that her mother wouldn't take her. Caroline could offer to do it. A special treat after being gone for so long. And then Caroline could go inside. See if she felt anything.

"I feel terrible that I haven't been here," Caroline said, the idea taking root, and she forced herself to slow down, forced the need out of her voice. "I'd love to make it up to her somehow. Do something fun."

Vivian had turned away, was pawing through her purse, already distracted, already placing herself in a place that was not the stifling quiet of the house. "Mmm. She would like that, I'm sure."

"Maybe Jazzland? She mentioned once that she'd always wanted to go."

"Jazzland. Good grief, that child has been going on and on about that place for the longest time. I *detest* roller coasters. Beth will be delighted, and maybe it'll snap her out of this funk. I never know which version of her I'm going to get. I can arrange getting the tickets. Would this Friday work?"

"That's very kind, but I can—"

"Don't be silly. Just so long as I'm not the one who has to take her." Vivian waved her hand. Caroline was relieved. She'd anticipated Vivian shooting the idea down immediately, but to have her support Caroline taking Beth to Jazzland and offering to pay was beyond what she could have hoped for.

Vivian walked to the stairs and called up. "Beth, Miss Caroline is here. And she has something to tell you."

Beth came tumbling down the stairs and squealed as she leapt into Caroline's arms in the kind of bear hug that normally only younger girls gave. "You're back! Thank God."

Caroline smiled down at her, and for the first time since her father had told her about her own disappearance, she felt a genuine sense of warmth. "What do you think about going to Jazzland on Friday?"

"No freaking way," Beth said, clapping her hands to her mouth. "Are you serious?" Beth darted her eyes back and forth between Caroline and Vivian. Vivian lifted her eyebrows but said nothing. If her daughter's perky demeanor was a surprise to her, she kept it to herself.

"So serious," Caroline said.

"Yes! This is going to be so excellent!" Beth said, and squeezed Caroline again.

Vivian gathered her keys and purse. "You two have fun today. And Beth, try to maybe get in the shower at some point. I can smell you from here."

Beth rolled her eyes as soon as her mother's back was turned, and Vivian waved a hand over her shoulder as she left.

The morning passed easily—Beth absorbed in her work and quiet—and Caroline sank into the comfort of her repeated movements, but as their session wore on, Beth moved more and more slowly, her eyes glazing over as she passed her brush over the canvas.

"You okay?" Caroline said as they cleaned up. A blotch of ochre paint was smeared under Beth's right eye, and Caroline reached out and dabbed at it with a paper towel.

"I'm fine," Beth snapped, turning away from Caroline's touch, and Caroline stiffened. Less than two hours before, Beth had hugged her, had seemed excited to have Caroline back. But now, she'd crumpled into herself, her face turned away and hidden behind a veil of stringy hair.

Moody. But I can't blame her. Not after everything that happened with that boy, Caroline told herself as she packed her bag. Beth stood at the sink, washing the same brush again and again. She wondered if she shouldn't leave Beth alone, but Vivian had told her a few days before her return that she didn't need to wait on her after the lesson ended anymore. She'd updated the security system. Beth would be safe. Still, Caroline hesitated, waiting for Beth to turn, waiting for her to say good-bye, but Beth's gaze was all dim paleness and milk. She kept her eyes trained on the window into the backyard, her mouth fallen slightly open, a thin line of spit stretching between her lips. Maybe she *had* taken her medication today.

"See you tomorrow," Caroline said, and Beth turned then, her eyes still focused on something that existed beyond. In the ether.

"Sorry. Just tired. I'm excited for Friday," Beth said, but her voice was atonal. A rehearsed series of words offered up to placate. The contrast left Caroline feeling unsettled, but she pushed the feeling away.

Caroline let herself out, punching in the alarm code Vivian

had texted her. If Beth tried to leave, or if anyone tried to enter the house, Vivian would be alerted, and the police would be on their way with the push of a single button. All very high-tech. Illusory security to help Vivian forget the faces of the missing girls, to delude herself into believing it would not happen there, not to her daughter.

She dropped by Helping Hands, but her father was sleeping heavily, the frailty of his body outlined by the sheet placed over him, and she did not think she could sit with him, watching the portions of him labor through the final acts of living. The receptionist stopped her on the way out, asking if Caroline possibly had her payment today? She knew they'd agreed to give her a week, but she'd be happy to take care of it if Caroline did happen to have her payment today, and Caroline had to shake her head. No, she didn't have it. The receptionist had pressed her lips together in a tight smile, had clacked away at her computer and mentioned someone would be following up with Caroline the following day. "As a convenience," she said, and it took everything in Caroline not to cry.

She drove home, determined to ask Daniel about the sculpture. If Helping Hands decided it was best for her to find another facility for her father, she feared he would not survive the move, and she would never be able to forgive herself. Vivian would pay her at the end of the week, but it wouldn't be nearly enough to cover all of her father's outstanding fees. But if Gemma bought the sculpture, Caroline could make it work, negotiate a payment plan, charm them somehow. She had to sell it. She had to. She repeated this to herself as she went up the front walk and let herself inside.

Daniel sat in the living room, his laptop open on his lap and a beer on the coffee table in front of him. He looked back at her as she came in, but he did not close his laptop. Still angry, then.

"How'd it go?"

She turned, slowly setting down her bag and removing her shoes with unnecessary care in order to buy a few moments for strategizing. She needed to tread carefully with Daniel. First, she had to convince her pissed-off fiancé to lobby his boss about her sculpture when he clearly didn't want to push the issue. And second, and equally importantly, she had to introduce the trip to Jazzland in a way that would help him understand why she needed to go there again, needed to be in that place even though he wouldn't like the idea of it. She had not told him she'd spoken with Lydia, had kept this secret from him, and she felt the need to keep it tucked away, to keep him from understanding her real reason for wanting to go to Jazzland.

"It was good. Beth was happy to see me."

"Everything good for you? All normal?"

"Everything was fine. Totally standard day." She took a deep breath. "Vivian even asked if I'd be interested in taking Beth to do something fun. As a welcome back." If he knew it was Caroline who'd suggested the trip to Jazzland, the rest of the night would be a fight she did not want to have.

"Something fun? That doesn't exactly sound like Vivian."

"I don't know. Maybe she's feeling guilty about keeping Beth inside all the time."

"Where to?"

Caroline forced herself to remain still, to look at Daniel directly, so he had no reason to imagine she was hiding anything. "Jazzland. Beth's always wanted to go."

"Caroline—"

"It's for work. I can't spend the rest of my life avoiding a place just because someone recommended it. I'm on my medication. It'll be fine."

"It's barely been a week, and you're already heading back to the place your *doctor* told you not to go to. How am I not supposed to be concerned about that? It's bad enough that you're already back at work, and now, you want to go to Jazzland?"

"I need the money, Daniel. And it's for *work*. Everything will be okay. It won't be like before," she said, and he went quiet, turning away to stare out the window. She opened the refrigerator, stared at the beer her medication would not allow her to have, and then closed it and leaned her forehead against it. Fuck it. She might as well say all of it. "Have you talked to Gemma about the sculpture?"

"The sculpture?"

"Yes, the sculpture. *My* sculpture. The one I asked you to show Gemma. The one you took pictures of."

"You still want to sell it then," he said.

"It's not a 'want to' kind of situation. Had I mentioned that I changed my mind?" Caroline let a moment pass and then another, waiting on Daniel to fill in what she needed to hear. All he had to do was tell her yes, he'd spoken to Gemma; yes, he hadn't ignored what Caroline had asked of him. Open his goddamned mouth and tell her he supported her.

Instead, Daniel said nothing, and another piece of her died inside his silence.

"Have you talked to her?"

"I did, but she hasn't given me a definitive answer yet. She was optimistic though. Said she really loved it, but she wasn't sure if she could find the right spot for it, so that's why I wanted to be sure you were still wanting to sell. These things can take a while, you know? Buyers can be fickle. But she really liked it. Said it was edgy."

Relief dropped over her, making her legs weak. "Do you think you could ask her again? Maybe mention that I need to sell it quickly?"

He smiled up at her. "Of course, Linny. No problem. I know how important this is for you."

They slept, their skins barely touching, the vapor of her agitation settling thick in the room. In the morning, she rose without him and then left him sleeping. She swallowed her pill as she drove toward the Kellums', her windows rolled down so she could taste the late bloom of sweet olive. The smell was cloying, and her throat felt thick, nausea threatening to overtake her, so she rolled up the window.

Daniel would talk to Gemma today. He understood. He knew she needed him to do it. And on Friday, she would be back in Jazzland, listening and watching for anything that would lead her back to the girl who'd vanished and forgotten where it was she'd gone. Everything would be fine. She told herself this as she parked, as she started up the walk to the Kellum house, as Vivian called up for Beth, and then bid them both good-bye.

After her mother left, Beth remained still, her hands limp at her sides, her shoulders curved so she seemed to be in the slow act of folding into herself. Caroline waited for the girl to move, to go and gather her paints, her canvas, their pattern so established Caroline had never questioned it, but Beth only stood, her gaze fixed on some distant point only she could see.

"You ready?" Caroline said, but Beth offered no response. "Go and get your stuff, okay?" Beth turned toward Caroline as if seeing her for the first time.

"I will. Jesus," she said, and rolled her eyes. Caroline noted how worn-down Beth looked. Sallow skin, limp hair, dark circles under her eyes. Maybe she was taking her medication more frequently, and it was having some negative side effects? She trudged back up the stairs, and Caroline knew from her pace that it would be a while before she saw Beth again.

Standing in the center of the kitchen, the house yawning silent around her, she rubbed her hands over her arms, trying to warm herself against the chill that had threaded through her blood. She and Beth would paint for an hour or two, Vivian would come home, and Caroline could leave. She was freaking herself out for no reason. Dr. Walters had given her medication to ensure she would never see things like that again. She had no reason to be afraid. Her uneasiness was related only to Beth's bad mood, to the deep quiet of the house. The nausea she still felt wasn't helping.

This room was real. Beth was real and safe in the house with her. Everything was fine. The likelihood of anything bad happening was slim. Those were real things.

Above her, Caroline heard a loud thump followed by the sound of laughter. She went to the stairs, placed her foot on the first riser. "Beth?" she shouted. A scuffling sound followed by more laughter. "Beth, you're supposed to be getting your stuff."

She placed her foot on the next stair, arched her body toward the second story, and waited for the girl to answer. For her to call down that she was sorry; she'd be down in just a minute. Beth didn't call down, the house fell silent again, and Caroline wondered if it was possible to drown in so much quiet.

She paused, her hand gripping the railing. If she went up the stairs, if she walked down the hallway with its empty hooks where photographs of Beth's dead father should be and stood and looked into Beth's room at the end of the hallway only to find it empty, she was afraid the final piece of her that was still intact would crumble under the anxiety pushing against her skin.

From the hallway, a voice lilted upward. Clear and sweet. Caroline caught at snatches of the words as the song floated down to her from the upstairs hallway. Singing. Beth was singing. That was all.

Caroline sank onto the bottom stair and tried to still her shaking hands. Then she left the stairs, left the sound of Beth's voice, and went back to the kitchen and paused. The basement door stood ajar, but that was impossible. She'd just been in the kitchen, had been gone only a few moments. The door had been closed. She knew it had, but now it stood open, and she walked quietly to it and placed her hand on the doorknob. Down below, the light had been switched on, and something scritched across the floor.

Turning back toward the stairs, she listened as Beth's voice shifted through the notes of her song. It sounded like Coldplay. Beth wasn't downstairs in the basement, but again, something shifted its body over the floor, and Caroline imagined Dr. Walters telling her it was only an animal. That she shouldn't allow herself to become worked up. Hysterical. Probably a squirrel or a possum had found its way inside, and either Vivian or Beth had left the light on the last time they were down there. All easy to explain. All plausible. But she couldn't bring herself to descend the stairs.

"This is stupid," she said, took a breath, and set her foot on the first step, making sure she made lots of noise as she went down, hoping it would frighten away whatever had worked its way into the house. When she reached the bottom, she swept her gaze from left to right, taking in the stacked boxes, the bean-bag chair and blanket where Beth read, but whatever had been making noise was gone now.

"See, Caroline? Nothing here," she said, and reached for the light, but when it turned off, she saw it. A dark form hunched in the corner, shoulders curved forward as if it could hide itself, as if she would not see it if it kept very, very still. Her breath caught in her throat, and she squinted into the gloom. It was nothing. A shadow.

She flipped the light back on, and the form vanished, the corner only a corner. Her heart hammering, she switched the light off once more, and the shadow reappeared, but it was closer, and in the darkness, she thought she saw a mouth open, long teeth reflecting back the light pouring from the top of the stairs.

Again, she flooded the room with light, but there was nothing there. Nothing hiding itself in the corner. Nothing waiting for her to turn her back. She turned away and scrambled up the stairs, leaving the light on but slamming the door closed behind her.

Her hands would not stop shaking, and she took deep breaths. She had not seen anything in the basement. She'd only imagined it, had imagined the man in the dark coat, the man with the mouth of a dog, was crouching in the corner, waiting for her to come to him. Waiting for her to notice that he'd never left her. It was a trick of the light. That was all.

She filled a glass with water, drained it, and then filled it again. Her stomach seized, and she breathed through her nose. From upstairs, Beth's voice lifted in a long, quavering note, and then fell again. Caroline had no desire to tell her to hurry anymore. She was afraid if she tried to speak, she would not be able to keep herself from being sick.

She pressed the glass against her forehead, but the coolness had not lingered. There was no relief in it. She shifted her weight. Closed her eyes. Let the breath in her lungs settle and then pulled air into her in a long, slow rush, and from behind her came the gentle sound of Beth on the stairs, the cool touch of her fingers closing around Caroline's wrist.

"You're ready to see it now. What I wanted to show you. The secret. Do you remember? I told you about it before, but you weren't ready." Beth's voice fell over Caroline in a harsh, ragged whisper. She stepped ahead, her fingers still digging into Caroline's wrist as she pulled her forward. The girl's touch, the sound of her voice, made Caroline's skin crawl.

"We need to get started—"

"You need to see it. The secret," Beth said, and tugged Caroline's arm, hauling her forward until they stood at the entrance to the family room. The room was large and a fireplace with a cedar mantel dominated the far wall. Some designer's final touch. Refined and rustic at the same time. Ivory couches and a pale shag rug in the center of the room attempted to draw light into the space. They failed. There was one window, but it faced the back of the house with its large trees and shaded yard, so the room stayed dark.

Above the mantel, pictures of Beth covered the wall. These were the only pictures Caroline had ever seen in the house. One of Beth as a baby, her mouth open in a gummed smile as she stared directly into the camera. A close-up of chubby hands wrapped around her mother's fingers, obscuring her gold wedding band.

"There. See?" Beth pointed at the line of photos, directing Caroline's gaze to the final piece hanging on the wall. It wasn't a photo at all, but a painting Beth had done. Caroline was surprised to see it hanging there. Beth had claimed to hate it. It was dull—a barren field done up in drab watercolor. Caroline tightened her grip on the glass—aware only then that she was still carrying it—and stepped closer to the painting. Her skin tingled, and the room dropped away as she stared into the swirled paint, the interior world seeming to shift and come apart.

Somewhere in the room, something breathed out a ragged snarl.

Caroline shrieked and jerked away from the painting, her legs moving to put distance between it and her body. As she moved, she bumped against an end table. Her hand closed involuntarily around the thin glass, and it broke from the pressure, the pieces clattering to the floor.

Beth didn't move to help Caroline, didn't jump forward to help her collect the broken pieces. The girl stood with her hands at her sides. "You're bleeding."

She glanced down at the blood seeping down her wrist. She must have cut it when the glass broke, but she stared back at Beth as if she'd been the one to do it.

"Did you see it?" Beth asked. Caroline opened her mouth and then closed it, her fear suddenly roaring through her, a behemoth awakened.

"I knew you would be able to." Beth stepped forward, and Caroline shrank backward. The girl paused, cocked her head.

"It's okay. You can tell me. It'll be our little secret. It's fun to have secrets. Isn't it, Miss Caroline?" The girl took another step forward. "What did you see? In the painting?"

"Nothing."

Beth frowned. "But I painted it. It's not nothing."

"That's not what I meant," Caroline began, but Beth drew closer, standing beside Caroline so their arms brushed against each other. The girl's skin was fever warm.

"What did you mean?"

The room seemed to shimmer, the periphery of Caroline's vision going hazy and blinking out.

"I don't know."

"How can you not know what's right in front of you?" Beth's hand pulled at her, tugged her forward until she was again inches from the painting.

"Do you see it?" Beth asked, her voice smooth and even. She was just a little girl. They were looking at a painting. That was all.

Beth tapped the canvas. Her finger lingered on a spot where long brushstrokes traced upward. A spot where grass grew tall and bent in the wind.

"I hid it here. For you." Beth removed her finger. "Do you see it now?"

Caroline looked. Her heart aching in her chest, the painting blurring, doubling and then tripling, while the grass seemed to undulate before some unseen wind. And then, she saw.

Hidden in the grass was what appeared to be a face. An outline of pointed teeth, the deep hollow where the eyes should be, but there were no eyes. A dark creature in the grass.

"I've always seen it. Always. Close my eyes at night and I see it standing there with its mouth open. Panting. Dr. Bryson says it's just a dream, but I know better," Beth said, her voice distorted, and Caroline blinked down at the girl who stared into the painting.

She scrunched her eyes tight, and tilted her head. "A beast just for me. And for you. I knew you would like it. It's a trick. Like your sculptures. How they're made of other things."

"What did you say?" Caroline could not help but absorb the word. *Beast.*

Beth pulled the bottom hem of her shirt up and pressed it against Caroline's hand. Scarlet blossomed against the pale fabric. The girl darted her tongue over her lips. The movement looked violent. Feral. "Be careful. There could be small pieces. I'll get the broom," Beth said, and walked slowly out of the room. Again, Caroline looked at the painting, but she could no longer see the face. Only long blades of grass.

When Beth came back, she didn't speak but busied herself with the broken glass. With careful strokes, she swept the floor, lifted the rug at the corners and swept beneath it as well, and then bent to collect the bits she'd found with the dustpan.

"Are you sick?" Beth looked up at Caroline from the floor. All concern. All compassion. Caroline pressed her fingers against her temples. Everything in the room had gone strange; she couldn't help but feel there was some peculiarity, some vileness or rot still carefully hidden away behind the smile she looked down on now.

"No. Not sick," she said. Her mouth tasted foul.

"Maybe some fresh air? That's what Mom always says whenever she isn't feeling well. That she needs some fresh air."

Or maybe she just wants to get away from you.

No. Caroline couldn't think that. If she let herself slip back into the old fear, everything would start over. After the seizure, the doctor and his information on dissociative periods, Caroline had assumed she'd been the one to drive back to Metairie to retrieve the dead dog she'd used for the second sculpture. But now, looking down at Beth, she needed to ask. "Beth . . . did you . . . that dog. The day you found the dog. Did you put it in my car? I won't be mad if you did."

"Ew. No way. Picking it up would have been too gross," she said, but her intonations were strange. Like a poorly rehearsed version of what she was supposed to say.

Caroline nodded her head, and Beth shrugged and carried the broom and dustpan out of the room.

Caroline's chest ached. She needed out of this room with its dark corners, but her legs wouldn't move, and she looked at the window. Since she'd come into the room, the gloom had grown, the light changing from the brightness of morning to the filtered gold of afternoon.

How much time had she lost? Frozen in front of a painting while Beth whispered in her ear about hidden faces. Finally, she moved, her legs shaky as she looked closer at the clock on the mantle. Noon. Three hours. She'd lost three hours.

Her knees buckled, and she caught herself, her fingers gripping the back of a chair. *Nothing happened, nothing happened.* If she told herself this enough, she could believe it. It had been her medication. She was still adjusting. Or Dr. Walters had messed up and given her the wrong dosage. An easy fix. Simple.

From the kitchen, Beth laughed. The sound was like ground glass against raw skin, and Caroline wanted to close her eyes and sleep forever.

The clock told her Vivian would be home in less than an hour. She could still maintain that she'd had a normal day. Everything shipshape and in line. The painting for today in progress. No strange blanks in the day, no broken glass or dried blood to explain away. Her medication could be adjusted before Friday's big trip to Jazzland, and no one needed to know any differently.

And that was exactly what happened. When Vivian pulled into the driveway, Beth was finishing her painting and hopped up to kiss her mother as she breezed into the kitchen.

"Good day today?" she asked, and Beth nodded enthusiastically. The strange mood she'd been in earlier had lifted, but Caroline had not been able to keep herself from wanting to stay as far away from Beth as possible.

"Glad to hear it. See you tomorrow, Caroline?" Vivian said as Caroline gathered her things.

"You got it." She turned to Beth, who held out her arms for a hug. "See you later," she said as she forced herself to embrace the girl. Beth drew her down, her mouth pressing to Caroline's ear.

"I'm glad you're good at keeping secrets. He told me you would be," she whispered, and released Caroline. She hurried down the hall, convinced if she turned back to look at Beth, she would turn to salt.

Caroline drove home and called Dr. Walters's office and left a message. What she'd seen was a shadow, but the lost time was more problematic. She thought maybe the dose was too strong. She didn't want to let him make any more decisions for her, but he was the one with the medical degree and the power to prescribe medication. She didn't have a choice.

In the fluorescent light of the bathroom, she undressed slowly, her fingers pressing indentations into the soft parts of her flesh, and how easy, how simple for something to slip inside. How breakable and tender. It made her shiver, and she pulled a T-shirt over her head. Beside her on the counter, her phone rang. Helping Hands. Again. As if she had forgotten the duty she carried with her whole body, how it had invaded her lungs, the wet beat of her heart, the stillness of her bones mapping out the small length of her. That shrill reminder of her failure echoing back as the front door slammed, and Daniel entered.

"Caroline?" he called, and she left the phone behind.

"Did you talk to her?"

"What?" He paused in the doorway, leaning against the frame.

"Gemma. The sculpture. You said you would mention it to her again."

"She's still busy, but she's interested. Said she should have an answer soon."

"How soon?"

Daniel sighed. "I don't know, Linny. There's protocol to things like this. Proper channels. Calm down."

She leaned forward and buried her head in her hands. "Don't tell me to calm down, Daniel. I don't have time for proper channels." Her voice broke, and Daniel was beside her, his hand rubbing her back.

"I'm doing everything I can. I promise. I'll try again tomorrow. Okay?"

She nodded. "Okay."

She thought she would cry, but she didn't, and her tongue tasted of salt and bitterness.

CHAPTER 19

LILA 2019

Jazzland. That single word burned into her, and Lila tapped her fingers against the edge of her mother's neatly made bed.

Her mother's laptop was on her nightstand, and Lila knew Caroline had the autofill function turned on, knew if she took the laptop and booked a plane ticket to New Orleans, she would be able to press a single button and let the computer fill in the credit card information. She moved quickly, swallowing back her nervousness and fear. She'd flown on her own before. There was nothing to be frightened of. She knew what to do, and she let the computer work its magic.

It only took thirty minutes for her to book the ticket and print her boarding pass, to grab her passport from the shoebox where her mother kept important documents. Even though she'd made the trip to New Orleans on her own five times now, she knew how the attendants and boarding agents tended to look at anyone younger than eighteen. It was possible they would be suspicious even though she'd seen plenty of kids even younger than her traveling alone.

She didn't bother with a bag but shoved her passport into her purse. Still using her mother's autofilled credit card, she scheduled a car to pick her up and take her to the airport. She waited by the door, her stomach fluttering with nerves. It shouldn't have been that easy, but it was, and she locked the door behind her when she went.

"You heading to the airport by yourself?" The driver waiting for Lila in the parking lot had a pink, round face. Smooth and hairless with pale eyebrows and pale eyes like the squirming pile of baby mice Lila had found under her bathroom sink once. The driver smiled at her in the rearview with rubbery lips slicked in a baby doll–colored lipstick that matched her skin, and Lila knew the woman was waiting for Lila to respond.

Instead, she lifted her shoulders and grunted. The woman's smile spread even wider, and she glanced away, clearly uncomfortable with this girl in her charge who wouldn't smile. Lila didn't care.

"You just seem a little young to be going to the airport is all. I'm Mary, by the way," the woman said.

"I do this all the time."

"Okay." Mary guided the car out of the lot but kept looking at Lila in the rearview mirror. "You're not taking any bags with you? Where you heading?"

Lila pressed her forehead to the window, her skin leaving a thin, oiled smear. "That's none of your fucking business. And you have lipstick on your teeth."

Mary snapped her gaze back to the road, and Lila could have wept for the quiet. Nausea rose up over her in a wave, and she swallowed against the heat building in her belly and closed her eyes. It didn't make her feel any better, so she let them drift open.

The car slowed as it approached a turn, and Lila looked out into the verdant sprawl of trees, trying to fixate on anything that would make the world feel like it was resting still instead of heaving beneath her feet.

Beside them, another car slowed, and the man driving turned his head, and he smiled and smiled, and the smile was only for Lila, didn't she see how he was smiling only for her? How there were too many teeth for his mouth, how they curved downward into fangs, and that was a smile just for Lila, and his mouth opened farther. Lila's stomach lurched, and she forced herself to look away, to breathe deeply through her nose, and when she looked back, the man was gone.

Mary didn't say another word throughout the entire trip, and when she let Lila out at the airport, she sped off, the car swerving back into traffic and then disappearing. Lila checked in and then moved through security without anyone giving her a second glance, and then she boarded, just another face, another number to be checked, and found her seat.

Lila chewed at her lower lip, pulled at a loose bit of skin until it tore away, the sudden sting feeling more pleasant than painful, the taste of blood on her tongue. The plane rumbled beneath her like a great animal, and then they were moving fast, her stomach dropping as they lifted into the air, and she bent into herself, suddenly aware of how alone she was.

Closing her eyes, she focused on the sound of the plane's engine and the mild hum of conversations around her. Her phone was in her purse, stowed underneath the seat in front of her, but she couldn't bring herself to move to retrieve it. Right now, she just wanted music; a set of headphones she could plug in her ears and drown out her thoughts—thick and heavy and swirling with *bad* things and a heavy bass line. Something as loud and screechy and angry as the feelings coming awake inside her now.

That awful red thing in her belly clenched again, and she dug her fist into the soft flesh of her abdomen. Instead of standing up and screaming, Lila clenched her teeth hard enough for her jaw to hurt and waited for the flight to be over. If she counted her breaths, maybe she wouldn't explode. She couldn't think about her mom or dad or Macie. Jazzland was the only thing, and she focused on it, but the anger was still there, a deep hurt she couldn't forget.

When they finally landed, Lila waited until the plane was practically empty before she stood. She didn't want to have to fight with the idiots who leapt up immediately to pull their bags from the overhead compartments and then stood there, staring at each other like cows. The attendants smiled as she exited, and her legs felt weak as she took the ramp into the terminal. She licked her lips. The air here tasted of salt. Of decay.

For a long time, she wandered through the terminal, unsure of exactly what she was supposed to do next. She had not had the forethought to schedule a second pickup for when she landed. *Stupid.* There was the twenty dollars in her purse—leftover birthday money—but she didn't think it was enough to get her anywhere close to Jazzland. It would likely barely get her out of the airport.

She'd passed the same security guard at least three times, and on the fourth pass, he kept his gaze trained on her, his hand moving for the walkie-talkie at his hip. She sped up, pushed her body toward one of the exits, the large panes of glass winking in the sunlight, and then she was out, people streaming around her, and the air was too hot, too thick, and she was going to choke. She couldn't breathe. She couldn't.

Why had she thought she could do this? Fly all the way to New Orleans by herself, without telling anyone, with barely any money? Her hands fumbled at her purse, and she pulled out her phone. Her mother wouldn't have gotten home yet, but there were text messages from her. Checking in. Making sure she was okay.

She glanced over her shoulder, searching for the security guard, wondering if she could go back inside. The automatic doors slid open and shut, the faces beyond blurred and feature-less except for one, and she knew him, knew now how his mouth would open, the teeth extending, and she *knew* him, but it didn't keep her from being afraid.

She opened her phone and dialed, listened as it rang four, then five times. He wasn't going to answer. She was in New Orleans, and he wasn't going to answer. On the seventh ring, the call connected.

"Lila?"

"It's me, Dad," she said, and darted another glance through the automatic doors, but the man was gone.

"Shouldn't you be in school? Why is it so loud there? Are you okay?"

"I'm in New Orleans. At the airport."

"You're . . . what?" He spat out the last word, his confusion dissolving quickly into irritation.

"At the airport." A car horn blared and then another, and Lila jumped.

"What the hell are you doing at the airport? Is your mom with you?"

"No." She paused, weighing out her next words carefully. "I wanted to see you."

"Where in the airport are you? I'm coming to get you."

She looked up. "Outside. By the West Sky Bridge."

"Do not go anywhere. You hear me? I'm leaving now. It'll take me about twenty minutes to get there. Nowhere. Understand?"

"Okay," she said, and hung up the phone, determined she would not turn around again to see if the man had returned. To see the opening of that dark, terrible mouth.

But she was here. Jazzland and all its secrets were close enough to touch. As she waited—the damp heat settling thick over her skin—her body sagged under a weariness she'd come to understand. She'd come all this way, but there still felt like such a long way to go.

CHAPTER 20

CAROLINE 2004

In the morning, Caroline waited for Daniel to leave, stood beside the window, the blinds cracked open so she could watch as his car pulled away. The queasiness she'd felt the day before was back, and she breathed deeply, waiting for it to pass. She hadn't eaten the night before, but the thought of food, of the physical, primal act of chewing, of swallowing, made her ill.

She'd woken in the night from a dream of her father, his body covered with a thin, piss-soaked sheet as he moaned and thrashed on a cot that was too small for him. She'd not been able to fall back asleep. Instead, she'd risen and wandered from room to room, unable to shake the vision of him, broken and helpless because of her. She'd made the decision then that she would call Gemma herself and explain. Daniel wouldn't like it, but she couldn't wait any longer.

She'd already put the number for the gallery into her phone, and she pressed Send the moment she could no longer see his taillights. "Gemma Gardner, please. This is Caroline Sawyer," she told the smooth-voiced receptionist who answered, and she knotted a fist against her sternum.

"Just a moment," the receptionist said, and then the line clicked and rang twice. Caroline went into the kitchen and leaned over the sink, her stomach clenching tight, tight, tight, her nerves hot and liquid and sliding through her, and her mouth watered. She should hang up, she should not be doing this, and she gagged once, but the line connected, Gemma's voice confused but bright on the other end, and Caroline swallowed hard.

"Caroline? Is Daniel okay?"

"Everything's fine. I was actually hoping I could talk to you for a moment. If you have time." Caroline forced the words, and they fell from her lips like dead things caught in the act of a resurrection.

"Of course. What can I do for you?"

"I was wondering what you thought of the sculpture?"

There was a pause on the other line, a shuffling of papers. Again, the queasiness rose up, viscous in her throat.

"You'll have to remind me. It's just that I see so many throughout the day. What sculpture is it?"

Her heart ached through its beats, and she forced herself to breathe. "My sculpture. The one of the woman holding a dog's head. Daniel showed it to you, and you told him you were interested?"

"A sculpture of yours? I'm so sorry, Caroline, but I'm afraid he never showed me anything."

"Oh. I see." Around her, the room blurred and came back into focus. Everything seemed set in stark relief, the edges of the curtains, the furniture too sharp; her anger and grief at Daniel's betrayal cutting through the haze of the morning sunlight.

"That doesn't mean I wouldn't be interested in seeing it though. I know Daniel works for me, but you've created quite a bit of buzz about yourself, too. You have pictures?"

"I do," Caroline said, and pressed a fist against the counter-top so she would not scream.

"Send them now. I'll take a look and call you back. This after-noon is crazy, but I have some time this morning. I can get back to you in a little bit."

"Sure."

"Perfect. Chat soon."

"Bye." Caroline hung up the phone and pulled up the pho-tos she and Daniel had taken together, the colors bleeding into each other as she blinked away her tears. Daniel had not shown Gemma the sculpture, had blatantly lied to her and pretended to care. Had he hated it so much he thought he could get by with ly-ing about it? With putting Caroline off again and again until her shame forced her to let it drop? Another thought floated to the surface, but she pushed it off. She couldn't think that; couldn't imagine a world where Daniel had not shared the sculpture be-cause he was jealous. Because he didn't want Caroline to succeed. Or, even worse, that he did not want her to succeed before he did. The way he teased her about being "Mr. Caroline," about how her shine spilled over onto him, and he would have to be satisfied with the scraps; was that how he really felt? Had he gotten so far away from her, so far into this new world he was so concerned with fitting into, that he could have done something like that?

She sent the pictures to Gemma, and then leaned down, placed her head against the counter, and wept, the tears coming hot and fast, her heaving breaths too big for the world, her hurt spilling out of her.

And then her phone rang. Gemma. She stood, swiping at her face and clearing her throat, and answered.

Gemma began talking immediately. "Holy shit, Caroline. Of course I want the sculpture. It's . . . incandescent. Dark and lovely and surreal, and I fucking want it. Immediately. My only question is when will you have more? Because I want those, too."

Caroline laughed then—a high, clear note—and sank to the floor, the phone still pressed to her ear. "Thank you. You have no idea—"

"If you bring it down today, I can pay you immediately. I want it up as soon as possible. If someone buys it for more, I'll reimburse after the sale. But I want it now, and cash always greases the wheels. Two thousand sound fair to you?"

"Yes, of course. I can bring it now. Sure. Of course. Thank you. Really. I'll bring it now." She heard herself rambling, her own words stupidly looping back on themselves, but she didn't care. It would be enough to cover her dad's bill. Enough to keep him at Helping Hands. Enough to keep her from drowning. "I'm coming now. Yes. Okay. See you in a bit," she said, and hung up without waiting for Gemma to say good-bye.

She threw on a pair of jeans and a bra, her emotions cresting through her. Fury and excitement and nervousness and fear. Daniel would be at the gallery. He would see her come in, see the sculpture, and she didn't think she'd be able to keep herself from screaming at him, from asking him why he'd lied. Why he'd sabotaged her.

She drove and mouthed her accusations, testing the deep barb of what she wanted to say to Daniel, and the city rose around her, the scent of urine and horse manure mingling with onions destined for gumbo and cigarette smoke filtering through the vents in her car. She glanced down at the sculpture. She'd wrapped it in tissue paper, and it stared up at her, the eyes and mouth obscured. The ghost of a face. She shivered and looked away.

Daniel was not on the floor when she entered Antoine's, and the holy quiet of the gallery fell over her as she cradled the sculpture to her chest and stepped toward the sleek, ivory desk where a receptionist smiled up at her.

"Are you Caroline? Gemma's expecting you. You can head on back to her office. And by the way," he lowered his voice conspiratorially, "Gemma showed me the pictures. It's truly fantastic. Ethereal."

"Thank you." She stepped past the desk but then paused and turned back. "Is Daniel here?"

"Gemma sent him on a coffee run. He should be back any minute."

Caroline nodded. It was better that he wasn't there. If he had been, she didn't think she would have been able to keep herself from making a scene.

Gemma stood as Caroline entered, her hands outstretched, and she grasped Caroline's shoulders and leaned forward to drop a kiss on her cheek. "You weren't lying when you said you were on your way!" she said, and laughed, pulling back to glance down at the tissue paper. "Is this it?"

"It is." Caroline bent and set the sculpture on the floor. Despite its size, it wasn't heavy—the materials ensured that—but when the weight of it left her arms, she felt emptied.

"May I?" Gemma rested a hand against the tissue, and Caroline nodded. Stripping the paper away, Gemma made small sounds of appreciation as she circled the woman, her fingers hovering above the dog's head, the dress made from leaves. "Exquisite. Truly."

"Thank you."

Gemma turned to her. "Are there more?"

"No. Not yet," Caroline said, remembering the other, more horrible sculpture still hidden away in her closet.

"When you do make another, I want first look." Gemma straightened suddenly, her gaze fixed somewhere behind Caroline. "Look what the cat dragged in. I knew your fiancée was talented, Daniel, but you've been keeping her from me. Shame on you."

"What?" Daniel's voice was quiet. Subdued. She did not turn to face him, did not want him to see her expression.

"The sculpture. I'm buying it. Right now, as a matter of fact."

Gemma stepped past Caroline and toward her desk. From the top drawer she withdrew a checkbook. "Two thousand, right?"

"Yes," Caroline said, and listened to Daniel's sharp intake of breath. He had not wanted this for her. He had tried to keep her from this. He did not deserve to see her triumph. Her hand did not tremble as she accepted the check.

Gemma beamed. "Take your fiancé to a nice lunch, Caroline." She threw a wink at Daniel. "She can certainly afford it with work like that. Listen, I have to dash off to a meeting about the Aversion Gala, but I'll be in touch soon with details. I'd like you here for the unveiling. I may be able to squeeze it in at the Gala. And thank you," she said, then brushed past them and out the door.

"Caroline—" Daniel began, but Caroline turned on her heel and walked past him without looking up to see the shock she imagined would be on his face. He followed behind her, but he did not rush, did not call after her. He wouldn't want to embarrass himself in front of the people he so desperately wanted to impress. Only when she was outside, already half a block away and almost back to where she'd parked her car, did he call out again. "Caroline. Would you please stop?"

She whirled to face him. "You didn't even mention it to her. When I called this morning, she had no idea what I was talking about. None."

"It's not that simple—"

"No. You don't get to talk right now. You knew how much I needed the money. You knew. And you go and do something like this? To me? The person you're supposed to love? How could you do something like that?" He stared down at his hands, and she wanted to make him look at her, to make him see how he'd hurt her. "Fucking answer me."

"You're right. I didn't show her."

"No shit. But why?"

"I . . . I don't really have a reason. I guess I thought . . . I don't know what I thought. That you weren't ready. Not stable enough yet. With everything that's been happening."

"You had zero right to make that decision for me. None. And I guess it had nothing to do with the possibility of me getting a little bit of attention? With me stepping back into the world you'd been making only for yourself? With protecting your bullshit, pretentious vegan lunches and discussions about the right kind of loafer and whose work is overrated and whose is not? Look me in the eye, Daniel, and tell me it had nothing to do with the fact that you were afraid I would take away whatever attention you so desperately need."

Daniel stared at the ground, his voice so low she almost couldn't hear it. "You don't understand. What it's like constantly being in your shadow. Even when you haven't been working, you're all people want to talk about. What you're doing now. When you'll start putting things out again. It's like I don't exist."

Caroline brought a hand to her mouth and covered it, bit down on the interior of one of her fingers to keep herself from any outward violence. "Oh, *fuck you*," she said, finding her keys, and leaving him standing alone in the center of the sidewalk. Only once she was in her car and pulling away did she allow herself to cry. So many years built on dust, and they crumbled beneath her, and she wondered if she had ever really understood Daniel, if she had ever really seen his true face. His ring burned on her finger, but she could not quite bring herself to take it off, to fling it from her in some final, symbolic end.

She drove with no real sense of direction. There was only this need to move, to get away from what had happened with Daniel, and quiet residential streets slipped past in blurs of gray and brown until the scenery changed into a more expansive landscape, the road narrowing and descending between arching trees, their limbs tangled overhead with weeping moss that draped over the branches like burial shrouds.

From her bag, her cell phone rang. Probably Daniel calling to offer her another bullshit justification for what he'd done. She let the phone ring until it went silent. She had nothing more to say to him.

When her phone rang again, she gritted her teeth. She reached for the phone, intending to tell Daniel to fuck off again, and glanced down at the screen. Helping Hands. The dark canopy over her broke, and the sun peeked through, but it was dim and pale, and it did not warm her. The bill. They were calling about the bill.

She forced herself to calm down, to rid her voice of its tremor, and accepted the call. "Hi, it's Caroline. Listen, I know I'm behind on my payment, but I can cover it now."

"Ms. Sawyer, this isn't about your bill. I'm so sorry." She didn't need the nurse to say what she was going to say next. Caroline had been waiting on this call for the past three years.

"No," she said, but denying it wouldn't change anything. Her eyes filled with fresh tears.

"I'm so sorry, but he's gone." The nurse carried on, but Caroline heard nothing. Dumbly, she drove with the phone in her hand, and the words came at her like a dull roar, and she felt herself closing the phone and throwing it, her hands gripping the steering wheel as the road rose and fell before her in monotone shades.

Gone. As if that was a place someone could go. Around her, the world blurred, and her father was *gone,* and there was nowhere to be. Nothing to do. No calloused hand to hold. Only endless days of nothing, and she felt herself begin to come undone, felt the scream working its way up through her gut, and she was ready to give in to it.

When the dog ran in front of her, her vision was still too blurred to make out its body darting into the road. At the last moment, she saw the tail—black and tipped with dark brown—but there wasn't time to lock up her brakes. The car lurched, once, twice, a sharp yelping as her tires thudded over the body, and then it was done.

She pulled onto the shoulder and focused on her hands. "Fuck. *Fuck,*" she said, and choked then, leaning into the steering wheel, her sobs caught in her throat. She couldn't bring herself to look into the rearview mirror, the horror of what she'd done smeared across the blacktop; blood and bone exposed to the air. She took a deep breath through her nose and then looked anyway. The slick, furred body faced away from her, the neck bent unnaturally. The paws scraped slow strokes against the asphalt as if what happened was only a dream and any moment the creature would wake up and run off into the woods. Her entire body shook, but she could not move, could not do anything other than watch the rearview mirror, her mind looping through the tangled snarl of her thoughts. Daniel. Her father. This dog and all the others.

The animal shifted its weight, heaved itself forward as if it could stand with a broken back, but its hind legs didn't move, and the sound of its pain echoed through the trees that surrounded them.

Don't. Oh, please, don't. She looked back at the dog. It had mercifully gone still, but a strange hum buzzed in her ears. *Leave. Leave this place,* she thought, but the noise changed. It broke apart and sounded harder. More clipped. She knew then what it was she was hearing. The wheezing sound of laughter.

In the rearview mirror, the dog's body twitched, the muscles drawing together into a heaving breath, and then, it stood. It swiveled its head and turned eyes the color of putrefaction and death on Caroline. Its right ear flopped, peeled away to reveal raw meat and white bone.

The dog was laughing at her. She was sure of it.

It opened its mouth, the teeth grinning wide, and Caroline still could not move. As she watched—a low whimper working up and out of her—the dog stood on two legs and leered at her, that mouth still peeled away and grinning, as it shifted and changed into the mouth of a man.

It gnashed its teeth, the muscles jerking under its skin, and Caroline remained frozen, able only to stare as her fear bent and twisted into something greater than she'd ever known. For so long, she'd felt haunted. Her memories or hallucinations or fears or depression, or whatever the fuck else anyone wanted to call them, were things she could not outrun. She was prey. She was nothing but meat.

Finally, she moved, her hands fumbling at the gearshift, the steering wheel, and then punched the accelerator. The car spun hard to the left, but then the wheels caught, and she watched as the creature disappeared behind her. The engine whined, a hard-edged sound of metal grinding down, and she backed off the accelerator.

Not real. None of it real. None of it.

She tried to slow her breathing, to will the horrible surging in her rib cage to stop, but her body felt separate from her mind. The synapses fired uselessly as she tried to convince herself to calm down. To convince herself that what she'd seen was nothing more than some kind of hallucination brought on by trauma.

But she saw the falsity of it. Even as she tried to hold her own flimsy rationalizations up as proof, she knew she would not be able to believe the lie. No matter how frequently she told it.

CHAPTER 21

LILA 2019

Exactly eighteen minutes after she called her father, his sedan pulled up to the curb, and he was out of the car and ushering her toward the passenger's seat.

"Get in the car." He slammed the door, and Lila leaned her head backward. The car smelled like coffee and unwashed clothes, and it made her stomach turn again.

Better to stay quiet. Better to keep her head down and let him rage at the world instead of saying hello to his daughter. She wasn't sure why she'd hoped for anything different. That dark, ugly thing stretched again, pushed at her, and it felt like she might peel inside out.

"I've tried calling your mom, but she must be in class because she isn't answering. Does she know that you're here?"

"No," she said.

He slammed a palm against the wheel. "Goddammit, Lila! You cannot be pulling stuff like this. Taking off without telling anyone and then just showing up unannounced? What if something had happened to you and no one knew where you were? You have to *think* before you do things." He wiped a hand over his face. "Hopefully your mom gets my texts before she gets home and sees that you aren't there. It's not like I don't have enough going on here with Brina. I can't drop that responsibility any time and rush off to save you from whatever stupid thing you've gotten yourself into."

Her father didn't speak again, and they drove on, the sun beating over them. The scenery changed from trees to small subdivisions, the neat boxes of all those identical bricked houses lined up, their yards the same cookie-cutter combination of boxwoods and scrawny palm trees. Daniel pulled into the driveway and cut the engine.

"Come inside. I'll try your mom again," her father said, and opened his door.

For a moment, Lila considered staying in the car, but then she too got out and followed her father into the house. The door opened onto a small hallway that led into the kitchen. To the right, a coatrack held a pile of raincoats, and several pairs of shoes lay scattered against the tile.

"Rebecca? Any news from the hospital?" her father called out, and headed down the hallway.

Rebecca stood in the center of the kitchen, a glass of water in one hand, her hair pulled away from her face with a navy headband. There were dark circles under her eyes, but she was still striking. Her cheekbones high and angular, her eyes large and long-lashed.

"No," she said and stared at Lila without saying hello. Her neck had gone splotchy. A clear tell that she was irritated with Lila for showing up unannounced.

"Go to your room while I call your mother, Lila," Daniel said.

Lila curled her fingers inward. "Are you going to send me home?"

"I said go to your room."

"It's not *my* room, Dad. It's some bullshit guest room you like to pretend is mine."

"We have Brina to worry about. I can't be dealing with you, too. Go. Now."

"You don't even act like I'm your daughter anymore. All you care about is that fucking baby."

Lila heard herself speak, but it felt like something else was using her. She knew the dark thing was speaking through her, but it was speaking in the language of her own fury. Better to let it talk. Better to let it say all the things she'd been holding inside but was too scared to say.

"Excuse me?" Rebecca said. Her father stood still, frozen, his hands pattering over his legs as if he could somehow keep the world from tumbling out of its skin.

"Oh, shut up, Rebecca. Like you know anything about it."

Rebecca turned to Lila's father. "Daniel?" she said, but Lila knew what Rebecca really wanted to say. *Deal with your daughter. Fix this. Fix her.*

"Lila," he said, and his voice was soft. The way he used to talk to her when she was little and hysterical. A scraped elbow or cut or bruised knee, her face gone runny with tears and snot as he bent over her, all fluttering hands and kisses to make it better.

"I hate this place. I hate coming here and seeing you pretend you give a shit about me. And more than anything, I hate that fucking creature that's rotting away in the hospital. It won't do any good, you know. Praying like you have. Things that are that weak are supposed to be eaten by something more powerful. She's *food*," Lila said, and Rebecca brought a hand to her mouth.

The room went hot. Everything pressed down and a dull roar

built in Lila's ears, so she didn't understand what her dad or Rebecca was yelling, and her teeth clamped down, and she was
laughing, high and clear, and her dad was pulling back his hand
and then bringing it down hard against her jaw, and the sound
was like the sky cracking open.

Then she was screaming, a sound that came from the deepest
part of her belly and didn't resemble screaming at all, but a low
growling, and her father had his hands against her back as he
forced her out of the room and toward the hallway. Toward the
little room they pretended was hers. Her entire life was nothing
but a series of her parents' make-believes. *Let's make-believe we
wanted a baby. Let's make-believe Lila wasn't a worthless fucking
mistake.*

He didn't speak as he pushed her inside, the door like a gun-
shot when he locked it behind him, and then she was alone, her
mouth still opened wide, a cold pool of spittle leaking out of her.

"I want her out of this house, Daniel. There's something
wrong with her. Get her mom on the phone, and then get her
on a flight back to Atlanta. Tonight," Rebecca said.

Her father spoke, the thin edges of his voice catching at
her, and she could taste his confusion. He didn't know what
to do. Didn't know what had happened to his sweet, obedient
daughter.

Rebecca's voice rose and fell. Still angry. Still talking about
Lila as if she were a thing instead of a person. Lila smiled and
listened as the front door opened and closed, the sound of a car
starting and roaring away. Good. Let her stay away. She pictured
Rebecca crashing the car—crunched metal and glittering glass—
and flames the color of a sunset.

Turning, Lila looked at the room. Everything beige. The bed-
spread and the curtains and the carpet. Nothing on the walls
except for a series of small prints. Herbs and their Latin names.
The dresser top clean and dusted. There was nothing to throw.

Nothing to tear into tiny pieces and grind into the carpet. Her fingernails cut small half-moons into the palms of her hands, and she hoped her blood would stain the carpet. Leave some color in this bleached-out place.

She heard her father outside the door, his feet dragging and his breathing ragged as an animal's. He paused there but then moved on, the sound of him loud and angry and confused, and then another door slammed, and all went quiet.

But she was here now. In New Orleans. And something had happened at Jazzland. The *before*. She would go there and find it out. Before her mom and dad could send her back.

Outside, the sun tipped toward darkness, and Lila sat on the cheap mattress and waited for the room to go black. She knew it would not be long, but the minutes ticked down, every one of them taking her closer to her dad getting her mom on the phone and booking a return flight.

When the light finally bled away, she rose and went to the window. This room had been selected for her because it gave her afternoon sunlight, and she looked out into the fenced backyard. Tucked away in a corner, a man in a dark coat stood. He waved to her and smiled. His teeth gleamed in the dim light. It was a mouth made for destruction.

Lila knew she should be frightened, but she wasn't. Not anymore. She knew him. He'd been with her ever since she left Atlanta. Excitement fluttered in her belly, and she covered her smile with her hand. She didn't want the man to know how happy she was to see him. Not yet. But of course he knew. He knew everything about her. He knew how good it felt to finally let her anger be louder than anything else.

Her father's voice sounded from somewhere in the house, and she heard him say her mother's name, heard him tell her mother that she'd come to New Orleans. Still, the man stood in the yard, and he beckoned to her, his hand flashing pale in the darkness. She blinked, and he was gone.

It was all connected. She knew it was. And she needed to go to Jazzland, needed to see for herself this place her mother was so frightened of.

She opened the window, darted a glance over her shoulder, and slipped out.

CHAPTER 22

CAROLINE 2004

The funeral was larger than Caroline had expected. The procession behind the jazz band stretched as far as she could see as they made the walk to the church. So many people who'd loved her father came to pay their respects, to touch her shoulder, their eyes misted over as they passed along their sympathies. As the service began, the minister asking all of them to bow their heads, she kept waiting for tears, to feel anything other than numb, but even as she climbed the steps to the podium to deliver her eulogy, her body felt mechanical, and she read from the paper before her without emotion.

She put her father in the ground, her fingers stained with the earth she tossed onto the coffin, and then it was over. A few hours and her father's life had been tucked carefully away.

In the pew, Daniel sat next to her, the air a thin barrier between them, weighted with her anger, her accusations, and her grief. He could not lessen any of it with something as simple as the reassurance of his fingers squeezing hers, his hand against her back. They'd not shared a bed since Caroline had learned of her father's death, and the pillow and sheets draped over the back of the couch were another form of her mourning. Gemma's check had covered the overdue bill at Helping Hands and helped with the cost of the funeral. The remainder that Gemma's check hadn't covered went on a credit card Caroline still couldn't afford to pay off.

Gemma had buyers eager for more of Caroline's work, but she'd put them off to grant Caroline some time to wrap up her father's affairs. Caroline couldn't bring herself to focus on anything when she could barely rise every morning, barely draw breath. The world around her was tinged with shadows that felt alien. There would no longer be a time in her life when her skin did not ache from so much loss.

She'd been dreaming about the man in the dark coat; dreaming about dogs with broken bodies; dreaming about men with cruel mouths, saliva dripping from their teeth that were too sharp, too plentiful for the ever-stretching skin that opened and opened, and there was no end to these nightmares. She woke in the night to rise, to vomit, only to return to the empty bed, fearful of the sleep she'd once longed for.

She went to an appointment with Dr. Walters a week after the funeral. He had given her medication that was supposed to fix her, but it had not. She'd started leaving the lights on at night, terrified she was going to round a corner and see the man crouched there, his fanged mouth gaping as it dripped saliva.

She sat across from him, her arms crossed tightly across her chest. "I'm still seeing things. In fact, it's gotten worse. I thought the medication was supposed to help," she said.

"We can adjust. Try something different. Response can vary from person to person." He frowned back at her. Already, the prescription pad was in his hand. Ready to throw another pill at her.

"So what happens if this one doesn't work either?"

"Ms. Sawyer. My job is to help you. There's no reason to question my expertise in this arena." He gave her a tight-lipped smile that was meant to be reassuring but instead struck her as smug.

Caroline bristled. She was already in a position that made her feel powerless, and he'd just chastised her like some schoolgirl for asking a completely normal question. She exhaled and let her shoulders droop. She was so tired. Of fighting. Of feeling powerless. Of feeling broken.

"Of course not," she said, but her anger had not cooled. She felt as if she'd fallen into a labyrinth with no exit. The medication had not helped because there was something inside of her that was irrevocably damaged. Whatever pill Dr. Walters gave her next would likely be one that left her drooling and quiet. Problem solved.

"Good girl," he said, and leaned over the prescription pad. Later that afternoon, she sat in her car outside the pharmacy and screamed until her throat felt raw. Then she went inside and filled the prescription.

For six days, Caroline wandered through the apartment, restless but not sure what it was she was looking for. She thought about Detective Doucette. There had been no more disappearances, but there hadn't been any girls returned either, and she thought of the bodies, those animal-like markings, the two women with their similar stories, the sounds people had reported hearing at Jazzland and how they mimicked her own experiences. She took her medication. She had no more delusions, just the dreams of the man and the dogs. She thought about Jazzland. She folded and refolded the blanket Daniel was using. She thought about Jazzland, and she dreamed about it, the dogs snarling around her as she wandered through the empty park, the coasters silent but the screams unending. She woke and fought against the gorge in her throat, and she thought about Jazzland.

On the seventh day, she called Vivian. "I'd like to come back. Tomorrow."

"Are you sure? It's only been two weeks. You can take more time, if you want it."

Caroline drew a deep breath and tugged at Daniel's blanket. He'd left it crumpled at the bottom of the couch. Not once had he folded it. It was always her. Always Caroline left behind to pick up whatever wasn't right. "It would be good to get back to something normal. Some routine."

"Of course. It was the same for me. After my husband died. Beth has an appointment with Dr. Bryson in the morning, but if you want to come after lunch, you can."

They said their good-byes, and Caroline snapped the phone closed, wondering if Beth would have forgotten her promised special trip. Caroline hoped she hadn't. With her father gone, the recollection of what had happened to her was a portion of her life she wanted finished. Her father had blamed himself for Caroline's abduction. She needed to understand what had happened to her, even if she was never able to tell her dad that it wasn't his fault.

That night, Daniel brought her sunflowers. He did not say he was sorry. Again, they slept apart.

The following afternoon, Beth was waiting for her when she pulled into the drive, and the girl jumped into the air and streaked toward the car.

"You're here, you're here!" Before Caroline could even climb out, Beth had wrapped her arms around her in a bear hug.

"I am," she said, and the girl only squeezed harder.

"You won't go away again? Not anymore?" Beth said, and another kind of guilt flared through her. After all of this, she hadn't considered how her absence affected Beth, how being locked away with only her mother for company would have driven her crazy. That maybe Caroline had been the only part of the girl's day that wasn't a form of keeping her in line.

"I'm going to do my best."

Beth dropped her arms and glanced down. "I'm sorry about your dad."

"Me too," Caroline said, tears threatening at the corners of her eyes, and she blinked them away.

Beth peeked up at Caroline through her lashes. "Do you think we could still go to Jazzland? Like you said? It would probably help cheer you up."

Caroline smiled down at Beth, thankful she hadn't forgotten. "As long as it's okay with your mom."

Beth squealed and clapped her hands together. "Tomorrow?"

"I'm fine with that. But you have to ask," Caroline said. Immediately, Beth ran into the house. Caroline followed, knowing that it would be okay with Vivian as long as it meant she didn't have to do it. After so many hours in the Kellum house, Caroline understood that Vivian was more concerned with appearances than she was with reality. As long as Beth looked and acted the part of a good girl and kept quiet, she was happy. It didn't matter how Beth actually felt.

As Caroline had expected, Vivian said yes. It took everything in Caroline's power to keep Beth on task and to keep her from flinging paint all over the kitchen, but by the end of her session, Beth seemed tired and distracted. Caroline had forgotten Beth's appointment with Dr. Bryson that morning.

"Feeling okay?" she asked as they stood at the sink rinsing their brushes.

"Fine," Beth said. She tilted her head forward so her hair fell over her face.

"Everything go well with Dr. Bryson?"

Beth's head snapped up—her jaw clenched and eyes momentarily darkening—but the expression quickly melted into an innocent smile. "Of course it did. Why wouldn't it?"

They fell back into cleaning up, but Beth's lie hung heavy between them. Even as Caroline gathered her things, she could feel Beth straining to keep up the façade that nothing was troubling her.

She drove home, her heart aching when she didn't make the turnoff toward Helping Hands. Daniel was already there, set up in the living room and spreading a light layer of gray paint over a canvas.

"Hey," he said, and she paused in the entryway, willing him to come to her, to apologize, to tell her he'd been an ass, and that he'd fucked up beyond belief, but he only stared back at her, his brush clenched in his fist. "How was the lesson?"

"Fine." She paused, willing him to fill in the silence, but he turned away, brought his brush back to the canvas. "We're doing the Jazzland trip. Tomorrow."

He paused, but she pivoted away from him, left his reprimands and irritation behind to fall into dead air, and from the bedroom, she listened to him slash at his canvas. He'd swapped his brush for his blade.

The next morning she woke up with the start of a headache and a nausea that forced her out of bed and into the bathroom, her hand clamped over her mouth so she would not be sick before she reached the toilet. When she finished, she rocked back on her heels, trying to think of what she'd eaten, to think if this could be a virus, but the nausea had been with her for a few weeks now. She'd assumed it was stress-related, had assumed it had to do with dealing with her father's death, but she counted back, and then counted again.

Nine weeks. She'd not had her period for nine weeks.

"No," she said, and stood. "No."

She'd gone off birth control the past year. No matter what she took, it made her sick, or made her hair fall out in clumps, and so they'd used condoms, and Daniel was always so careful. But there was the night she'd bitten his lip, and he wouldn't have been wearing a condom, and her stomach clenched again. She bent, throwing open the cabinet under the sink, her hands blindly searching for the tiny box she knew was there. They'd had prior scares, and she'd bought the tests mostly for her own peace of mind, had put the box back under the sink when she saw the negative result.

The box was still there, a single unused test tucked inside, and she pulled it out and glanced toward the door. Daniel had already gone. She'd heard him gather his keys and the door open and close, but she still felt he was there, able to come in at any moment and see her standing there with the pregnancy test in her hand.

She opened the sealed package, her mind racing as she squatted and placed the stick beneath her. Nine weeks was enough time for something to come alive inside of her. She set the test on the counter and then sank onto the bathtub ledge, unable to watch as the liquid seeped across that white field, that first pink line brightening, and then what? She could not look, could not watch her future unfold in those achingly slow minutes, but there was Jazzland, and she couldn't spend the rest of the day locked in the bathroom.

She crept forward, her eyes on the floor until she reached the countertop, and then she looked, and she looked, and there were two lines there, and her knees buckled.

Two lines. Positive.

She sat, her hands fluttering to and away from her abdomen. Inside of her, another heartbeat.

"Hello," she whispered, tears on her cheeks, and she wondered if her own mother had felt the same way. Helpless and terrified and exhilarated and somehow in love with something she couldn't even see.

And she felt it. Love. She did not think she would have, not at first, but already, it was there. Pure in all of the ways love was supposed to be, in all of the ways described in that old Bible verse she'd had to learn when she was a kid. No jealousy. No anger. No envy. It just *was*. Accepting and all-encompassing.

But there was Daniel. Daniel who had lied to her; who had tried to damage her career; who had not believed her or the reasons for her fears. Daniel whose child this was as well, but even as she touched her belly, she knew she could not be with him. Even though she was carrying his child, she could not be with a man who discarded her thoughts, her feelings; who actively sought to take away the only thing that had ever brought her joy. A man threatened by the very things that were the core definition of who she was.

"I'm sorry," she whispered to her baby, to Daniel, to the silence around her, but she would leave him, and she would raise her baby, and she would put this part of herself in the ground and build something new. Something better.

She buried the test in the trashcan and showered, swallowing against the bile in her throat, and then dressed and drove to the Kellum house, where Beth waited.

CHAPTER 23

CAROLINE 2004

The parking lot for Jazzland was still mostly empty when Caroline and Beth arrived. The blacktop was already sunbaked, and the air smelled faintly of tar. Beth had spent the entire car ride bouncing up and down in her seat and chattering about which rides she'd go on and in what order. Now, the girl pulled Caroline from the car and dragged her toward the main gates. Caroline's head throbbed, and she was still queasy, but she followed along.

The lurid red and green metal of the gates sprawled overhead, and Beth continued to yank at her hand. "You have the tickets, right?"

"Yes, I have the tickets," she said, opened her purse, and withdrew the two printouts Vivian had handed her that morning.

"Bought them online," she'd said, and then waved them off.

Everything here was too bright. All that twisted metal refracted the sunlight into a thousand pieces, and cartoonish colors bled over every building fashioned to capture some long-forgotten feeling of Americana. Squinting, Caroline took in the front of the park, waiting for some recognition to come, but there was nothing.

At the entrance, a short, round woman with a flabby chin that ran directly into her neck took their tickets, and then Beth pushed Caroline through the turnstiles.

"Come on! The line for the Mega Zeph is probably super short right now!" Beth darted ahead and doubled back before lunging ahead again. Over and over the girl danced away from her. Caroline didn't bother with telling Beth to stay beside her. Already, her armpits were damp and her shirt clung to her back. It was the end of Jazzland's season, full autumn now, but there'd been a heat wave, and the humidity breathed out a deep summer intensity. If Beth was going to spend the entire day running, it was fine by her. It would give her more of an opportunity to examine the park alone. To try to remember.

The park was practically empty except for a few groups of children with frazzled moms in tow. Tucked in the darker corners were groups of teenagers who'd cut school. Some of them paired off, their arms and tongues tangled together as they mauled each other's faces in the name of love. Here and there, park workers in circus-colored uniforms stooped to sweep up bits of paper.

Ahead of her, Beth twisted to the left, away from the swings and the Ferris wheel. "Kids' rides," Beth had called them in the car. "Waste of time."

As they passed the Ferris wheel, Caroline listened as children squealed, and her head pounded. Faintly threaded under the children's shouts was a tinkling, music-box version of jazz. Caroline froze. The music coming from the Ferris wheel was familiar. The notes were both jubilant and melancholy, and her body broke into goose bumps despite the heat. She paused, wanting to hear more, to see if there was anything that would help her remember anything else, but Beth had already dashed off, her blond hair glinting in the sunlight. Caroline closed her eyes, willed herself to remember, but even as the music played on, there were no sudden revelations, and she followed after Beth before the girl disappeared. Had she heard that music all of those years before? On the day she'd reappeared, were those notes playing over and over as she stumbled through the park?

By the time Caroline caught up to her, Beth was already in line, the snaking, wooden structure of the Mega Zeph towering over her. She waved to Caroline and shot her a thumbs-up. How was it possible for Caroline to remember nothing? To have been in this place and not recall anything that happened to her?

They made their way through the park with Beth running ahead and Caroline plodding behind, trying to go back to that day, to remember her father going inside their house to get them a snack, to remember being here, confused and alone as she wandered, but there was only the dim outline of her fear and nothing else. She forced herself to listen carefully, to go beyond the screams and the music, but there were no sounds of dogs. She wiped at her forehead and trudged on.

Outside of each coaster, Caroline waited for Beth to emerge exuberant and red-faced and declare that she was going to ride it one more time before the day was out. But as the morning bled away, Caroline felt increasingly ill. With the heat and the sound of people screaming and the myriad of smells—fried foods, sweat, garbage—her headache grew worse and nausea threatened to overtake her.

After Beth had ridden the Jester and the Zydeco Zinger and the Mega Zeph multiple times, she slid her hand into Caroline's and looked up at her. "Thank you for bringing me," she said.

Caroline knew she should warm to the feel of Beth's hand tucked inside her own, but the humidity was invasive, and her head buzzed with pain, and she couldn't feel anything else. She cupped Beth's hand in her own because there was nothing else to do, and when the girl loosened her grip the smallest bit, Caroline let her hand drop.

As she sat outside the rides waiting for Beth to finish, Caroline felt as if the screams pouring from the mouths of overexcited children had somehow found their way into her brain. Her head felt swollen with screaming and heat, and the same uneasiness she'd felt before when she'd come with Daniel settled over her. That same distinct feeling something bad was going to happen. There had to be something here. Something she wasn't seeing.

When Beth emerged from yet another coaster, Caroline waved the girl over. Her fear was palpable now, so much worse than it had been, and she wanted to be somewhere enclosed, somewhere where the sky wasn't so large. "Let's get some lunch."

"Pizza! And ice cream!"

Caroline nodded, and she breathed warm air and kept walking.

The restaurant was cold. They kept the doors closed, and the air was like a wall. Caroline shivered. Plastic booths—red and flecked with glitter—dominated the floor space. The front end of an old Cadillac jutted from one wall, a booth tucked inside, and doo-wop played over the loudspeakers. They hadn't been the only ones looking to get out of the heat. The restaurant was crowded. Kids shouted at one another across the booths while the adults shot them looks that said to calm down right this minute. Her head was pounding, the room sliding in and out of focus, and she blinked rapidly, willed herself to stay with it, to stay in the moment. She was overheated. She was pregnant. There was a reason for the dread building inside her. It had something to do with the park, but she couldn't figure out what.

"Find us a table, okay? I'll get the food," Caroline said.

"Cheese pizza, please," Beth said, and then the girl was gone.

The line moved slowly. The smells of grease redolent in the air. Caroline focused on the cool air blowing against the back of her neck and turned to look for Beth. She'd found a booth beside the window, and the sunlight streamed through and haloed around her. Beth smiled and waved, and Caroline turned away.

Again, she heard those echoed screams, and she rubbed at her eyes. She would feel better after she ate something. Would be able to go back into the park and keep looking. But for what? The question looped in her mind, and she bit down on her cheeks to keep from shrieking in frustration.

She placed the order and shuffled to the side to wait for the pimpled employee to stack their food on the burgundy plastic tray. Around her, kids ran back and forth, shouting and laughing and tussling together, and the room felt too small, as if it couldn't contain all the energy it held, and she turned again to look for Beth.

The sun pouring through the window glinted harsh light through the space. It momentarily blinded her, the booths and outlines of kids gone white, and she blinked rapidly against her blurred vision. Beth still sat in the booth, her hands folded against the table, but she wasn't alone. A man wearing a dark coat sat across from her. A shock of oil-black hair swept over his forehead. He was tall. Thin. A mouth drawn back in a smile that revealed straight, white teeth. He too had his hands folded against the table, the fingers long and tapered. Hands for snatching up little, delicate things.

Behind her, the cashier called her order, but she couldn't bring herself to move, couldn't breathe as she stood not even twenty steps from Beth and the man and watched him reach across the table and trace a finger along the girl's cheek, watched him lift a lock of her golden hair. His mouth opened, and an ill chorus of snarling erupted. Even as the sound of the dogs fell over her, still Caroline could not move.

No one noticed Caroline standing there. They streamed around her, gathering their trays and plastic forks and napkins, and they didn't see her watching as the man took Beth's hands into his own and leaned across the table to whisper in her ear.

Caroline knew what she was supposed to do. She understood what was expected of her in a situation like this. She should be across the room, her arms around Beth, shouting at the man as she pulled the girl away. She should be finding a security guard, a park employee, anyone who would listen.

The man leaned back, and Beth smiled at him. Caroline's heart beat slow and steady, and she watched because she knew what this was. She knew what was going to happen. The room seemed to swell, to shift and change into something that had grown out of a nightmare, and she watched as Beth turned to her, watched as the man lifted a finger to his lips.

But what turned to face her wasn't a man's face. The thing that looked back at her was all fur and lolling tongue and sharp teeth and blood. The head of a dog on the body of a man. The dog she'd hit and left behind on that winding road. The man she'd seen so many times now. Hiding in the shadows. In her dreams. The man who was not supposed to be real. Around her rose the terrible sound of mouths opening and closing, of snapping teeth and snarling.

Caroline stumbled, her mind completely coming apart, and she tried to run, to shout for Beth, but the world went hazy and dark, and she fell down into it, Beth, the man, the sound of the dogs fading away until there was nothing except the beating of her own heart.

CHAPTER 24

LILA 2019

Lila walked too close to the edge of the interstate, her feet stumbling over the white line. Trucks honked as they swerved to avoid her, and she lifted her hand to wave at them and laugh. She couldn't remember how long she'd been walking, only that it had always been night, and her father probably still had not come to check on her. Fuck him.

Twice, a car had pulled over, the taillights gleaming bloodred in the dark, but then the driver had taken off. Probably realized they couldn't pick up some random girl. Realized what that would look like. Lila was counting on the person who didn't care what it looked like.

Her hair was damp with sweat at her temples, and her shorts were too short and chafed at her thighs, but she kept walking and watching for the right car to pull over, the friendly, toothy smile from behind the glass. It would come. She just had to be patient. The thing inside of her was fully awake now, and she wondered if this was what it was like to be possessed. It wasn't so bad. Like she could feel and say the things she'd always wanted to but had never been allowed. Like finally taking a breath after spending a lifetime buried under what other people wanted.

When the right car finally came, it wasn't a car at all, but an old pickup with the mirrors and tailgate knocked off.

"Where's a little lady like you headed?" The driver's hair was bleached blond and brushed the tops of his shoulders. A tattoo peeked out from under his T-shirt. The grinning mouth of a skull with butterflies pouring out of its teeth.

"Cool tattoo." Lila forced a smile.

"This old thing?" He lifted his sleeve. "You should see the other ones."

"Maybe if you're nice," she said, and he flashed a mouthful of yellowed teeth.

"You eighteen?"

"Is that how old you think I am?"

"Question is if that's how old you want to be?"

She shrugged, and he leaned over and popped open the door. "Climb on in."

The interior light in the truck was broken, and she slid onto the seat and was thankful for the dark because it meant he wouldn't see how young she was. At least for a little while. The interior of the truck was littered with crumpled beer cans and discarded packs of cigarettes. A silver lighter and a screwdriver sat in the cup holder along with a plastic cup filled with something that smelled cloyingly sweet.

"Never said where you're headed," he said.

"Jazzland."

"The hell you want to go to that creepy-ass place for?" He glanced over at her, and she shrugged.

"I got reasons."

"I reckon I can help out a little lady with such a pretty smile. I'm Brady," he said, and stuck out his hand. His fingernails were dirty.

"Caroline," she said, and didn't take his hand. He put it back on the wheel. The thing inside of her delighted in the lie, delighted in the fact that she chose *this* name—her mother's name—to feed to the man.

"'Sweet Caroline. Bum—bum—bum,'" he sang, and his laugh sounded like a wheeze. "But really. What sort of trouble you trying to get up to over in Jazzland? Maybe I'll join you."

"I'm looking for something," she said, and her own annoyance—separate of the voice inside her—rose up hot and insistent. She didn't like him, even as the voice whispered that everything was fine, that she should just take it easy. The voice had been part of her for so long now, but her revulsion fought against it. He leaned toward her, and her lungs burned with the effort of holding her breath against the animal stink rising off him. Fuck that. She didn't like Brady, and there was nothing the voice could tell her that would change her mind.

"Ain't we all," he said, and his eyes, slick as oil, slid over her body. She clenched her fists, and the voice murmured, sweet and smooth, and *Didn't she want to be a good girl? Didn't she want to be* nice *for this man who so clearly wanted to help her?*

"I was looking for something too once. Still ain't sure I found it. Reckon you could maybe help me out with that, sweet Caroline?"

She put her hand against his arm, squeezed the loose flesh there, and the voice was happy with her, happy to be in control once more, and *that was good.* He was older than he looked. "You going to be nice to me, mister?"

"Sweetheart, you ain't never been with anybody nice as me. Soft and sweet and quiet. That's what you mean, ain't it?"

"Yeah. Soft and sweet and quiet. Just like that." The seat was covered in a ratty Navajo blanket and was rough underneath her. She shifted back and forth, and he laughed. He was a stain, a fucking blight on humanity, and she could taste the stench of him. But the voice was there, telling her to be sweet, to be a *good girl*. Her head lolled on her neck. Everything was too hot, and everything inside her mind was too big for her body.

"You make yourself comfortable. Let's get to know each other a little first, say, honey? You can tell me a little bit about all of the things you like, and I'll tell you a little bit about how pretty you are, and then it'll all be good, and we'll go to Jazzland and see what kind of hell we can raise. Yeah?"

"Yeah," she said, and thought about how she wanted to reach into his mouth and snatch up the pink, wriggling tongue and then tear it out by the root. He turned on his blinker and guided the car into the left lane. Above them, the sky stretched on and on, and dead pine trees lined the earth, running alongside the blacktop like a row of jagged teeth. For miles out, the trees carried on, and she imagined herself walking inside them, her bare feet pressed into the dirt and dead leaves.

"Too hot," she whispered, but Brady hadn't heard her. She could feel his thoughts thrumming off of his skin. Violent things coiled deep inside him that waited to leak out through his pores, and the voice told her it would be better to be still, but her skin itched, and she couldn't.

"How old are you really, little girl?" he said, and his hand snaked along her thigh, found its way to the crest between and settled.

Isn't that nice, the voice sighed, but it wasn't nice, and her throat constricted, and it wasn't fucking nice at all. She couldn't speak though. The thing inside wouldn't let her, and her mouth stretched into a smile, and it hurt, and she fought against it, and it *hurt*.

For miles, he drove with his hand between her legs, his fingers playing with the edge of her shorts, and he hummed tunelessly as Lila inwardly squirmed against his touch. He turned a final time, and Jazzland appeared before them. The bricked entrance crumbling and weeds and plants growing up through the asphalt. Nature forever returning to reclaim what was rightfully hers. Graffiti covered the once brightly colored buildings that had faded to a dull pastel, and trash piled in the corners. He guided the truck toward the back of the lot and into a corner shaded by overgrown trees.

He brought his fingers to his nose and inhaled. "Ain't you sweet."

Lila bit down on her tongue until she tasted blood, and in that moment, the voice quieted, and she could move again. She leaned forward, pressing her weight against the console as Brady grinned.

"Clean as the day you were born," he said, and she wet her lips, lowered her voice, as her fingers searched for the thing she would need.

"How many girls have you hurt, mister? How many of us have you pinned down until we couldn't move? Until we couldn't breathe? Until you convinced yourself our screams had nothing to do with our pain or fear but were some kind of fucked-up clue about how much we wanted it." She panted, and the voice ran through her blood, and it hurt, and she wanted it out, wanted to shriek and tear until her thoughts were her own again, but it wouldn't leave, and it *hurt,* and she knew there would only be so long she could hold it off.

"Hey, now. It ain't as bad as all that. It can be real nice. Or it can't. That part's up to you, darlin'. Sometimes, the screamin' makes it more fun."

She leaned away from him and rolled down the window, gulped down mouthfuls of air that tasted of soil and the damp promise of rain. Lila's head swam, and the words coming out of her mouth were hers but also not. She didn't recognize the cadence of them, but the anger and the disgust were hers alone. "No. I won't scream."

If he'd looked at her closely, he would have seen her tip her head back, the muscles flexing and shifting in her neck, the tendons corded and tight, and he would have seen the color of her eyes shift, seen her grip the screwdriver in her right hand, but he was looking down, fumbling with his belt buckle, his zipper, the pale mound of flesh already in his hand, and he didn't see.

"I'll be sweet. The sweetest you've ever seen."

She opened her mouth, but no sounds came out, and then she was on him. The world went black and red, the voice inside screaming, and she sank the screwdriver again and again into his neck, the blood pouring thick over her hands. When she'd finished, she opened the driver's side door and pushed him out onto the asphalt, and still the voice screamed because *she hadn't listened, hadn't been a nice girl, and look what she'd done,* but she ignored it because it had felt good to hurt him, to hurt this man who took from other girls, who took things that did not belong to him. She tumbled from the truck, her legs and arms weak.

The sound of claws against asphalt came from somewhere behind her, and Lila shook her head, but the air buzzed, the dark threatening to overtake her. Behind her, a creature panted and shifted, its fur brushing against her arm, the air suddenly filled with the warm, fetid scent of its breath. Dog and man. Beast and blood bound up under flesh and teeth fashioned for cruelty. For violence.

The dark rose up around her, and there was the sensation of teeth along her shoulder. Beyond, hundreds of eyes reflected back at her, their voices tangling together into snarling and howling.

What have you done? We'll have to clean up your mess. *You should have been sweet. You should have been quiet. It could have been so simple. So lovely. Now, there will be pain. So much pain.*

CHAPTER 25

CAROLINE 2004

The casket at the front of the church was too small. Caroline stared, unable to imagine Beth inside it; unable to fathom that her body could have ever been that insubstantial.

From the altar, the minister asked for every head to bow, for every eye to close, but Caroline could not bring herself to pray. Beside her, Daniel dutifully followed suit with the rest of the funeralgoers. Only Caroline and Vivian kept their heads raised, their eyes locked on the casket with its spray of white roses. White for innocence. White for purity.

But the reports that had come back had been the same as the others. The tearing at the thighs. The mutilated sex. And the rumors spread no matter how Vivian insisted her daughter had died without defilement. White roses, then.

Caroline had sat in the back of the church, slipping in only moments before the service began, and the room was large enough that she could fade into the background without Vivian seeing her. Even though it had not been her fault, even though

the security footage cleared Caroline of any responsibility associated with Beth's disappearance and murder, she feared the
accusation she imagined she would see reflected in Vivian's eyes.
If only Caroline had not pushed herself—too long in the heat so
early in her pregnancy—maybe she wouldn't have fainted, maybe
she would not have provided the distraction Beth needed to
slip out of the restaurant unnoticed by those focused on the
unconscious woman on the floor. Maybe Caroline would have
been able to stop her before she got to the park's exit, before
she vanished from the security cameras, her body discovered
three days later in a ditch not five miles from the park.

Caroline had told the police about seeing a man with Beth—a
man in a dark coat—but they'd only shaken their heads. She was
confused. They'd reviewed all the footage. Beth was alone in the
booth. She was alone when she left the park, slipping in among
a series of families and then vanishing. There had never been any
man in a dark coat. There had only been Beth.

The news reports in the following days ran rampant with
speculation. The Cur had claimed another victim—this girl
who'd left Jazzland behind for reasons unknown and then
stumbled into a nightmare. For days, Jazzland was closed as
the police conducted their investigation, and mothers throughout New Orleans appeared on the nightly news, wringing their
hands, and repeating themselves over and over. *How awful, how
awful, how awful, howawfulhowawful.*

Since Beth's murder, there had been no other disappearances,
but doors remained locked and parks were empty of the sounds
of children at play. Parents hiding their children away from a
monster they had not seen. But Caroline felt that she *had*. No
matter what the police said, or Dr. Walters said, or Daniel said,
as she sat in the pew, readying herself to stand, to leave as soon as
the benediction was finished, Caroline felt she had conjured the
monster herself.

The final amen echoed through the church, and Caroline stood among the mourners, her hand tugging at Daniel's as she exited the pew and then out the doors into the vestibule that smelled damply of mold and wood polish.

"You should have gone to see Vivian," Daniel said as he started the car, and Caroline secretly cupped her belly. How long before he noticed? How long before she wouldn't be able to put off telling him anymore?

"Don't," she said, and he didn't press, but jerked the car violently as they left the parking lot.

They had not slept in the same bed for so long. Caroline was glad for it—this shedding of a life she had imagined she wanted. She would not long for his physical presence when she finally worked up the courage to look into his face as she told him the truth. She was going to have a baby, to be a mother. He was going to be a father. And she would not be with him. She could not.

That night, she slept alone and dreamed of the man with the dog's mouth. Dreamed of his teeth on her thighs, his tongue tracing a line of blood across her rounded belly, and she tried to pull away from him, to protect her baby, but he was inside her, and he was tugging and tugging, and she screamed without sound, but it did nothing to stop his rooting. He would take from her—this precious thing—he would take it away, and his mouth was filled with her blood—her baby's blood—and then there was the still, blue body falling out of her, and she did scream then, waking to glaring sunshine, her feet cold against the sidewalk in front of the house. Sleepwalking. She'd been sleepwalking.

Her belly grew. She covered it with large T-shirts and avoided showering when Daniel was in the apartment. He asked no questions. He did not notice. But the nightmares and her sleepwalking got worse. She started going farther and farther, leaving the door open and unlocked behind her so Daniel stopped sleeping as well, kept awake so he could gather her up and bring her back inside. She saw Dr. Walters and told him that no, she hadn't been hearing any more voices; no, she hadn't seen anything that wasn't actually there. Only the nightmares. *Always* the nightmares, but she knew how to differentiate those from reality. Life had fallen back into the dull grays of normalcy since Beth. Yes, everything was fine. Yes, she was taking the new, pregnancy-safe medication he'd prescribed. Yes, she would call immediately if anything happened. She'd given in totally to whatever he prescribed. Anything to keep her nightmares from appearing in the waking world. Anything to keep her from seeing that mouth, those teeth.

Twice a week, Gemma called with news from the gallery. Caroline's sculpture was garnering quite a bit of buzz. Three weeks after Beth's funeral, Gemma reached out, her voice high, and breathy. "I wanted to call and tell you before I forgot. There was a gentleman here this morning—I'm blanking on his name now—but he was very interested in your sculpture. Asked a lot of questions. Turns out, he's a dean at an art school in Atlanta. I didn't think you'd mind, but I passed along your email. He said he'd get in touch with you this week."

An hour and a half later, the email came through. Dr. Foti, dean of Academic Affairs. He was hoping Caroline had a portfolio? Ms. Gardner mentioned she'd been enrolled in a program previously. Each year, the school offered a full scholarship to a senior who demonstrated promise so that they might focus freely on their work for their final showcase. In exchange, it was expected the recipient would serve as a mentor for other students. The program was specifically designed to foster an interest in teaching, and it was possible that participation could lead to a part-time teaching position upon graduation. He was hoping Caroline would be interested, and he looked forward to seeing more of her work.

Before she could find all the reasons why she shouldn't,

Caroline pulled up her old portfolio—the images of the sculptures looking various and without cohesion. She wished he had not already seen the dog sculpture at the gallery. It was her best work—the only thing she'd done that seemed to mean something. But she attached the portfolio anyway along with a note that she was interested, that she was flattered he'd thought so highly of her work, that she'd be willing to do whatever was needed in order to be considered, and then she closed her laptop.

That night, she dreamed in mute gray, but there were no nightmares. No sleepwalking.

And she did as she'd said she would. She filled out an application, had her transcripts sent, and Daniel was there in the background, floating in her life as a reminder of so many failures.

When the call of acceptance from the Atlanta School of Art came, she realized she had outgrown even her largest shirt. There would be no more pretending she and Daniel could carry on this way. Two ghosts floating through a house, through a relationship, that had once worn the face of love.

Finally, she waited on the couch for him. Dozing, she dreamt of what it would have been like to draw a veil over her face before reciting their vows, her lips damp and tongue cloying with champagne. Would she have been happy? Before all of this? She liked to think she would have been. The two of them coming together like pieces of flint, their spark catching the world alight, and her skin warmed by the heat. It was a thought she still clung to, but she waited, her hands wrapped around a sweating glass of water she couldn't bring herself to drink, and she repeated the words she needed to say over and over.

When he came in, he didn't seem surprised to see her and came to sit next to her, his hands folded and resting against his thighs. She could taste the memory of those hands pressed against her, and she wet her lips and reminded herself she would not feel them again.

"The Atlanta School of Art offered me a scholarship."

Daniel exhaled loudly and rubbed at his forehead. "Of course they did. Of course." He paused, waiting for her to say anything else, but the words remained frozen on her tongue. "Are you going to take it?"

She held out her hands, her palms facing upward. "Yes."

He leaned backward, his breath rushing out of him as he stared at her. "I'm not leaving New Orleans, Caroline. This is my life—*our* life. It's here. My job, my art. *Us.*"

She stared down at her hands. "Just me. It would be just me who goes."

He pressed his lips into a thin line, his jaw set firm. "What the fuck is that supposed to mean?"

"Daniel. Please. You can't act like you haven't felt this. We're . . . broken. We have been for a while. I can't trust you. Not anymore."

Daniel put his hands over his face, and she forced herself to be still, to face this. He inhaled. Exhaled. Through his hands his voice was muffled, but she heard what he said. Every syllable. "And when were you going to tell me that you're pregnant?"

"What?"

"Give me a fucking break, Caroline. Like I haven't noticed you trying to hide it in those tent-sized shirts. I didn't want to force you to tell me, but I didn't realize the goddamn reason was that you were going to leave. That it would mean so little to you; that *I* would mean so little to you. It's fucked up, and it's selfish. What kind of person does that? Doesn't tell her fiancé she's pregnant with his child and then just drops it on him, and oh hey, guess what else, she's leaving you to move out of state?"

"That's not fair."

"Do *not* talk to me about what's fair and what's not."

"You want to know what's not fair? You lying to me about Gemma. You trying to damage the only thing I've ever been any good at and resenting me the entire time. You not listening when I talked to you about anything important. Telling me my dad could go in a home that was less expensive; telling me to listen to Dr. Walters even though he treated me like a child."

"This is about a stupid sculpture? You're upset because of something that fucking *trivial*? Jesus Christ." He laughed and stood, running his hands over his hair as he turned to stare out the window. "You know what? Fine. Pack your shit and go to Atlanta, and pump out mediocre art at a mediocre school. It's what you would have done anyway, but at least now it won't be with me."

Caroline flinched, tears stinging at the corners of her eyes, and she wiped them away.

"Fuck this," he said, and turned away quickly. When the door slammed, the sound ricocheting through the apartment, she didn't jump. And like that, it was over.

Caroline had been living in Atlanta for two months when the rain started in New Orleans. Daniel had already left the city. Taken what he needed and flown to Ohio to stay with a cousin who had an extra room. Now that Caroline's due date was only three weeks away, he called her every few days to check in. For months he called to apologize for what he'd said, to tell her he'd never needed anything but her, that he'd been so, so stupid. "Come back. Come home," he told her, but there was nothing left for her there.

Caroline watched the news reports, the lines of cars stalled out as they made their way out of the city, and she thought of the things those waters could pull up. So much death brought to the surface only to recede again, back into its own form of quiet oblivion. After Katrina was over, she saw the ruin, the city laid flat, Jazzland flooded over, and she was thankful not for the disaster, but that Jazzland had disappeared under the floodwater. She hoped they tore it down; the land left to whatever ghosts haunted it.

She pasted on a smile, and she went to her doctor's appointments and to class, and she took her prenatal vitamin and ticked off the days on the calendar and wondered how she was going to do this alone. Every night, she drank a glass of ice water and lay down on the couch and waited for her baby to kick and punch and move, not because she thought the feeling was sweet but because she was terrified the baby had died in her belly. Sometimes, she dreamed about Beth and woke up with a scream dying in the back of her throat and her face and pillow wet. She'd have to heave herself out of bed and drink glass after glass of water, and still her heart felt like it was in her mouth. The images wouldn't leave her. The dog with its mangled face. A man with sharp, bloodied teeth. Beth's hair with dark stains, and her arms reaching out for something that would not hold her, and the baby would kick and kick and kick.

She woke and slept and woke and slept and taught herself a new pattern, and Daniel, and Vivian, and Beth, and the man with the dog's face were sharp edges she learned not to think about. Whatever had happened to her when she was a girl, whatever had happened to Beth, they were separate, horrible things. She had to believe that. There had been no creatures. No man with the face of a dog. She had seen no other delusions, and there were no more news stories about missing girls. She had to believe, had to accept that Dr. Walters had been right. She took her medication and forced herself to think of other things. She did not want to pass whatever sickness remained curled in the sleeping parts of her brain on to her child.

When the baby came, the nurses marveled at how Caroline did not scream. They cleaned the baby. Weighed her. Tested her eyes and ears. Everything normal. Everything as it should be, and when Caroline looked down at her daughter, she did not see Beth's eyes reflected there as she had expected to. "Lila," she said when the nurses asked for her name.

Daniel was there, and he lingered after Lila was born, trying again and again to craft a family that didn't exist. For the first eight years of Lila's life, Daniel would appear every so often at her doorstep, flowers in hand, having flown to Atlanta to try again after all this time to win Caroline back. But just before Lila's ninth birthday, he met Rebecca, and they married a year later with Lila as a junior bridesmaid. After that, Caroline felt that she could finally take a breath; the life she'd created something she could cocoon inside, and Caroline learned all the small things that fill up a heart to the point it aches. She memorized the sound of her daughter's laughter, and she carried it inside her as if it would shatter. She prayed to a god she didn't quite believe in to keep Lila safe, to erase her memory of the things she'd seen. She raised her daughter to be good, to obey the rules, because obedience meant safety. She waited for something terrible to happen.

For thirteen years, she learned to forget.

Almost.

CHAPTER 26

CAROLINE 2019

"What do you mean she's in New Orleans?" Caroline stood in her office, the phone pressed to her ear as she threw everything into her computer bag and grabbed her purse.

"She called me from the airport, and I picked her up. What the *hell* is going on, Caroline? Somehow she manages not only to book a flight without your knowing, but then get on that plane, fly all the way here, and then I can't even get in touch with you?"

"Don't you dare try to blame me for this. Don't you fucking *dare*. After that bullshit you pulled the last time she was there—not even being at the airport to pick her up—don't even think about blaming me for this."

"She said some terrible stuff to Rebecca. Truly awful. If there was something going on with her, why wouldn't you tell me?"

"I *have* been telling you there was something wrong, or don't you remember?" she snapped before jerking open her office door and hurrying down the corridor.

"No, you were telling me about news stories that had nothing to do with Lila. Nothing to do with whatever the fuck is *actually* going on. You should have heard her. She sounded like an animal."

"Put Lila on the phone. Now." Caroline walked, intent only on getting out of the building and back to her car. She listened as Daniel's muffled voice called Lila once and then twice, listened as a door creaked open, and then only silence that was somehow louder than a scream.

"She's gone. Jesus. Her window's open and she's not here," Daniel said, and a cold panic crept through Caroline's guts.

"Is she anywhere else in the house?" Caroline's palms were slick as she unlocked her car and slid behind the wheel.

"No. I would have seen her come out. I locked the door."

"How long has it been?"

"Ten, maybe fifteen minutes? It hasn't been that long. Maybe she's just outside. She can't have gotten that far," he said.

Before Daniel could say another word, he hung up. She dialed his number—at least five times—but he didn't answer, and she drove on, back to the apartment she knew would be empty. She pulled up Lila's number, but there was no answer, and she screamed, striking the steering wheel with the palm of her right hand until it ached.

Running through possible scenarios, Caroline sped toward the apartment. Daniel would find Lila. He had to. She should have known, should have understood that what was happening with Lila went far beyond having an argument with Macie.

She sped into the parking lot and ran upstairs, imagining that somehow she would find Lila in her bedroom, that all this was a nightmare, and if she pretended Lila was inside, everything would be okay. But of course Lila wasn't there. Not in her bedroom, or the kitchen, or sitting at the dining room table with her earbuds in as she did her homework.

Caroline wandered back to her bedroom. Her laptop was

sitting on her bed. She opened it and scanned the screen, the ticket Lila purchased still displayed, and she sank onto the bed. For so long, Caroline had kept Lila sheltered from her past—everything that had happened at Jazzland, Beth, her own forgotten childhood—all portions of herself meant to be kept locked away. She'd imagined she was protecting Lila, afraid her delusions would somehow become part of Lila's dark inheritance. But now her hallucinations had bled outward, and she thought of Beth, of the man she saw lead her away. She pictured Lila; pictured herself watching as the man took not Beth, but Lila; pictured her daughter's face as she turned back to look at Caroline one final time.

Her cell phone rang from where she'd left it in the kitchen, and she cursed herself as she ran down the hallway for not bringing it with her. Daniel. She snatched it up, and he was talking before she could get the phone to her ear.

"She's not anywhere by the house. I've looked everywhere I can think of to look. And she doesn't have her cell phone with her. She left it on the dresser," he said.

"Call the police. I'm getting on the next flight. I'll be there in less than four hours." Caroline grabbed her purse and keys. Checked her wallet to be sure her credit card was tucked in its lonely slot, and then hurried out the door.

She called the airlines first, but there were no flights out to New Orleans until late the next afternoon. That would take too long. She could make the drive in six and a half hours. Six if she sped, putting her in New Orleans around two in the morning. She steered the car onto the interstate, followed the same path that had brought her here to Atlanta, and the miles ticked away behind her as the road stretched on, and the taste of death rose in her mouth, and she swallowed it down to fester in her belly. Still, she kept her hands locked on the wheel and watched the white lines unravel as they led her toward everything she'd run from. She called Daniel to tell him she was driving instead, and there was still no Lila. The police said they'd keep an eye out, but that they couldn't technically call her missing just yet.

Her eyes burned from watching the side of the highway. Rounding every turn, her heart would surge as she looked for a girl with dark hair even though she knew it wasn't possible for Lila to be on the side of the interstate. The miles passed, and the highway was empty save for a few other cars, and she cranked the air conditioning and pinched her thighs to keep herself from drifting off.

Her thoughts always cycled back to Lila. She could have just been angry, intent on punishing both of her parents, but her thoughts also traveled to the more terrible, crushing idea of a man with the face of a dog, of teeth tearing at her daughter's thighs, her chest, and it was stupid to have ever believed that all these things weren't connected. After Beth's disappearance, she'd spent so long convincing herself that her addled mind had been seeking a solution less terrible than the idea of a human doing something so awful, but she couldn't ignore it anymore. What-ever had found her and Beth, had found Lila. She was sure of it now. She thought again of the women in Detective Doucette's file; their insistence there were beasts that took girls, their intent to silence their tongues, to teach them to be compliant. What they would do if the girls would not fall into line.

In the distance, the dark roiled, the moon emerging but spilling no silver light. Caroline should pull over. Should find a motel and get a room with a hard mattress and sheets that smelled of age and bleach and sleep for a few hours. As the road unraveled in front of her, she told herself these things, but she kept driving. What was ahead of her could not wait. Scrubs of trees stood to her right, and in the median, illuminated by her headlights, wildflowers lifted bright faces to the sky. Something to cheer weary travelers as they made their way on and on, but seeing them sway in the wind didn't make her feel better. Too often, their crimson petals looked like smears of blood.

When she crossed into Louisiana, something inside her broke. Her chest went tight, and her vision blurred. No other headlights appeared, and she flipped on her high beams. The road curved, the trees rising as if out of nothing as she approached New Orleans. The outskirts of the city were changed. Marred and fragmented. Dead hulls left behind to carry ghosts. Graffiti on stained concrete walls and metal jutting toward the sky. The skeletons of a life swallowed by water. Even years after Katrina had pulled the city apart, everywhere there was the smell of things decomposing, the air tinted dark as ink as Caroline drove down streets where people had tried their best to stitch their lives back together with broken thread. Some parts of the city had recovered after Katrina, but there were still forgotten places on the edges, still places where it seemed as if the water had only just receded.

If it were a different time, if she were a different person under this banner of black sky, she would have cried. Her homecoming tainted and spoiled as the garbage mounded in front of houses with shattered windows, maggots teeming in their rich depths.

She rounded a corner, her headlights illuminating an overgrown front lawn, and a pain racketed through her head as a memory drifted up from a long-buried place. The itch of grass beneath her legs. And the man. How he'd stood across the street from her and waved. She felt she'd known him for so long, and she'd stood, her book tumbling to the earth, and followed him. Then there was only darkness. An enclosed place that smelled of decay. The feeling of teeth against her legs. The sharp scent of blood and a sensation of floating as something rooted between her thighs. Tasting her. Telling her what a sweet, good girl she was. Telling her to keep quiet even as a deep pain took root in the tender parts of her.

Her vision swam, the road before her doubling. The deep, nauseous stink of fried food and spun sugar filled the car, and she gagged, the car swerving over the white line and onto the shoulder. Around her rose the sound of children screaming and dogs snarling.

Somehow, she was able to pull over and throw the door open before she was sick. Terror ran through her like electric shock. Trembling, she sat up and rested her head against the steering wheel. She grasped at the edges of her memories, tried to push herself to remember more, but there was only the ghost scent of sugar lingering in the car. Like funnel cake. Like cotton candy.

"Jesus," Caroline said as awareness flooded through her. She knew where Lila had gone.

CHAPTER 27

CAROLINE 2019

Her eyes burned as she turned off the exit. The way was dark, but she remembered it. Soon enough, those ancient, twisted arcs and loops spilled over the landscape. Jazzland. After so many years, she was back here. She turned off her headlights and guided the car forward. She imagined cops patrolled the area frequently, looking for kids who hoped to find trouble exploring the wrecked amusement park, their faces shining in the dark as they whooped and ran.

The entrance was still there, the once-lurid painted gates gone dull, and the buildings beyond were streaked with brown water stains. Oxidization had tarnished the metal gates, and she imagined they would crumble under her touch. Overgrown trees and bushes crept across the concrete. The coasters rose behind like great metal beasts. Caroline sat in her car and looked out. Her heart pounded in her chest, and her mouth tasted of iron. At the back of the lot, an ancient pickup truck sat. Likely abandoned.

When she stepped out of the car, the wind caught at her hair, and in it she smelled burnt sugar. The old ghosts of what the park used to be. "Lila," she said, and her feet carried her forward. She did not know how to be afraid. Not anymore.

The park was quiet. A fine layer of dirt settled over the abandoned bumper cars and graffiti crawled over every exposed surface, the black and green and red paint faded in the dark. Dust filmed over her skin, her mouth, and she tasted inside it the little deaths it carried. She fought the urge to spit. There were warnings posted everywhere. No trespassing. Violators prosecuted. In spite of these warnings, there were plenty of defaced walls inside, along with the detritus of teenagers and young adults sneaking here to live dangerously and party away from prying eyes. Daring themselves to stare into the face of a place that was once designed for joy and now only looked like a nightmare that had pulled itself out of the earth.

There was a part of her that believed she had never left this place. That if she traced her way back to that restaurant, she'd find herself still standing at the counter watching a little girl with blond hair laugh at a man dressed in black, his teeth and fur obscured by too-pink skin. Imprinted forever, like a film reel unspooling.

So she walked on, her feet finding the same route she and Beth had taken all those years before. She listened for any sound, but there was only the wind and the scrape of her feet along the broken asphalt. A flurry of movement to her right made her heart accelerate, and she whipped her head around, trying to see beyond the rise and fall of shadows. Something near her shifted, and she turned again, her eyes searching for what it was that had moved.

A large dog padded toward her, its mouth open and snarling, and her muscles clenched, readying herself to run, but the mouth shortened as its legs elongated, and when she blinked, it wasn't a dog before her at all but a man in a dark coat, his mouth open, his tongue lolling as he grinned.

"Hey," Caroline yelled as she stepped forward. But the man turned, dropping to all fours and then loping away, the movements skittering and unnatural. She ran after him, but he was so much faster, his body bent low to the earth. Her lungs ached from use, and her muscles burned, but he had disappeared into the twisting labyrinth of the park. She screamed, again and again, her frustration and terror and anger made audible; she lifted her voice, until the only thing tumbling from her lips was Lila's name, but it was no use.

It had been real. All of it. The delusions, the snarling dogs she'd heard here so long ago. It was all real. The man and his transformation proved it. For years, she'd been medicated, her truths explained away, and still, she'd seen him. All of it had been real.

Around her the park breathed in and out, and whatever secrets it held would die inside it. She walked, her gaze sweeping over broken glass and crumbling brick, but there was nothing. For long minutes, she wandered, and when the sound of another living creature finally came again, it was behind her. She froze, her face lifted to the night sky. Whatever was behind her, it was panting.

She turned. The man stood so near her that she could feel the warmth of his breath over her cheeks. "Hello, Caroline." He lifted his face, his nose flaring as he scented the air.

Caroline stepped backward, stumbled. "It's you."

Dr. Walters spread his hands before him. "But of course it is, dear." The edges of his lips lifted in a smirk. "Who else would it be?" He threw his head back, his mouth opening and opening into an impossible maw. Around his eyes, his skin blackened as the flesh stretched and changed as his head lolled backward and then snapped forward with an audible pop as the planes of his cheeks, the slant of his nose, the color of his eyes morphed rapidly through a series of faces. Some she recognized—Lila's school counselor, the psychiatrist she'd been seeing since she moved to Atlanta—but most she didn't. His head twitched, and he grunted as his face contorted through many faces. All of them older, white, well monied, arrogant. Placating smiles and snide, curved lips. Again, his head twisted violently, and then the face looking back at her was once again Dr. Walters's.

Caroline panted, the air thick in her throat, and she blinked and blinked, but her head felt light, too filled with the reality of what faced her. Again, she drew breath, willed herself to stay conscious.

He cocked his head. Smiled his awful smile with those innumerable teeth, and Caroline thought of the scars on her thighs and the bodies of all those discarded girls. She didn't bother trying to stop the tears.

"There never was a serial killer. The Cur was never real. It was always you." She blinked rapidly, and her vision swam, the man's body doubling and tripling before resuming its normal form. She thought of all those lost girls. The many forms he must have taken to grant him access to the inner workings of their minds. "Tell me where Lila is."

"But don't you know? Don't you remember?" His was the voice of legions, a dull, hissed growl that burned in her ears. "I brought you here, to the Kingdom, once as well, but you were a *good* girl." He clucked his tongue, and his face blurred. Salt-and-pepper hair. A sharp nose and lips that seemed too large for the weak chin. Caroline's mind flashed to an indistinct memory of herself, too small for the chair she sat in, her legs dangling. His face across the desk, smiling down at her, telling her that she would be fine. That she didn't need to see a doctor anymore. That it was okay if she wanted to be quiet. Wouldn't she like that? There was no need to fight.

"Swallowed your pills like you were told. Confused and sad

and quietly angry in all the ways that bring us pleasure. That feed us. Just as your mother once did. And her mother before her. And now dear, *sweet* Lila."

"Don't you fucking touch her."

"Oh, but haven't you raised such a good girl, Caroline? Compliant. Obedient. Because you imagined it would keep her safe. That by keeping her close to you, keeping her innocent, you could keep her mind intact in all the ways yours isn't. Same old story." He shrugged. "Mothers, mind your daughters. Keep them sweet and polite and mannered, and it will keep the teeth from the door. Your mother served so wonderfully in that regard. Didn't want anyone to think her daughter was strange. And how beautifully you fell in line with your little sticks and twigs. Always feeling there was something locked away. Never good enough. And if you ever did make anything . . . more. Well. It was simple enough to fix."

He leered at her, and she curled her fingers into her palms. "The sculpture was so lovely, wasn't it? The dog? We gave it to you. Like a gift. Or maybe a small reminder to keep quiet so no one would call you crazy. And you did keep it quiet, didn't you, Caroline? Because people would have seen the teeth and claws. And it would have revealed you as . . . well, someone capable of *monstrous* things."

"You . . . you made me do that. You made me take the dog and make that *thing*."

"You poor dear. You poor *lamb*. You didn't like how we took your talent—the thing you love so much—and . . . what's the word here . . . warped it? Made it perverse? And you gave in after that. Took your medicine. Stayed quiet like you're supposed to. Our sweet, delicious girl."

"Fuck you," Caroline said, and the man chuckled, the sound low and deep in his chest. "So that's what you do? Keep us scared and feed on us. Make us think we're crazy, so you can use us up until there's nothing left. Until we're just rotted husks of what we could have been."

"How simple you make it. Your fear. Your confusion. Terrified of what you've seen and heard because you know to give voice to it is its own kind of doom. They'd label you broken and put you away. So you stay silent, and what a glorious feast you give us."

She gulped air. "And what about the ones who aren't good? The ones who don't listen?"

There was that voice again, a multitude of muffled roars Caroline felt under her skin, answering her questions. He shook his head. "You'd done so well. How long Lila kept herself hidden just to please you. Her insecurities. Her anger because she never quite seemed to fit anywhere. Couldn't have done better if you'd served her up to us on a platter. But what a mess she's made. She has become . . . problematic. She didn't listen. Like Beth. She didn't listen either. You remember though, don't you, Caroline?"

"You kill them," she whispered.

"It does little to satiate our hunger, but any girl who is unusable, who doesn't obey . . . well, we tear her open. And her blood is enough. At least for a short while. Until we find another who is more suitable. We call out to them, and they come running. Jazzland is only one of the places we've claimed as our own. Places where blood has spilled. Places where so many voices have been forever silenced. Witches burned or hanged. Women locked away in small cells." He smiled, revealing endless rows of teeth.

Heat flushed her neck, her cheeks. In the dark, she snarled at him. Lila was with these creatures, and they had not been able to control her. Lila with her anger and her silence because she hadn't been able to tell her mother, been able to tell anyone, the truth of who she was. Like Beth. Like Caroline. All of them angry because there was some intrinsic part of them they had to bury.

"Where is Lila? Where is my daughter?" she said.

"She is for us. Only us. I am one of many, and we share the spoils, so to speak."

"Then take me instead. If you're so fucking *hungry*. Take me and let her go."

He stepped forward and leaned toward her, his face against her neck as he inhaled. "You have had your monthly blood. For many years now. You cannot serve us in the way that she can. Not as fully. Her silence tastes best."

Her hands shook behind her back as he breathed her in once more. The girls they took would be so young—taken before their bodies matured—and she wanted to hurt him, to take him apart with her hands, but if she tried, Lila would die down among those terrible creatures.

The man gazed at her, his eyes sharp and wet, the pupils too large. Caroline counted the spaces between her heartbeats as she kept her eyes locked on him. She would not look away.

"But your blood is still sweet in its own way. Perhaps we will have you both." He opened his mouth then, and there were too many teeth, and she remembered then. How they had marked her as their own. How they had infected her with their control. Their mouths on her thighs, biting down, the deep smell of her blood, and then her own screaming that went on and on until there was nothing left. She had broken under them because she wanted the pain to stop, would do anything if it only meant there would be an end to it. And she had fallen in line. Because she'd imagined it would save her somehow. Keep the ever-present dread she carried in her blood from spilling outward and infecting everything she touched. But it had happened anyway, and for years, she had fed them with her silence.

"Yes. Both, I think." He stepped aside, and standing there amid the gloom was Lila.

Caroline gathered her strength and slammed her shoulder against the man, pushing past as he fell, and then threw herself at her daughter, crushed the girl's body to her as she touched Lila's arms and face. "I'm so sorry. Oh God, Lila. I'm so sorry. I should have told you everything from the beginning. How they took Beth. How they took me. All of it. I didn't know what it all really was, how it all connected, but I still should have told you."

Lila's eyes rolled backward into her head, the whites shot through with burst blood vessels, and Caroline kissed her and smoothed her hair. She hugged Lila to her chest, the weight of her daughter's body the only thing she ever wanted to feel again.

"It's going to be all right," she said, listening as the man rose behind her, his breath ragged as he moved.

"You *bitch*," he said, and then Lila's voice was close in Caroline's ear.

"I did something bad. I'm so sorry. There was someone, and I hurt him, and I did something *bad*."

Caroline's mind filled with images of Lila as a little girl. Her dark hair clouding around her face as she spun under a faded sun and fell laughing into green grass that covered her up so Caroline couldn't see her. The color of her eyes when she opened them in the morning. How they looked just a shade darker. The feeling of Lila's body cupped against hers on nights when she'd had a nightmare and come crawling into Caroline's bed; her skin flush with the honey-scented smell of sleep.

Lila's eyes fluttered, the irises rolling, and then they were locked on Caroline.

"Momma?"

Caroline touched her face, her hair again, and she remembered the softness of Lila's skin when the nurse had laid her on Caroline's bare chest. Beneath her, the asphalt was broken. The ridges pressed painfully against her knees, but she knelt over Lila, her body tensed as she searched for what she needed. Finally, her fingers closed over a large piece that had come loose. She gripped it tight and slid it away from the man's view. It wasn't much, but it would have to be enough.

"Everything is going to be okay, Lila. Listen to me carefully now. If I tell you to run, you need to do it. You need to get as far away from here as possible." She did not know why the man was not already on them, but she could only assume he was taking his time, enjoying the anticipation, delaying his fall upon them because he took enjoyment in the expectation of violence and blood. She could only hope it would buy her a few more seconds.

"I can't leave you here." In the dim light, Lila's face sparkled with tears, and Caroline reached her free hand to wipe them away. Lila leaned into her touch, and Caroline's chest heaved with love and regret and sorrow. She would not be there to see her girl become a woman. There would be so many things she would miss. For thirteen years she'd been a mother. A thousand years wouldn't have been enough.

The man stepped beside them, and Caroline stared up at the yellow, winking eyes. "How touching. How sweet your combined flesh will be when it breaks together over our tongues," he said, and his voice was the voice of thousands.

Quickly, Caroline pushed Lila away from her, and it felt like something inside her had been severed. "I love you, my girl. Everything is going to be okay," she said. *"Run."*

Lila hesitated, and then she turned, her hair streaking behind her as she fled away from the man. Away from Caroline.

The man roared and leapt forward, his hands groping after Lila, but there was nothing to catch but air.

Caroline laughed, and then she was screaming, and she opened her mouth wider. "You *motherfucker*," she screamed again as she stood and swung her arm in a wide arc. The piece of asphalt came shuddering down, and there was the spongy give of flesh and then a sickening crack.

Before Caroline could lift her arm again, the world lit up in fire and teeth and hurt. She twisted and screamed her daughter's name aloud as everything came crashing down. Her memories and blood soaked the ground where she lay, and the beast opened its vast mouth to devour her.

She spoke Lila's name and Beth's and her own name again and again until even drawing breath was an act of infinite pain. But there was the memory of Lila, the sight of her hair as she ran.

Caroline smiled and then the world went black.

CHAPTER 28

LILA 2019

"She's not dead. I can see her breathing."

"Must be on something. Let's just go."

"You're such an asshole, Camille. We can't just leave her. She's bleeding. Like she hit her head or something."

"So what do you want to do? Carry her out of here?"

"Maybe somebody hurt her. Dumped her here. You ever think about that?"

"Hey. Girl!" Two fingers snapped above her, but Lila couldn't open her eyes. There were still many parts of her that weren't responding, and her body was heavy. She couldn't move. Not an inch. That dark, fevered part of her, the voice that had been louder than anything else, had gone quiet and now all she felt was exhausted.

"We have to go. If the cops catch us here again, we're beyond fucked. It's just a bad trip or something. Her friends are probably around here somewhere."

"We've been all through the park already. There isn't anyone else. Besides, she looks super young."

The two voices were high-pitched. Female and slurred.

"If she's hurt, we need to tell someone. What if there's something seriously wrong with her, and we can't see it? What if she dies, Camille?"

"She's not going to die."

"You don't fucking know that for sure!"

The deep taste of blood flooded Lila's mouth, and she coughed, spurted so her body jerked, and both girls screamed. She opened her eyes.

"Hey! You okay? Can you hear me?" One of the girls knelt on the ground beside her, and the other stood with her arms crossed over her chest. Both had hair bleached white and then tipped with violet, the same elfin faces and arched brows. Twins. Mirror images down to a starburst of a scar on their right and left cheeks.

"Did you take something? Did someone hurt you?"

Their voices bloated and expanded, and Lila could hear her mother screaming, could feel it in her blood. She reached out, her arms flailing, but her mother wasn't there.

"Where?" she choked out, and the kneeling girl grasped her arm.

"Easy. It's okay."

"Something isn't right," the other girl said.

"They're killing her," Lila said, and both girls went pale, their faces like bleached meat.

"Call the cops, Camille."

"But we'll end up—"

"Just fucking do it!" the girl said, and the other fumbled a cell phone from her back pocket.

Lila could feel the beasts taking her mother apart. Her body opened like overripe fruit and left to bleed. Discarded like waste, and she screamed, and there were other voices, too. The Kingdom of beasts answering her. Lila curled her body into itself.

It wouldn't be enough. The police would come and flood this place, but nothing would change. Lila sobbed, and the girls hovered near her, but they did not speak to her again.

When the police came, they wrapped Lila in a silver blanket and helped her to her feet. She could have fought, could have lashed out so they wouldn't move her, but it didn't matter. She could sit in this spot until her body gave out, but her mother was gone. There was no use in lingering, so she let them push her across broken pavement and out of the park.

They sat her in the back of an ambulance to clean the cut on her head—she must have fallen and knocked herself out. They told her everything was going to be fine, but they needed to know if she'd come in with anyone, if someone had brought her there and hurt her.

"My mother" was all Lila said, and they turned away, spoke into the walkie-talkies clipped to their shoulders, and she leaned against the seat, drained with the effort of that minimal movement.

"Okay, sweetie. I'm Officer Gilbert. What's your name? Can you tell me?" The officer who leaned over her was female. Petite. Her hair tucked under her hat was dyed a dark auburn.

"Lila. Lila Sawyer."

"That's a beautiful name." Officer Gilbert repeated Lila's name into the walkie on her shoulder along with a command to run the name through the endangered children list. "You came here with your mother tonight? Is she the one who brought you here?"

"No."

"But she's here?"

"She came back for me."

Officer Gilbert knelt in front of her and waved a hand at the other officers who gathered behind her. "Can you give us some privacy, please?" The group scattered.

"Where's your mom right now, Lila?"

"Still there. She won't ever come out."

"Still in the park?"

"No."

"Is that her car? Or the truck?" Officer Gilbert pointed at her mother's dark sedan and then the truck, and Lila remembered blood on her hands, and she could not speak; she could do nothing except shake and shake.

"Lila, did your mother hurt you?"

"No."

Officer Gilbert rocked back on her heels. "Can you tell me what you were doing here?"

"I brought her. She was looking for me."

My fault. My fault.

"Lila? Why did you come here?"

"She stayed, and it's my fault, and I—" She broke off, and Officer Gilbert patted her knee.

"It's okay. We'll find her. Don't worry." A flurry of commotion broke out behind her; the officers' walkie-talkies crackled, and then shouts. Officer Gilbert glanced over her shoulder and then back at Lila.

"I need for you to sit tight for me, okay? I'm going to close the door. I'll be right outside. You'll be just fine." Two officers broke apart from the group and jogged back into the park with their heads down. A dog barked from somewhere deep in the park—two brief peals that echoed across the night air—and Lila shrank back into the seat. She had done something bad, could remember the edges of it—the blood, the feeling of skin beneath her fingernails—but her head was thick, and every time she settled on a thought, another intruded, and she couldn't focus.

More shouting. More lights from more cars as they pulled into the lot, and Lila's stomach turned. Her mother had come looking for her. And now . . . even amidst all the confusion, Lila understood the weight of what it was her mother had done.

The door opened again. "I'm so sorry." Behind Officer Gilbert, the other officers watched, their expressions grim, and Lila tried not to see them, tried not to look, but their faces burned themselves in her mind, and fear bloomed hard and cold in her chest.

"I'm so sorry," Officer Gilbert said again, but Lila already knew what it was they had found in the park. The Kingdom took what it needed and spit what it didn't back out like waste. Lila tipped her head back and looked up at the stars. Hard fire wrapped in night, and she took all that cold inside herself, and her tears leaked out of her like water.

"I want to see her," Lila said.

"Oh, honey. I understand. But she's not the same."

"I don't care. I want to see her."

Officer Gilbert paused and scrubbed her face with her hands. Lila let herself go rigid. "I don't care what she looks like. I'm her daughter, and I want to see her."

Officer Gilbert sighed, pausing for a beat, and then she nodded. "Come on."

The other officers went still as Lila passed, their heads turning as they weaved their way through. Each individual piece of their sympathy separated itself out and settled on her shoulders.

Officer Gilbert wound through the park, her footsteps quick and clipped, and the sky watched above them, silent and vast. Ahead of them, another group of officers huddled, and the woman paused and turned back to Lila. "Are you sure about this?"

"Yes," Lila said. Officer Gilbert went among the group, and they parted, their faces cast down or up. Anywhere but at the girl who came forward, her arms locked against her side.

Officer Gilbert kept her hand on Lila's shoulder as she advanced on the form that lay against the asphalt. Her mother's face was turned away, but Lila could see exposed bone on her cheek, a flap of skin sagging along her neck. And everywhere were jagged gashes where she'd been opened up.

Lila knelt and let her hands creep through the air to hover over her mother's face, the lips parted so she could see the teeth both pearled and stained with streaks of crimson. "I'm so sorry," she said, but her mother didn't turn to look at her. Didn't turn to smile and draw long fingers through her hair. Never again, and Lila's chest heaved. She dropped her hand.

"I want to go home," Lila said, and Officer Gilbert came forward and helped her to her feet.

"We'll need to take you to the hospital. To be sure you're okay," Officer Gilbert said.

They went back through the park, and Lila didn't fight as she loaded her into the ambulance. She listened as people came and went, their voices shouting, and then the back doors opened once more, and a woman stepped in and closed the doors behind her. She was dressed simply in a pair of black slacks and a navy button-down that shone against her dark skin, and her hair was braided tightly and fell around her face. She smiled at Lila, and it was a careful smile. The kind you offer something that could bite you.

Lila only stared back at this woman who advanced on her now, one hand held up in a gesture of surrender.

"It's okay. I'm Deborah. I'm a social worker, and I'm here to help you."

Lila settled back on the stretcher, and Deborah crouched beside her. "Can you still feel them? The beasts?" she asked.

Lila could not bring herself to speak, could not believe it was possible that this woman knew about *them,* but she nodded, and Deborah patted her hand.

"It'll be like that for a while. But with time, you won't feel them as much."

"How do you . . . how do you know about them?" Lila asked.

Deborah clasped her hands. "They took me, too. When I was a girl. It took a long time to figure out what was happening. That the things I was seeing and hearing were real even though I had plenty of people telling me they weren't. I met another woman who had a story similar to mine, and the pieces started falling into place. And now, there's a whole group of us who remember. We watch out for survivors, help them deal with it in the best way they can."

"They killed my mom."

"I know, sweetheart. I know, and I'm so, so sorry."

"They don't like it when we fight them. When we don't listen. That's why they killed her. That's why they were going to kill me." Lila's voice cracked, her anger and her grief forcing itself up and out of her throat with a sharpness that ached.

Deborah lowered her voice. "That's what they do. They attach themselves to us like a parasite before we can learn to have a voice of our own. They look for that fear and confusion and anger and feed on it."

Lila thought of Macie, of how she'd hidden the truth of who she really was away, and of her anger. Deborah looked back at her, amber eyes winking in the dark. Lila could still see the quiet girl she must have been, but there was a fire there, too. If Deborah had been taken, there was still a part of her that had survived; a part that had not been drowned in blood and then devoured. "What about the ones they kill?"

"They were the ones who wouldn't fall in line. We think what they want is to force us to be silent. They want the ones who could grow powerful. Strong, loud voices. They feed on our passivity. Our fear. And if we fight back . . ."

Lila nodded. "I could hear him. In my head. I thought I was losing my mind."

"That's how it started for all of us. After they took us, it was hard to feel much of anything. We could still do some things that made us happy or content, but it felt dulled. Anytime we tried something larger or tried to put up a fight about something, we'd start seeing and hearing the beasts again. We'd be terrified, and it shut us up. It's how they keep us submissive. By making us think we're losing our minds. Dismissed as crazy or hysterical and drugged up. And then the cycle repeats. The quieter our voices become, the greater their feast," Deborah said.

"If you've learned to get them out of your head, why wouldn't they just come and kill you, too?"

"Every day is a fight. I'm scared a lot." She shrugged. "Maybe my fear is still enough for them. And I still keep quiet in my own way. Because no one outside our small circle would believe me."

Lila bent forward at the waist, her head drooping, but she could not control the tears flooding out of her. "Can you not stop them? Since you know what they are? Kill them and make all this stop?"

Deborah squeezed her arm. "I wish I could tell you we knew how. I wish that more than anything. The one thing we have figured out is *when* they come. That's why I knew when the call came in tonight that what was happening out here had something to do with them. From the best we can figure, they come in fifteen-year cycles. Girls start going missing. And we can feel them coming awake, too. We dream. We see or hear things. We think we might be losing our minds, but it's just their power, reminding us to keep quiet."

"Can't you just tell the police? Catch them in the act somehow and then show the cops?"

"We've tried. So many times. But what little we've turned up has been shrugged off. It's easy to blame what happens to missing girls on other things. Animal attacks. Some pervert on the loose. A serial killer. And then the ones who come back with the beasts inside them, the ones who seem confused or stop talking or have strange episodes or don't seem like themselves anymore? Well. It's easy to shut them away. To keep them quiet in the exact way the beasts want. To marginalize them and everything they say as unreasonable and lock them in hospitals, in asylums, in kitchens. It's what men have always been doing, isn't it? Shutting us up anytime we say or do anything that doesn't fit into the nice little box they want us in." Deborah's voice went hard and then she shook her head. "But that doesn't mean we'll stop trying."

"Will I always hear them?" she asked.

"Yes. I won't lie to you."

Lila hesitated and then spoke again. "Are you able to keep me safe? To keep them from hurting me?"

"No. I can't do that." Deborah looked directly at Lila. "I can't save you. But I'll be here to help you, to guide you back when you feel them. To fight when they try to confuse you. That much I promise."

Through her tears, Lila gazed out the back window, looking for the beasts, a man, her mother, anything. But there was nothing but Jazzland, empty and quiet, lit up in the blue, alien lights of the police cruisers. Deborah's hand squeezed hers once more, and Lila remembered her mother's voice.

Everything is going to be okay.

CHAPTER 29

LILA 2034

"I lived with my dad until I was eighteen. He wasn't the greatest parent before my mom died, but her murder was a wake-up call for him, I think. He was a different person after that. Kinder. A listener. We're still really close." Lila blew across the surface of her coffee. She'd ordered it black, the way she liked it. Bitter on the tongue and hot. A reminder that the taste of it was real.

Wendy sat across from her, an untouched muffin on a plate the color of sunshine. Her fingernails were the color of sludge, and Lila wondered what they would look like pressed against her bare skin. They'd been on a handful of dates now, but Lila never went back to her apartment with more than a lipstick stain on her mouth and a pitted feeling in her stomach. For the first time in a while, this thing they were building felt real. Substantial. Nothing like the string of failed dates and one-night hookups that had dominated her early twenties. She was ready for something more, and when she was with Wendy, it felt like forever. After everything, she felt like she deserved such happiness.

"He told me, after Mom's funeral, that he felt like it was partly his fault. That if he'd just listened, maybe she would have lived. That if he hadn't been so wrapped up in dismissing everything she said . . . anyway, he promised me he would always listen to me. That I could tell him anything, and he would accept it, without judgment. And that's exactly what he did. For me and for Brina. I ended up leaving New Orleans for a while. I wasn't sure I could live here. But being away from this city didn't feel right, either, and eventually I found my way back. You know. The whole song and dance. The prodigal daughter returned. My dad was excited. Knowing I'd 'come home,' so to speak. He always said it would have made my mom happy to know I was back."

"Did they ever figure out what happened to her? Your mom?"

"No. Eventually, the police filed it as a cold case murder. There was a serial killer back then who abducted girls. The Cur. They think he targeted me, and lured me away, but somehow my mom figured out he had taken me to Jazzland. He killed another man who was at the park, and then my mother. Their bodies were both . . . mutilated, in an almost identical fashion. I don't remember how I escaped." She took a shuddering breath as she remembered that night. Her mother's fingers in her hair. The feel of her arms as they cradled her. *I love you, my girl.*

Lila wiped at the tears forming in her eyes, and Wendy grasped her hand. "I'm so sorry," she said.

"It's okay. Really. I've learned how to deal with it. Years of therapy. Lots of hours in beige offices, sitting across from doctors who looked at me like some specimen under a microscope. In the end, none of it really mattered. None of it could bring her back."

Wendy lifted the mug to her lips and sipped, and Lila watched her mouth and teeth. Maybe tonight there would be more than the kiss good night; more than her body pressed against Wendy's lean form, left burning and empty when she pulled back.

"They never arrested anyone? At all?" Wendy said.

"No. I try not to think about it anymore. Know what I do think about though?" Wendy shook her head. "I was thinking about your mouth."

Wendy flushed and tucked a strand of curling, dark hair behind her ear.

"But don't worry. I have an excellent therapist, and whenever I feel wobbly, she gets me back on track. And I also have Deborah. She was the social worker assigned to my case after everything happened. She's the reason I decided to become a social worker, too. Without her . . . I'm not sure what would have happened. She became like a third mom. I thought it would bother my dad and Rebecca. How close we were. But she ended up becoming part of the family. Came over every Sunday night for dinner." Lila paused. She'd not intended to tell Wendy about Deborah. Not yet. Maybe eventually she'd tell Wendy the truth of everything, the truth of what had happened to her and her mother so long ago at Jazzland, but for now, she wanted to leave this coffee shop behind and lose herself in Wendy's body. "So I'm not going to come unhinged one night and start screaming. And I don't bite. Unless you ask," Lila said, and flashed a feral smile.

Wendy tipped her head back and laughed. Lila wanted to curl up in the sound, safe and warm, and never leave. "I still think about my mom all the time though. Pretty much every minute of the day. I miss her a lot. Even now, all these years later," Lila said, and Wendy nodded.

"I know what you mean," said Wendy. "There are mornings I wake up and have had a really weird dream, and the first thing I want to do is call my mom and tell her about it. Every time it's like losing her all over again. Remembering that she isn't there. Like another death."

"Yeah."

They finished their coffees. Wendy left the muffin untouched, and Lila wrapped it in a napkin and stuffed it into her purse. A snack for later. They walked in silence, and the night settled around them, but there was no fear in it. Only quiet.

When they got to Lila's apartment, Wendy pulled Lila to her, her mouth hot against her neck, and whispered, "Let me come inside."

They tumbled into each other, and Wendy's body bent and moved around hers. Lila wondered if this was what it was like to drown. To hold her breath like this so that someone else could have the air.

When Wendy fell asleep, Lila whispered to her, words she'd never said to anyone other than her mother and father, and then to Rebecca and Deborah, but she thought she knew what they meant now as her heart beat a painful pattern against her chest.

Outside, the sounds began again. As they had, on occasion, after her mother had died. Now, Lila watched and waited for other girls in the way Deborah had watched and waited for her.

She rose and went to the window, pulled back the blinds, and looked out into the dark. Yellow eyes winked back at her. In the distance, something howled. Long and mournful. The sound of a mother keening. The sound of a beast coming awake. It was a sound Lila understood. Even so, she was not afraid. She was ready for the fight she and Deborah had spent the past fifteen years preparing for.

She turned back and looked at the woman asleep in her bed and smiled.

She closed the blinds and tucked herself back into bed. Cupped her body to Wendy's.

And she slept.

ACKNOWLEDGMENTS

Writing this book has been a journey unlike anything I've ever experienced, and there are far too many people to whom I owe my gratitude. To my amazing editor, Alexandra Sehulster, and the entire team at St. Martin's Press, a million thanks for your enthusiasm, faith, and dedication to this book. To Stefanie Lieberman, Molly Steinblatt, and Adam Hobbins at Janklow & Nesbit for seeing value in what this book has to say and for pushing me to refine and polish until it was just right. Your guidance and advice have been invaluable, and I could not have done it without all of you helping me along. To my beautiful friend and colleague Damien Angelica Walters, who has read far more versions and drafts of this book than anyone should have to. I feel so privileged to have you as a friend. Thank you for reading every woe-begotten email I've ever sent you and for celebrating every victory as well. To Erinn Kemper, Robert S. Wilson, and Michael Wehunt for reading drafts and portions of the book and offering their thoughts and advice. To Lisa Kroger and Jon Padgett for answering my questions about New Orleans and providing the kind of details that made the NOLA sections come alive. To Sadie Hartmann (Mother Horror), for being not only a wonderful person but also the best cheerleader I could ever ask for. To every reader who has ever enjoyed anything I've written, thank you from the bottom of my dark little heart. To my dear, dear friends who listened patiently and cheered me up on the tough days: Amy Foti, Jen Sellman, Samira Bregeth, Annie Bolton, Ariana Jordan, and Sam Rickard. I feel so lucky to have all of you in my life. To my family, who have always encouraged and supported this dream of mine. I love you all. And finally, to the two Js. You are my heart and my home.